BRAIN GUY

It is the Depression and Hell's Kitchen rent-collector Bill Trent has just lost his job. But Bill is a smart guy. He figures right away that if he hooks up with McMann, together they can make a bundle holding up the businesses that used to pay him rent—McMann's got the muscle and Bill knows when the safes are loaded. Then his younger brother Joe comes to stay, and it's hard to keep up a respectable front for the kid, particularly when plainclothes cop Hanrahan gets wise to the heists. McMann calls Bill the brain guy but how smart can you be when you've got nobody to trust, no way out, and no place to go but down?

PLUNDER

Joe and Blacky are two AWOL GI's in post-WWII Manila. They've escaped the stockade and are loose in the world of pom-pom houses and sweet buy & sell deals. And Joe has plans—big plans. He's going to get a piece of this action. Posing as officers, Joe and Blacky begin to build a little financial empire for themselves. But Joe isn't satisfied with a small piece. He wants it all, whether it's black market goods or someone else's woman. And all Blacky wants is an end to the conniving. Between Joe's schemes and Blacky's conscience stretch the obliging back streets of Manila. The rape of the Philippines has begun.

BENJAMIN APPEL BIBLIOGRAPHY

FICTION

Brain Guy [reprinted as The
   Enforcer] (1934)
Four Roads to Death
   (reprinted as Gold and Flesh]
   (1935)
Runaround (1937)
The Power House (1939)
The Dark Stain (1943)
But Not Yet Slain (1947)
Fortress in the Rice (1951)
Plunder (1952)
Hell's Kitchen [stories;
   reprinted as Alley Kids] (1952)
Dock Walloper [stories] (1953)
Sweet Money Girl (1954)
Life and Death of a Tough Guy
   [reprinted as Teenage Mobster]
   (1955)
Alley Kids [stories; orig pub as
   Hell's Kitchen] (1956)
Teenage Mobster [orig pub as Life
   and Death of a Tough Guy] (1957)
The Raw Edge (1958)
The Funhouse [reprinted as
   The Death Master] (1959)
A Big Man, a Fast Man (1961)
A Time of Fortune (1963)
The Enforcer [orig pub as Brain
   Guy] (1972)
Gold and Flesh [orig pub as
   Four Roads to Death] (1972)
The Death Master
   [orig pub as The Funhouse] (1974)
The Devil and W. Kaspar (1977)
Heart of Ice [adapted; fairy tale]
   (1977)
Hell's Kitchen [novel] (1977)

POETRY

Mixed Vintage (1929)

NON-FICTION

The People Talk
   (1940; reprinted 1972, 1982 as The
   People Talk: American Voices from
   the Great Depression)
We Were There in the
   Klondike Gold Rush (1956)
We Were There at the Battle
   for Bataan (1957)
We Were There With Cortez
   and Montezuma (1959)
The Illustrated Book About South
   America Including Mexico and
   Central America (1960)
Shepherd of the Sun:
   The Story of the Incas (1961)
With Many Voices:
   Europe Talks About America
   (1963)
Hitler: From Power to Ruin (1964)
Ben-Gurion's Israel (1965)
Man and Magic:
   Magical Practices in All Ages
   Throughout the World (1966)
Why the Russians are
   the Way They Are (1966)
Why the Chinese are
   the Way They Are (1968)
The Age of Dictators (1968)
The Fantastic Mirror: Science Fiction
   Across the Ages (1969)
Why the Japanese are
   the Way They Are (1973)
Ben Shahn: Prophet With a Brush
   [article] (1974)
Across the Zodiac:
   The Story of a Wrecked Record
   [ed by Percy Greg; abridged &
   afterword by Appel] (1978)

BRAIN GUY

PLUNDER

BY BENJAMIN APPEL

STARK HOUSE

Stark House Press • Eureka California

BRAIN GUY / PLUNDER

Published by Stark House Press
1315 H Street
Eureka, CA 95501
griffinskye3@sbcglobal.net
www.starkhousepress.com

ISBN: 1-933586-01-X

Book design by Mark Shepard, www.shepgraphics.com

First Stark House Press Edition: November 2005

REPRINT EDITION

Table of Contents

INTRODUCTION
BY CARLA APPEL

I never read introductions to novels. I'd rather just read the novels. So it seems odd to be writing an introduction for this volume of two works by my father, Benjamin Appel. Besides, if he were around, he would scorn a literary introduction. "My books speak for themselves," he would snort, making sarcastic remarks about so-called experts with their academic credentials. But since he is not around to introduce himself, I will, waving the non-academic credential of being his daughter.

It was difficult for any of us to think of Bennie—that was what we all called him, daughters, wife, friends—as distinct from his writing. It was impossible for me to separate father from writer. He was the parent who was home all the time, writing all the time. My mother was gone all day teaching second grade. Bennie worked at a desk in his bedroom. I don't remember ever being told not to bother him while he was writing, I just knew it. I knew he was there if I needed him, I knew he'd stop work at noon, come into the kitchen, make me lunch, go back and write some more. When I was old enough to go to school, I knew he'd be at his desk when I came home. If I were sick I'd be comforted by the sound of his typewriter coming through the wall next to my bed.

We lived in a small town, Roosevelt, New Jersey, population about 1000; most of the families knew each other pretty well. My childhood friends knew Bennie well enough to expect live entertainment if they came home with me for lunch. Bennie heated cans of Chef Boyardee Ravioli with accompanying puns, spontaneous poems set to song, and fantastic stories told with a perfectly straight face. He had an unending, irreverent sense of humor and a bottomless imagination. He liked kids, liked talking to them, teasing them, checking to see if they took him seriously. He behaved the same way with adults. He didn't believe in age-appropriate boundaries; he never talked down to kids, nor did he "write down" in his juveniles. People were people, no matter how old, or what color or what nationality. Bennie was an equal opportunity teaser.

He was also a great encourager, of any kind of talent. He encouraged his daughters to write, but did not ram it down our throats. If we brought school compositions to him for his opinion, we'd get the full editorial red-pencil treatment, but we were free not to ask for his opinion. He didn't have to encourage us to read because we never considered not reading. Books lined the living-room, hall, and bedroom walls; if we asked for suggestions we got them. Some of them took and some of them didn't. Balzac, for example, I didn't like; Thomas Mann, a great favorite of his, became a love of mine. I don't remember the context of being handed *The Magic Mountain* when I was around 13. Bennie had to translate the French, erotic parts for me, which was perhaps embarrassing, but he persisted because he didn't believe in censorship.

He had a phase of reading Shakespeare plays aloud after dinner, with us each taking parts. He had a phase of reading split editions, English on one side and Italian, Spanish, or Russian on the other side, depending on which language he was trying to learn just then. He had a good ear for poetry, a wonderful ear for dialogue, and a tin ear for learning other languages, but that never stopped him from trying.

Bennie was one of those lucky ones who always knew what he wanted to do, lucky, too, in his parents. My grandfather, a Polish immigrant plumber, was not much of a reader, but he and my grandmother believed in and supported their oldest child Bennie the Writer. They did not impose other aspirations on him, so he was spared having to think about, or to pretend to pursue another career. By age 24 he had won an award for a one-act play, produced a book of poetry, and published a short story in a Columbia University Press collection. *Scribner's Magazine, Esquire, Redbook, Literary American* and *The Anvil* featured his stories. Many were set in New York's Hell's Kitchen, the setting of his own life from age three. The hard-boiled stance of the stories was not a phony pose for a writer who grew up in that neighborhood. Hell's Kitchen was a tough place. "Tell us what you did when you were little" elicited remembrances of how he and his brothers sneaked away to swim in the Hudson River off the West Side piers, not telling his mother; of swiping apples from pushcarts in Paddy's Market on Ninth Avenue; of checking out books from the public library, walking home and facing gangs of Irish kids who vandalized the books, taunting the "book woim" and making him fight.

"Write what you know," he would advise others, and followed his own advice. *Brain Guy*, his first novel, was one of eight to use a New York City background. *Plunder* and *Fortress in the Rice* resulted from his first trip out of the U.S., to the Philippines. He'd been ghost-writing for Paul V. McNutt in Washington, D.C. and traveled with him as journalist when McNutt was appointed U.S. High Commissioner there in 1945. During the years Bennie worked on *Fortress* my family was poor, living on my mom's salary and buying groceries on credit. Ironically, *Fortress* was, later, the only one of his novels to be turned into a film, starring Rita Moreno and Van Heflin. *Fortress* and other books were translated into other languages, including Russian, Spanish, Portuguese, Italian, Czech, Roumanian, and German, selling well in foreign countries, often better than at home.

One of Bennie's longstanding jokes was: "What's the definition of a creative writer? One whose wife supports the family." It wasn't a joke if you were my mom, but neither were his own self-discipline and unwavering focus. Bennie didn't believe in writer's block. He even wrote a poem in Princeton Hospital during his last illness. He was lucky to be able to spend his whole life doing what he liked best.

SEPTEMBER 2005
WASHINGTON, DC

BRAIN GUY

BY BENJAMIN APPEL

CHAPTER ONE

Who could he shake down for some dough? In the Italian table d'hôte he cracked the last walnuts with a spiteful feeling that the meal had cleaned him out, but who gave a damn? Eighty-five cents plus fifteen cent tip. That skunked a buck. Hell, he needed money. It'd been a jinx all day. None of his horses'd come in. The numbers'd been n. g. And pay-day was a mile off.

The cashier took his last buck. He strode back through the palms with the warlike solemnity of a fellow returning to tip a waiter or a barber. "Thanks, Mista Tren,'" said the waiter. "You got horse for me, mebbe?" He slid the dime and nickel out from his fingers. "Horison is the fourth."

The waiter appeared as if he'd been rewarded by a spendthrift.

On Forty-second Street and Eighth Avenue he paused in the thin fog floating in from the river. It was almost nine. From the side-street brothels and hotels the Greeks were going to their coffee-houses for a night of gambling. Hell, he needed money.

Eastwards Forty-second was a foam of yellow light. Following its course with his eyes, he somehow felt broker than hell. He was the crème de la crème to waiters, but the world's biggest mug anywheres else. His face was Christless as a panhandler's. He thought about shaking down one of the speaks or joints that he managed discreetly as a real-estate collector. Who could he shake down without too much of a squawk? Crowds passed before him as if pinned immovable to metal strips. The crossroads of the world. Hot air. He killed time. The city of a million bugs chasing their behinds off for a few nickels. He was a louse, too, always broke, always in a panic to get some dough. Fastened to the fate of the metal strips, endless men and women were having their impact on his vision. Where were they going? What were their lives and what the hell was the difference?

He pulled up his coat collar, griped with himself for being groggy. He remembered his kid brother. He'd never had a good influence on the kid. Maybe it was too bad the kid was coming to town real soon. The kid was soft. He was hard-boiled. Being soft was nothing in the pocket. He decided to shake down Paddy, feeling swell inside as if he were turning over a new leaf. His face was beautiful with hope. Hell, Paddy ought to come across.

He hurried north, playing with two pennies in his pocket. Whose fault was it he was nuts about money? It was the fault of the Big Stem, fault of the Big Stink. You simply had to have dough. Paddy ought to be good for ten bucks.

Entering the side street, he shuddered. The El was at the end of Paddy's block. The tenement rows with their bleak staircases, the silence mean as a beggar's, impelled him to mind his own business. The smell of the Hudson was in his nostrils. He'd be one swell guide for a kid brother from a hick town.

His hand slid along the banister. He seemed to flit upwards through a smell of cats. On each landing there was a solitary lonely light. On the third floor he knocked at Paddy's door. The door slanted open an inch. Paddy peered out. The door edge cut down across his lips as if silencing them. The man whispered with the bitter humor of a stubborn wise-guy: "Ain't I glad? Phenagling Bill. Hell."

"Hello, Paddy." He pushed past the hostile paunch. The stench of rotten whisky stood behind him like a doorman. It was damn cockeyed. Since when did Paddy chuck parties?

He saw all together, swiftly, the three small square rooms of the railroad flat, the peeling paint, a big trunk. A radio was howling. Two couples were dancing. The men were slim ginzos who appeared to be trying to stick their bodies into the women. They stopped a second and glared at him with animal eyes. He didn't like their looks. Wops weren't up his alley. He nodded at the women. Bobbie and Madge were Paddy's whores. He grinned. He wanted dough, but those ginzos were after kife. One of them was shouting at Paddy, implacable with lust, suspicious. Bill was disgusted. Hell, he didn't want no piece of those dames. The ginzos could keep them. He appealed to Paddy. "Let me see you private."

The mick shook his big face. Sandpapered by age, his cheeks were large-pored. "Beat it. This is private." But just the same he led Bill into the last room, slamming the French door. They were alone even if the beds spoke for Madge and Bobbie.

"Listen, Paddy, did I or did I not get a cut in your rent? Right. I did. And no one's wise your joint's here."

"You got fifteen bucks outa me two weeks ago."

"And was promised twenty-five. You think it a cinch keeping the boss from getting wise?"

"You eat money." Paddy confronted him with the littlest of blue eyes, his face a pokerface all of a sudden. "You lousy heel."

"Quit belly-aching. Give me the dough."

"Yeh, yeh." He flung the door open, announcing: "This guy's Bill. He's O.K." Coming out of the room that led to the fire-escape, the others accepted him. It was different from coming in off the street. Since when did Paddy chuck parties, the chiseler, thought Bill. He didn't like it. Was Paddy figuring to pay him off in merchandise? The pimp was rubbing his clean red jowls, sidling over to him with the comradeship of one stag for another. "Bill, you're a guy." He pulled up his trousers so the crease'd keep. "If I weren't a good guy myself, I'd call you a lil sonufabitch."

"How about my dough?"

"Sweat for it. I did. Who'd aguess it with that goodlookin' mug of yourn. Madge is nuts about you." He smiled at the dancers in the cleared space. The long hairs of middle age stuck out of his nostrils. His shirt was blue silk, his manners the old-fashioned ones of a pre-war bartender.

"All dames are nuts on me, but who gives a damn? Got my dough?" He peered sideways at the big nose and chin of Paddy, whispering: "Since when do you chuck parties? Fishy, ain't it? If I didn't need dough real bad, I'd get the hell out."

"It'd be healthier."

"You don't faze me."

"Don't talk so loud."

The radio stopped. Out on the floor Madge was telling her partner to take a good flying trip for his guts, hurrying off into the last room, where she sat down on the bed. In the faces of the women there was the strained impatience of plotters approaching a climax. Bill shivered. He felt as if he'd missed a signal. Behind him Madge's eyes were forged steel-like with fear. And all the talk was stupid. The conversation seemed to be lagging behind, out of it all. Madge's deserted partner complained bitterly. Imagine chasing out on him. What was wrong? Did he stink?

Bobbie hugged the other ginzo. "I won't run off, Tony."

Tony laughed like a fool. He was in luck. His dame liked him. He squeezed her hand, his eyes innocent, betrayed. He was thinking of a good time, and the others, staring wickedly, thought of something else. Tony was pitted against them all.

Bill's heart pounded. Something was up. Even Madge, young as she was, was hep. The shades were pulled down behind her. He hardly felt Paddy's thumb jabbing into his side or heard the leering crack. Something was up. He had stumbled into it. Whatever was to be would be soon. Bill's head ached. The silly talk was unbearable. Fascinated, sick, he observed the spectacle of a man blind to the hostile eyes, the thumbs turned down against him. The others faded from sharpness like figures in an old photograph. He knew that Bobbie and the two wops were there because they had existed a half-hour ago. But out of that time nothing was clear except Paddy and the kid sulking in the third room. These two were cut out of his agonized awareness. His back was turned on Madge, but he was seeing her in the dress the color of a green cordial. Wavering on thought like a reflection on water, he saw the thin girl face, the woman's body. It seemed to him then, not seeing her with sight, that he loved her. Sure he did, and no use kidding about it.

The two ginzos were gabbing with fat Bobbie, while Paddy's head, colossal because all their words and motives behind the words emanated from him, nodded pale and evil, the eyes bright, the lips cold with the humor of a murderer. These two, Madge and Paddy, were the omens of what was to come. Bill puffed on his cigarette. He thought: Bobbie is twenty-five. Her words are false. Her mouth is false. She is not a woman who has been a fake to many men. She is a whore. Tony is a fool if he can't see how she's faking him. He was horrified at dumb Tony pawing her, his teeth a flash of life. He is to die, thought

Bill; they are to kill a man, I don't know why. It doesn't matter. Tony and Bobbie were dancing, their veins beating blood, the woman squirming her hips. Oh, there was something cockeyed in the flat, and everybody was wise except Tony. Paddy thumped his hand on Bill's knee. He grinned, fraudulently delighted. "You're a corker." He poured rye into his glass. "Why'nt you beat it?"

"What you going to do to Tony?" He felt slimed to be sharking for a few lousy bucks when death was in the flat.

Paddy rolled up out of his chair with the finality of one leaving on a steamer, waving the bottle of rye, gleaming brown facets of light. There was no bringing Paddy back. He was gone.

Bill wanted to scream out: "You dumb ginzo, get the hell out before you're carried out." Tony was dancing at his own funeral. Twisting his eyes into the rear room, he saw Madge still sitting on the bed. He wanted to say to her: "Aren't you sorry? At least we can be sorry." She lowered her eyes, a mad pretty kid. He was thinking of the Irish eyes of her, the long, sweet, white limbs. In his heart there was desire and pity. Why didn't he beat it while he had a chance? He couldn't move from his chair, nerveless, morbidly curious, laughing when Paddy asked him if he liked the young un. Tony flopped down in a chair, Bobbie on his lap, her dress above her knees, her legs hanging. Her cheeks were blown full with song, singing in a loud nauseously sweet voice. It was to be. Now. Paddy eased across the floor, his body stiff, polite. Bill leaned forward. Paddy, who rarely raised his voice, was bellowing. Paddy was in love with noise, increasing the radio's volume. Tony's pal crept behind him.

Bill distinctly heard his heart miss a beat, then another. Madge was singing, her voice all quavers. He started. Why not holler, too? Holler holler, oh, my God! Across the way, people were shouting: "Shut up, for Chris' sake." Voices from the flats above and below threatened: "Shut up." "Can the racket." "Cut it." "Get the cops." All the potential violence of their bodies exploded into noise. Bill wheeled round. Avoiding his eyes, Madge sang with the persistence of a set-off alarm-clock. It was impossible to think.

Dark-haired, both ginzos. Both must have hairy chests. The assassin stood directly behind Tony, stood in time itself that second like a statue on a pedestal. Paddy's mouth was a rubbery circle changing shape. The statue moved out of inanimation. The knife was out. Tony's pal lunged. Paddy winked at Bill as if to say: You'd hang around, huh?

Madge sobbed. Bobbie shot off the lap of the corpse.

It wasn't a corpse. Yes it is, thought Bill. He was stunned to see death catch up so fast with what had been such a fine animal. A minute ago Bobbie had snuggled up against the ginzo, walling him with her fat flesh so that his face was hidden, and all there was of a man were the two legs in their trousers. The legs are dead now, thought Bill. He is dead all over and lying on the floor all over. The sleek head was on the dirty carpet. The assassin wiped his blade. Even Bobbie had no guts for this, her rouge a mask plastered on pallor. The radio sang with the complacency of a robot. "Couldn't get you out, you sonu-fabitch," said Paddy. "You're in it."

Over and over again the slaughter re-acted itself, grinding his nerves like a needle stuck in a groove on a phonograph record. The chair in which Tony had sat was ventilated. Empty space cut through the middle by a decorative slice of wood. The knife had been lunged through the slit. What the hell was wrong with him? That was a dead man on the floor, no tailor's dummy. But still he didn't give a damn one way or the other. The wop was the pawn in a game he wasn't hep to. He heard himself saying: "I'm not in it. But how crazy to spot Tony with all this gang about!" This was what struck him above all else. To murder with such a crowd about. Holy Moses. That was dumb. There was a thing called the law. Tony wasn't a cow that could be killed legit.

Paddy was interested in the same problem. The two of them seemed to be debating in a forum. "They ain't no witnesses. You ain't one. Gene ain't." (Gene had finished wiping his knife and was dragging the trunk from the corner. He'd snapped up the top, dropping the bloody handkerchief to the bottom with a casual elegance as if it were a flower.) "The dames ain't witnesses."

Bobbie crossed herself, sitting down on the bed next to Madge. Both women were leaning on their elbows, a fatalistic chorus, scented, lewd, hard. Bill wondered how much there was in't for Paddy. Gene said: "I won't be no strongarm for him no more." He peered down at the corpse he'd been paid to protect as if remembering their business together. This was the only clue. The killing was over, ended forever. They were all safe and tomorrow would only be another day. Paddy stepped over. They lifted it off the rug, the weight running into the hips all of a sudden, lowering it into the trunk. The head hung back desperately, getting a last look. Paddy shut down the top, pulling the straps tight. He circled back to the chair, searching for stains, for any proofs that here a man had lived and died in a second, Gene lit a cigar. What was that? Christ. A fist pounded on the door. Bill gasped as if the corpse had decided to come out for another look. Paddy sat down on the trunk. "All you bastards," he said hotly. "Talk. Damn you, talk."

"A swell party," Bill said, punch-drunk. "How're the girlies?"

"Go to hell," said Madge.

"Open up. Open dat door." The fury of the tough domineering voice smacked through the door. Only a cop could yell like that.

Gene let him in. He was a fat man, tramping in with a stride as if he were on his beat. "What the hell's the row?"

"What row?" said Paddy.

"You got no ears? With the block callin' the station." His eyes circled about. "Ain't it classy?"

Paddy kicked his heels against the trunk. "Gwan home."

The cop was amazed. "You lousy pimp."

"You lousy flatfoot, ever hear of Kerrigan? He's my friend. He can tell you how to spot a joint. A coupla plainclothes rats knock the dame off, then pull the marked two bucks outa her sock and they got a pinch."

"I'll pull you in for riotin.'"

"See how far it gets you." Bill thought that under Paddy's behind there was the electric chair. "Don't be dumb, cop. This ain't a joint. This feller's the rent-collector. Ain't that proof things are oke?"

"What's your name?" the cop growled.

"Gwan, Bill," shouted Paddy.

"Bill, what else?"

"Bill Trent," said Paddy. "He collects for Stanger."

Bobbie giggled. They all seemed to be saying: You see what you get fooling around with Paddy, you see.

Bill choked. Yes, that was his name. The cop scowled at Paddy, neutral. He'd find out if Kerrigan was wise. He was gone, sore at not getting five bucks.

"Why'd you tell him my name? I'm liable to get in dutch if the cop sees my boss." The cops had his name. He was an accomplice. He couldn't rat. If the office got wind of this he'd be out of a job. How things broke.

"Chase after the flatfoot. Hey, flatfoot, me name is Bill Trent." Paddy was delighted at his fun.

"Your hot joke's liable to cost me my job."

"I'll stick a brassiere on you and peddle you to the boys."

"You're funny as hell."

Paddy glanced at Gene seriously. "McMann's waiting. Tenth and Fiftieth." He'd forgotten about Bill, speaking to him now with little interest. "Inside with the dames. Gwan."

Even now, Bill thought, in a fix and all, my job in the air, I pick my dames. He grinned sickly at the fool who sat down on the bed next to Madge and not next to Bobbie. He was afraid the pimp'd bawl out: "You like the young un, don'tcha?" He shook his head. It'd all happened to him, no fooling. He'd barged in for a shakedown. What a shakedown he'd got!

Paddy switched the radio on, stretching out on the couch, his eyes on Bill. Bobbie read a tabloid. The two men and two women were silent. The atmosphere was a family one even with the trunk pushed up against the wall. My heart's in that trunk, thought Bill, like hell. "You like the young un?" Paddy remembered. His brain was split up with different thoughts. The women and Bill could only think of the trunk, waiting for Gene to return, but he had other ideas. "I love her." He seemed to be speaking to himself, his lips shut, his head an auditorium in which talk roared…You were calm at the killing, so calm I admire you. You are Bill. I am Bill. You were smooth even with the cop snooping. He struggled to get inside of himself, to feel that Bill was himself, that he wasn't an outsider to himself, but a real fellow called Bill. His job was in the air. He was a witness. Here he was sitting on the bed, the kid close to him. He was balled up. What a joke, shaking down Paddy. He listened to the radio, trying to get hold of himself. Maybe the trunk was empty? He believed the murder and consequent events were a matter of hearsay, staring at the old-fashioned trunk with its broad straps. Madge was trembling. Poor kid. She wasn't more than sixteen. She wasn't shivering for nothing. Murder.

Bobbie read her tabloid with the stupendous peace of morons, the murder as forgotten as last week's customer. She was fake. He wouldn't touch her for anything. She was already filling in the time until the next excitement. Paddy grinned. If it weren't for Madge groaning a little, he'd never believe the trunk held a corpse. The radio played. Bobbie chewed gum. Again Paddy ribbed him about liking young uns. And what would the boss say? "You're fired, Bill, because the cop says you're a rat, and didn't you rent a flat to a pimp against my orders?' What a fix. And his kid brother coming to town. Joe Trent was the name of his brother. Joe was a decent young kid. Joe thought him a wonder. He was Joe's hero and therefore had both their lives to consider. Joe was the type of kid who thinks himself independent, but invariably follows the leader towards either good or evil. He'd be one swell leader for Joe. Dear God, he prayed, let me not spoil him.

"You like Madge?" He doubted whether Paddy had really spoken. Madge was a nice kid. He said: "Hey, Bobbie, what does the paper say?" It was difficult speaking. Through talk, through imitating the actions of a living man, he would finally move into life out of his doped dreaminess.

"Nothin' much," said Bobbie. He wanted to talk of headlines. He knew some. Tony The Wop Wiped. Paddy The Pimp Sought. Bill The Rent Collector Implicated…He was amazed at her reading the muck of other crimes. The blood was still hot in the poor ginzo. A short time ago he'd wanted things. Tony had gone home. The guy in the trunk was somebody else. The trunk was empty, maybe. It was easier to believe ties and shoes were there. That was customary. If the tabloid had said: There's somebody in a trunk in Paddy's joint, it would've been different. Murders belonged in newspapers. Clothes in trunks.

"We're all conventional," he said.

"You're crazy," Madge said.

He wasn't crazy even if they didn't get it. It was the most natural thing for Paddy and the whores to be conventional. "It's tough on you," he whispered to Madge. The murder was real for her even if the papers hadn't announced it. She didn't answer and he thought the murder was a fake. There would be no future consequences. It was a perfect job and nobody would ever find out. He had nothing to worry about.

The radio was in the middle of a jazzy number when Gene entered with McMann. McMann was thin, with a face of hard contours as in the photos on taxi licenses. The flat was crowded. They were all a little excited. McMann was the second shock to Bill that night. He was significant to him. He didn't know why. It was just so. It was like seeing the one face in a crowd that means something, that shocks one into thinking: Somehow I ought to meet him or her, or

I have met him long ago and can't forget. He breathed hard, baffled at the yoke uniting him with a stranger. McMann glanced at him, his eyes far away. The red-brown eyes held neither recognition nor interest. "What the hell you lookin' at?" said McMann.

"Don't mind him," said Paddy. "Want a drink?"

"Yep. that trunk heavy?" Bill knew who McMann was. McMann was Bill. McMann was the flowering of the seeds in him. He knew with the knowing of instinct that McMann was hard, ruthless, courageous. These qualities were in himself. He was pulled to this stranger like a sun fragment to its sun.

"Who the hell you lookin' at?" exclaimed McMann.

Paddy grimaced. "He's just a snoopin' weasel."

"A brain guy, huh?' He grabbed one of the trunk's handles, Gene the other. They complained it was pretty heavy, tugging it to the door. There was nothing in that trunk but clothes. Bill listened to them clumping downstairs. A man had been killed, but it was of no importance.

Paddy glanced at Bill. "You phenagler, see a damn?"

"Nothing. I'm worrying about my job."

"You gave McMann the once-over."

"Who is he?"

"A hack. Here's ten bucks. You'll be needin' it if you get canned." He laughed some more, thinking only of the fun of the moment, not confusing the fun with the murder.

Bill pocketed the bill. "If that cop sees my boss—"

"There was no cop, sonny."

"Can I go?"

"Sure. Unless Madge wants you?"

"Naw." He lingered as if he really ought to write his name in some visitor's book. Was there someone special he should say good-by to? There was no one. He was thinking of putting his coat on, but it was on. He'd worn it all night.

Even Madge had no use for him. Her eyes were blue dark in the whiteness of her face. Well, he'd seen a ghost too. Damn her. He'd like to give it to her where it'd do the most good. Everything was rotten, spoiled, stinking. The hell with the fake of her youth. He slammed the door. For the first time feeling gay, giddy. His heart sang in his breast. He was free. The fear that had hooked arms with him let go and skulked out of mind. It was easier than hell to kill a guy and dump him in a trunk. He was alive. He hurried down the tenement stairs. Out on the street he rubbed his eyes. "That was a party, Christ!" he exclaimed.

A few cabs were parked waiting for stray drunks. The mist hadn't thickened or lessened. It was exactly as it'd been. He whistled, stepping big steps down the street of speaks, garages, clip joints, and tenements of poor respectable folk on whom the vices had been quartered like a conquering army.

Was he glad to be alive? Thinking of Paddy, McMann, the women, was thinking of a strange race visited in a distant land. This was New York. This was nineteen hundred and thirty-one. This was getting on to the New Year. He pitied Madge more then ever and all the other kids sold for profit. On Forty-second and Eighth, the Franklin Savings Bank upset his pity. If he had five thousand in that stone pile he'd do something. He'd clean up things. Why kid himself? You needed about fifty million and different hearts and brains in people to make life decent. And that was out of the question. As long as men were men, the world'd be lousy. Best thing was to make some dough, and the hell with the world. His solution oppressed him, his soul full of decay. He was ashamed for men. By Christ, how could they sink so low? It was the fault of the plutocrats who allowed graft and white-slaving. He laughed bitterly. All human lice had mothers, all had homes, all had come in contact with something saving. Hell, his sociology was cockeyed. Yet Eighth Avenue was answering his doubt, even if the answer was silence, a finger on lips. What a petty grafter he'd been! He'd shaken down joints and crap places, but, by God, he could never sink into the real scum. He could never kill or white-slave. He remembered McMann, who probably drew the line nowhere. McMann was himself, his traits developed.

He laughed and laughed. In his pocket he had Paddy's ten bucks. It represented the mathematical number of times some machine had come across. It represented Madge's earnings. And he had pitied the damn little slut. He had had the gall to pity humanity. He had pitied the queenly bitch of a New York. He ought to pity himself instead, a louse if there ever was one. What about his job? He shrank to the tiny stature of one on a breadline. The city was queen again. If he lost his job it'd be pretty tough what with his brother coming to town. His brother was bringing a dog. A dog. A puppy. That just showed you how innocent Joe was.

He choked with hysterical laughter. Not once had he thought of ratting on Paddy, or actually wiping out one bit of filth in the filthy world. Aw, what was he eating himself up for? If he lost his job he'd make dough in some other way. He was one guy that wasn't going to starve. Guys like McMann never hit the breadline.

CHAPTER TWO

A paralysis of hate stiffened his limbs as the boss recited why "I must dispense with your services just at the present." The boss made an efficient picture in his swivel chair, the photographs of the real estate he owned hanging on the wall behind him. Flanked by all these possessions, each of which symbolized so many regiments of dollars, the army of which he was the general, he naturally girded up his loins as the interview progressed. For some time he'd been a collection of newspaper headlines. DEPRESSION CONTINUES. INDUSTRY SLACKENS. PRESIDENT HOOVER COUNSELS AMERICAN SPIRIT. BANKS FAIL.

The light came back to where they were like an old man applying for a job. The boss had yellowish hands that went swell with what he had to say. Bill hated himself. How comical and cool he was, behaving just like the Mr. Meek and Mild of the comic strips! He could give the boss a headline. MAN FOUND IN TRUNK. Let him put that in his pipe and smoke it. He had to speak up. No use letting Stanger go on forever. The boss was inspired by the stern morality of the depression. He spoke of the American Will, and how depressions came in cycles. His dyspeptic face had the haggard cheeks of a woman-hound. The boss is old, Bill thought; I am young if that's any satisfaction without a job.

"I realize all you're telling me, Mr. Stanger. What with foreclosures and tax sales we're losing many collections. Business is punk. Conceded. But I'll take a cut gladly." He stared at the boss as if the boss were an animal in a trap. Stanger nodded. No use. The trap wouldn't hold. "I'm sorry, Bill. But we must do without you entirely. Damn the times. Put yourself in my place. You know how the office's been hit."

"I wouldn't have lost my job if it weren't for that mess. I appreciate your reticence, but that cop did spoil it for me. I heard all about it, how he said we were maintaining a nuisance at 348 and I was wise to it. If that cop hadn't found out, I'd still be here."

"Well, we all know that houses down here in the west side are loaded with all kinds of joints, but, the point is, our knowing isn't official. I'm not blaming you. Most rent-collectors tax these joints. Why not? With real estate shot to hell, nine landlords out of ten are damn glad a brothel or a crap joint's paying rent for a flat that'd otherwise be empty. A rent's a rent. But I can't keep you now. If I did, the cops'd watch all my properties like hawks. They'd be out to hang up one of their nuisance signs. Therefore, if a collector of mine gets caught he must go."

"That clears the ground." He had an idea the boss was more glad than sorry. The damn hypocrite got a pleasure out of the mistakes of others, smirking now because he'd got it in the neck.

"I probably would've been forced to let you go anyway. The little landlords are getting squeezed out, and with their properties reverting to the banks and mortgage people, I'm losing out on customer after customer. And the decline in insurance. What would you do in my place but stifle all feelings, despite my friendship with your father. I can't help it, Bill." He was happier, his heart contained in the formula, sacking Bill the second time. He shifted his eyes towards the ceiling as if asking God to approve of his humanity.

"I guess so."

Bill listened. What would McMann've done? Spit in his damn face. His heart suddenly banged with a fear of the boss reading his thoughts. He tasted an almost physical nausea on his tongue. Oh for the guts to cry out: "The hell with your damn job and your damn fight talk. Shove both up." But something might be gained from the boss, something might be gained yet. The mission strangers in town wouldn't help him with a dime. He felt suave, like a fellow everybody admires at a party. Where'd the calm come from? McMann couldn't've been smoother. He put the job behind him. It was the edge, but he refused to jump off.

"If my father were in your place he'd act the same way." That was it. Force some sentiment out of the dry man before him, who had nothing but lust. Sentiment. Try, try until you succeed. "The times are against all of us." He observed the effect of this with the scientific scrutiny of a kid waiting for the rocket to flare.

The boss lit a cigar and thought of Bill's far-away father. He'd been dead fifteen years in time and many centuries in memory. "Your father was a fine man," he conceded irritably as if speaking of George Washington, reluctant to make the admission, suspecting his ex-employee of some game.

"He spoke often of you. You were his best friend." This was putting dart after dart into the boss's conscience.

The boss trembled. He was like a woman resisting a ravishment, fighting memory. It was no use. He couldn't order Bill to shut up. There was a Sunday code a fellow had to respect even if it hurt like hell. "Yes yes," he said as if saying no no.

"He used to speak of your days at college, always sorry he couldn't live in New York. When I finished college he was happy to send me here, away from home, to work for you." He didn't curse the hypocrite. He just tied him up. The boss couldn't move a muscle and now Bill jabbed him with dose after dose of "memory" as if from a hypo. The boss fidgeted. Pink spots appeared on the ivory of his yellow cheekbones. It was a pleasure to contemplate his agony, for that's what it was, the agony of someone in a hell, in a past irrecoverable but still meaningful. It had held Bill's father, an old friendship still holding some truth for the man Stanger had become. He stared the longest time at Bill, the smooth-shaven face smelling of lilac and talcum, the crisp jaw lines, the full mouth, the blaze of blue eyes balanced finely the straight nose. He was envious, and regret wrinkled his face. This Bill was a ladies' man, and so young. So young and handsome. He thought of Bill's father when he too had hummed with animal energy, had been a man. Wonderful to be young, needing no stimulus. He was sick to be reminded of the fertility pills he took, hating Bill for shoving him back into the world before the war. It was gone and no use haunting it. He suspected the young man was seeking for an advantage. It was all right for Bill to try to put one over with his talk of the past, but it would not be all right for him to be a sucker. He glanced at Bill as if he were a landlord asking for a loan he wouldn't get in a million years. The boss felt better. "Since I didn't give you notice and because of our connection, well, this envelope is a month's salary." He grinned benevolently with an unspoken comment: There, you can tell your old man I'm not so bad. "Thanks. I'll be needing it. My young brother's in town. We'll need it to live on."

"Joe in town? Why?"

"It hasn't been so good for him since my mother died. You know how it is. Living in a small dinky Pennsy town like Easton. It was no go. He's a proud kid and couldn't hit it off with our cousins. Without parents, well…" He was heaving his darts openly, shameless, stabbing sympathy into the boss. He could imagine the boss thinking: The two poor kids, no father no mother, orphans orphans *orphans* in the cruel world. Bill quivered, gloating at the reactions of his target. Say "orphan," and the boss'd react one way. Say "whore," he'd react another.

"But couldn't you two go home where you have relatives? If I weren't tied up I'd like to do something. But I'm in the red and this is a rotten town to be in without a job or family."

"Impossible. We'd rather starve or sleep in the park than go home." The boss sighed, his eyes sad and tragic. He became limp like a woman who has fought her attacker and at last surrenders. It was a rape. "I'm sorry, Bill. If I could help—"

"You can help. You've many properties full of empties."

"Well?"

"My brother and I could stay in one until we got work. It's a nerve, but I'm remembering your friendship for my father and my family. Why, Joe's always regarded you as an uncle." He felt cheap, ashamed at his peddler's psychology.

"Taxes and interest are sky-high."

"We don't want to move into one of your good houses where you've a chance of renting."

"Yes?"

"How about those properties of yours off the El, near Greenwich Street? The houses on Leroy that are always empty? I've heard you say a thousand times they're worthless."

"You'd move into one of those?"

"Better than sleeping in the park."

"Hell, if you're willing to live down there you can stay as long as you want. You're kidding?"

"No. They're better than the park or a flop-house."

The boss was plaintively eager to shy away from talk of money. "For the sake of our special connection— Why, Bill, only too happy." He seemed cheerier, hearing himself recite to friends *what he did* for the sons of his old crony. "The best of the lot's one on Leroy, between Greenwich and Hudson. A slum neighborhood, but it's a clean house. Stay there as long as you want. It's a roof at the least. Maybe something'll turn up."

"Thank you, Mr. Stanger. Thanks awfully. It's swell. My father couldn't't've been more decent." They gazed ironically at each other, reviewing the game that'd been played. Both appreciated Bill's glibness. The boss seemed to see Bill's father hovering on angel wings over the ink-well. It did a fellow good to do good.

"I'm sorry I couldn't have done more. The janitor's a Mrs. Gebhardt. Have her phone me for instructions." He smiled, admiring Bill. "You're a conniver working me up to a free apartment. But I don't regret it. Not in the least. I owe something to the sons of my best friend." He paused as if about to add: Remember me to the folks. "You and Joe drop around for lunch any time. No need to go hungry. Come up for dinner, any time at all."

"Good-by and thanks."

"Good-by." He fumbled with a letter, a dodge he always resorted to to end an interview. Bill went too far with his wisecracks. He ought to respect the dead. The job was wiped out. His bravado flamed into zero. He'd die before he'd ever eat one of Stanger's salvation hand-outs. "Good-by." He might need the boss again. Everything was fair in war. Hunger was war. He shut the door, smiling at the outer office. He had the sack. What a skunk he was to rake up his father's bones for charity! But a fellow had to live. None of the other collectors were around. They were all out hounding tenants, shaking down joints. The three stenographers, with the wisdom of those whose jobs are still solid, guessed he'd got it between the eyes. Their faces were three pennies.

Hell, if he wore a brassiere and rouged up like a fast number or a dame ready to be convinced, he'd be set too. Stinky Stanger and the damn stenos. He was sorry for them. "So long, kids. Best of luck. I'm out in the snow and got to find a dame to keep me."

Miss Tassio laughed. The lean redhead who always looked hungry stared straight at him. Miss Kornitz, who lived over on Avenue A, hung her head, ashamed. He patted her shoulder. "Don't mind me, kid. It's a lousy world, and no one can help what they've got to do. People got to eat." Why'd she hang her head? Better to look up into God's mug and give Him what for. He shut the door.

The dust roared up the street. The New Year was just entering people's consciousness. Although Christmas hadn't tinseled into sight, he seemed to feel the New Year. Ring the bells. It's coming. Horrah! The stenos were watching him through the plateglass window. Then they began to work. Typewriters clicked. He laughed. Time must go on, and Progress. What grand sayings! He studied his reflection in the glass, the camel coat and snapbrim felt. That was a good build he saw, handsome face. it was himself and it wasn't. This reflection was a ghost bidding him good-by from the office. He walked free from a self that had been. The Bill walking away was his new self, mysterious, strange to him. He'd been newborn. The old was dead. His new life was undetermined, unlived. Maybe Paddy'd get a job for him. Easy dough wasn't bad. A fellow had to live. Life must go on. You bet. He thought about his brother, Joe. What a lie! Joe wasn't due in New York until after New Year. Joe and the pup. By New Year he might be in the dough. You never could tell. One thing, he was going to get his hands on dough, he didn't give a damn how.

He had forgotten completely about the murder at Paddy's. And really there was no reason to remember it. It was just another one of those things that never make the papers and leave no impress on the minds of the performers. The star of the show is got rid of, and that's all. When he thought of it, it was simply an unimportant accident that had caused the loss of his job. It was a banana peel and he had slipped. Hell, a guy needed dough. Dough.

CHAPTER THREE

The November sunshine was so bright on his eyes they felt shot to hell. He acted as if he had nothing to worry about. Yet he had the God-damned gate, and what was he moping for? He was aware of the granite city, and all things, masses, lights, people, were scratched on the surface of his eyeballs. He put his hand on his breast. What was the use? Forget it. He entered a Horn & Hardart. The money changer slid out two nickels towards him. He took them with a feeling that his cash was going, that he was flinging his money into air with drunken fists. More than ever he needed dough. The tiled eating-place was haunted by the presence of the bus-girls cleaning up the tables, treading silently. Here was a place to hug his misery. The food displayed behind glass was a museum exhibit bought by men who neither smiled nor frowned. He bit into his doughnut with a lonely intensity. He was right at home. He wasn't the only one in the boat. He sipped his coffee with the cheeriness of one who has begun to accept his misfortune. The hell with it all. He was young. The world was full of easy money. Maybe it was a good thing he had lost his job. Maybe he could coin more dough if he was on his own. What thoughts! Who the hell did he think he was?

He wondered what was to be done? He had no money in the bank. He'd spent every nickel fast as he made it. Salary, graft, shakedown money. And Joe coming to town after New Year. Joe and a pup. Just a happy family. Joe depended on him. He had twenty bucks in the dresser at the hotel room. A month's salary. Fourtimes twenty-five plus twenty. One hundred twenty. That was dough. That was something. What a sucker to think he was licked! He had a place to live in. Two guys could buy a lot of food for one hundred twenty bucks. He grinned at working the boss into a free flat. Why, he was a bloated millionaire. Near him an old man with eyes protruding like old ivory cane-tops was guzzling soup. The old man murmured to himself. Bill laughed. Christ, he was young, smart, strong. He had some money. The city was jammed with a million devils worse off than himself. No one paid any attention to him laughing. They were used to anything. What he had to do was simple as pie, a cinch. He had to shake down as many speaks and joints as he could before everyone wised up that he was canned. When he stepped into the sun again, he had walked out of respectability. His fate was floating loose as a cloud. This Forty-second was a new street in a new town. His life was new. He passed Hubert's Flea Museum, the posters of legless women and bearded men, the burlesques with the big color portraits of tenement girls who'd made good and were stripped naked to prove it. A huge sign read: TILLY PIPICK FROM THE BRONX. He was accosted by the sexiness of a street turned whore, bragging of a good time for little money; the radio stores, the burlesque queens, the cafeterias, dance halls, and cut-price haberdasheries pleaded for his attention. He'd been in a murder. He'd lost his job. So what? He hit Ninth Avenue and Paddy's Market. The wagons of yellow and orange fruit, the apples and bananas, shone their bright primary colors under the drab bridge of the El. The only immaculate things were the fruits, the piles of silvery fish, the masses of coffee beans. Bill pepped it up, briefly helloing the barbers, grocers, and other tenants who knew him and still thought he was the rent-collector. He said to them: "See you tomorrow, Wiberg." "Too busy, Gus." "Got work to do." Up the sidestreets yellow and cheap with sun, where the cars were parked from corner to corner, the tenements also in lines, but forever immovable with the eternity of squalor, he chased the dollars.

A fellow was gabbing with one of those skinny hot girls who eye every male. Bill brushed by them in the doorway where they courted, thinking of Madge. The perfume of the kid, the smell of her, belonged to Madge, though the girl was someone else. He knocked at many doors and chiseled Jewish and Greek gamblers with flabby card-sharp hands, owners of brothels and speaks, all the easy-money boys in shady rackets. "Hell," said Herman. "You leech. I lose all my cash to some Greeks—"

"If it ain't Billy. No dough, Billy."

"Five's all I can spare," said Pete.

"Come nex' week."

"Go to hell."

"Wednesday. O.K. Positive."

"Come next week."

"Come next week."

"Wanta tear off a piece? Dough's scarce."

"Cop yerself a sneak."

"Nex' week."

"One sawbuck's all you get."

"I'm tired shellin' out."

"Come next week. I ain't no Morgan."

"Take a drink like a good feller."

"The hell with you, you bastard. Beat it."

"I'll give ya ten when you move me."

At the end of the day he had over forty bucks. The boys had belly-ached, but forty wasn't bad. So long, easy money. When would he be seeing it again? It wouldn't be bad making a lot of it. A smart guy always could. And was he smart? He was smart.

The next morning even the loafers on the corner were wise to him. The word had got around that Bill Trent was canned. Angelo, the bootblack, tipped him off the bookie was out to collect. The little wop ran out of his parlor, stuck on to the building proper like a coffin-shaped wart. Ninth and Tenth Avenues, that he had bossed as the landlord's representative, were comically hostile. They were sorry, but laughed just the same. He'd slipped on the banana peel. Just too bad, Bill. Tough luck, Bill. What you gonna do, Bill? The hundred and twenty bucks didn't look so big. Yesterday's shakedown money didn't help much.

He was dispossessed and put outside the walls of the rich city. He was outside, no more one of the employed, one of the host of inside men, the bankers, butchers, gamblers, streetcleaners, who all had some function in the city and were paid for it. He moped the morning away. He checked out of his hotel. They could shove their room and bath and circulating ice water for eleven bucks a week up their behind. He'd go down to Stanger's joint on Leroy and pick out his duplex with toilet in the yard so you could get fresh air any day or season.

He took the downtown El, getting off at Christopher Street station, hurrying along the platform with its urinal old New York smell. He was bust, but he wouldn't stay that way. Loads of dough in town. He'd shaken down enough pimps, gamblers, snow-peddlers, to realize that. Guys like Paddy or McMann always had plenty. Ninth Avenue, twisting southwest at little West Twelfth, had become Greenwich Street, completely covered over by the El. The light slanted between the crossties, holding the gloomy sun. As he walked, the sun darkened. It was colder. Could you beat it? He was always thinking of McMann. Far up ahead, Greenwich, somber, deserted, seemed to end in a grayness without bulk or dimension. Warehouses, machine-shops, trucking offices, with their great wagons backed right up on the cobbled sidewalk. It was a district of huge brown horses and heavy men, remote from uptown New York. It made him think of pennies, of men in caps. Three blocks west, the Hudson was a multitude of hoarse river voices crying up of facts hard, bitter, turbulent.

He tightened his fists, pushing his jaw forward. By Jesus Christ, he wasn't going to be licked. He pulled his hat brim lower over his eyes, holding anger in his hand like a blackjack. Didn't he have plenty contacts with the easy-money boys? Take Paddy for instance. He'd known Paddy two years. Maybe Paddy'd show him a few things, especially since he was in on one of Paddy's little jobs. Leroy was between Hudson and Greenwich Streets. Opposite Stanger's house a printing plant and a warehouse divided the entire side. Small red three-story houses went from corner to corner. There were battered ash-cans. No doubt a spinster and a cat lived in each little house. His new home. Hoorah! He missed the push of people; smoking on the sidewalk, his guts flowing out of him. His lips hung slack. Where was everybody? This part of town, destitute, forgotten, a ghetto of solitude, was outside the walls, cast out from the prosperous boroughs. To the east autos were speeding to South Ferry. On West Street the elevated highway was crowded with wheels beating it away. He smiled at his home. The paint on the red bricks was peeling. The crinkly edges like a plant growth. Wasn't he a lucky guy to get his rent free? That bastard Stanger. No wonder he'd been so liberal. In the vestibule he rang Mrs. Gebhardt's bell.

She was a tall woman. Her eyes were blue and clean. Her teeth protruded slightly. Catholic buck teeth, he thought, but she isn't Irish. She was blond, with the scrubbed cleanliness of the poor. "You certainly keep the house spick and span, Mrs. Gebhardt," he said. "I used to be in real estate. I'm going to live here and Mr. Stanger wants you to phone him for instructions."

She acted as if she wanted to retreat a step, watching him with a tension that was almost fear.

"It's no racket, lady. You call Mr. Stanger and you'll see." He glanced at the four letter-boxes on each side of the vestibule. There were name cards in about half of them. "Plenty empties."

"You say I call up?"

"Don't be so nervous. I'm one of the boys from now on."

"No phone here."

"Let's go to the corner, then." She got a coat and they went out. On the corner of Leroy and Hudson, there was a coffee-pot and six or seven kids hanging out. They looked at Bill and Mrs. Gebhardt with the sexy appraisal of guys with nothing else to do. Mrs. Gebhardt flushed and muttered: "Loafers."

He agreed with her. Those kids never worked and always had some money. He wondered how many brats Mrs. Gebhardt had. Her hips were so wide, her hair so yellow, her flesh so clean, she was the type to have six or ten, all with yellow hair and clean as washed pigs. Maybe some daughters in the lot, and no wonder she was sore at the gang. Those kind of kids fixed many a dame's wagon. Inside the coffee-pot, the pay station stood stiff as a cop. He gave her a nickel. A pimply cashier smiled at him. Every floozie was nuts about him. Now he listened as Mrs. Gebhardt dialed his office. Good-by to the office.

"Hello," she said, while he waited. "Can I speak to Mr. Stanger, please?" Finally she hung the receiver up. "Mr. Stanger says for you to pick out any flat you like." They returned. He was thoughtful. How many times would he be coming down to his home from Hudson Street, passing the gang of kids?

He inspected the old railroad flats, three rooms emptying into one another. The corridors were hushed. It was a house seemingly deserted by its tenants. The heavy woman preceded him into rooms dry and hard as bones. He wanted to shout: "I've seen enough." And was it himself, at last, who selected a front flat on the third floor? "This'll do."

"You sure? Well, if you need me, we got the flat back of the stairs."

"Thanks. I want to plan my furniture, my baby grand and library."

She laughed. He was alone in his three rooms. Home sweet home. The paint was in fair condition. The floors were scrubbed clean. Hell, it wouldn't be forever. Once he hooked into real dough, once…He'd have an electric bill. There was no steam heat, but the middle room had a small gas radiator. Another bill. There was a gas range in the kitchen. Where the hell was the toilet? Christ, only the one on the floor to be shared with three other flats. But Mrs. Gebhardt said only one of the three was occupied, by an old man with some sort of pension. Not so bad. No kids to mess up the seat. And he could always use hotels or the Grand Central. One room was the kitchen, the middle room'd be his parlor, the room on the street'd be bedroom. He looked out at Leroy, feeling secure looking from the inside out. He had a roof at least. Across the way, trucks were loading up in the yard of the printing plant. A great iron gate was raised as if prisoners were preparing to depart on the truck. What an ideal place for a murderer! What a hide-out. What was he thinking of?

He had come down in the world. Free rent. He'd have to buy a bed and furniture. Poor Joe, still in Easton, in a big sunny room on a street with trees, didn't even guess as to his future. He ought to write a letter and tell him to stay where he was. A big nice room wasn't worth throwing away.

He saw his brother's face as if it were a death mask. Life had come to this, to seeing things as still and dead. This nice big sunny room. And trees. Let him stay home. But the kid was to set on living with him. He forgot Mrs. Gebhardt, betrayed by a dream of childhood, a long, slow memory of green things and a town and parents. He stared out on Leroy Street, his heart expanding into a vagueness, precious and vanished. Tears shot into his eyes just as they did when he was touched by some movie. He didn't fight the tears as he did at movies, where the dark was full of eyes, but let them roll down his cheeks. What was the use? There was easy dough. It was his job to connect. He felt so bitter, so wolfishly alone in the world, his self-pity was almost a hate. Inwardly he was shaking his fist at everything that had happened. Now miraculously he was at ease, sitting at his deathbed, the death of his old life, mourning silently, reconciled to his loss. A fellow like McMann was always in the dough.

CHAPTER FOUR

The next few days wasted away like those when one is coming out of flu. His heart was numbed, but the body continued its adventure with living. On Ninth Avenue he spent a bartering morning in the shadow of a second-hand furniture store. The proprietor was a fat ugly Jew who didn't wear a derby tilted on the back of his head, but appeared as if he should. "Vell, vot do you vant mit my life? Here's a loffy double bed mit a dresser, new, ain't it, mit chairs like iyon." Bill dickered with him, his body roused up to the duel of money. He sunk his fist into mattresses, cutting the dealer's price with the virtue of a man who knows he's going to be gypped anyway. He almost had a good time as if there wasn't a damn thing to worry about, buying what he needed, playing at settling down all afternoon. He arranged the furniture, put the linen and towels in the dresser, hung his ties on a rack, had the gas and electric companies turn on their services after a flying visit to their immaculate museum-like offices on Irving Place. He got settled. His body had done the trick even while his brain remained aloof.

And one morning when he gazed out on the iron gate and the truckers, his heart was sound again. The new life into which he had dropped like one from the sky was his life, and accepted as such. Only a guy like McMann would've been at home in ten minutes, but it had taken him three days.

Mrs. Gebhardt was a great help, cleaning the flat when he was out. "The boss says to make you comfortable." And he, who'd been motherless a long time, considered that it was nice of her even if it was a pain. Why'n hell should she mother him? Sometimes he loitered in her flat a few minutes. It was clean as a peasant mountain hut. On Leroy Street her flat was a fairy-tale.

He got acquainted with the family. Mr. Gebhardt worked among the fruits and vegetables down in the produce markets near Washington Street. He was a big raw man, crisp as lettuce, with hair like dry straw, and a red smiling face. The four children he divided into two groups. One group consisted of the three little ones, with indefinite sexes, hands usually free from dirt, similar in size and texture as cucumbers. Then there was a big sister, big Cathy, sixteen and virginal. The domesticity of these Bavarians in the steel of the city was a peace about him, the names of the children a song of decency and the green earth. Frederick, baby Carl, Gertrude, and big girl Catherine. Freddie, Gertrude (no one abbreviated her name, somehow) Carlie, Cathy.

Then, completely settled, he worried about his dough. He better look out. He ought to see Paddy instead of sitting on his pants. He still dropped in on the Gebhardts with a chocolate bar for the kids, but even Gebhardt guessed his alert sharp manner wasn't the nicest thing. The first communal glow was gone, the feeling that he was involved intimately with them like one of a shipwrecked party. Cathy began to blush when he helloed her. Cathy had a swell build. If he wasn't such a good guy and grateful and so on, he'd like to lay her. All these tenement kids were easy.

He wrote to his brother, itemizing the flat, the gas radiator, the outside toilet, the poor chances, advising Joe to stay where he was. How was he to make money? He'd called on a number of real-estate firms and agencies, wanting a job in the jobless city where the employed all looked like soldiers not knowing when they'd get theirs. It was 1931. In another year the nation would vote on Hoover's policies. Next November there would be the dubious sort of hope all Democrats experience at the polls. What good did that do him? He spoke to the pale swarm of interviewers and bosses, who listened, smoked, and uniformly moaned about business. He produced letters of reference. There were no jobs. Men much longer in the real-estate field than himself couldn't land a thing. Real estate was plain lousy. The banks and mortgage companies were foreclosing right and left. In 1930 some eighty millions of properties had been foreclosed. Thirty-one was twice as bad, and he wasn't the type to find work. He wasn't the stubborn-chinned, light-blue-eyed type who have the guts to make the round of agencies and offices day in and day out for weeks and months with a courage superior to that of dying. He was too soreheaded, too spineless, for the endless Spartan ordeal. And always there was dream of easy money. How could a fellow take a job (he had just one offer) for ten bucks a week, to collect forty houses, when that job was worth thirty bucks at least? When, given a break, a fellow could pick it off the streets? Why sweat for pennies when the greenbacks were waiting to be plucked? He'd have to starve before he'd work for ten bucks. He turned the offer down.

He ate in cheap cafeterias where everybody wore their hats and coats; speculating about Paddy, McMann, all the dead-eyed crowd of hangers-on, the bookies, pimps, good-time boys, who earned such a fine living with less brains and guts than lice. He had picked up too much easy sugar, had grifted ten bucks in ten minutes. How in hell could he work an eight-hour, six-day week for a lousy stinking tenbuck, where he'd be checked up with no chance to shake down anybody? That was no job. That was slavery. The thing to do was see Paddy. Paddy only gave him a few minutes to explain, and then laughed like a hyena. "You sonufabitch, so you got your peeps open for the main chance?"

"I need some dough. Why the hell don't you give me a break?"

"You?"

"Sure me. I don't need to be on any probation. Who wants to hang out on a corner for years, shooting pool, crapping around for two-cent jobs." Damn right, he didn't want to be one of the reserve force who never work, herding together, waiting for the chance to make good.

That day Paddy was wearing a blue shirt. He was nodding like a father, tickled to be handing out advice. "You might get a break with Duffy and Spat's mob of kids. Try them. Speak to Duffy."

"Not for me. I know some of them kids. Ray, Schneck, Mike. I've shot pool with them. They're kids. I've got a brain in me. I don't want to mope around with them."

"You're in a helluva hurry."

"Why not? The town's full of easy dough, full of sporty guys who sleep late, eat well, and spend their afternoons doping out horses. I'm not going to hang out with Duffy's kids. They're heels. I want to do business with you."

"With me?"

"Sure. Like we done in the past."

They thought of the murder. "Yeah?" said Paddy, hiding behind that. "Yeah" like a kid round a corner.

"We got something between us. You could trust me."

"You've got too many ideas. Come around tomorrow." He winked. "The young un's nuts about you. I'm nuts about you myself. You got nerve. If they don't murder you, you lil sonufabitch, you'll be a big shot. I'm getting old and gray. I need a smart feller like you."

"You're a lousy liar, Paddy. Don't kid me."

"You got my number, kid."

"I wish I had."

Paddy said: "Tomorrow, smart guy."

CHAPTER FIVE

The women were out, but some of their things were lying on the bed. "It smells like a department store where all the customers are dames."

"Hello, Bill." Paddy's hair was pomaded. "Afternoons ain't worth a thing. I let them off. But if I knew you were coming I'd akept Madge home."

"You knew I was coming."

"How did I know?"

"You didn't get me here to kid around?"

"Maybe. I like a good joke." Big-jowled, impressive, Paddy was the pump, ruddy sort who are usually expansive, but now his discretion was that of a lean killer. He looked steadily at Bill. About him and the flat there was a stale odor of women and the busy night-times. The linoleum reflected a glassy light.

"I was sacked account of you." He frowned. "There's no work."

"You ain't the only one."

"Christ sake, you can give me a break."

"Maybe I could." He was grinning, as if he had determined on this facial expression and was resolved to keep it. He picked his creased trousers an inch higher, whistling with the monotony of a calliope.

"I'm ready to do anything. Hell, I was smart enough to shake you down regular."

"Yeah. A real smart guy."

"Then we got that trunk between us."

"You said that last time. Listen. Get yourself a job with a real-estate bunch. There's no room for you."

"There aren't any jobs." He spoke with the hysterical urgency of a man with one hope, and beyond that the breadline. "A fellow in your racket can use somebody you can trust. You're liable to get in dutch any day, and then who'd stick by you?"

"You bastard," said Paddy. "The hell with teachin' me what to do."

"You can use somebody you can trust."

"How do I know I can trust a smart guy?"

"Give me a break." He imitated Paddy, not ironically, but through some instinct for preservation. His features masked into a hard face. His eyes were cold balls. He sucked in his upper lip, biting on the inner flesh. Neither said anything, listening to words unvoiced, to intentions secret in brain. The kimonos lay soft and whorish on the bed. A smell of disinfectant. In the room on the fire-escape the sun glared. They waited for their paths to cross again. "You're first rate," said Paddy without admiration. "You got nerve. You talk tough, but I wonder if you got guts." His blue eyes swam on the tops of their pouches. "You wanta flop into something soft, but it ain't easy."

"No use heeling around with Duffy's kids."

"You're in a hurry."

"I'm no dumb kid. You see them in pool parlors or on corners. They get nowhere 'cause they got no guts. They eat. Sure. And a little job now and then keeps them in cat money."

"You got things sized up." He seemed like an elderly man, the poise, the hard eternity of the criminal dropping from him. "You're a nervy bastard 'cause you don't know better. Dumb, but what's the diff? Fact is you're nervy. I'm in right, but there's no tellin! Mad dogs always on the loose." He sighed, his eyes distant as ever so that it was impossible to say whether he was putting on an act or not.

"That's what I want. An even break."

"You'd be nix carrying a rod. See? I know. Hell, you're a funny guy." His laughter boomed up, false and hollow. "Here's an address. It belongs to Pop. You go down'n see'm. See? Wait for me."

"I don't get it."

"You're American, ain't you? You're no dumb Yid or ginzo or mick. Cut the bunk." He smiled benignantly.

"It's not clear—honest, Paddy."

"Either you do it or you don't."

"It's a go." He offered his hand.

"Shove it up," said Paddy, "with the rest of the collitch stuff."

"Thanks for the break."

"I ain't promised you nothin'."

"Christ, I'm glad. One business is like another to me."

"Oh, beat it," Paddy said wearily, "before you queer yourself altogether."

CHAPTER SIX

This was the beginning. He snorted at something theatric in the whole business. Maybe Paddy was tricking him? The flight of El stairs ascending to the level of the platform was his first stride towards opportunity. He'd have a job at the end of the ride. Who wouldn't feel the nuts? The El snaked towards South Ferry between the tenements crowding close to the rails. The conductor bawled the stations. A sexy thrill ran through his marrow. He stared at the women who came on and went off. It was as if he had dosed himself with a drug, cocky, impudent, striping the women naked as they sat. "The dead thrall of doing nothing was at an end. He'd be in the dough. He knew plenty storekeepers who had cash-boxes to raid…The train curved into the brightness of South Ferry. Far across the gray flat of water, the Statue of Liberty stood gripping her torch with the stubbornness of a small child. Salt smell in the harbor. The hearing of harbor sounds. The sight of the autumnal trees. He got off, jostled by the bodies of going somewhere as if in search of their minds left at home. He boarded the Second Avenue El, finally walking down the flight of iron stairs into a strange city.

The people were smaller, fatter than the Irish German American residents on Leroy. They smelled rich, oriental, crowding the ghetto sidewalks. Peddlers sold shoelaces, pretzels, herring. Slabs of pink smoked salmon, fish in tubs, kosher butcher stores. And thronging and bargaining on the streets was a city of Jews.

Peering inside the window of the address, he felt his spine taut and rigid. He went in deliberately, now that he was committed. It was three o'clock. Kids were loose from public school, playing ball, chalking the sidewalks with information about Izzy who loved Anna. The door opened before him, yet he still remembered the first sight of ghostly men behind the plate glass. He, Bill Trent, had business with Isaac Markow's Rumanian Tea and Coffee House. That was something it wasn't easy to get over.

It was a long, large room with small marble-topped tables about which men in caps and hats were playing checkers and pinochle, sipping Turkish coffee from demi-tasses. He hesitated on the dirty floor, wondering why tough guys always wore their hats so low over their eyes. Where was Pop? A man with a bulldog face and a paunch held tight in a buttoned sweater too small for him swaggered over. "Yeah, mister, what you want?"

"I'm supposed to meet Pop."

"You know him you find him." His eyes were stupid, shining immaculate as artificial eyes. He dug his hands into the pockets of his sweater. A thick thunder of Yiddish, cracked by sharp and sudden laughs, hung over the tables. He searched among the mustached and clean-shaven for a stranger. Dark eyes glinted at him over saucers of tea. In the rear at an immense wooden table an old man was watching him, leaning on a cane.

"Pop?" called Bill. The old man nodded.

"What you want?" He was in for it now. The bulldog had changed into a kibitzer at a card game. "Paddy sent me to you. Did he telephone? I'm Bill." Pop had the most surprising blue eyes. They gleamed in a whitish stiff face, with a heavy gray mustache. He was dressed in serge, his hat straight on his head. His neck was very thick, as if he'd been as strongarm in his youth. "I hear of you. Paddy say you good worker. Come." He led the way behind the table into another room, secretive with emptiness. The tables were covered with red checkered cloths. A bar was in one corner. The laughter alone had followed them from the coffee house. Bill listened to it, the raw hawhaws of gambling men. They laughed like Duffy's Irish toughs. These are Yids, he thought amazed, Yids. He couldn't believe Yids could have such nasty mugs or that all Yids weren't tailors and such meek guys. He couldn't get over this ghetto rathole where everything should've been different and wasn't. A fellow like McMann wouldn't've been fazed, but he was green as hell. Pop had nothing to say, breathing in the afternoon air, heavy and defunct here, where all life began late at night. There was nothing to be learned from Pop's eyes except an uncompromising vigilance.

"Did Paddy explain why he sent me?"

"I do anything for Paddy."

"He's a fine fellow."

"I write him bonds, tens'n tousands bailbonds." He rapped on the table, calling out in an old tired voice: "Sammy, Sammy, schnapps." The waiter hopped out of the kitchen in the rear. He wasn't in livery, but was dressed in a Canal Street suit—a skinny man with wide lips pulled away from each other and taut on a small, almost chinless head. His complexion was a ruddy brown, the nose flat, the eyes holes in the skull. He set down two glasses and a bottle with treacherous dexterity, and retreated to the bar, where he began to polish the wood, never glancing at them. If that guy doesn't carry a gat, nobody does, thought Bill.

Pop poured out the drinks. Bill swallowed, gasped. Pop was white and flabby as if he'd never drunk.

"Paddy a gud friend," said Pop. speaking carelessly in a low tone. "Nottink I not do, and you his friend. You wait. We see." He didn't give away much information, leaning on one arm as if whisky had some effect after all.

Bill lit another cigarette. What the hell was he supposed to do? Sit over the old mummy until he became alive again? Pop shut his eyes, almost dozing. Sammy swished his cloth up and down. Sammy's brown was wrinkled, but he was still thin as a school kid, as puppishly fashionable, his feet twinkling in brand-new shoes. He was a nice guy, that Sammy, like hell he was. Pop slept. This was one swell way to make five grand.

The laughter from the coffee-drinks knocked against the wall. Time slumbered with the old man. It took a long time for him to thaw, yawning, pulling out a card from his pocket. "Call him up. Pattini do anything for me. Say Pop wants to see him."

What was he, an errand boy? This was getting hot. He propped the card up on the top of the box in the phone booth, dropped in the nickel. Five cents in the red. One swell way to make dough. He glared at the names, numbers, initials, the vulgar phallic pictures scratched on the wood by primitive men. He listened to the thin contacting buzzing, the echoes of his voice sounding pure and English in this place of dialect. Somebody said Pattini was out and who was calling? "I'm speaking for Pop. Pop says for Pattini to get in touch with him soon as he can. It's important."

"Oh, Pop," said the voice in a vanishing crescendo.

"Pattini's not in," he said, moving back to the old man through the atmosphere that held them all as in glue, the bar, the electric bulbs, Sammy working like a dissolute mechanism.

"You got twenty dollar like Paddy say?" said Pop.

It was a sock between the eyes. A premonition was upon him. "He didn't say anything of that to me." The old man turned his living eyes downwards, so that his face was dead, an enigma without emotion or thought. "You got it or ain't you?"

Bill took the chance. "If he said so, O.K." He was the lousiest sucker the world'd ever seen. Pop folded the banknotes and stuck them in his pocket. He leaned on his fist. They waited.

Time ticked unendurably, his mind doped by the quiet, by Pop's immobility, by that other stillness of Sammy, ghostly for all his pushing the cloth. The laughter from the coffee house seemed not to belong to men.

The phone shrilled clear and metallic. Pop awoke, beckoned him to answer. "Hello," he said, feeling the cheer of his voice. It was Pattini's steno. Pattini was on a bond in the Bronx; soon as he came in she'd ring Pop, to tell Pop. Bill sat down. Sammy stole into the booth and put out the light he'd left on. This was the second time Sammy'd switched off the electricity. Bill stared into the empty holes that were Sammy's eyes. There were eyes in the holes, staring at him, shrewd as a monkey's.

He wound his watch. Time had some use elsewhere. He'd been down here almost two hours and nothing'd happened. He was out twenty bucks and five cents. What a rooking! It was nearly five, and here he sat like a pig's behind, his brain dusty, shelling out two tenbucks as if they were butts he was offering a bum. Holy Jesus, what a sap! He was so damn easy. You bet crime was a business for smart guys. Where'd he expect to shine in? And he'd figured crime as nothing because some apes and morons rode around in yellow Packards. How the hell did they do it? His head ached with a desire for sleep. Far away like a dream waiting to occur soon as he shut his eyes, the Leroy flat was being built in consciousness. He'd coin dough. The determination in him, ugly and sore as a cancer, to make dough, to make it quick and easy, surrounded him in a cloud like sleep. His day-dream built itself higher, hauling material from the remote reaches of his brain. Paddy. The ginzo in the trunk. Trust Paddy? McMann…everybody knows Kelly, Kelly with the green green tie, His hair is red, His eyes are blue, He's Irish through and through….

He almost dropped off, awaking suddenly to danger. He heard footsteps. Pop, leaning his forehead on his fist, was listening. He was such an old man, ready to die any minute in this desolate room with the spotted red cloths. The door opened and Pop actually smiled, his lips pulling back on his teeth. It was Paddy, his voice marching ahead, loud, insolent. He sat down next to Pop, his fists on his belly, the thumbs hooked in his vest pockets. His face was shiny with wind and high-class barber service. "Hello, Pop. Hello, Bill. You guys havin' a good time? Me? I'm on the blink. A man can't earn an honest living any more. They don't let you set fire to a house or pick a pocket or run a joint. Hey, Pop, what can an honest feller do these days? Madge sends her regards to you, Bill."

"You keep that line up long enough and I'll be falling for her."

"Hey, Pop, how's he look? Should we give him a break? How's he look?" The three of them were glancing at one another with the secrecy of a group where one is kept outside. Bill was outside their knowing, trying to penetrate the pact between them. Paddy placed a tiny package on the table. It was wrapped up carefully, tied with peppermint-striped string, and sealed with thick red wax. "It's a match-box," said Paddy.

"What's it got to do with me?"

"It's yours."

"Mine? What's in it?"

"I'm not sayin'. It's your first job. You're to fetch it over to a little cigar store tonight. You're not to open it."

Bill was wide awake. "Dope?"

"You got a tongue on you. I'm not sayin'. It's a Swede match-box."

"What's the sense bringing it over when you can do so just as easy?"

"Maybe that's why I want you to bring it over. You on?"

Was the reason straight? Probably a rotten one like the time when Paddy'd told the cop his name. "I'm not carrying dope." He seemed to be looking backward towards old aversions. "And what about my twenty?"

"You damn fourflusher. Want your dough'n you can have it. I mighta known you'd belly-ache."

Pop leaned his forehead on his hand again. He seemed tired, as if he didn't understand their language.

"I'm not reneging."

"What then?"

Pop gave Paddy the two tens. Paddy held them up.

"I don't understand."

"If you want your dough you can have it. Well? I'll see you tonight." Paddy got up and walked out.

A fake, a nightmare, that's what it was, but he was out twenty bucks. He picked up the wrapped, sealed match-box. "A helluva lot of mystery. I don't get it." Pop said nothing. Paddy was gone when he walked out on the street. Early winter lay in bluish frosty twilight. Shawled women huddled at the pushcarts. The wind held the teeth of winter, not biting yet, but showing white and hard. The match-box was in his pocket, a third eye given to him. Through it he looked out on another world. He turned around with a wild sudden fear of pursuit. Did he expect to see Pop trailing him? The peddlers' voices chanted religiously. The sky was dusty deep blue. He was shaking something very light but solid. His fingers crawled out from his pocket.

Uptown the tower of the Empire State held north. The skyscraper was the visual proof of another New York. Around it were the department store, Fifth Avenue with its furred shoppers. He thought of the cleaner town, again gripping the matchbox, fierce, eager, shamed. He was in for it. He'd done it. He'd become part and parcel of the rotten slime. He was carrying dope. Cocaine. Heroin. He was a criminal. He stared at the swarthy tribes moving in a dimension outside his own, negative to his worry. Their code was not his code. His code was five thousand bucks. That was enough of a code for anybody.

He hurried away from the masses of fish, the women thicker shadows. With a strong magnetism his mind conceived the matchbox. Sometimes it was miles away, in somebody else's pocket. His destination was unknown. He thought he was progressing towards an unknown and equivocal goal. Why kid himself? He carried the future, the tomorrow, inside his pocket.

Getting off at Christopher, he hurried down to where the last wagons were lumbering. The huge brown bulk of the post office squatted on Greenwich and Christopher like a mammoth cave. He walked south to Leroy. Had any guy interested in him got off the train? He stared backwards for the pursuer born in mind from movies and crime stories, from kid memories of Sherlock Holmes and Arsene Lupin. He saw the winter night that would be until the spring, and the next winter and the winters after. High on its stilts, Christopher station, green-wooded, slant-roofed, was perched like a tiny mountain villa.

He slipped into his own house. This was home. Had been sanctuary for three weeks. He went up to his flat. The dark corridor, with the wallpaper torn like a poor woman's skirt, ended on his own door. He paused, leaning against a vast hollow space, panting with the eternal fear of the nemesis, the doom come home before. He turned the knob, knowing what he would see.

It was Cathy. She lifted her body that had been stooped with cleaning, gazing at him with the full understanding of a man and woman surprised. She stood in the yellow electricity as if in the middle of a sea.

"Hello," he said. "I heard you inside and for a second I thought it was a burglar." He gripped his match-box, furious, concealing his impatience. "You're almost through, aren't you?"

"In a second." Slender, her light hair plaited, her neck, pale white, rising strongly from her dress, her hands also white, she stood in an infinite distance of pallor, in her own pale beauty. He thought she was a virgin. By Christ, what a virgin!

"No need to rush, Cathy. Take your time."

She poked her broom under the bed. The purity of her movements tore at him. He fingered the strings tied about the matchbox, sliding his thumb across the wax.

"You're pretty." His heart beat to the lust pounding in his blood. He'd like to squeeze her all over, to touch the pale curves of her body. Must be the match-box. Fault of the match-box. It held his evil spirit. Cathy was only a kid. He was twisted inside with curiosity, making small sly talk because of a need to kill time. Across the way, through the windows, the iron gate of the printing plant was the entrance to a dungeon. The gate was down, and between the bars the yard, behind, was desolate. He stared at the bold brutal building. But the thing he'd like to do best now was to seduce Cathy, to put his hands on her young girl thighs. Christ, I must let her alone.

The future was in the flat. The match-box held the sewerage of life. Cathy was the purity. He hesitated, too young yet in heart, too young with remembering his father and mother and brother, the kid still sweet with the old Sunday-school life, the old decency, to venture to her. He thought: I ought to smash the matchbox. Crush it in my fist, be clean of Paddy. He held the box between iron fingers. The box was concealed, his purpose was concealed. What he was becoming was also hidden. The proof of it all was that Cathy didn't notice a thing wrong, finishing up her work, her childish eyes blue, serene, innocent.

"I'd like to kiss you, Cathy. You're getting to be a real pretty kid." She blushed as he gripped her hand. He let go. She shut the door. Another time and he'd yank her back. Why did he think that? He felt the thought a huge and gross surrender. You leave Cathy alone, he said to himself.

He put the match-box on the table. It probably had a yellow foreign label and blue paper sides. He pulled the window-shades down, sneering at the insensate desire for secrecy. There was no one across the way to spy but the smudged faces of workers. He walked around the box like a beast about a bonfire, feeling it clumsily. No use shaking it. That didn't tell him a damn. But again he shook it madly, hoping to find out. The box said nothing. Wrapped up, sealed, it was indifferent whether its contents were dope or salt or matches. Suppose he untied it, broke the wax; what of it? How easy it would be! Cut the strings. Cut loose from Paddy. But why spoil his chances because he was sappy in the bean? The last clean resolve was gone as utterly as Cathy. He placed the box in a drawer, scared at the big scratching cat of his curiosity. No use ruining himself with Paddy for keeps.

He went downstairs, tapping at the banister. The stairs retreated before him. On the ground floor he thought of Cathy. She was some kid. Some build. He'd like to inform her in a deep voice: "Quit cleaning my flat. It'll be best for you." At the Gebhardt door he hesitated, wanting to knock. The heavy dark wood faced him like an enemy, and, suddenly transparent, he imaged Cathy behind it, saw her limpid, a reflection in water, the slim limbs, the blue eyes, the hard yet soft young girl flesh. He didn't knock. If it was her luck to clean the flat with him around, well, that was that. Leave it to luck. His good luck. Her bad luck. He flamed hot again thinking of the next time. It'd be better for everybody if he fixed himself up with a kife. There was Madge. He tiptoed to the street like a death that has decided the time isn't quite ripe. Jesus, he was getting to be one swell guy to have around. It seemed as if he had been indoors for hours. The street had a forlorn appearance as if he were seeing it at midnight or early dawn. Down on Greenwich, some overtime trucks were close to the sidewalk, the names of towns written on them like timetables. He read Allentown, Scranton, Wilkes-Barre. That was home territory. On another he read Hoboken, Ridgefield, Hohokus, Jersey City. He was rested. Not a soul was on the street. The hell with Greenwich and the El. He was sick of it. Him for Hudson. The opposite avenue diked in the narrow tide of Leroy. His head was clearing from thought of the match-box.

On the corner he winked at the cashier inside the coffee-pot. She was a new one, rouged, dressed in black. The boss had got a new one, must've tired of pimples. He hurried down past tailor shops, coal cellars, paint supplies. A stout woman in a red sweater hovered in front of a news-stand. He looked at her minutely, although she had no interest for him, then boarded the uptown trolley. At Fiftieth and Eighth, he got off. He had an idea he'd like to size up Duffy's kids. No reason attached, but he'd like to look them over. Up from the ranks. That was him even if he had never been in the ranks.

He entered a combination of shadow and intensity that had no relation to the alarm-clock world or to the grubby little businesses surrounding the pool parlor. Two of the three tables were in use. The players were young and looked alike. Some were blond, others were thin and dark, but about all of them there was an identical mass appearance, the duplication of a herd. They were Duffy's kids. When they weren't shooting pool, they hung out on the corner, smoking, spitting, winking at the dames. But pool was serious. They had dough up. Their hats were perched on the backs of their heads, almost falling off. They all seemed long-chinned and sly, laughing with the decorum of people on a subway train. Bill stood within the door, spotting the kids he knew, Schneck who was supposed to be strong as a horse, Ray the smart aleck. The proprietor observed everybody, a middle-aged man in a gray suit with a face round and shiny as a billiard ball. Bill eased round to where the ranked cue sticks stood in their racks like rifles. "Hello," he said.

"Howya?" said Schneck, nodding as if this were the first time he'd met Bill.

"How's tricks?" The dumb bastard. What a life! Killing time in the dog afternoons, hanging around for the next day, week, month, the break that had to come. They both watched the pool game.

"I hear ya got canned."

"I resigned."

"In your hat. You got fired."

The kids roared, Mike, Ray, all proving their ears were sharp and pointed. He contemplated the lot of them, all the dumb bastards with their faith in a fabulous future. "I got a new job, and one of these days you'll all be working for me." No one was interested. A job stank. Why the hell work? The three pools of glare from the low-hung table lights flung down on the crazy ivory balls. The faces of the players were shadowed, terse, tight of lip, leaning over their cues, steadying them up and down before each shot like pistons. He imagined the matchbox on the green baize cloth, staring at his resolve focused before him. What would the kids've said if they knew? It'd be nothing to them. Ray'd give him the horse laugh. He concentrated on their faces, reading in their hidden brains other secrets, other match-boxes, knowing them through and through who pretended to be iron men. Hell, Schneck or Ray'd sell their souls for his break. "So long," he said.

"So long," they said.

He departed the blue smoke, the clicking of balls, the guarded comments. Was it because he was a stranger, not one of them? After all, he hadn't gone to public school with them or raided the Greek frankfurter men or lined up some dame in a coal cellar.

The winter night covered the avenue of a thousand shops. Honest proprietors peeked out for trade. The poor damn fish. What chance did they have to beat the boys?

He opened the drawer in his room. The match-box was still there, patient and devilish. He walked up and down the flat, the suspended mirror throwing back his double. Another Bill was circling the fellow he knew as himself. He winked at the mirror, slow, childish, serious, receiving the wink back. He laughed, knocking his ring on the gas radiator, the symbol of heat rather than its actuality, shivering in the kitchen with its single chair. His trunk was against the wall, hat and coat chucked on it. He turned into the central room, with its second-hand couch and lamp and book-trough full of novels read long ago, ending up in the bedroom with its double bed, two chairs, and dresser. What a lay-out! He leaned against the window, staring down the length of his flat, the three rooms tied up one to the other like freight cars. What a joint! He was frightened at the sparse poverty he recognized at last. Good God, he had to get out of it somehow, anyhow. For the first time he knew himself as poor as a mouse, remembering his job as a distant luck, a sheer blessing, a paradise accidentally entered, from which he'd been accidentally kicked out. His dough was going like hot cakes. He had to do something. He shut the drawer that held the match-box, his curiosity vanishing out of him like a gasp. What the hell did he care? He was broke. He wasn't becoming a rat for the hell of it. He'd make some dough, a couple grand and quit. A few breaks and he'd leave the Big Stink. It could stink on without him. His thoughts were arduous as prayers. And now that God was placated, he began to figure how he could force the break. No use waiting for it like Duffy's kids, sitting on your behind like a dope. He had to be of use to Paddy. How? A rent-collector like him. That was it. It'd be a pipe sticking up a Yid. In his joy he whispered: "Thank God" as if he were a devout person granted a miracle. At eight-thirty Times Square was going to the theater. Cabs honked into the theater streets. A minority of the ritzy gang were coming on time, black and white waiters and ladies in no evening clothes. On Broadway the city had conglomerated in a great, laughing brilliance of faces. He was fingering the match-box when he went into the cigar store. The window held a rectangular display of empty boxes. Inside, an aisle sneaked past the counter. It was the sort of place where the backroom is the reason for being. Paddy was puffing a cigar as if he had been here forever, his feet up on a disk table, privacy thick about him as smoke.

"We alone?" said Bill. Paddy nodded. He produced the match-box. Paddy tilted his hat back.

"Christ, you're a prime. Set for the initiation." He broke the strings, cracked the seal, ripped the paper off. There was nothing in the box. Bill stared from the empty coffin of space to Paddy. "You rat," he hard Paddy shouting. "You took it."

"I didn't open it. I did not." His protestations were piling up faster than their utterance, yet he stopped short, shaking his head as if dazzled, shaking free from a queer lethargy. He saw Paddy's lips tighten about the cigar, his lips freeze away from humor. He guessed. There'd Never Been Anything In The Box. A trick. A lousy joke. He blurted fast and almost incoherent: "Cut the comedy, Paddy. I knew all along there wasn't one grain in't, but I let it pass."

Paddy gave him his contemptuous laughter like a mouthful of spit. Paddy roared as he stood naked and abashed.

"The twenty bucks was a joke, too. You knew that too? You sonufabitch, you knew all about it. A nice lil joke. Twenty bucks. And carryin' the box all day, and reporting. Jesus Christ." Each laugh had pounded him like a fist. He lingered there gazing down at a prostrate bloody body; the body was himself. He looked down at himself, at the beaten fool. Then he laughed louder than Paddy. They had a grand time, but not at the same joke.

"And you thought you were stringing me, didn't you, Paddy? Ask Pop if I didn't belly-ache about handing over the dough."

"Did you bite?"

"Listen to me. I wanted to get in with you even if I had to act the prime dumb bastard. I knew that match-box was empty. You think I toted it all day? Things aren't done that way. I figured if I did as you said, give you your laugh, maybe you'd feel I meant it about a break. Fact is, I was at Duffy's pool parlor. Ask Sch- neck, Ray. That's how much I fell for your match-box."

"Before you wised up, feller, you said you didn't open it once."

"Why should I? I knew nothing was in it." He discovered, as his heart qui- eted, that Paddy's eyes were slanting at him, speculative. Behind their bright gaze the bulky man leaned his head on a big fist. "Your going out of your way to play a joke on me proves—"

"Proves what a sucker you are."

"Proves I can be of use, Paddy."

"Proves I hate you enough to rook you."

"Hey, I'm sick of 'proves'; let's play something else."

"Sit down. You're a funny guy."

"Give me a break. You shook me down for twenty bucks. I've shaken you down for much more. But that's over." Paddy presented a surface like granite. "Stick to your own game."

"No jobs. I had one chance for ten a week, but it wasn't for me." Paddy said what he'd expected to hear, what a million echoes sounding into his brain from movies and magazines predicted he must hear. "Ten ain't dough. But what can you do? There's plenty guys holding the bag."

"I can make dough."

"Who's stoppin' you?"

"I need your help."

"Yeah?"

"I've been collecting rents a long time. I know a mess of shop-keepers on Ninth and I know where they keep their dough and when it's around. That's worth something."

"Maybe."

"Quit stalling, Paddy. I don't intend knocking off poor slobs. First it don't pay, second there's plenty cheap bastards who can afford to hand a little over." He guessed Paddy approved his sentiment, Paddy the Irishman, Paddy the Tam- many Robin Hood who chipped in his share of coal for the poor every winter and paid for his share of barrel turkeys, but didn't bother a damn about grab- bing the sons of the poor or corrupting their daughters for his pocketbook. He loathed himself for his cleverness, for putting over the proposition with such a Christian and piratical fervor. Paddy's brow knitted, his eyes mechanical, stilled, his lips spreading wide and pinkish. "You're talking now. Break in reg'lar Do a guy a favor and he owes you a break."

"I've got the inside dope on lots of them. Some of them dirty Jews stink with money."

Paddy offered him a cigar with a bland free attitude as if he were the devil, giving him the world. It's only a stinking ten-center, thought Bill. He had to be careful. No use spilling the beans unless he was in real sure. No use being doublecrossed.

"I've other ideas, too, Paddy. I know a stack of whorehouses and joints loaded down with cash. If they aren't friends of yours we can hook them." Paddy suddenly didn't know him. He was a stranger, muttering: "You better stick to real estate."

"What's wrong?"

"You sonufabitch. A mad dog, huh? Your ideas are lousy." He retreated into his granite like a mobster into his hide-out.

Jesus, he was dumb. He couldn't learn to keep his trap shut. This was a strange room and he didn't know who might be listening, what eyes watching. "Don't mind my hot air, Paddy. Who wants trouble? I was kidding."

Paddy's face was drained of all blood. "You young squirts talk rough. We'll stick to the Jews." And swiftly, his lips not moving, the ghost of a whisper (it must've come from him, even if he was listening to it after it was over, disappearing while spoken; "…you bastard, shut up…"). Who had said that? Paddy?

"I've been blowing hard." The plain brown walls; this hole in which they sat seemed hemmed in by ears and eyes. "All I want's a piece up your place."

Paddy approved; his voice had a shade more color in it. "O.K. I got a swell piece. Madge. She likes you even if you're a sonufabitch." They smiled, thinking of the young girl, bargaining over her body become an escape, retreating steadily from the menace of Bill's crazy crack about hijacking joints.

"So long. I got to beat it."

"Come around tomorrow. I'll fix it up." He passed down the narrow corridor, the sweat of fear under his skin, hating to turn his back. Betting his life on the card of a dumb ass crack. That was bright, that was the action of a smart guy. In the cigar store, two men glanced at him, dour, significant, their thoughts furtive. He opened the door, hurrying into the crowd.

It was after the theater hour. The lifetime spent with Paddy, including danger, wealth, and greed, had endured a half-hour. He returned to a forgotten life. Limousines traveled effortlessly up the streets, silvery bright shapes inside. Crowds piled the sidewalks, young men gripping their girls' arms with the possessiveness of spendthrifts about to hit a movie. He followed his path among them, jostling against a soft hip or a hard elbow. He was ashes. He was an urn, his guts and heart ashes. These Broadway flies, he was stupid as they. Live and learn. You had to learn to keep your mouth shut. What storekeeper could be held up? Would he need a gun? It was all up in the air. There was Wiberg. Or Soger the pork man. Metz. Not Metz. He might get a job for his kid brother from Metz. Holy hell, Christmas right round the corner. It hadn't snowed once, but his heart was white and wintry all over.

CHAPTER SEVEN

He decided Wiberg's Dress Shop was the best bet for a beginner. Beginner was hot stuff. This was the second day he was looking the place over. It was becoming a routine job. He thought of the letter he'd received that morning from his kid brother. Joe would be in definitely after the New Year. "Next year I'll be with you," Joe had written. A regular kid letter. The dumb kid. His descriptions of Leroy Street and poverty with a capital P hadn't scared him any. Joe'd rather live with him than stay home where it was a cinch. Joe was thick. Back home he had a nice room, a lawn to look out on, good food. He was crazy, a nut to leave high school and a real good time. For what?

He dropped in at a drug store. "Pour me a coke, stinker."

"Working yet, Bill?" asked the clerk. Tall, pale, he grinned behind the counter with the casual gigolo attitude of drug-store clerks, his light eyes blinking under carefully tended eyebrows. He approved Bill's suit, his shirt and tie. Bill was a dresser.

"I'm making hay while the sun shines."

"Your hay's all wet. You're canned, guy."

"Hay's for horses and hicks. The real-estate game's cracking up."

"I got a good tip, Bill. Marge in the fifth."

"That's a sucker game too."

"Yeah, what do you do, wise-guy?"

"I'm buying up Ninth, including this crummy store." They laughed quietly in the interior of prescriptions and remedies. It was an old-fashioned place with the soda counter stuck into one side and not bossing everything in sight as in the chain drug stores.

"Ain't you heard of the crash?"

"Never crashed for smart guys. You still see plenty limousines, don't you, stinker? Don't forget it." Outside he thought of Joe's letter again. Could you beat it? Maybe Metz'd give Joe a job. He knew how to do a little favor for Metz. He strolled down Ninth. The pushcarts obtruded their orange and yellow colors high against the light, impregnating the dusty air with a fecund earthliness. Sun poured between the ties on the El tracks. The air was crisp, with winter warmed into autumn. He peered into Wiberg's Dress shop. Three outside cases. The big plate window displaying dresses at 1.89, 2.89, 3.89. Between the counter and a rack hung with garments, Wiberg himself was reading, the fat scholar's nose with the thick glasses nailed tight against it. He wasn't a bad guy, but business was business. The upper avenue of the El ran straight and undeviating, en route to a distant goal. There was no need to spy on Wiberg, but it made him important and necessary. Paddy didn't have to know it was a pipe. Later, back in his flat, staring across at the printery, he thought his life a putrid one. What a way to kill time! His life was lonely. He had been with himself almost exclusively. No wonder he was griped. No dates. No wonder he sized up Cathy as a possibility before dropping off to sleep. A fellow had to live or else must dream of Cathy, Madge, the world's women, spilling his seed in bed. What a life! What a damn bastard of a life! No job. Nothing. He was unchanging as the printing plant with its huge gate. He leaned out of the window. He needed money. He needed women as much as any wealthy lice. He thought of the Only Things in Life with animal relish as if women were all of life. What the hell was he griping for? Things were due to change. Let Joe come. He'd get a job for him with Metz. Joe'd be out of the way. He'd be free for anything. He needed money, and Wiberg had it. It was a luxury to sit alone like a cripple. The hell with such luxuries. Action. The murder at Paddy's, Stranger giving him the sack, the match-box, had a dreamy far-away shimmer. They'd been exciting. His heart had beaten so terribly over these dead things. The past was gone. All over with. The trouble was, his new life hadn't begun. He hadn't started yet. Sneaking around Wiberg's didn't mean a damn. When he was a kid he used to plan out how a bank could be robbed. Action. He never considered there was still time to heel out, still time to remain an Honest Man. He glanced at a newspaper, opened and shut a book, reread his brother's letter, yawned, his attention elsewhere like an actor busy with small talk behind a lowered curtain. Tomorrow night Wiberg was to get visitors and he didn't even know all the details yet. Lucky as hell Cathy didn't show up.

Mrs. Gebhardt was polishing the mail-boxes in the vestibule. He touched his hat and said: "Why clean my flat so often?"

She was surprised, not because she saw him in the afternoon with the men all working, but with a greater surprise stretched over weeks, seeing him with a grave comprehension as if he were a menacing stranger. "No trouble at all. And since Mr. Stanger says—"

"You work hard enough without bothering about me."

"But I like to help."

"Arbeit macht des Leben süss, huh? How do you like my German? I had a year of it at college. But all work and no play makes Jack dull. That's more sensible."

"Work is good."

"Take it easy." He hurried down the stoop, guessing she was looking after him. "By the way, my kid brother's coming to live with me soon. Cathy'll have a boy friend."

She didn't like his Joe in the least. The next night, a little before twelve o'clock, things were set. It was the sleepy hour of closing. His hat slanted over his eye, the tiny red coal of his butt preceded him like another sight, calmer than his own. He felt a terrific mounting sensation. The El roared out of the cave of quiet with a monstrous noise. Many stores had closed. Fifteen minutes ago he'd observed the blue coat and stick of the law swagger down the avenue.

He passed a butcher shop, a man in a white apron holding up a string of sausage and arguing with a Polish woman. The clerks were yawning in the gents' furnishing. The windows of the pawnshop were empty of diamonds. Then he passed Wiberg's. Again he saw the fat scholarly face surrounded by glare. He was reading a newspaper in his store. Bill hurried to the corner. McMann sat at the wheel of a long-bodied car. Two men were at the back. When they saw him coming, they leaned their slim urgent faces forward. "Clear?" said McMann.

"Clear. He's alone."

"O.K." Immediately Bill crossed the trolley tracks, gleaming redly from the tail-lights of cars. Across the way, with the gray guarding El Pillars between, he waited. He was alone. Wiberg was alone. The two men who had been in the rear of the car finished their walk. One of them paused outside the dress shop. The other entered. He saw this, his eyes speeding towards another incredible vision…Paddy, his kid brother, or thought he saw them beyond the actuality, swift and deadly. McMann was floating up in front of the shop, his timing fascinating and beautiful. The long black auto body prolonged itself from the corner, where three wops were talking in loud voices. The car went right up to Wiberg's. It had been parked on the corner. Had been. This was it. This was the life. Christ, what a guy McMann was! He was terrified, green inside and sick. The passers-by didn't know him from Adam. A sullen couple, the woman pleading with her husband, began to bicker. Just at that second, the holdup guy outside Wiberg's flipped his butt away. The one inside, like a machine animated by the cigarette's arc, terminated his talk. All this in one second. Wiberg turned his back as if looking for some article. Wiberg crumpled. The one inside ducked his blackjack out of sight, interested in the cash register.

All done. He'd done it. Wiberg sloughed because he'd known that on Thursday nights the storekeeper always held his cash for deposit in the morning. He thought of how the fat face had flopped on the chest, the body slumping behind the counter. The visitor wasn't interested in the register, chasing out, trailed by the lookout man. They hopped into the car just floated up. The gears sang. It was a finished job.

And what the hell was he moping around for? He hesitated, proud and curious, like a little boy elated over his first success. McMann and his helpers were phantoms. Poor Wiberg lying behind the counter, and no one the wiser. What the hell. They'd all been invisible. That was it. A successful job left no feelings in the criminal. If no one saw you, you weren't seen, and if you weren't seen, it'd never been. The ginzos on the corner were still hollering. The embittered couple glared into the window of a furniture store, the man glowering, the bewitched woman pointing to a plushy set in red and green. Poor Wiberg was lying there.

He walked a few steps away, cocking his head back. A deeper quiet was on the street. The El's thunder was possessed of the menace of noise heard past midnight. Steel wheels hammered. A trolley was approaching. He stepped over to an El pillar, streaked wet from some bum, holding up his hand. The motorman stopped. He flipped a nickel into the cash-box. The traffic light beamed its great benignant green eye. He sat down in yellow light on the yellowish brown seat. The trolley jerked forward. He was the only one to notice a woman entering Wiberg's. Only he heard or thought he heard her scream. The motorman drove remorselessly away on his inexorable duty. The other passengers were reading tabloids or else swayed punch-drunk. Looking back into a vanishing world dynamited with activity, the ginzos were running. Ten to one they'd phone a cop. In a few minutes the neighborhood'd be a beehive of radio cars, buzzing blue, authoritative. The families in the tenements would be poking their heads out of windows, crying out, thousand-voiced: "Ain't those cops wonderful with dem raddyo cars? What chance's a crook got?"

No one in the trolley had any idea of what had happened or was about to happen. Their blind peace was magnificent. Suppose some eagle eye had spotted McMann's license number? Suppose? For the first time in his life the police were on the other side.

It was enough to make McMann scream with laughter. He was standing, red-faced, brash, in Paddy's flat, a glass in his hand, when Bill popped the question. He roared himself out of his usual photographic calm. His observing stilled features curved away from sharp teeth. Paddy's dames had been sent out. The men passed the whisky bottle, laughing at Bill. Bill was confused. McMann was the supreme mystery of a covered heart. He understood the others, but didn't get McMann at all. "Suppose they spot the license?" said McMann. "It ain't my car." He threw himself into another spasm with a hysterical, almost decadent relish. But his laughter was an act for the eye. Bill thought that all the time McMann was wondering how the others took him, laughing at them all with a private laughter that made no sound.

Bill grinned. "It went off like clockwork. The way you eased up that car."

"Nothin' at all. That wheel was pie. Whatta swell wheel! I'll miss it."

Paddy counted out the money. "About a hundred eighty bucks. That ain't nothing for a mob." He glared at Bill. "Hey, kid, it wasn't worth it."

"Wiberg should've had double that. Just my luck." He was a sap coming up so late. Likely there'd been double one-eighty, the real dough divided by the four of them.

"I'm takin' twenty," said Paddy. "Chicken-feed. Fifty for McMann. O.K.? We were waitin' for you, Bill. That's hundred'n ten left." He glanced at the pair who'd pulled the job, both sullen, expectant, like a pair of wolfish dogs. "You guys'll take forty-five each." He pushed the ninety bucks, mostly in fives and tens, to the pair. They divided it, muttered s'long, disappearing out the door like smoke. "That leaves twenty-one, twenty-two to be exact, for Bill." Bill picked up his share.

"Them guys're in a helluva hurry," said McMann. "The sore bastards. Forty-five ain't enough. They got guts bitchin'. Christ, we could've borrered a couple Duffy's kids for half the dough."

"Duffy's kids are trigger-crazy," said Paddy.

"I don't like them bastards. I hocked the car." He lit a cigar, sitting gingerly, ready to spring at a touch.

"I don't like to kick, but my share isn't much, Paddy. I got the dope. The job'd be impossible without me." Paddy winked profoundly at McMann. "I was waitin' for the sonufabitch to raise a stink. Can you beat his gall? If they don't kill'm he'll be a big feller. Let's get down to facts. What'd you do? You didn't risk your neck like McMann and the boys. What'd you do?"

"I got the inside dope."

"Sure, you louse, but what'd you risk? They packed the rods." He scowled, irate as an annoyed father. "What you want? Twenty odd bucks' dough. Weren't you belly-aching the only job you could get was one for ten bucks a week?"

"But watching Wiberg for days?"

"Watchin' your ear." They lapsed into a hypnotic silence. Bill felt his blood shoot hot into his head. He glared at them through a mist. McMann didn't have a speck of dust on him. McMann was the devil, his eyes almost invisible. Paddy took his drink hard, fighting the burning in his guts with stiffer drinks. Paddy was over fifty. Paddy was beginning to feel his age.

"Thanks, Paddy. Thanks for nothing."

"You got your nerve speakin' to me like that." His mouth hung open, his skin finely wrinkled. "Believe me Jeez, he's the champ. A Yid's ambition, the bastard. Sucking around for a break and me fool enough to get you an' a coupla boys to fix Wiberg, and this sonufabitch with the gall to gripe."

McMann bowled, having a good time. Bill imagined McMann approved his gall. "I'm glad for the break, but why rook me?"

"Rooked? Holy Moses, I rook'm by givin'm the chance to make twenty-two bucks."

"Why'nt you guys shut up?" shouted McMann. "Me'n Bill's takin' out a coupla dem dames. That'll square it."

"Like hell."

"Don't be cheap. Give'm a ring."

Paddy phoned. "Yeh, this is Paddy. Say, Madge, you and Bobbie come right over. Yeh. Hop a cab." He was still gaping at Bill. "I feel like hell givin'm free lay."

"Aw, you're a good guy. N' you got twenty bucks 'cause your name's Paddy. No wonder the kid's griped." He winked at Bill, his red hair cropped close, his tiny blue eyes the only soft things in his hard bony face. He gave an impression of being all jaw and cheekbone, all stone surface flushed pink and handsome with a brutal reckless youth. Bill liked his approval, excited by the thought of a night with Madge, almost pitying Paddy, the poor damn pimp. He drank, sorry for the old man. That was the road of sin, S, I, N. You lived, you died, before you looked around you were old, taking guff from McMann. It was swell to be tough, biting at old Paddy. Again he was being champ fool. They'd double-crossed him sure as fate. Wiberg had more than one-eighty. Paddy had been too quick calling up the women; it was a rook, arranged before he got there. The idea was if he got Madge he'd forget the doublecross. What a dopey bastard he was! Yet Paddy, eying them steadily seemed to be on the up-and-up, Paddy replenished his glass, his head capped by the flare of the floor lamp, obsessed by their youth. Bill couldn't help thinking that, gyp or no gyp, he had it all over Paddy. He was young. He'd make other breaks. He had it all over Paddy.

"Let's forget it," he cried. "It's done with. There's plenty more dough. I got the habits of these storekeepers down pat. A cinch. I know when and where they keep their cash. More than that, McMann. I'm wise to the guys with the joints." He bragged carelessly, his eyes on their non-committal faces, day-dreaming of fortune, of himself as a Napoleon of the Underworld, owner of yellow Packards and of whores de luxe. McMann's thin lips were fitted one to the other like two edges of stone.

"You know lots," he said.

"Sure. Gamy guys can knock off some real dough. Why fool around with shopkeepers for nickels?"

"You through?" said Paddy.

"You bet I am."

"Quit hollering about knocking off joints."

"Nothing's wrong with that." He almost sobbed at his craziness, but after all what was the diff? They could go to hell. He wasn't going to be tied down to chiselers all his life.

"Nothing's wrong squatting in a coffin with a bullet through your bastard head. I told you once already, but you can't hold that tongue, can you?" Bill grinned like a man condemned to death. "That ain't so hot, that coffin part."

"You poor louse," said Paddy.

"Maybe it was his fanny speakin'?" said McMann.

"Maybe it was."

"No guy can be so dumb," said McMann.

The old disgust lurched into his heart. He'd said too much. Now McMann knew. "I'm just nuts with booze. I don't mean a word. Who the hell'd kid around with guys with gats?"

"Blab some more and you'll need one," said Paddy.

"Need what?"

"A gat."

"Don't make me laugh. Me with a gat? I couldn't hit a fly."

"A fly's a tough shot," said McMann.

Bill poured sick laughter out of his mouth, impressed by his importance. Talk of certain things, dare certain things, and you became a big shot. McMann and Paddy were just conservative business men, differing very little from grocers. They minded their own business. What tissywockers! All he had to do was brag, expand holdups into hijackings of mobsters, and they got cold feet. Talk like a wolf and they ran for cover. God help him. He was a fool. They knew what death was, knew his bite, listening somber and disgusted as he screamed with the puffed-up nonsense of an office boy figuring up millions. Christ, they knew how tough it was to pick up a grand.

"I'm nuts," he said contritely, "but I can't help thinking of the easy dough in this town."

"You sonufabitch," said Paddy with the monotony of an almost impersonal contempt. "Don't you think a million guys haven't itched for the dough in joints? But who wants to get wiped? You're a baby, a dope. It ain't like taking a storekeeper."

"But it ain't so hard, Paddy," said McMann. "It's a pipe. You get a gat. You knock off a coupla joints. You got luck and you're set."

"Don't be giving him ideas. The sonufabitch's nuts enough as is."

"It's a pipe. Don't get clipped and you're in the dough. Two, three, six months and they'll be feedin' outa your mitt. King of the crap-house."

"Cut it. He's nuts enough."

"Maybe he ain't so nutty. Maybe it's the smart thing. I dunno."

Paddy sighed, utterly shocked. "You're hopped."

"Maybe getting' hopped's smartest."

Bill was wild. McMann on his side. With that guy on his side anything was possible. "You bet it is."

"Holy smoke!" exclaimed Paddy. Somebody knocked at the door, the three of them lifting their heads like conspirators, hearts beating at the door yawning open, two women slicking in, rouged, powdered, proud of their hips, groggy with booze. "Hello," said McMann, brushing his thick red hair. A glow seemed to emanate from his good health. Madge and Bobbie stared at him with the serious measured regard of women expecting a hot time. Paddy disintegrated, his big head outlined in the background with the innocuous innocence of a figure faintly drawn and removed from the main scene.

"You old horse," said Bobbie, tapping McMann's flank.

"Howya?" said McMann. Bill thought: So Madge's mine. A break. It was hard to remember the holdup. Wiberg's smacked-in skull, with his flesh turning hot and tight. Hell with the cops. Hell with them. He was glad of the booze he'd drunk, glad Madge's lips were so red, brightly painted with a blood that was not blood. His joy had no relation to what had happened or to any time but this single exultant meeting with the girl he was about to lay. It was Madge. That was plenty to think about. Her roundish face on top of the heavy collared coat was so small a face, so lacking in the solid meatiness of Bobbie (Bobbie's big-chinned full-cheeked face proclaimed she was a woman, a swell piece and don't let anyone forget it) that her long legs, sensual in their stockings, were an unexpected break. He thought: She's not a kid, even if she looks like one, she's a woman. "Come on, Kid," said McMann. "Get your coat. The ladeez're steppin' out."

Paddy, smoking a big cigar, vanished gradually behind blue smoke. His voice issued from no body, like God's voice. "Free stuff," he moaned. "Jeez believe me, I'm givin' it free."

"Cut the crabbin'," said McMann.

"Ain't Hoover talkin' of morytoriums?" He banged his hand against Bobbie's hip. "You ole pizzazz, I ain't seen you a long time."

"I'll shove your face."

"Jeez, baby, no foolin'." Bobbie slipped into the coat she'd taken off, somehow clothing herself, she'd been so naked in the thin silk dress. "Blowhard, McMann."

"Always did like the young uns," Paddy shouted to Bill, tottering behind her.

"Merry Christmas," said Bill.

"Chris'mas? Holy hell!" exclaimed Madge with profound unbelief. They hurried through the tenement smell, down the dark corridors with the pair of doors at each end like blind hopeless eyes. McMann pounded down the steps ahead of everybody. Bobbie giggled.

Out on the street, Bill's head cleared. The clean river wind hurled a smell of salt and rotting piers. McMann took Bobbie and went on ahead. Bill snickered at the swagger of her hips, the good full-meated zest of her, the shapely poundage that had once rested on the lap of a corpse. Me for that, he thought; fannies for me and I'm for fannies. He grabbed Madge's arm. "A long time since we played around, and you're it."

"Yeah? So what?"

"You're it and you have got it?" She was young all right, not more than a schoolgirl nor much older than Cathy. And here she was walking with him in the dirty city. His drunken mind evoked other newspaper headlines: YOUNG GIRL ATTACKED IN HALLWAY. CHILD OF EIGHT STRANGLED. She was too girlish to be a whore. He thought of schoolgirls, long-braided, greasy of snout, smelling of adolescence, of virginity. He almost puked, letting go her arm.

"Have you got it?" she repeated like a wicked child. Her head was lowered, downlooking like a nun's, the features in profile soft and delicate, the Irish tilted nose, the harmony of her lips and eyes reminding him of pictures of women painted long ago. He trembled. Holy Christ, he was shaking all over.

"How long you been with Paddy?"

"Mind your business."

"You're not so bad for a kid. Of course, you're not a real woman." Every young snotnose that'd ever lived had to go bugs over a whore at one time or other.

"Don't you pester me."

"I don't want to pester you. I like you."

"Go hop yourself, then." She smiled.

"Sure, if you help along."

She laughed. "I seen you lots of times at Paddy's and you never give me a tumble but a couple times only."

"How old are you, Madge?"

"Almos' seventeen. Jeez, you're a nosey guy."

"Who taught you to talk so tough?"

"Go to hell."

"If you come along."

"That's old. Say, Bobbie," she called down the street, "this sonufabitch's pesterin' me."

Bill laughed. "Everybody calls me that. I'm most getting to believe it."

"You must be one, then."

"No. I'm too smart." Again the two couples were walking decorously towards Eighth Avenue, as if happily married and en route to the movies. The corner glistened with a thousand shoes. Eighth flowed with light, with Neon signs jazzing up their hearts with the music of the Big Town. "I like you, Madge. It's swell to be with you. Who'd've guessed it two months ago?"

"What's so funny about that?"

"I'm not used to the fast life and fast dames like you." She liked that crack. "You're some kid." He suddenly blazed with laughter. "I almost forgot and I bet you did too. Remember the night at Paddy's when Gene fixed that ginzo?"

"I saw nothin'." He was a mug to spoil a good time. How could you like a guy like that?

"I only saw you. I like you; that's why I'm so nosey. C'mon, sister, tell papa about yourself."

"Bobbie said I musta been dumb as hell. I musta been. Bobbie says even the girls they pull outa the schools is smarter. I was dumb. I lived in Brooklyn."

"That's awful dumb."

"Don't let 'em kid ya. Brooklyn's a lively burg." She laughed proudly. "I knew the ropes. They were linin' me up two years ago and yet I fell. I was dumb."

"I don't get you."

"It's this way. One night I goes ridin' with a coupla fellers, not kids I hung out with reg'lar, but strange fellers. They brought me to Paddy'n he paid two hundred for me. But, Jesus, was I dumb? Bobbie says even the school kids knows better, most of them, than go ridin' with strange fellers they never seen before." She glanced at him serenely, her face calm, with a quality like innocence. "Now, you punk, don't bother me. Bobbie says every stinker's always wantin' to find out about a girl."

"You're smart now."

"Cut the oil."

"Where's McMann going?"

"To the Greek's. He nuts about Greeks'n their cabbyrets. Them Greeks stink. Coffee ain't bad, naw the lamb chops. But me, I like Broadway. You're a queer," she said simply. "You're a queer."

"Give me another chance, honey."

"You're a new guy, ain't ya? You usta shake Paddy down. I saw ya. You was a rent-collector or somethin'."

"I'm a dummy. I'm cockeyed. I'm a baby. I'm singing my hymns and feeling sorry and I'm a fool for that. By God, I can't get it straight in my bean that every business is a business. Only dummies don't know that."

"You give me a pain."

"I'll give you more than that." She squeezed his arm. McMann had turned the corner into a sidestreet. Three stone steps descended from the sidewalk towards a curtained door. The narrow window was lettered in Greek. Madge whispered they meant a good time. A glare came through the curtains. They stood a second like supplicants waiting for charity. McMann knocked again, cursing the damn Greeks for keeping an elegant party like them kicking their heels. The door opened on plaintive wailing music.

"I like jazz," said Madge. "This Greek stuff is lousy. Cats in a yard." Bobbie meowed, and they laughed with the idiocy of people ready to laugh at any crack. The music whined out of a big brown victrola. Twenty tables surrounded a cleared space in the center. No one was performing right now, although the crowd was staring at the waxed space hopefully. It looked as if some act were just over. The diners were mostly Greeks.

A skinny waiter, with an oily skin that reminded Bill of anchovies, got them a table. He was happy, hungry, glad to be with Madge. She was a swell kid and it was him with her. The joint was fun. Foreign, but fun. Little Greece. The swarthy gambler faces, the black eyes gleaming over tiny cups, reminded him of Pop's down in the ghetto. He was moving in highclass circles. Most of the Greeks had women with them, blond American or Irish women. The Greeks were boozing them up. It was a relief to glance across the spotted cloth at McMann's redness; his gang was white. Was Bobbie German or German-Irish or German-American? Black bottles sprouted up on their table, and he was surprised to see his forgotten fist lifting a glass of red wine.

"Mixing drinks is no good," he said.

"Aw, what the hell?" said McMann.

"Well, if you say so, but it's against my better judgment." McMann could make him do anything against his better judgment. First, he didn't own a better judgment. Second, Mac was a funny guy. Nothing could faze McMann. And Bobbie was German. Don't forget that. Madge was out of Saint Pat's whiskers. And McMann? The devil himself, asking him now how the wine was, his knees bumping against Bill's under the table. He declared he liked Greek dumps. Bobbie said he was a Greek himself. She licked her lips and demanded that he fill up her glass. McMann guffawed and offered to do something else. What a joke that was! A joke de la crème de la crème, terribly funny coming from McMann's thin lips. But Bobbie had an idea it was so old it stank.

"Fillin's old as the hills," said McMann. Bill laughed to see Madge laughing, her head tilted back. She seized her glass, her lower lip pushing forward to support the rim. He stared at her throat, the too delicate throat of a young girl, as some hot lewd power squeezed his knee. His blood rushed forward. He bit his lip to keep his expression from changing. Madge was goosing around. He touched the hidden hand, small and eager, stronger than his own, lifting his hand to her lap. He was too slow for her, too slow for all this business. He was a soft dill pickle. McMann's fists were out of sight. He trembled at the images in his mind. What was McMann doing to Bobbie? He wasn't soft. Madge shifted her chair nearer to his own, her fingers creeping under the lower part of his vest, her face not an inch from his own. The palest of freckles crossed her nose; her eyes were darker than blue in the dull light. A little red lamp like a tiny lighthouse stood on their table. Each table was alone with its light.

The waiter brought food, plates of lamb chops broiled brown, cups of Turkish coffee, bottles of wine. They smoked and ate. Both hands free, McMann attacked the food lustily. Bill took his cue, pushing his dame away. Hell with women, food came first. That McMann knew how to live the real life, the caveman modern life of grub, dames, murders. Bill held a greasy bone in his fingers, tearing at the meat with his teeth, his lips slimed with animal fat. Bobbie and Madge were no slouches either, packing it away. All of them were like animals eating as if they weren't sure when they would eat so hearty again. Someone shut off the main flow of light. In the mysterious room each table was alone in space, solitary as an island in the night, the red lamps burning. The small and large glowing eyes of cigarettes and cigars shifted about like wild eyes. Bill blinked, still seeming to see the fat oily Greeks, polite, dissolute, heeling their women.

McMann shouted: "Hey, kid, not here. For Chris' sake," his voice laughing with Bobbie's. The dark had one memorial usage. Before he actually realized what he was doing, Bill grabbed Madge, his hand kneading her small breast, kissing her full on the lips. "You sonufabitch, your lips' greasy as a pig. Phew, you greaseball." A spotlight stabbed quick, instantaneous as lightning. Here and there skulls were picked out as if the spotlight had struck them dead or half-dead the eyes black holes, the cheekbones savage and gaunt. The glare traveled around the room. Opposite him, McMann's head was a geometry of planes and angles. McMann didn't seem human but a devil put together of hard woods. Bobbie was almost comely, a plump ghost, but Madge was the same. The dancer sidled out, her long powdered legs moving to the heartbeats of the spectators. She was almost naked, her body dead-whitened with powder. Her black hair loose upon two breasts solid as apples. She did not dance, but swayed to the erotic sighing music. At all the tables the men smoked or sipped wine, their male gestures a chorus.

As the woman's body sang of its beauty and desire, the solid apple breasts wavered in Bill's mind. Her heavy fecund thighs followed the winged naked feet, white and strong, the five toes distinct from one another and anciently beautiful. His own toes were prisoned one to the other. Summertimes the beaches were ugly with thousands of female feet civilized in tight shoes. He whispered groggily something about the glory that was Greece, not these greaseballs, the ancient Greece with all her glories.

"You gimme a pain in the behind," said Madge.

"I'll bust you in the jaw."

"Sh," whispered McMann.

The dance ended, his heart remembering the apple-breasted woman in her stark moment of beauty. The house applauded. He clapped his hands, confused, as if the dance had happened somewhere else, and drank more wine. The lights flashed on like sharp slaps. The place was jammed with anonymous good friends, guzzling, smoking. He sat with the pals of a lifetime, immortal buddies of his. McMann had slipped his arm about Bobbie. Madge squeezed pretty tight against him, her hands teaching him her kind of love, humming a song similar to: "I can't give you anything but love, baby."

They all staggered out finally, up the three stone steps into a cab spinning out of the night. The men flopped on the seat, holding the women on their laps. Bill was insisting he couldn't let Mac treat, no sir, when the cab seemed to hit a wall, stopping, McMann pushing everybody out. Madge and Bobbie jigged on their heels, it was that cold. They were on Twenty-third Street. Bill said the Greek's had been warm, and this weather was a blizzard, and he was going to divvy up or know why. The cabbie slipped McMann his change. McMann announced he was glad to put dough in circulation. The cab rolled west under the El. Ninth Avenue was only a half-block away, the station lonely above the street.

"You're spending all your dough."

"Aw, dry up. It ain't mine."

Bobbie shivered and wanted to go where it was warm. "Whose dough is it?" Madge asked, pressing tight against Bill. He gripped her around the waist and told her to mind her damn business. It was a donation. The crosstown trolley banged down the street and he thought of Wiberg falling down like an empty suit. On this very night. He stared at the street, the quiet rows of brownstone fronts across the way, the tailors and Chink laundries spaced in dark stone, and then they were all trooping upstairs. McMann unlocked the door of his two-room apartment. It smelled male. A pair of silk stockings hung on a chair. McMann hauled off his overcoat. The bedroom faced the street. The second room could be used for sleeping. Bobbie yanked off the cover of the studio couch and made it up as a bed, plumping down the two couch pillows, tucking the blankets in. Not the first time for Bobbie, thought Bill, but was Madge always dame number two? "Hit the hay, kid," McMann advised, "and don't fix her more'n fifty times. Jeez, I'm tired.." He unbuttoned the shirt on his white chest. He didn't wear an undershirt. His red hair tousled like a married man's at bed hour, he walked into the bedroom, trailed by Bobbie, her hips broad and matronly. She shut the French door and began to undress behind the curtains. She might've been concealed by a high wall, already out of her dress, yawning from the wine, in a pink brassiere and step-in. A second later he doused the lights. Bill sprawled in one of the chairs. "What a guy! He's burned cig holes all over the joint." He was talking big because he felt uneasy, his heart bursting. His body wanted to shake violently. Maybe because he didn't go about these things in just this way? He had to get used to it. And then a fellow shouldn't stay on the wagon so long.

Madge sat on the studio couch, her thin green dress folding over her legs. Her thighs were spread far apart. She nodded her head, the narrow triangle of face with the slightly oriental eyes staring at him with some female knowledge that almost provoked him into shouting: What the hell you thinking of? "Hell with landlords," she said.

"I'm nuts about you." He pulled his jacket and vest off, aware she was observing him with a knowledge more certain than truth. What the hell was she finding out? He was plain crazy. Why should he feel she was getting into the core of him? It was a lousy trick of women when about to give themselves. The only way to hide himself from her was to fix her. Damn her, so young and acting so smart.

He imitated McMann, chucking his shirt on the table, his bare arms haired yellow, stuck out of his jersey.

"Hey, you," he said, "get outa your dress."

"O.K." She lifted it over her head, naked as a nymph, her young breasts in a tight band. She leaned back on her elbows, her ribs showing faintly.

"You're a skinny runt."

"Nuts to you."

"Hell, you're tough." He hated the idea that she had lived more strongly than himself. "C'mon, strip."

She crossed her white legs, again contemplating him with her immense calm. "You're a bad boy, ain't you?"

He thought of the crowds that had slept with her, youth or no youth. What was her idea about things, about himself? He was just another guy. "You think you're slick. You're just a kid."

"Yeah, what you think?"

He glanced at her who was serene with living. She knew more than him. She knew ten times as much, kid or no kid. He remembered her story, the lineups in Brooklyn, the abduction, and now whoring it regular. His knowledge, gross with age, with stale usage, with death. Yet her body was slim, a flower stalk almost virginal, her body years distant from maturity and womanhood. Naked

above the waist like an old-time boxer, he mourned for her youth, a pity in him
that included himself as well. He heard McMann laughing softly and the
stealthy male movements.

"Cmon," said Madge. "What you mopin'?"

"I'm wondering."

"About what?"

"About you, you poor little bitch."

"You got fever sure as hell. Aw, come to bed. You're a corker. You act worse'n
a kid."

"I'm thinking I am one." His voice was soft.

Her eyes lost their diabolical sure knowledge of the male animal, her nose
wrinkling like a puzzled child's. "You're a funny feller. You're diff'rent."

"I'm Save-a-Soul Billy." Wiberg hadn't happened last year.

"You're nuts."

"You like me?"

"How do I know how you act up in bed? I seen some of the huskiest turn
out punks."

"Let's find out." He laughed, switching off the light, stumbling down the
black room, his bare feet sliding along the rug. He sat down next to her, feeling her cold thigh against his own. "You poor kid."

She hugged him. "You crazy galoot." In the dark she was made of silver and
he wasn't sorry for her or himself any longer. "What you gettin' me for Chris'-
mas?"

"You chiseler." Other Christmases, his kid brother, Santa and the reindeer—
thinking with the sad determined sentimentalism of a person whose life has
changed, whose anniversaries are to be different.

In the night they were two kids hugging together against the loneliness and
cold. Dawn was pressing its pale fingers against the two windows. Tomorrow
couldn't ever come.

CHAPTER EIGHT

He awoke to McMann's hand shaking his shoulder, snapping awake with that sense of loss of one sleeping in a strange place. McMann yawned, although his hard-surfaced face showed no fatigue. Bill got off the couch immediately. "Hello."

"Sh, Bobbie's still snorin' inside, the ole pig." He winked like a small boy. "I like 'em hefty. Madge's skinny, but she'll be all right in a coupla years."

"I'm glad to hear it."

Madge was asleep, turned on her side towards the wall. He marveled at the quietude of her face. A voice like Mac's ought to wake the dead. Even his whisper had guts to it. It was early afternoon, the air frosty and clean. "How'd you wake up, McMann?"

"My belly hurt. I near starved."

Bill scrubbed his face in the bathroom, soaking his hair and sleeking it down. They were cozy inside the bathroom, just the two of them, McMann boasting of his private toilet, the class to it, no chasing out in the halls for him, he liked to live nice. Bill squeezed a pink worm of toothpaste on his finger and mauled his gums, combing his hair. They gazed kindly at one another with the peace of men after a night with women.

McMann shut the door gently behind on last night's old smell, walking downstairs into sunlight. The crosstown tracks glinted. People's cars were nipped red. The windows of the stores were bright with sunny winter. The hanging wooden flags, advertising furnished rooms, swayed in the wind.

"Le's grab some food, kid."

"You bet. You were saying how you like to live nice. What about last night, then? Suppose you get pinched or shot?"

"Gotta make a livin'." That didn't have nothing to do with living nice. The best thing was not to worry and not to expect too much. "An' here's another thing. Forget Madge." That dame wasn't settled down like Bobbie. He wanted a dame to stick by him. They saw each other in daylight the first time, their eyes shining two kinds of blue. McMann ordered bacon and eggs in the corner coffee-pot. It was a male place, although a floosie was sitting at a table watching the guys feeding at the counter.

"I don' like stinkin' around with women when I got no use for 'em," said McMann, monastic, healthy. He always beat it out early as he could. When the dames cleared out, he went back for a nap. They cut into their eggs, the yellow dripping on the hot bacon. Maybe he should've let Bill sleep? But he figured Bill figured the way he did.

It was exciting meeting this new McMann, who wasn't drunk or tough, but was almost gentle, a *human being*. McMann wasn't more than twenty-five or six. Last night he'd seemed ageless. Bill sighed, one buddy with another. "You slug, Mac, I'm paying for this. Last night nicked you for plenty."

"Hell, if I didn' wanta treat I'd asaid so. I don't go blowin' my dough away for nothin.'" They got up from the counter, chewing on toothpicks.

"Want to come over my place?"

"Naw. I'll chase them skirts out."

"Well, I'm beating it. Kiss them for me."

"Sure thing, kid."

"Don't you kid me. I'm old as you."

"O.K. See you at Paddy's some time." Spitting out soggy bits of toothpick, he added casually: "You got stuck the other night, but them guys had to get their slice. Nex' time we'll do it ourself or maybe borer Duffy's kids. Get me? Me'n you can knock off a joint easy. Lotsa stores. That dairy guy Metz got dough. S'long."

McMann was the devil and he'd been fooled because the sun was out. He foresaw himself led by McMann into the unarrived tomorrows. That was swell to think about. What could he expect? McMann knew his inside dope was worth something. His dope'd help Mac to live nice, to pay for the private toilet. He walked up Leroy Street as Mrs. Gebhardt came out into a world not his own. He distinctly felt the difference. The light eyes in her peaceful face angered him. She'd gone to bed at ten and guessed maybe he'd been bumming. "Every time I see you you're fresh as a daisy." She didn't thank him. It wasn't a compliment.

"You don't see us so often."

"I'm busy buying Christmas presents. Sure, a present for myself. I bought myself a job." He went upstairs and undressed. McMann and him could make dough. Was he a sap? Saps had thought the same thing and been socked with lead. How many saps'd been bopped because they thought they were wise? He was getting to talk like McMann even. Hell. The luck was with him. He'd be careful and luck'd do the rest. His veins were rested. He was healthy, tired, successful, even if only to the tune of twenty-two bucks. He hopped into bed, his arm feeling for Madge, and fell asleep with the profundity of one whose heart and future are arrogant with youth. Did he dream of Duffy's dopey kids shooting pool? The dopes waiting for a break, Schneck, Ray, Mike, shooting pool? Did he dream that he was the boy who gave them the break? His pipedreams broke up into darkness. He slept.

He awoke differently this time from an unknown nightmare to see the sun outside in one fat yellow bar. He bolted upright, his heart shaking. He had a terror of McMann, imaging the high-boned face, pink, impassive, the small blue eyes in pinkness that weren't windows of the soul, weren't anything, the lids constantly narrowed as if he didn't use his eyes for sight. What went on behind those eyes, in that boxer's skull? Damn his loose tongue. McMann might be stringing him along for a sucker. Christ, if he didn't feel yellow as a louse. But

Mac was T.N.T. and was no joke. Bill's brain ignited into a flash of inspiration. McMann was out to get control of Duffy's kids. That was it. And he was the way to do it…His body reacted normally to the night before. His eyes were puffy, intricate with tiny red veins, the back of his neck ached. His tongue hung heavy in his mouth yet slid across something nauseous. He put his head under the clean fury of the jetting water, got into a fresh shirt frayed at the collar. It was almost five o'clock. Across the way the sidewalk sloped down to the gutter in a gradual diagonal, trucks and wagons backing up close to the building. The huge boxes on wheels were loading up. They were always busy across the way. The guy that owned that joint was one lucky stiff. The truck-drivers were working with the laborious grubbiness of their class, hefting and lifting. The black bars of the raised iron gate were shaking as the wind tore and shook them. He went downstairs into the afternoon. Beyond Greenwich, higher than the El, the autos sped down the elevated highway. Everything was overhead, trains, roadsters. The world beneath was trivial. Past the El, blocking out sight of the river, the great greenish gray buildings of the steamship and railroad companies usurped the lower sky. A flag was waving and his heart was desolate. The only path leading out of hell was the path of McMann's…

He was tense with resolve, wondering at his fight for the right thing even after so many blunders. He had a flat rent-free, and now he had an idea for a job for Joe. He waited on the El station for the uptown El finally rattling in, square and snaky-jointed. In the small pilot box in the first car the motorman was pale and steely. He got off at Forty-second. On the far side of Ninth, Wiberg transacted business. He grinned, fascinated by the granite endurability of the place they'd robbed. It showed no sign of last night's holdup. Metz was a former tenant of his, his window architectured with round red cheeses and slabs of Swiss. Eggs were piled up, peculiarly and grotesquely similar to huge worthless pearls. Inside, the floor was fresh with sawdust and the smells of cheese, butter, milk. Two clerks in white aprons were behind the counter, their cheeks red. He thought of the story that Metz never permitted his help to go outside for lunch, compelling them to lunch on pot-cheese, rolls, buttermilk. What a diet! Joe'd be healthy working for Metz. Metz himself, wearing the straw hat that somehow was his official dairyman's guild token, smiled, a small dark man with an unctuous flashing of teeth and a ceremony of hairy hands. "Billy Trent, ain't it?"

"What you think Metz? Cmon in the back. I want to see you private." He grinned, not expecting Metz to spill the beans about Wiberg, but hoping he might. "How's geschaft since I quit hounding you for rent?"

"So-so," said Metz, his hands adding a commentary of: It might be worse. "You working?"

"Part time for a friend of mine."

"Dot's something. I always said it, the whole world can be on the breadline, but this Bill, he'll have something to do."

"You're wondering now why I want to see you privately. I want a Christmas favor from you. When I had the chance I did plenty for you."

"You should a Jew been," said Metz, frowning with admiration. "I give you plenty Christmas presents, not only Christmas, but in July too."

"I want you to give me a break now. I don't make much dough and my kid brother's coming to live with me after the first. He's nineteen, huskier than me, and not afraid of work. You got three stores. Give him a job."

"How can I, Bill? These fellers are all cockeyed relations of mine. My stores're full of my wife's relations. She should an orphan've been."

"You can take on one more clerk. He's a goodlooking kid. He'd bring you trade. Don't your Irish Dutch Wop customers complain about those schnozzolas?"

"So long's the merchandise is good I got no complaints."

"I can do you a favor, Metz."

"Lemme hear."

"How'd you like to get your rent cut again?"

"Why not?"

"This is a real Christmas gift. I know some facts about the people who hold the mortgage on this house and how a smart guy can get his rent cut."

Metz was still sleepy behind his glasses. "You always know plenty things," he said heavily. "I wonder why you're not a rich man."

"It's the times. I'll be rich. Don't worry." He stared at Metz. He had damned good dope, and the Yid ought to chip in cash as well as a job. "First I want twenty-five bucks. I'd ask for more, but since you're hiring my brother I'll let it go."

"Much obliged."

"How much rent you pay, Metz?"

"You know better'n me. Four hundred for this rotten corner, with the peoples all moving away to Long Island'n Brooklyn."

"I want your word I get twenty-five and my brother that job."

"I ain't ever disappointed you." He wrote out a check for fifteen. I cash it soon you tell me, right here and now."

"Gypping me already."

"A job's worth money. You don't buy them."

"Keep this under your hat. The landlord's in hot water. Yeh, Delhota, even him. He expects to drop this corner. Taxes and interest aren't met by the rental. Strike him hard for a reduction and you'll get it. Show him the color of a few hundred and you'll get a nice new lease. He'll be foreclosed anyway. What does he care?"

"If it works out so, your brother gets the job. I'll break him in. Twelve dollars a week. Nothink for overtime." They went out to the cash register. Bill had a swift glance at the stacked greenbacks. "I keep my word."

"You're a sap to keep all that dough in there. You might get robbed." Metz glared hot and wild for a second. "Ain't you heard? Wiberg was hit on the nut last night. Took seven hundred, the bummers."

"That's bunk. Where the hell'd he get seven hundred? Probably took five smacks and he claims the rest for the insurance people."

"No no no." He waved a finger. "He's dying for a cent, but I know they take three hundred for sure." And he'd got twenty-two bucks. He'd been double-crossed. "How do you know it was three hundred and not one-eighty? You seem positive." Metz smiled bashfully. "Take my word."

"Did you loan it to Wiberg? Did you loan him any?"

"You should a Jew be. Some of you goyim is more Jewish than the Jews. Send your brother around, but if it don't work out mit Delhota, no job."

"If you weren't sure, you'd never shell out dough."

"Du bist a Yid," cried Metz. "A Jew, nothink else."

Outside, Bill thought of McMann. He was lucky to get any money out of the Wiberg holdup. He felt smarter than the gang of gyps because he knew definitely he'd been rooked. Oh, boy, if McMann knew Joe'd be working for Metz…He wouldn't take Metz for anything. Even if he had plenty.

Wiberg put down his paper, his ancestry of Talmudists evident in his bearing. "You work yet? Bad times not working."

Bill was sorry for the gentle fat man, sorrier for himself who'd been rooked. He was chill and confident. Wiberg had represented so much money. In that second, possessive of this shrewd knowledge of himself, he straightened up, proud of his clinical attitude. That was the way to be. No softness, to work at crime as a scientist works in a lab. The hell with people. "I hear they've been working on you. Tough luck."

Wiberg had waited for the chance to explode. "They always pick on a poor man. Bang me on the head. A feller asks me for a pair lady stockings when bing! And I had lot of money. How they know cin Gott allein weisst."

"They get much?"

"I should say. Seven hundred."

He stuck out his lower lip. "You been eating dope. Don't kid me. When the hell did this shop net you that in a year? You'd have to put dresses on half the behinds in town for seven hundred. Why, that's seven grand these times."

"They took it, I tell you." He picked up his paper. "The police. Phooey on them with their radio cars. Who they catch? Nobody. But I remember that feller."

"Forget him. You're insured. Maybe that holdup's a Christmas present—that is, if they give you seven hundred."

He left the shop. He'd been rooked. He couldn't forget it, thinking of McMann and Paddy with the cold calm ferocity of a scientist contemplating necessary guinea pigs. Otherwise it was a good day's work. Fifteen bucks and a job for Joe. Metz wasn't a bad guy. Neither was the dough in his till. On Saturday nights around midnight Metz ought to be good for five hundred. That was dough. He wondered how the kid'd fit in with his future? The clean honest kid, thinking of cleanliness and honor as qualities similar to skin pigmentation or the shapes of noses. He'd forgotten to interpret honesty either ethically or spiritually.

He was a champ chiseler and Christmas Day he dropped in at the office. He was the prodigal come home, and everybody was tickled to see him. Christmas Day Stanger had a fatted calf for everybody. It was an old custom. A bottle was on the table and they were drinking conservatively under Stanger's happy but moral eye, the rent-collectors and stenos gazing at one another, standing up like human beings and not shorn in two, leaning over desks like exhibits out of the Flea Museum. There was no fatted calf for Bill, but many handshakes and wonderings when he'd get a job. "I just dropped in to wish you all a merry Christmas and happy New Year." He smiled so charmingly that Stanger called him into his private cubicle and slipped him ten bucks, despite strenuous protests that he'd dropped in for the spirit of the thing. He had a tough job keeping a straight face.

"They're all getting presents," said Stanger. "I want you to take it. Why haven't you been around for lunch with Joe? Mrs. Stanger has asked me many times to get in touch with you down on Leroy, but there's no phone and somehow I never got around to writing."

"Thanks, Mr. Stanger. Thanks for the free rent. It's swell of you."

"Listen, you must come around for dinner."

Later he said: ; "Merry Christmas" again. No use losing a contact like Stanger. Ten bucks…That night he went to a party with Madge. McMann was there, and so were a few of Duffy's kids, Schneck and Ray. He'd noticed Schneck and Ray were thick friends. Duffy of course was too big to show up. McMann told him on the sly he'd invited the kids up. "Might be needn'm soon. Free booze and grub and they'll be eatin' outen our hands." After the party, McMann, Bobbie, and Madge and himself went to a nigger joint in Harlem. The ten bucks went like a light.

CHAPTER NINE

Bill put down the valise and opened the dog-box his brother had lugged in from Easton. For a moment the two brothers didn't look at each other, tacitly filling in the strangeness of meeting after so long by concentrating on a third and neutral object.

The dog was a mongrel puppy, normally happy with an inane blue-eyed youth, but now disconsolate. It ran about the flat, lifting its nose in sorrow for its abduction to a place that didn't smell of grass. Its white coat was spotted with black like a Dalmatian, the ears and eyes those of a sad hound.

"He misses the country," said the kid brother.

"What'd you bring him in for? A dog in the city—hell."

"You're not sure, Bill?"

"Did I say I was?"

"I'm awful glad to be here."

"You were always a lover of animals."

"So were you. Don't you remember?"

"It's so long ago I've forgotten." The brothers raised their eyes from the puppy waddling on its inept legs, from Joe's single shiny valise, and stared at each other across the distance of two years. The distance was infinite because Eaton was less than a hundred miles from New York and Bill could have easily visited if he'd wanted to. Their faces were queer to one another. Both had returned from the death of parting to be joined again, solemn, wondering how much each had changed. Seeing his flesh and blood on Leroy Street, Bill thought of his own appearance. Joe wasn't a mirror likeness of himself, but there was enough duplication for him to feel a sudden distrait longing, a certain sense that this boy was his brother and no one else. The kid's hair was lighter than his own, almost yellow, but he was not quite as husky or as tall. His eyes were the same color of blue. He was his brother all right. He ached at the impact of Joe's youth, the nineteen years that were enough like himself to cause the glacial years to retreat, leaving something green and sunny in heart. In a way he was seeing the Bill that had been four years ago, seeing himself not in memory, but in the flesh. This smooth eager face, this courageous kid that was now his brother, had once been himself. The bitter age that had nothing to do with five or ten years, but was ageless as time, now lay on his shoulders like an impossible burden.

"Well," said Joe, "it's the New Year. 1932 and I'm damn glad."

"So am I." For the sixth or seventh time since he had met Joe down at the Pennsy station under the immense roof of glass and steel, with the redcaps bugging all over the place and an imminent sense of trains and departures abbreviating all lengthy talk, he asked: "How's everybody back home? I don't care much, to tell you the truth, about anybody but you."

"It's a long time since you were last in Easton. The girls missed you. Honest."

"How's College Hill? Everything sleepy as ever? You've grown. Last time I saw you—that summer two years ago, it was—you were a head shorter."

"We had a dandy time that summer."

"Things are different now. I lived in a hotel then and we did the town like gentlemen, but now I'm poor as a mouse. Poorer."

"I don't care, Bill. I'm tickled to be here."

"How are those relatives of ours? Not so hot?"

Joe insisted they were all right. "Like hell they are," said Bill. "They probably made you feel punk once in a while." Joe seemed bewildered at his talk, the queer stresses upon quiet words shaped into sounds of things ominous, sounds echoing of Paddy, of McMann, of his brother's new life, cold, brutally phlegmatic. He said Bill seemed changed a lot. He had big pouches under his eyes. He patted the dog, who stopped moaning to lick his hand.

"Spotty doesn't like it here," said Bill.

"It's the city," said Joe apologetically as if to say that Spotty's reaction wasn't his own. "I'm glad to be here. Back home they were decent, but somehow— well, I wasn't in the way, but somehow I felt I was in uncle's wife's way a little bit. There wasn't anything definite. She was decent. I don't know if I'm making it clear. I hate to sound like a crab or to have you think I was some orphan at the mercy of hard relations. Not that at all. They were decent. Maybe it was my fault. I didn't feel close to them nor they to me—not very close that is, for we all liked each other. Honest, I'm glad I'm here, though." His eyes shone. He patted the double bed. "We'll sleep together like when we were kids."

Bill gulped, and the old kid times of father and mother streamed up from his blood and marrow. "You bet."

"We'll start in together, Bill. Just as you wrote. The rent's free and you have a little money and then this Jewish fellow has a job for me. Gee, you must be a wonder to get a job. Back home they don't exist."

"It wasn't anything."

"Who lives in this house, Bill?"

"Hardly anybody. It's half empty, but there are some poor families with kids, all plugging. And the Gebhardt family. They got a pretty daughter." Joe laughed. "I wish I could get a job for myself. Everyday I see some important people, and if I get a break I'll be in the money again. Then, as I told you at the Pennsy, I make some side money doing some nighttime bookkeeping. Don't worry, we'll get along."

"That's why your eyes are shot. You ought to take care of them. That bookkeeping must be hard on them."

They smiled at each other, over the ridiculous puppy sniffing at musty floor smells, their eyes meeting and remembering a fogged sad time of kid days, looking into the future, puzzled, Joe a little sentimental, Bill wondering what Joe was really like. A nice kid, but what was under Joe's skin? Joe could never guess what a bunk artist he was.

"We're in Greenwich Village," said Joe.

"Hardly. The artists are further east. It's poverty mostly." He sighed. "I'll be back at six. I'm going to see Metz."

"I'll go with you."

"No, you better not. I've got to see some other people after that. You wash up and then we'll have a regular meal, spaghetti, antipasto."

"Can we afford it?"

"The Ritz is our next stop, kid." He buttoned up his camel-hair coat, edging down the three small rooms to the door. From the bedroom Joe looked as if he wouldn't see him for a year. He narrowed his eyes with the wonder of it. Joe was nuts about him. What a good kid! "So long, Joe."

"Hurry it, Bill." He wouldn't drag Joe in the dirt for the world. He grinned sickly, feeling, knowing, that somehow or other he'd get Joe in dutch. It always happened that way. It was the natural thing. What a big brother he was! By Christ, he wouldn't make a play for Metz if it was the last store on earth. He hoped he'd keep this New Year resolution. The El pillars on Greenwich were bolted right in the sidewalk. Almost above his head a train hit his sight with the might of a movie train pounding straight at the audience. He felt tiny inside. So Joe had come to town. Hoorah! It didn't make so much difference. He was awed at the velocity of his direction. Would McMann be home? There was another store lined up, and Mac ought to hear about it. He had a hunch Mac had a good bean on his shoulders.

At six they rubbed their wet faces dry with towels, smelling like new suits, and went downstairs for dinner. Icy air blew in from the river. Beyond the elevated highway, the cars zizzing home from work, the west wind humming in steady. The river was out of sight, but Bill guessed Joe was dreaming of the river's immense gray sweep. He was that kind of kid. Joe was excited, his eyes jerking up to the warehouse and printing plant, seeing with so new a vision that Bill also realized their significance. It struck him that these eight-story fortresses, the opaque windows wired for strength, in contrast to their own shabby down-at-heel house, were the goals of all endeavor. Their house. Christ. The stoop with the black cast-iron rails, the iron picket fence, the garbage pails, all reiterating the poverty of the "last of the Trents"; rubbing destitute elbows with other junky tenements on either side, all of them a row of beggars kowtowing and sucking around before the industrial brutes across the way. A fellow had to get his pile by hook or crook. Anything was fair. The only thing that counted, as the churches and colleges and government knew, was dough. "We'll get out of here soon," Bill said.

A speakeasy had moved into the tenement on Hudson and Leroy, next to the coffee-pot. Inside, the kids were staring through the window covered with the ice lace of winter, the kids also dreaming of dough. Joe's eyes had the far-away abstraction of one peering ahead to a legendary freedom. He'd get used to it. He'd get used to the city and to Bill. On Hudson Street a wire meshing ten feet high surrounded the school playground. Beyond the yard, full of the gray miserable cindery gravel of city playgrounds, the school was shuttered up. They followed Leroy eastwards. Elegant high-stooped houses like those on Washington Square, red brick, the brass polished, with a sense of dark rich corridors and servants, gave way to tenements. Leroy curved on itself towards the Village and spaghetti. Joe nearly always followed the same street afterwards, even when he didn't see much of Bill, stepping in the footprints of that first night. Leroy was always a winter street to him, of dusk and pleasant hunger.

The streets of town, spinning out from their flat like webs about a spider's home, entangled him forever. The city. The sense of being caught in one spot while the glamorous web of activity spread to the ends of the world. Beyond Leroy the immense town was endlessly beautiful. Yet after he was working for Metz, the city betrayed him. It held promise, but no fulfillment. Bill betrayed him, too. It was as if Bill had moved back to Easton because he'd come to New York. After the grind at Metz's he was alone. Bill came in late at night. He'd be asleep usually, but when Spotty lifted his pointed head, growling, barking, he'd snap awake to see Bill grinning at his grogginess. He'd say: "G'night" as Bill patted Spotty, his hand saying: It's me, mutt. Sometimes Bill'd ask how the slave was, and say maybe he ought to quit. "Go to bed, Bill." "No fooling, Joe. I think it's too hard on you. Quit." He'd beg him to let him sleep. Or Bill'd curse, stating it was a pain to get up at six as Joe did and then get in at eight or nine at night. Joe was no nigger, was he? But he'd be talking to a corpse. Joe'd be sound asleep. The job was no cinch, but perhaps it was best for the two of them to be separated in the working, planning day.

Joe would get up, shutting off the alarm and switching on the light. Spotty, of course, would be wide awake, his behind shaking like a hula dancer's with the terrific love of a dog greeting its master after the night. The long white tail lashed like a whip. Spotty tried to walk, mad to kiss Joe's face. He'd pour milk in a bowl, crumbling up a piece of white bread, his eyes red, his heart somber. The puppy was growing up with a thick chest and huge feet. When the dog had eaten, Joe'd stare at Bill, wash up, and go downstairs for breakfast. He'd got into a habit of studying the dull sleeping face. All wasn't kosher in Denmark, as Metz'd say. Bill was awfully pale. He smoked and drank too much at his bookkeeping. He whored too much. That bookkeeping job was a swell job. Yet, whores, Joe thought with the virginal condemnation of a young boy who's had a few affairs, and those with housemaids, mostly, in a park. Bill was a sight for sore eyes. It made them sorer. The nose and mouth built in clay (his features were handsome, but weighted) were getting gross. Bill's clothes would be thrown all over the place. And there'd be a foul smell of tobacco and booze. The windows were kept shut in the winter. What a job he had! Wished he had a job like Bill. Even the whore part of it wasn't so bad. He was sure of Bill. He knew Bill. When Bill drank, there was always a dame along.

Joe'd yawn into the mirror, his yellow hair wet from the tap, patting Spotty, who immediately after eating sprang into bed next to Bill as if he were taking Joe's place. Joe smiled, gathering up the wet newspapers spread every night as a temporary dog's toilet.

He walked rapidly down Leroy to Greenwich, and then uptown to Christopher. The morning air was like fresh apples. Through this underground district with the El ties prisoning out the sky he'd be thinking of Cathy Gebhardt and how pretty she was. Bill hadn't kidded him any about her looks. He liked thinking of her early in the morning on this street of machinery and chemicals and mowing trucks. There were dozens of hauling firms trafficking with all the distant cities. Almost every other office hired out trucks or ran buses or had a daily business with the towns of America. Mahopac, Paterson, Kerhonksen, St. Louis, Memphis, Toledo. Boards and charts tabulated the places visited. It was swell. The names were swell. What a life to be holed up on Leroy when all the world was moving! Joe exhaled the sharp air. His eyes weren't sleepy. Near Christopher El station, going north on Greenwich, the street slanted from east to west, the gothic archway of St. Veronica's Church always hitting his eye with the sudden beauty of a tree, a church, or something not absolutely necessary to business. It was Cathy's church.

He drank his man's coffee and ate his ham and eggs in a large cafeteria full of workers. Everything gleamed white, tile and walls and tables, and everybody, with the exception of the counterman punching holes in meal tickets or roaring into the kitchen, alert, sleepless, was dressed in dark working clothes, the tall blueshirted longshoremen, Irish, Swedish, Polack, the German and Bohemian butchers in the wholesale meat markets, a host of workers in all the trades that compelled him to think of the far-away. The workers of the far-away. Ships on the river, railroad terminals, trackers, shippers, meat workers handling the huge naked corpses of cows and pigs slaughtered in Chicago. After breakfast he rode uptown to Forty-second, standing outside on the toy platform between the El cars. Every time the El stopped, the conductor squeezed into zero, opening the gates, hollering in a voice of whisky and cold weather. But the El never traveled to the far-away places, or he didn't at any rate, always getting off at the same station, sometimes thinking of the rails penetrating to Columbus Circle, the Eighties, the Bronx. He'd go to the Bronx with Cathy one of these days, to the end of the line. The Bronx must be some place. Running downstairs, he'd report for work.

Metz started the same way. At seven sharp, little Napoleon would pop in, take off his felt, get into white apron and straw hat, the special livery he kept in the rear, glaring at the three clerks like a general at his army, preoccupied, figuring profits. "O.K.," he commanded. They'd fill a bucket of water and clean the window, the water trickling on their hands. Ninth Avenue was beyond life, a plateau of beautiful loneliness. Nothing could be as lonely as a city when the sun shines and nobody is stirring. The oyster-wagons, the fruit-peddlers, had not showed up yet. Washing the window was working in a city everyone had left. After this they swept out the store, Metz dropping the fresh sawdust with his own hands as if it were manna from the skies. Then spick and span in their white aprons, the clerks and their boss waited for business. Soon the first Polish woman came in for milk and rolls. They cut butter, sold eggs, passing down this and that, wrapping up, smiling at the Irish, Greek, Italian housewives.

The Irish were never tired of ribbing the boss, asking questions about that good-looker. Oh, he was a dandy. Joe'd grin; the two Jewish clerks'd grin affably, long-nosed, swarthy; Metz smiling in his strange bashful way, pleased the customers were pleased. The morning went up like a house afire, the three of them slicing the salt butter, weighing the cheeses, making dough for Metz. Every now and then, Joe'd be picked to go downtown with Metz in a dark rattling truck. There in the market, in the outside vigor of air and sun and the things of the earth eaten by men, Metz'd purchase tubs of butter, boxes of cheese from the wholesalers. Joe would help other workers load up the truck. In the beginning his muscles ached, but among those Slavs and squareheads, sinewed, uncomplaining, the doing men of the earth, he soon rejoiced in the heroic betrayal of youth, using his body wantonly. It was impossible for him to tire. They'd drive back, and Joe and one of the clerks'd unload. They called him Der Starker because he was taller than they, and his chest and shoulders were more spectacular, but he noticed they worked as well as himself, the thin Jews.

The afternoon was another morning except that the things sold weren't as barnyard simple as eggs and milk and butter. Under the steady control of Metz, the clerks, who appeared to be attached by countless wires to the canned goods crowding the shelves, moved like puppets serving the customers. Around noon when things slackened, they'd snatch a roll, cut off a hunk of butter and cheese, drink a bottle of milk, and then work arduously all the day. Metz didn't permit smoking in the store. At intervals they'd rush out into the yard, choking on furious puffs, returning all smiles as if they'd never left.

It was always a surprise to Joe when Metz, dark and gnomish, never changing in appearance, never showing fatigue or the progress of time, would shout to him: "Hey; Joey, you'n Sam can go home. Tomorrow you'll stay a little later." He'd scramble for the rear stockroom where the shelves were a thousand shining tins, the cases and boxes piled against the walls. He'd Houdini out of his apron, hurrying onto the street. On the alternate days when he stayed later it'd be almost nine; he'd be happy and a little sad for the livelong day that had vanished hellward so swiftly. The incredible long day, begun at six, was gone. How nice it was early in the morning getting his breakfast, fresh and crisp in the bustle of life, the trucks shooting towards far-away destinations! The fourteen-hour day was over. Jesus, that was going some.

"All gone," said Joe to himself.

Now this Ninth Avenue, so empty when they washed Metz's window, was crowded with folk who'd already eaten their last supper meal. Families gazed into the gleaming winter windows, young couples were hotfooting it for the movies. Everybody had eaten and was full-bellied. He hadn't. When he woke, the world slept. When he ate, the world was sated. Bill's life was more fun. Bill had a good time. Bill slept as late as he wanted. What good did he get out of it all? His job wasn't worth a lousy twelve bucks. Boy, was he tired? It was getting on to nine, but it was twelve midnight, as far as he went. After he washed and got something to eat, it'd be time for bed if he was to rise at six.

Dark lonely Greenwich sounded his footsteps. The businesses were shut down and lights were scattered. The river smelled of the night. The tugs sirened. He cut up into Leroy, into a city of the dead, the warehouse and printery lonely pyramids. The row of houses glimmered with lights remote as camp fires.

"Hello, Spotty," he said in the empty flat. Was that kiyoodle wild to see him! He sat down on the rug, the pup biting his hair. A fellow's only friend, and that was no dumb crack either. Bill was out busy with his bookkeeping or whatever it really was. He'd be in bed when Bill came home. The only time he could see him would be at six; and sometimes Bill wasn't even in then, sleeping out with the ledgers. Or he'd have the pleasure of his company on Sunday. He should've stayed in Easton.

He washed up and knocked at Mrs. Gebhardt's, entering into the snug warmth of the place as if into a brother's heart. Hulky Mr. Gebhardt was reading a German newspaper, the kids doing their homework, Mrs. Gebhardt already glancing nervously at the gilt clock on the mantel. The dishes were dried, the red clean cloth spread on the table, the family sitting in the parlor like an illustration of domesticity, their cheeks shining, their eyes bright with industry, patience, and religion. They smiled at him with the patriotism of other workers, Gebhardt lifting his paper with bony red fingers, smiling with eyes small as a pig's, blue with a stamina for the year-in year-out grind with only a few turnverein picnics and beer parties. "How's vork today, Joe?" He understood the boy.

"I made a million."

"In the market?" He continued with the sympathy of one banker quizzing another about a bond issue concerning them both.

"We brought back enough cheese to feed every rat in the world."

"Hawhahhaw, you hear dot, mamma?" The kids laughed with him like dutiful white mice.

"Metz does a whale of a business—"

"Where you go? You eat here. You ain't here a long time. Mamma give him zu fressen. Dot means to eat."

"I was going out. Honest."

"A home meal harms nobody." said Mrs. Gebhardt, rushing to the gas range.

The three younger kids, Frederick, baby Carl, Gertrude, smiled at him, yellow-haired, almost formidable with their collective honesty. Joe winked at the three child faces, at the do re mi of kindergarten Carl, eight-year-old Freddie, twelve-year-old Gertrude, so young and yet so patient for the working lives waiting for them. He could shiver at their courage, the unconscious strength of children who will and must follow their parents' way. Sleepy, listening to the comfortable newspaper rustling (he didn't mind Gebhardt's absorption, understood he must hit the hay soon and this was his only chance to read the world news), watching the wakeful kids peeking at him from the table, their yellow heads inexpressibly beautiful, their industry predicting that some day society would follow the road of knowledge. They were omens of the new life, even if their bodies would be coerced to the slavery of their sires. Mrs. Gebhardt brought back a steaming plate of goulash and browned potatoes simmering in hot heavy gravy. In a separate bowl she poured out a cabbage soup. She was glad he was hungry and had such good things to eat.

Cathy, who'd been busy in the bedroom, finally showed up. He realized why he'd dropped in without dinner. To see Cathy. She led baby Carl away, slender but almost as motherly as the broad-hipped Mrs. Gebhardt. Baby Carl didn't complain even if his face was sour, his pale plump cheeks pouting. "How are you, Cathy?" he said. She was all right, and soon as she put little nuisance to bed she'd be with him. "Little nuisance!" exclaimed Mrs. Gebhardt, very much shocked. He ate his goulash, chewing meat and potatoes and drinking the cabbage soup at the same time. They smiled delightedly with the happiness of folk converting a foreigner to their ways. Gebhardt declared he was a Deutsch already. The Mrs. laughed, the kids sneaked another look at him. How was Bill, the Mrs. wanted to know. Joe stated he hardly ever saw Bill. Bill was a busy man. Again they all nodded sadly and sympathetically, workers with regular hours and routines, considering one outside their class. If Joe was tired he shouldn't ought to go to the movies. "I'm not tired. How about you, Cathy?"

"It's very late."

"Stay home," said Mrs. Gebhardt. "So cold outside." She thought that if Bill would've wanted to take Cathy to the movies she would've been frightened, and more frightened to have Bill stay home with them, with his sharp weary face. Ach, mein Gott, Brüder!

"I can't stay home. I'm restless." Mrs. Gebhardt looked at Joe. He was Bill's brother. He could be for good or bad. He was Bill's brother. She was afraid for her Cathy.

CHAPTER TEN

Bill stared out of McMann's window at the neat block of brown buildings across the way, the shades lowered in the apartments and furnished rooms. Behind one shade, light glowed through and he saw the shadow of desire, a woman's shape to be lusted for because her face and age and life were unknown. The shade was very old and thin. The street lamp hung its huge white pearl over the sidewalk, and Twenty-third was womanless except for a shadow. McMann was speaking through one corner of his mouth. He wanted to know why they should divvy with anybody. The Wiberg job, there was him, Bill, and the two bastards, and Paddy. Five guys. "I don't want to get too mixed up." He glanced at McMann's face, so pink it seemed chipped out of stone, at the humorous treacherous eyes, so small it was hard to realize cunning could be held in them.

"If it's us two, that's less mixed up?"

"Not the way you're working it. Given a break and you'll be making a play for the Duffy kids." The bathroom door was open, the enameled interior visible like a distant perspective. How unreal the scene was! And was McMann growling he had cold feet? Maybe it was because Joe had come to town, hardworking Joe. What a life! He hadn't been living since Stanger'd kicked him out. He'd been existing, hopped up for a life that contained many deaths every day. Maybe he ought to quit right here and now before real danger'd smack his head off. McMann was unreal as Paddy or Madge, who weren't in the apartment "You're getting' yeller," threatened McMann.

"Holy Christ, where's your whisky? You're giving me a tin ear." He drank a shot of rye. "I know I talked big as a house awhile back."

"That was man talk. You had guts."

"I'm not busting up now. I'm just wondering if it's best for us to go ahead and take the long gamble?"

McMann didn't know. But he'd been making money. Bill grinned. McMann had a sense of humor. Twenty-two bucks. Why divvy, McMann insisted. Take the long gamble. Make or break. Either be in the dough or get wiped. No use lousing around.

The shot of booze wrapped his belly in hot bandage. So Mac thought he had him buffaloed. He knew he'd been gypped at Wiberg's. Mac'd gyp anybody, ready to cut out Paddy for a nickel. "Soger's next."

"Thatta boy." His guts felt soft. Like a sentry on duty he had watched time pass, his eyes strained, cautious, curious, peering into the shadows of time. The shadow life. Damn it all. Poor Joe. Never saw him. Let him rot at Metz's. That cheap Metz. Ought to grab his till. What was he thinking of? He said dully: "I don't want to get mixed up too much."

"I'll go nuts."

"We'll get in dutch if we try to steal Duffy's kids. Duffy'll wipe us."

"No guts. And all that big mouthin' about knockin' off clip joints and speaks for real dough. What the hell kinda talk? It's safer just us two'n more dough. I hock a car. You take the wheel. It's a cinch, kid. I pull off all the business with the gat. We beat it off. Them storekeepers are a cinch." He walked to the bottle, coatless, his taut belly seeming to be held in a corset, his hips small, his chest arching, his long stone head nodding in a way that made him appear like a horrible bloodless monster.

McMann had him going. If he had real guts the best thing to do would be to kill the rat. To get rid of him once and for all. McMann wouldn't stop now until death. "I won't carry a gun. It's a lousy laugh. Every day I'm getting more mixed up, just like the storybooks."

"Who toldya to come in? Quit crabbin.' Won't Paddy raise a stink? They'll all be suckin' around. They'll work for us. We're going to be boss. Big shots, you'n me."

"That's what I'm scared of." He had a vision of the Duffy kids in their pool parlor like parts of machinery waiting to be assembled, the hard, soulless kids, pale broad Schneck, Ray, who was like a younger McMann, the others, bits of steel waiting to be put together in power, waiting for the strongest to direct them. It was Duffy. I could be McMann. Those kids were waiting for the strong finger to start them clicking. And McMann was the devil to do it. He would do it. He would if he lived.

"Do we take Soger, kid? You need dough."

"I guess so."

Two nights later Bill drove the car, a five-passenger Chrysler, downtown from Columbus Circle to Forty-eighth Street, parking a hundred feet above Soger's Pork Store. He was alone. It was ten sharp. Where was McMann? God Almighty, where was Red? He put the car in neutral, turned off the ignition, shivering in the dead auto, waiting. The tiny dashboard light glowed on his knees, Christ, he couldn't hang out here all year where some guy might spot him. He lifted his coat collar high about his face, pulling down his hat brim, shrinking into his coat as if hoping to bury himself from sight like a kid ducking under a blanket. Lucky it was late January, a high howling wind roaring around the El supports, standing like resolute beggars in mid-winter.

He looked at the linoleum shop with shiny coils of carpet, the Jewish butcher store with Hebrew letters saying: "Kosher Kosher" (or "All Jews can buy here," grinning at Metz's translation). He gripped the wheel tight, glancing past the Swiss watchmaker's hole in the wall, the bald head in the front of the tiny window, glass in eye; the second-hand furniture shop, the cordial shop with a window full of crepe and artistic bottles; Soger's Pork Store. Soger's. Where was Mac? Poor Soger. Many a time he'd cut him a swell sandwich, two huge slices of bread with a hunk of liverwurst the size of a fist. It was ten minutes after ten. He'd hurried downtown with hell after him to be on time. "Ten sharp," Mac'd said, "a hundred foot above Soger. You'll see me coming down from the opposite corner. Start up the boat when you see me. Put it in first. Soon as I come out, roll forward, and don't forget to keep the back door open…" He thought of his instructions with a misery he hadn't known since college exams, sweating under his arms, burdened with heat…What a ride downtown in the hocked car, knowing every second it was stolen, dodging trucks, afraid of every cop who might be Eagle-Eye Gus with a million numbers memorized (McMann said Gus hung out on the bridges mostly), shaking and dry-mouthed when the red traffic lamps like mad beast eyes compelled him to stop. Where was McMann? Was the guy planning to frame him? How many years in the coop for a hocked car? To a passer-by he looked like a young fellow on a date, moping for his broad to come down from one of the flats above the linoleum or pork stores.

His heart rushed forward as if he were in love and McMann his approaching sweetie. McMann at last sauntering down the street, not fast, not slow, wearing a big felt yanked down almost to his eyebrows in Greeky fashion. Bill's body quivered. He pushed in the clutch. The gears ground, the car was in first. Frantically he put it in neutral. He'd forgotten all about the ignition. Christ! He switched the ignition on, starting up the car, the motor singing. He put the car in first, his foot depressing the clutch and ready to ease up. While he'd fumbled getting ready, his eyes concentrated on the dark pit of the footboard, he'd somehow kept glancing up and down the street, knowing Mac'd gone into Soger's, a customer in a pulled-down felt. The door opened, he had a sense of stout Soger falling over, all mixed up with another storekeeper who'd flopped the same way (was it Wiberg?), but not really seeing Soger, just thinking he must be falling like Wiberg. Mac hurried out, slamming the door. He started forward. Mac yanked the door open in the moving car. (Christ, he'd forgotten about the door.) "Step on' it. Round the corner. Down Tenth." He slumped back in the rear. As they turned the corner into solitude, he crawled over the driver's seat with the dexterity of a snake. Bill was doing thirty miles an hour, honking his horn at the dark tenement street with the windows glistening and the lost sky directly above and ahead like some vast sanctuary. They bowled out on Tenth, the tires noisy. "Put it up to forty," said McMann, "and down Eleventh."

"O.K."

"There's a cop in a damn cab follerin' us. Lucky we got the head start." The glory of speed after all the waiting zizzed out of his bones. He turned limp, non-muscular, remembering now what should never've been forgotten, the sharp crack heard a second ago, the sharp malevolent spitting of pistol fire. He glanced sideways at McMann, hatless and nodding as if to say: Yeh, it's a gat. He jerked his head around. "That bastard hack can't do more'n fifty. Hit 'er up." Bill swerved into Eleventh Avenue, speeding across the railroad tracks. A huge locomotive was chugging down at him with one immense yellow orb. He heard the clang of the locomotive, saw the shining black steel, saw the indignant white face of a fellow in a roadster twisting out in panic from between Bill and the slow but terrible moving hill of steel. The meshing of tracks held yellow light, and he was swinging down Eleventh between the warehouses and auto-assembling plants, morbid and lonely, the car bouncing on the rough going.

"We duck the cab?"

"Jus' made it. We'll screw'm."

"What next?"

"Up Eleventh. I'm going to take the wheel. Get it. I'm takin' it. Don't let go the wheel. Shift over. Get it. And keep your foot on the gas." Bill heard the cop's gun bang once. In his mirror he saw the reflection of the cab's big lamps. They still had a good lead. "Up Tenth," said McMann. He headed for Tenth again, now feeling McMann's hard buttocks on his lap, his voice shouting to keep the gas going. McMann's hands held the wheel while he shifted from under, the car clipped of its wings. McMann sat in the driver's seat. He rammed his foot down on the gas. The night leaped forward. They curved into Tenth. "We gotta ditch them bastards. Radio cars. We'll park'n beat it."

Bill watched the slower cab hurtling after them. He wiped his brow. In for it. In for it. Good for him. Served him right. All crooks got—Mac jockeyed the car down Tenth, swinging the heavy tonnage like a fist towards Ninth Avenue. His recklessness had them on two wheels for a guts-falling second; then they coasted down the sidestreet. He jammed on the brakes, rolled the car up to the curb, tugged back the emergency. "Step on' it."

The street was emptily gripping winter. There were a Lutheran church and many respectable basement stoops populated by shopkeepers and old-fashioned Germans. Bill and McMann legged it for the corner. "Don' run," said McMann. "Easy, kid." Far below, at the beginning of the street, the lights of the cab flared at them. They were safe on Ninth. A cab was waiting on the corner. They'd just made it, piling in. "Gran' Central," said McMann calmly. "Step on' it, buddy." They breathed easily, the danger left behind them in the stolen car.

Lucky there was a cab parked, Bill thought. The cab cut down with the green lights to Eighth Avenue. They never saw the pursuing cab. He'd never know, thank God, whether it'd stopped at the abandoned car or pushed down Ninth still chasing the Chrysler. He lit a cigarette, dull with calamity, obsessed by a tracking fear. McMann was gabbing about Bobbie and Madge and the swell time they'd have (for the benefit of the hack; yet he was afraid of McMann, the icy bastard). "Wake up," said McMann.

"It's crazy gambling the way we do."

"The breaks is with us. Seven eleven."

"We almost crapped out."

Eighth glittered with the suave bulks of the new hotel; the theater vistas opening down to Broadway. Signs shot their thousand bulbs at them, yellow, green, red. It was true. They'd got away. He breathed with difficulty, but breathed, not gasping, tasting the blessed air. Their cab stopped for a traffic beacon. In this anonymity where no one was known and no one was in pursuit, he spoke defiantly. "I'm tired knocking off Madge, the little slut."

McMann grinned. He was wearing his hat differently now, tilted back at its usual cocky angle. His yes glinted. He paid off the hack. Grand Central shoved its clock at Forty-second, insisting on time and punctuality. Men were getting into cabs or hailing them. Everyone wore the same face. "Time for coffee before the train leaves for Atlanta," said McMann. Their cab moved up towards Fifth. "Tired fixin' Madge. Hell, that hack must've figured you a big shot."

"Like hell. He listens to crap all day."

"Not that hack. He can tell the difference."

They went into the Thompson. "Two coffees'n apple pies." The brown coffee spilled promptly out of its tap. "Jus' right. When beer comes back I'll give ya a job."

The counterman smiled. "Beer ain't never coming back." They sat down in two chairs. The sidearms had been swollen into miniature tables. "You're the nuts," said Bill; "if you aren't kidding about Madge in cabs, you're pals with that counter guy."

McMann gobbled pie. "Talk friendly to guys and they sorta don' see you. When you're frozen in the puss, every guy's got his peep out for you."

"Why'd you take me tonight? A beginner like me, to take a chance on me. I even forgot to open the door."

"You did all right. That shows I guess right. You got the start of a brain guy, no foolin.'"

"I almost flopped."

"I'd abeen wrong then."

"Don't you brain-guy me."

"When we're boss of Duffy's kids and own our clubhouse, you'll be the brain guy."

"Sounds the nuts, but what of Duffy?"

"Nothin' about him. That cop never even touched our tires'n the pork feller didn't like me at all."

"The dough."

"Safe." He seemed to be looking back as if holding tomorrow's morning paper, reading the paragraph about the holdup…At about ten o'clock last night, two unidentified men held up Soger's Pork Shop. One of them struck Soger with a blackjack, escaping in a stolen car. Pursued by Officer X in a chartered cab, yet the gangsters escaped with their booty. Soger claims he lost ??????…The newspaper boys'd write it up like that, but with more kick. How much?"

"How in hell do I know?"

"Two to share. That part's swell."

"That's talkin'. I'm sayin' it once'n for all, with your dope on these guys, we'll be king o' the hill."

"You bet. I know when they got the paperbacks."

"Don't I know it?" He beamed as if Bill had slaved years for his information, as if it were the result of brilliance and endless patience.

"Any rent-collector'd be as smart."

"What's the diff? You know. The thing is you're wise."

His psychology was certainly a funny one. Bill thought about it, fooling with his cup. All result and end with McMann. The redhead didn't give a damn about the how of things. The idea was to snatch the sugar, to put your mitts on it anyhow. How you did it or whom you gypped didn't matter. His cue was to make Mac feel that he was needed, to build up his own importance, or else some day he'd be bopped on the head for two cents. Mac was a first-class American business man; he had no use for anybody that couldn't be of use. He glanced up, his lips tight against his gums, almost as wolfish as McMann. He understood business, didn't he? "I got a hunch, Mac, we're due to be in the dough. It'll be seven eleven with us. Duffy better watch his step…Hell, Soger wasn't a bad guy."

"One good sock fixes 'em all alike."

He wondered whether Joe was sleeping. Both of them had put in a swell day's work. He ought to see more of Joe, the resolve an atonement, a washing-clean of his betrayal of an old friend. "I've been thinking how lucky we were with that cab just there."

"I told him to wait. We owe him ten smacks. I was nuts enough to stick up the joint myself, but not too nuts."

"You bitch," cried Bill. "Is that why you switched the wheel on me? And chasing up that block?"

"He couldn't be all over the joint."

"Who was it?"

"Schneck."

"Can you beat it?" Sure, he'd fixed things up. Schneck's brother was a hack. The story was that Schneck swiped the cab so in case things got stinky, Schneck's brother'd be clean. Schneck's brother was a respectable guy. Sure, that's how it was.

"I wondered about you talking about Madge and Bobbie when you could've used fake names."

"I was tellin' Schneck what ginks we are." It was in the cards for them to grab Duffy's kids. Wait'll Schneck spreads the news. They had a pocket full of dough and they'd be boss soon.

"And I didn't even recognize that Schneck's mug."

"We're due, kid."

"Maybe."

On Sunday he took Joe out for dinner. It was a punk meal. Joe was griped, insinuating Bill must be in a racket. "Why?" said Bill. "Because," Joe answered. "Why because?" "Because." It was a regular kid argument.

Hell, did Bill think he could pull the wool over his eyes forever? He wasn't that dumb. Bookkeeping. Like hell. He never knew a bookkeeper with Bill's hours or his boozy smelly breath.

"Let's have it," said Bill.

"Sure, why not?" Bill must be a racket.

"Why not? Lots of rackets within the law?"

It wasn't much of a meal and when Bill said he had to beat it uptown, Joe snickered and said for him to go ahead. Bill said he was sorry, but he had to go, it was business. Joe sniffed, sulky, said business was hat. "Here's ten smacks," said Bill.

"Why not?" Joe wanted to know. If Bill gave him two bucks more he'd have a double week's salary. It took him six days, twelve hours a day, to earn twelve bucks. The other salary he made in a minute. Bookkeeping wasn't so bad.

"Don't be so sarcastic."

"It's the truth."

"Go to hell." He ran out of the restaurant. Joe'd have like to rip up the ten-dollar bill. He pocketed it. You don't rip up a salary. And then why shouldn't he get it rather than some crummy whore? He felt like crying. Bill was tickled to be alone. He didn't feel too hot. Sure as fate, he was spoiling Joe. Aw, the hell with him. He was bitter at any hindrance, at any hand grabbing at his coattails. He was on the way up. Joe'd have to lump it. If it was in Joe to be honest, he'd stick honest. He had a square job. If it was in him to be a crook, it wouldn't make any difference. Bill grinned. His reasoning was hypocritical, but what the hell? It looked as if he had a hunk of conscience left. "The hell with everything!" he exclaimed. "I got enough trouble."

CHAPTER ELEVEN

It was the slow hour of afternoon when the cards stick and solitaire doesn't kill time but seems to perpetuate it, spreading it thin and miserable. Paddy continued playing, although he had a visitor.

"We ain't splittin' with nobody. We made up our mind," said McMann. "The pork guy netted us almost a hundred each."

"What beats me is why a guy like you is traveling around with that green bastard?" His flabby jowls were gray-white with powder. His hair was slick. He looked sick.

"Because it's a hundred a man. Then we give Schneck ten smacks—"

"I heard you. Duffy'll be givin' you ten gooses.

"I'll be goosin' him."

"You and the green guy."

"Yeah. He forgot to leave the door open when we took the pork guy, but he was smooth as silk when we took the wop grocer. That wop was spaghetti, that wop was. Bill's oke for the rough work. An' he's a brain guy. He's wise to all them storekeepers."

"A brain guy's hot. He'll be havin' you in oil with Duffy; then this brain guy'll have you easin' into a joint. If you guys live, you'll be big shots. If you croak, what the hell?" He placed a card down.

"We ain't pullin' rough stuff."

"What's Duffy?"

"He's diff'rent. His kids is gonna be mine. They belong to anybody can grab 'em. String along, Paddy. Take a chance. I give you a tenner from the pork guy and ten from the wop, though that wop netted us less'n one-fifty. I'm keepin' in with you. You keep in with me. I ain't gonna be a wild dog, but the breaks-s're comin' my way. I know it. Bill's got ideas'n beginner's luck. An' what's the use phenaglin' in the scum for pennies when the big dough's waitin'."

"What about Duffy?"

"Nothin'. His kids are all for me. A nervy guy can chew off plenty with a coupla breaks." His voice slipped out the hard r-sounding syllables, his yellowish-red eyebrows lifting over his eyes, staring Paddy so strongly in the face that Paddy forgot his solitaire, gripping the card in his hand loosely.

"Who's speaking? You or him?"

"Both of us. He's greener'n hell, but he's got some brains. All I need's a guy like him for the first push. He needs me. What the hell? I been six years scum-min' since I got outa reform. I can puke. I ain't much better off than the kids shootin' pool. Schneck and Ray and them dopes is almos' good as me. They knock off a lil jack, mebbe a kife helps 'em out, they got free tail, and I ain't much better. So I make double what they makes, and riskin' a stretch, with them corner kids riskin' nothin'. A guy like me's dumb not to make a play for the big dough."

"Is it you or him speakin?"

"It's me. That kid Bill's given me opportunity. Can you beat it?"

"Gwan lose your belly. Don't listen to me."

"I'm listenin', but a guy's gotta gamble, Paddy. The west side's nobody's. Three or four big fellers got all the rackets—"

"You'll be the fifth big guy."

"I'm nothin'. I want a break. There's dough in Bill. He ain't smart as he thinks. He thinks I dunno where he lives, but one day I got Ray to foller him home. Lives on Leroy Street. Some joint. He don' fool me, but he's got ideas'n luck."

"Ray belongs to Duffy."

"He'll belong to me."

Paddy shuffled the cards. "I seen wise-guys galore get wiped out."

"Yeah, what about those that don't? A guy gotta gamble."

"That brain guy'll get you killt. You see."

"His idea's me and him don' hafta hold up stores. He says we figure the details, and then the Duffy kids can do the job, me and him takin' the big cut. You never get killt doin' that."

Paddy cursed, chucking down the cards fan-wise. "Don't you see it, you sap? He thinks it a business. Like bonds or real estate or somethin'. Work hard and you're bound to get ahead. Like hell."

"Chiselers get no place."

"Chiselers don't get wiped out." He filled two glasses, tapping the bottle with his ring, smiling. "Believe me. Jeez, he's got nerve. Always had, the sonufabitch, shaking me down."

When Madge came in, McMann, as if he'd been hanging around for her all the time, crossed the room, grabbing her tight about the waist, squeezing her against his body with a persistent power. "Howya, kid? I been workin' that Bill to hand you some dough. A gal gotta live, I says, give her some dough. He says naw, she makes more'n me."

"Push off, willya?" said Madge.

"I'll push on."

"Hey, Paddy, make'm quit."

He pressed her tighter, bending her backwards with a steady mechanical application of pressure. "You don' mean it?"

Paddy's face was sardonic. "You red bastard, that's why you shelled out the wop's dough, so you can get it for nothin'."

Paddy shuffled the cards. Madge kicked at her attacker. He tugged and dragged her to the bedroom. All three felt a grinning admiration for power. In that narrow flat there was an atmosphere of brutality, a sense of muscles and drunken wills. The shades were lowered, the light flowing through with the sad shadowing that seems to emanate only from tenement backyards with their long clothes-poles hung with washlines, their sheds and garbage cans. The dismal rear end of the house apposite stared its windows blankly at Paddy's secrecy.

McMann partially shut the door, flinging her down in her coat, her wild slanting eyes glaring. He took her who was fresh from the street, the wind's red fading from her cheeks. Paddy could've witnessed the taking, but he turned towards the table, starting a new game of solitaire, seeming blind, deaf, and dumb, a eunuch except for the smile on his lips, a smile that was an awareness, an appreciation of power.

When McMann was through with her he said: "Keep your coat on. We're gonna see a coupla friends of mine."

Paddy hollered. "You red skunk. It'll cost you dough."

"Like hell." Madge powdered her face. "I get five or nothin' doin.' What the hell you think?"

"You'll get it."

"Who's the friends?" said Paddy. "Duffy's kids?"

"You're smart. Ray and Schneck."

"Holy Jesus, he means it." Madge and McMann left. Paddy was overwhelmed with admiration. McMann was a peach. If he didn't croak he'd be sitting pretty.

At police headquarters Hanrahan, the plainclothes man assigned to the Ninth Avenue holdups, had the theory that Wiberg and Soger and the wop grocer had all been hit by the same bunch. There was a unity in all three cases. All three had been robbed when they had an unusual amount of money on hand. Hanrahan was thinking some guy—who the hell could it be?—some guy had wind of this fact. Like all logical lazy men he loved unity. One stick-up man was easier to find than three.

CHAPTER TWELVE

Sunday was like an autumn day. The wind blew swift out of an ice-blue sky. It might be home," said Joe, "with the leaves sailing past the lawn." Bill was tying the laces of his shoes.

"We got river air down here," he said, tense.

The puppy had grown a great deal, running up and down the flat, barking at the brothers as if they were both at fault.

The great iron gate was shut down like stubborn lip.

Joe went to the gas range, flipping in the slices of bacon. "Three enough, Bill?"

"Plenty. How's the grind?"

"It's no grind."

"Why didn't you eat breakfast instead of waiting for me?" He yawned. Despite the shower, fatigue dominated his face, his eyes blurry, his features gross, his lips dry. "How after the grind — Hell, I'm groggy — And you don't even sleep late on Sundays. What time's it?"

"Past noon."

"How do you get up?"

"I was up at eleven."

"He calls that late. You're an iron man."

Joe cracked open the eggs. The coffee smelled black and strong. The dog sat down on his haunches, gazing up at the smell of food, mixing food up with Joe, food was Joe, Joe was food, his sad hound eyes learned and patient, his long white tail dragging. Joe looked fine. Hard work wasn't harming him any, his cheeks red, strong as a horse, thought Bill. "I used to lick you," he said regretfully, "when we were kids, but I bet you could lump me with one fist." Joe sliced the oranges, peering at the halves with their firm glinting orange color. He felt strong as iron, but his loneliness crippled him. He seemed to be leaning on a crutch, he was that lonely, anticipating the moment when Bill'd heel out.

Bill snapped on his felt, wondering what Joe'd say this time. "Sorry." Damn kid brothers. They acted like girls, like sweethearts. Let 'em stand on their own feet like men.

"Weren't we going to a show?"

"I thought we were, but it's off. I'm sorry."

"You're always sorry."

"I can't help it. I've got to tend to something important. Take Cathy out. She's a nice kid. You'll have a better time. Because I'm busy, don't you think I don't notice things."

"You're damn smart."

"Christ's sake, let's not fight again."

"Cathy's a good kid."

"Who's saying she ain't?"

"I didn't like the way you spoke of her."

"I didn't mean a thing." Already in thought he was hurrying down Greenwich to Christopher. The busy life. The paint shop on Ninth was due. The gink had dough. Would Duffy loan his kids for the job? Showdown soon. Soon the showdown.

He took out a ten-spot. "Have a good time." Joe wouldn't take the money. He put the two fives on the table.

"You make money pretty easy," said Joe.

"Let's not go into it again."

"Sunday's the only chance. If I ever saw you awake any other day I'd die."

"Didn't we cover it all last Sunday? Cut out the whining. I've got enough in my mind without you nagging."

"Enough that shouldn't be there."

"You're pretty clever."

"We're brothers." They stared at each other, forgetting they were brothers, like two men meeting the first time. Bill put on his camel-hair coat. From under his felt his lean handsome face, thinner now, with the nose and chin jutting out more strongly, confronted the rounder fairer face of his brother. Their eyes were the same blue. This was the one resemblance, the only thing that made them brothers.

"I advise you to mind your business."

"Don't make me laugh. You're in something fishy and I'll say it all I want." He grinned at the barking dog, running up and down with the optimism of animals that nothing can be wrong.

"So long, have a good time."

"See you next Sunday." He was alone in the flat, prisoned by the slamming door. He patted the dog's head with an uncertain hand. He looked like a kid brother now. He hadn't told Bill what was really important. Ninth Avenue was gossiping about the robberies, admiring the guys who pulled off jobs just when there was the most in it. Wiberg. Soger. Petrucci. Who was next? Those guys were the nuts, just happening along when the storekeepers were flush. But Bill would have said: What's that got to do with me?...It had lots to do with him when you were a brother and knew he'd collected rents all over Ninth, when you knew he wasn't working, what with his funny hours, when you knew he had lots of jack. The other day Metz had told him: "See, no robberies when your brother collects them fellers, and now when he's gone, one hard luck after another." Wiberg. Soger. Petrucci. All three had been collected by Bill. That was a coincidence. He'd thought he'd die, but Metz hadn't meant anything. He took the fives on the table. Bill set a swell example. Maybe he ought to set Bill an example? And return his dough? Maybe not. Money was money.

He sweated a week to find that out. He'd show Cathy a good time. He hollered at the pup to shut his damn face. Money was a funny thing. Even dirty money could do good. A good time with Cathy was something.

He made up the room, glancing around with a Sunday hostility in his eyes. His city home. It stunk. He punched the pillows, reversing Bill's. Bill was using olive oil to stop his falling hair. His pillow was dark and greasy. Staring at the stain. Bill seemed to be lying there in bed, his face haggard. He socked that pillow. Christ all hell, what sort of life was Bill leading? The stain was a reminder. He washed the dishes and went downstairs.

The Gebhardts had returned from St. Veronica's on Christopher. Every day when he walked to the El, the church's doorway was a hush of peace. Behind the El structure the doorway was all peace, all green things, all the Gebhardts…

Mr. Gebhardt was rocking himself, stiffish in his Sunday suit, the pants so sternly creased that the peace of the Lord was suddenly comical, a fashion show. Mrs. Gebhardt sailed the white cloth over the table. "Good Sunday, Joe," they said. The preparations for dinner continued, sanctified in that shadowed room with the shaftway light subdued, filtered quiet from the yellow sun. They all seemed participants in a merrier, more domestic mass. The light was meek as prayer, the adults prim and happy, the kids reading the jokes, their soft blond faces gleaming like choir boys', in the flat become a cathedral, Gertrude, baby Carl, Fred, all alike somehow, sexless, pure, churchly.

Cathy was in the kitchen part of the dining room, bending down, the gas-range door open, her manner observant and wifely, her nostrils indrawn from sniffing at the roasting chicken.

"Dinner soon," said Mrs. Gebhardt, patting down the cloth. "You eat with us. Sauerkraut. Chicken. Noodle soup. Kartofflen. Apple Kuchen."

"Nein," said Gebhardt, "him and his brother better eat spaghetti, that ginny food." The kids laughed.

"I'm meeting Bill for dinner," Joe said. "Thanks just the same, Mrs. Gebhardt." He felt lonely without a home, without Bill, without the Gebhardts. He'd beat it now, mope around, and come back later when they'd be through eating. "Say, Cathy, Bill isn't going to a show with me as we were supposed to like I told you. Want to go?"

Cathy wiped her hands on her apron, glancing at her parents. "Sure, if Pop and Mom say I can."

"Go right ahead," commanded Gebhardt, autocratic as the Kaiser. The kids laughed. His wife smiled at Joe, her placid head with the high cheekbones, the dry yellow hair parted in the center, making her seem more than ever like a farm woman instead of the janitor. The bedroom window, looking out on the backyard, was bright, jeweled, stained with sun streaming in upon all of them, the strong man, the woman near her white cloth, the three kids turning the papers, Cathy floating in the space between the range and the table, her hair glinting. He felt the strong Sunday peace enfold him, this sanctity of their lives relaxing on the Lord's Day so that it was easy to imagine a ghostly presence in their home, the merry presence of Jesus blessing them all in the flat smelling of soap, chicken, sauerkraut. "I'll be back around two, Cathy. So long."

The sun advanced upon him like a glaring face when he opened the street door. He blinked on Leroy Street isolated in the Sunday vacuum, detached from purpose and work. The warehouse and printery were deserted by men. No raw truckers shouted. No vans trundled up on the sidewalk. An El was speeding north on Greenwich, the windows rattling, the fleeing roofs of the cars traveling, under a huge and measured blue vault. The faces peered down at him, the eyes of strangers uninterested in the train's destination, Burnside Avenue. That was in the Bronx. With Bill's money he was going to have a good time. The best time would be traveling to the Bronx. He laughed at ten bucks being made so unnecessary for a good time. He crossed under the El, the light zigzagging through the ties, walking through a constant eternal series of light-shafts, all slanting and full of sun motes. His life was a deep and foul rooting in narrow places. He hurried past the trucking offices ready to resume their traffic with a hundred cities, come Monday. He was wasting his life. What could he do? Maybe Bill'd get him another job. Or a job like Bill's. To drink, live danger, to know lots of hot tough women; hell, that was life anyway. The grind at Metz's was an insult to any guy with spunk. He pushed his legs out vigorously, leaving Greenwich, striding into the sun again, westward to Washington Street and the smell of the harbor.

Many buildings had been razed here by the landlords and mortgage companies. Washington Street was an area devastated by war; a battlefield, the few remaining buildings presenting cracked windows, disused. Business had collapsed, lost foothold and position. Eastward the massed city behind Hudson Street spread to the East River, South to the Battery, north to Times Square. He was happier near the river. The wind unconfined, lurching into the lots, picking up the tag ends of paper. Families were strolling. The street had the aspect of a park lane. The city had retreated. And he wished Cathy were with him.

He had intended going down to the river, beyond West Street, the railroad terminals and steamer berths, until coming to the last land he might sit on the dock, staring at the greasy heavy water, foul and green. Here a man could look the river in its face, the red tugs, the anchored leviathans, at New Jersey's opposite shore, the roadway out of New York, the start into the plains and mountains of America. Not today, he thought, recalling lonely Sundays when he had sat with the waters. He'd go to Burnside Avenue. Uptown with Cathy. He was cheered at his own daring like one embarking on journeys. Devil take Bill and blue Monday. He liked Cathy. She liked him. What more could a fellow want? He day-dreamed, his eyes slitted against the sun like half-closed shutters, thinking rosily of uptown and gleaming cities. Hell, he'd forgotten to take the poor mutt out for an airing.

CHAPTER THIRTEEN

He left the dog with the Gebhardts, the kids mobbing it enthusiastically, baby Carl murmuring bawa bawa, holding out his hand as if towards a jewel of price. "Have a good time," cried Pop and Mom.

The two of them hurried down the corridor. She was ahead of him, the nape of her neck fluffy with tiny blond hairs. The flight of stairs, each step edged with a shining strip of metal, seemed to push him at her. In this gloomy transit between home and street he grabbed her from the rear, kissing her protesting face. She blushed down to her throat, ashamed and surprised. He thought of all her pale body, crimsoning, her breasts and thighs and toes, until she was rose-beautiful all over. He let loose and they were walking to the door as if nothing much had happened.

"You shouldn't," she said.

"I like you. You didn't say anything when I kissed you in the movies."

"This is too near." Her eyes were so miserable he imagined the ghostly fathers of St. Veronica, the Gebhardt home, the doctrine of sin and a thousand other religious inhibitions.

He flung the door open on sunlight and fresh air and had his answer, breathing deeply. "You're bugs. Don't you like me?"

"I like you."

"What you mean then? Shouldn't I kiss you if I like you? Your family kisses you."

She giggled. "You're a faker."

"Liking's liking. If I like somebody, I kiss them. You ought to be glad I like you." She blushed as they went down the stoop. She didn't know what to say, feeling his lips on her cheeks, thinking of her parents. She'd never been kissed before, even if he wouldn't believe it. She liked kissing, flushing redder. She was in the second year at high school. When she was a kid she'd cried and prayed many nasty things away. At public school she had heard all the bad words many times, seen them scrawled in chalk on the yard walls or whispered in the classrooms by young sports. You couldn't shut your ears, although she brought her legs together, shuddering. Then, walking home from school at three o'clock, the boys used to rush past her and the other girls, whipping out Tartar hands against their black-stockinged legs, sometimes jumping full of them like men leaping from horseback, pressing their hard nasty bodies against the girls. Then, lots of her friends petted. She'd even seen a boy lying on a girl behind the stairs, both of them sort of undressed and naked somehow. There were many nasty things. Going to high school, men'd wink and young fellows'd make cracks. High was wonderful. There were no boys, only girls, no one to get fresh except strangers on the street, and the loafers on the corner.

But all she said from this lifetime's experience with males was that he shouldn't do it, he should behave.

What dumb ideas she had! Back home, he told her, all the girls knew what kissing's for. But then, she was a Catholic. His eyes were wicked, as if he had hit the reason. "But lots of girls I used to know were Catholic and they knew their onions." His voice was the metallic worldly one of nineteen, wise about women because he's had a maid on her back on a summer night. Hell, what didn't he know about women? Cathy walked dumbly by his side, her head lowered as if he were one of those almost forgotten public-school kids whispering in her ear when teacher wasn't looking, whispering a brutal ravishment. She'd been raped that way so many times she was wiser than he. She knew more about men than he, the taker of a few cheap bats, knew of women.

"Plenty girls'd like to know me, smiling at me in the El, and in the store, too." It was a pain for him, a man, to be treated in that kiddish way. But her downcast head with the calm curve of forehead balancing against the straight fine nose and rougeless lips, the line of neck swelling out into her budding breasts, her virginal beauty, created the first agony in his heart. He was nineteen. His heart pounded, his eyes were almost veiled with tears of joy, tears for his own youth and her youth, and the wonder of their springtime on this blowing cold day. He forgot the wisecracks, jerking the words out. "I love you, Cathy. Honest I do. When I said I like you, gee, I meant I love you." Hell, he wasn't a man any more, the tough wisecracking fellow the clerks down at Metz's called Der Starker, who could lift tubs of butter like nothing. He was just a kid speaking for the blood humming in him, speaking for the life, the youth, the male fertility in him.

They walked silently up to Hudson Street, the poor-folk shops were closed, the delicatessens, the butchers', the corner chain stores with their gilt signs. In front of a coffee-pot four or five boys were stamping their feet, smoking. They spotted the dame and the boy-friend. The dame was oke, not classy dressed, but oke, a good build, none of your chickenbones. The boy-friend was a hefty kid, nice-looking. "I knew that dame in school," one of them said. "Boy, was she the iceberg! N'now she's flopped. They all flop." He laughed like a philosophic rake.

"Where we going?" said Cathy. "To the fish teayter or the Museum?"

"No fish teayter for us. We're stepping up to the Bronx. You on?"

"Sure I am."

"Thatta girl."

"The Bronx's all Jewish and Irish," she said. "It's Abie's Irish Rose." They laughed.

"I've never been there." He grinned at Cathy glancing at herself in the mirror of a chewing-gum machine on the El platform. "Jesus, you can beat any ten girls blushing. You want to grow up." But he felt swell for him to be the reason.

"Don't kid me. You like me the way I am."

Hell, you couldn't guess what a woman'd say next. The train crashed in. The steel wheels stopped rolling. They sat down in one of the double side-seats, putting their feet on the seat in front. It was riding in a private compartment. The conductor made a face. "He's a donkey. Cmon, lemme hold your hand. Carl holds your hand and you say nothing."

She laughed. "That donkey's watching us."

"I can lick any mick alive."

They sat close together, Cathy next the window. The El started up the tracks, slicing the district like a knife through butter. On either side, tenements lined the tracks. They went calling on many homes. A longshoreman was smoking a corncob in one window. A gray fat woman was leaning out of a top story, watching the train with the implacable curiosity of a small-towner. A kid gripped her doll as if the El were the bogy man. They stared into the privacy of lives, seen and forgotten. A young woman arguing with an unknown. People eating. But mostly the windows were curtained, and they seemed to be sneaking by at night.

Joe squeezed her palm. Holding hands was nothing. Not after you kissed a girl. Holding hands had been some stuff walking down the Museum aisles. Now it was nothing. He'd kissed her. His breath came hard, thinking about it. He wanted to take her in his arms and hug her to death, kissing her pale face all over. His eyes were far away on the sun-gilded tracks flashing by. Tall semaphores with red and green flags rocked by them. The El stopped; the conductor bawled: "Fiftieth Street. Nex' storp, Fifty-ninth…" People slid in and out. A young man took the double seat across the aisle, riding backward so he could sneak a look at Cathy. He was a sensitive fellow who always picked his seat within sight of a pretty woman so he could while away the gripe of the long ride. He lived in the Bronx and wondered whether Joe and Cathy would get off in the Eighties. They looked like Irish-German-American somebodies living on Amsterdam Avenue. He glared sadly but with resolution at Cathy's slim legs and flushed bright face. She liked her fellow. Hell, he thought.

Joe sobered up with the audience. His heart pumped like a son-of-a-gun but he was getting used to his excitement. His shoulder touched Cathy's. She was leaning her elbow on the sill. His shoulder was so wide his body didn't touch her anywhere else. He put his arm about her, yanking her towards him, his teeth wanting to rattle when he felt her hip and side press into his own. That'd give the nosey guy something to think about. Did he like Cathy, not even knowing it until today? "I love you."

"You're kidding," she said.

"I'm not."

"You are." Her yellow fringe of hair was smooth beneath her blue hat. He hadn't known he loved her until he kissed her in the hallway. What a sap he was! He'd been making blunder after blunder about love for weeks. What a sap! Every time the El ground steel against steel, or jerked ahead after stopping, she let her body's soft natural impact caress his own. It was the first time she let her body do what it wanted. Up to this Sunday she'd flexed herself so that she wouldn't bump him when the train started. They sat close, happy, united, gazing foggily out of the window at the press of grim hard poor lives through which the El was roaring like an artery. Now they were climbing higher above the street, peering into the fifth-floor windows, reading the stone lettered inscriptions carved near the roofs. The Shenandoah. The Glenby. 1985. 1904. They were riding through the long-ago when these houses had been stylish. On the right the roofs flashed their tar coverings. Beyond the chimneys were the trees of Central Park. Eastwards the tenements and boardinghouses were gradually giving way to the canopies on Central Park West. Much to the young man's surprise they didn't get off. At 110th Street, the tracks shot round in grand curves, the El ready to fly off in space. Walled behind the heights of 110th Street, the Park was left behind.

"Morningside Park," said Cathy. "We had picnic there once."

St. John the Divine. Tall arches, brave spires, and steel scaffolding. The central green coppery dome was a beauty.

"Down there," said Cathy, "are the Negroes."

The conductor growled: "Hunerd'n Sixteenth." New York shoved its black faces against the windows. It was as if he were on a river liner penetrating a jungle full of savages. Big blacks. Coffee arms like hams. Rows of kid heads. Browns and yellow-browns. With here and there an Irishwoman's head where the white race was continuing triumphant. Joe wanted to know why the whites didn't move out. Cathy said the rents were cheap. Now and then, in a Congo tenement, a mulatto with a thin white-featured face hurt him somehow. So white and yet a Negro.

The young man concentrated on Cathy. He made the trip every day. Negroes were nothing new. A pretty dame was something else. Joe gripped her hand; greater than all the novelties of the far-away, he sat holding love in his hand, the five fingers of Cathy, a Woolworth ring on the finger next to the pinky. She said she was glad he and Bill hadn't gone out today. She was glad to be with him. Bill was always busy, wasn't he? Sure he was. Bill was a high-power business man with cockeyed hours. Bill was smart. She glanced at him, baffled by his tone.

"Have your parents ever discussed Bill?" He smiled. "Not that I'd blame them. He's skating on thin ice. When we were kids Bill could do anything on ice." Ten bucks of Bill's smart money was in his pocket. He was sore. "We're taking a taxi back."

She was stupefied at his princeliness. He mustn't. A cab from the Bronx'd cost three dollars almost.

He told her to mind her own business. He had plenty of money. Bill made a lot as a bookkeeper. He wouldn't waste his dough but Bill's dough was different. Anyway, he was the boss. He looked like Bill with his eyes sharp and commanding, his chin thrust out. A slow creeping languor weakened her bones. She was soft as jelly. Three dollars, my! The young man was disgusted. That couple, hell. They looked engaged, having fun together. Damn. These poor Irish-German-Americans had fun when they were young. No waiting for them. They lived. The young man was a German. He attended New York University Heights Branch. The girls he knew couldn't be got, coached by their old ladies to lie low until they got a wedding ring. The young man hated to fork over two bucks when he got hot. It wasn't decent, romantic, or profitable. It made him taste rubber. He didn't like it. Damn those poor people who were regular pagans. He had eighty-two cents in his pocket. Damn the poor. A cab wouldn't be bad. In a cab he could make love. It'd be worth Bill's dough. He worked ten to twelve hours for two bucks. Bill's dough was easy, a different kind of dough. He'd like to make it himself. Gee, what a city New York was! You needed dough in a city like New York.

Cathy thought he looked a lot like Bill.

CHAPTER FOURTEEN

Pushing open the door of the pool parlor, Bill forgot about Joe, the poor kid. All the way uptown he had confused Joe with the dog, sorry for both with the luxurious regret of one intending to do nothing about matters. What could he do? The big yellow lights flared down on the tables, picking out highlights on the ivory balls. The proprietor, a lanky man wearing a striped shirt with plain white attached collar, yanked up his lowered eyes from the Sunday sports section. "Howza boy?" he said.

"McMann here?"

"In there." He jerked his thumb to a door in the rear. He put the wrestling dope aside, staring at Bill as if to get his mug down once and for all. A couple of lazy pool-room boys, hanging around for a sucker, drinking pop with the phlegmatic calm of petty gamblers, gave him the once-over as well. He felt photographed, important, uneasy, thinking for the last time of poor Joe. McMann had been arguing with Duffy and Spat, sitting in a chair tilted against the wall, smoking a cigar as smoothly as a junior executive. Bill was embarrassed by the convergence of cool measuring eyes, almost as impersonal as the eyes of cameras. He pulled his lips taut on his clenched teeth, grinning, seeing Duffy and Spat the first time, silently figuring what there was to him. McMann was as stony as the others, as if he were taking judgment too. Duffy was a skinny man with a dead white face, his hands long-fingered and corpse-like, his brown eyes flecked with fire, the only things alive in his burnt-out energy. Spat's mouth was crooked; shouldered like a wop laborer. They were each about twenty-five.

"No use stalling," said Duffy. "Schneck rode that cab for you. He shot off his mouth about it."

"And said what swell workers you guys are," said Spat.

"What about it?" asked McMann.

"You're using our kids," said Duffy.

McMann smiled like a conscious good fellow. "Let's get together. No stinkin' aroun', Duffy. We get the dope and the kids pull the job off. That's on the square."

"You're trying to start a mob by using ourn. Hell with that." His eyes blazed at both of them, the freckles on his nose standing out dark. He pulled up his trousers, showing ankles small as a girl's.

"We're not trying anything of that sort," said Bill.

"That's what you say."

"Let me speak. We're on the square. It happens I'm wise to plenty jack. I know when, the hour when the storekeepers got it."

"Yeh," bawled Spat, his big chest wanting to burst from his tight vest. "It's no secret who's workin' the avenoo."

"Schneck musta told you lots," said McMann.

Spat glared like a wild stupid animal. "Huh? Don't have ta tell us. It's you'n him."

"So what?" said Duffy. "What you driving at?"

Spat smacked his fist on his knee. "It can be done."

"You're thick," said Duffy.

Spat was dumb as whale crap, thought Bill. Duffy was the guy to win over, Duffy the corpse, with his small brown eyes darting swift as if trying to escape his inert body. It boiled down to this, Duffy declared. He didn't doubt their dope was O.K. As Spat had said, the town was wise to their raids. He didn't begrudge them a cent but when it came to horning in on his kids. And he didn't want to split with anybody. The hell with it. Suppose they took the dope and the kids pulled off the jobs, the risk'd be his, Duffy's. He didn't want none of it.

"What you crabbin'?" said McMann. "You know damn well you'n Spat play safe."

"So what?"

"You got a mobba hustlers."

"They're mine."

"Who says they ain't?"

"What of Schneck driving that cab for you?"

That was an accident. Nothing else. Sure it was, said Duffy, hitching up his trousers. Say the kids don't get nabbed, they break clear. They got to be paid. Spat and him had to be paid. Then McMann and Bill had to be paid. Christ, they weren't holding up any banks to get enough dough for such a mob. And with the depression, those storekeepers didn't have so much. Bill felt better. Duffy might be convinced or he might pretend he was convinced. He'd never forget about Schneck, but the easy money might win him over.

"Yeah," said Spat. "That's the point. Too many guys to share." He didn't foot anybody into thinking he was smart. He nodded his thick head with the small ears pinned tight into the hard bone.

"Suppose I find a ten-spot in the gutter," said McMann, "and split it four ways. That ain't much, but why turn it down?"

"What's that gotta do with it?"

"Spat, you're a lunk. Ain't it pickin' up dough?"

"Don't you call me lunk."

"I was kiddin'."

"Cut it."

"Aw right," said Duffy. "For the sake of the hell of it, a coupla kids stick up a store. They net some dough. How much? O.K. Let's say two hundred. Them kids are worth fifteen each."

"Ten," said McMann.

Spat sneered. "You wouldn' work for no lousy ten."

"I ain't no lousy green kid."

"Aw right. Fifteen each. Thirty for two kids. One-seventy left. Spat'n me keep a hundred. You guys get the rest."

McMann poured drinks, the bottle staunch on the round table, surrounded by their glasses and Spat's fists. "You're beginnin' to talk. Them kids are mopin'. You gotta slip 'em a fiver once awhile to keep 'em goin'."

"Gotta keep 'em satisfied," said Spat like a father. "Gin we give 'em. If they don't fix themselves up, we gotta get 'em a dame to line up. Those kids are good." Duffy puffed at a butt, the tiny coal brighter than his eyes.

"Necessities of life," Bill said.

"Sure," said Duffy.

"What's wrong, then, with them earnin' their keep?" McMann had him there.

"Well," said Duffy, "it don't pay for a coupla smart kids to get nabbed for ten cents."

The kids were plantation Negroes, thought Bill, the plantation the town of the Big Stink. The kids were worth so much a head. They were worth dough. He and Mac'd never get anywhere without help. Mac was right. No use puking around. The big gamble. Duffy's kids were the stake. With them he might make a few grand. "What's keeping you back, Duffy? Is it you think we're trying to start a mob by stealing yours?"

"We think what we want," said Spat.

Duffy, languid, hardly moved. What a pair they were, thought Bill, a corpse and a wild man! "I said it. Ain't it so?"

"No," hollered McMann. "Who wants your kids? We'll give ya the dope in advance."

"Go on."

"You pull it off as if it's your job. We'll take a chance you don't pull no doublecross. What more you want? Ain't that square?"

Bill thought it wasn't so hot. They wouldn't get more'n some change out of an arrangement like that. Was Mac nuts?

"Why you so square?" said Duffy.

"'Cause I'm a square shooter. Ask Paddy, anybody."

"I'll ask Bill. Hey, Bill, your pal square?"

"I don't know." He laughed.

"It sounds good," said Duffy. Spat's fist reached for the bottle. Bill, catching McMann's eye, wanted to speak with his eyes. Oh, if he only could! His stare said: They'll doublecross us. But McMann was pinkfaced, cold, unreachable. Duffy said the proposition suited him. It looked on the level. It proved they weren't trying to hook his kids. And the times were bad. Spat heeled his boss, insisting the times were lousy. Why, they had eight kids and a bunch of others and there wasn't work for most of them. When a kid had the chance for something better, he lamed out. Last week a kid got a respectable job running errands for a whorehouse at fifteen a week. Showed what things are. Two years ago that same kid was knocking out forty slugs working twice a week, rest of the time free for whoring.

They grinned at Spat, even Duffy's lips snarling upwards, incredulously amused at the harangue.

"Why don't you quit?" said McMann.

"Me?" He waved his hand in a grandly stupid gesture of pride. "I count. I'm a book. I got sidelines. I'm in numbers. I make eighty a week average." Duffy was smiling like a dead man. He wanted to know what the dope was on the first job. Bill didn't like his lazy voice with the vicious devil hiding behind his restless eyes. What the hell was wrong with McMann? McMann stared at Bill. "Give'm the dope. We'll see how he makes out. Bill's the brain guy, Duff. He figures the dope." Duffy was interested. "Yeh?"

I'll give him a joint in the neck, thought Bill. No gold mine for that bastard. And Mac calling him brain guy to boost his reputation. What for? "This store's on Ninth near Thirty-sixth. A paint supply. He's got two men working for him, but don't pay them on Saturday. Thursday morning he pays all his bills. At ten o'clock in the morning. The money's in a little bank in the rear. He's usually got a couple hundred for bills and salaries. When he draws the dough from the bank he takes some for his wife. A week from this Thursday he pays his rent."

"I don't like that business about the bank. That why you give us the job?"

"You want it on the counter?" said McMann.

"This job's lousy. If he don't open up at a gat, what then? New. It's n.g."

"Why'nt you let me finsh? I've real dope. The kids'll be outside. The first collector drops in to get paid. The boss opens the bank. That's the time to knock him off. You get what he has in the bank, plus what the collector has."

"You're a brain guy," said Duffy.

"It gives me a headache."

"That job would need three kids," Spat declared. "Two to cover the paint guy and the collector. One outside to lay puts." "Four kids," corrected Duffy. "One at the car, one outside the window, two inside." It was a good layout, but risky. He wanted twenty bucks for each kid, everything over to be split fifty-fifty. Duffy walked out, followed by Spat, led like a bull.

"How's Madge?" said McMann. It was a Duffy joint and they were going to pull an act for anybody snooping.

"I haven't seen her in weeks. You ask me about her too often. You making a play for her?"

"That skinny piece?" He winked, the outer surfaces of his red eyes glinting jovially while the body of each, set hard in his laughless skull, shone angrily. When they were hurrying east to Broadway, McMann cursed his heart out. That bastard Duffy. The world's crookedest skunk. He wouldn't trust him for a jit. They'd get rooked sure as hell. But they'd get some dough out of it. Could they pick up dough for nothing? You didn't see dough lying on the streets. That's why he went partners with that louse.

"Anyway, I gave him a real hard joint to crack."

"You're a brain guy."

"When you say that, I feel dumb as Spat."

"Maybe you are." The El cut from Ninth to Sixth Avenue. Behind its ugliness lay the bawdy beauty of Tin Pan Alley, Broadway, the Paramount Building. The streets were clean. A few actors from the sidestreet boardinghouse were hoofing it, panning the new models in the auto windows. But most of the Broadway crowd didn't get this far north, the grifters, chiselers, fakers, fags, business men on the tear.

"Maybe you're dumb, too." They smiled, hostile. The white wings hadn't neglected this grand street of America. If any dough'd been lying around, it'd been picked up.

"We're all dumb."

"You're dumber than dumb." He smiled. "What's to stop pal Duffy from freezing us out?"

"Naw. He wants other stores. Question is how much. The big boys let Duff coast. The west side's nobody's and he ain't big. His mob's all kids, hustling at the gin mills and gambling joints, doin' odd jobs, the lousy small-time business the big boys don' want."

Duffy didn't make booze and didn't sell it. Maybe he sold a tin of dope once in awhile. He was strictly a small stinker.

"What the hell are we?"

"The smallest stinkers in the world. I get griped. Christ, maybe we oughta raid a coupla big joints. Maybe we oughta cut Duffy out."

"He's wise."

"Sure. He knows we're afta his kids."

"Why does he go in with us?"

"The dough. N'a strong guy thinks he gotta be strong all the time." Bill nodded gloomily. "He isn't so wrong."

"We'll fix the rat." It'd be pie. He wouldn't monkey around with a tough mob. Duffy only had a bunch of wild kids, younger'n hell, no brains, ready for anything. Did he get it? They'd work in close to Duffy. Let the rat rook them. The idea was to get in; then they'd kick him out and have a bunch ready for anything. The kids were wild. Pep 'em up with talk of real dough and real dames and they'd make a grab for the King of England.

They strode below the El into the smug moneyed heart of Broadway, where schemes about making money sprouted as one walked into dream fulfillments. They'd get hold of Duffy's kids. If things broke they'd be set. McMann suggested they get some grub and take out a pair of dames, not Madge and Bobbie; he was sick of their stuff. He turned his brutal-chinned face. "Nex' week you'n me'll make a call. I gotta friend with a shootin' gallery. We'll fool around for the hell of it. You know nothin' about a gat? Well, you will."

Twice that week he stood in the long cellar of McMann's friend, out in

Brooklyn, pointing the pistol at the target. It was fun, like when he'd owned an air rifle. All you needed to know about a gat, said McMann, was to get the feel of it. Most shooting was at close range. He came in Saturday on the B.M.T. and went home. It was after seven. Cathy was cleaning up. He hadn't seen her for a long time. He laughed. "How do you like Joe?"

She said she liked him all right. He laughed louder. She was a good clean little piece. If Joe had any sense he could have a good time. She said she'd be back later. There was no need to leave on his account. But she seemed scared, going towards the door as he hurried forward. He smacked her soft buttock. She ran downstairs. He'd given her a send-off. Taking off his pants, he thought of the pistol practice and the holdup due Thursday. That'd mean dough. Things were moving. Duffy better watch out. He'd finished shaving when Joe came in. "Holy Christ, what you doing here Saturday, Bill?"

"You're early yourself."

"Metz let me off. I got a date with Cathy. It's almost eight. I got to wash and dress."

"I wonder if you know she's pretty."

"I know it."

"If you feel that way—How's Metz?"

"In the dough as ever. I saw him put a load of dough in his tin bank today back in the storeroom—" He stopped short. "He felt good. That's why he let me off." He regretted the crack about money. "Don't you be taking up anything I said."

"What you mean?"

"I've meant to tell you a long time. The Avenue's talking about those robberies. Wiberg, and Petrucci and Soger."

"You poor damn fool, do you think I'd do anything that dumb? Think I'd risk a stretch for a few lousy bucks? Get it out of your head once and for all. I'm in a racket. Sure, I'm keeping books for a bootlegging outfit, a regular job, and I'm safe as hell. I'm beating it now, but remember what I said. And give Cathy a good time." He sounds sincere, thought Joe, but just the same I oughtn't've spoken of Metz. Hell, he couldn't phone Metz and tell him to take his dough out of his bank.

CHAPTER FIFTEEN

"Leroy and Greenwich," said Joe stiffly, not used to cabs. He admired the twinkling of Cathy's foot, piling in. The cab started down Fifth. Behind the low park wall the woods, paths, fields, lay chilled and hard bitten. Apartment houses blinked in endless rows, complacent as dowagers at a dance. She said he shouldn't take cabs. "Don't you be crazy. We don't spend anything all week except a thirty-cent movie. And what we do Sundays? Nothing. Poking about and spending nothing." He grinned, always getting even with Bill when he rode in cabs. Cathy alone in a cab was worth something and he had Bill to thank. The twilight seeped into the streets, violet and hushed. Riding in cabs was rubbing elbows with the rich. Swell to be rich. He was getting used to cabs, this was his fourth, the heads of the drivers jutting big ears. He pulled her closer, her lips protesting, kissing her until she was limp. They sat up away from each other, breathing hard like fighters separated at the referee's bell. She said he was too rough. He said love was rough, grabbing her again. Ten more blocks clicked off. The taximeter indicated to the nickel how much this love scene had cost Bill.

The cab-driver thought they were just a pair of kids. Nuthin' else. Chris' sake. Only kissed her. He knew what he'd adone if he was back there. He'd agot his money's worth. Any slob could kiss a girl. Hell, but them Greenwich Villagers were goofy.

Again the boy and girl hugged with the desperation of their youth and virginity. Behind them rolled many cars. Traffic was scooting along the Drive and curving through the Park. On Madison and Lexington and Third Avenues, on all the twilight avenues of the town, in this interval before parties, before movies, the cars were traveling and the city's thousands were hugging, kissing, making love as the motors carried them to a thousand destinations. Joe and Cathy were part of the city design, natural to the city in that twilight…At this moment Mr. and Mrs. Gebhardt were talking of their daughter and Joe and how the two seemed to be in love; what was to be done?…Paddy was kidding a crowd of fellows waiting their next. In small rooms Madge and Bobbie were making one buck their share…McMann and Bill were drinking beer. They had schemes. There was the paint store, there was Duffy, there were other things…In a neat apartment Mr. Stanger was neatly informing a circle of friends of what he'd done for the sons of his best friend, how he'd given them a free flat on Leroy. "Where is that, Mr. Stanger?" asked a lady who donated to the Salvation Army. "Over in Greenwich Village," said Stanger; "not the neighborhood for us, but for young men, hahaha…"

"Where the hell are we?" said Joe. They were below Fifty-ninth, speeding between jewels, furs, antiques. The green traffic lights gleamed luxuriously. A few bargain shops had sneaked on Fifth, but wealth glared from most of the shop windows. Joe was so influenced he contemplated the meter with indifference. They held hands, bunching together like puppies for warmth. The cab shot below Forty-second, the Library lions dim dusky stone. Below Thirty-fourth, Fifth Avenue had many empty stores and lofts. The Flatiron Building on Twenty-third stood up like an immense distorted cut of pie, triangular, with narrow base, as if the builder had cut too stingily. The sachems and millionaires lied in the apartments below Fourteenth. Washington Square was a lonely winter waste variously surrounded by Knickerbocker stoops, garages, hotels. They hugged in the dark. The hack piloted them westward to Greenwich. Fifth Avenue, ducal, romantic, persisted like a dream street in their thoughts, where they had walked in sun and entered sunny mansions. He had bent her far over his clasped arms, distraught by the lovely half body of her, the tight belly, the young panting breasts. This half body, as if an entity in itself or attached to darkness or to a lower fish shape like a mermaid's, was magical to him. His lips groped sad and tender. He loved her, desire flaming up in him not from a young man's fancy, but from a man's maturity. For the first time his hand squeezed down on her breasts like a kiss.

More like it, thought the hack, seeing them almost prone on the rear seat. If he wants to kiss her the subway's plenty good. "O.K., mister, here you are." They got out. The street was tunneled through loneliness. He paid and the cab swerved up Leroy to Hudson, passing their house. Maybe their ghosts were still inside the cab, waiving to the house where the Gebhardts were waiting. He was tired of being poor, tired of his job, irritated that after the millionaire day he must return to a hole. Cathy said she'd have to tell the priest. "Tell him what?"

"That you, that you held my hand…"

He didn't give a damn if she blushed ten years. "You tell him I kiss you and all?"

"Yes."

"You cut it out. You tell him and we're through. Love the way I feel is our business, don't you see? I like you so much I don't want anyone to know. You haven't told your mother? Christ."

"No." He patted her hand. That was fine. And it wasn't the damn business of any priest. She said he mustn't speak like that. They argued, passing the exterminating store with its red sign and drawing of a white calm rat. Oh, nuts to her. She was nuts. It's a wonder she'd got over their petting in the cab. They walked up the stoop, and in the corridor he grabbed her again, his hand creeping to the edge of her breast. "So long. I may be down later after you eat." Gee, he loved her. He ran up the two flights. Bill was home, smoking a cigar. "How's Romeo?" said Bill. "I hear you been promenading with Cathy." Joe slammed the door. "What the hell you doing home so early and on a Sunday?"

"Take a big look."

"I am."

"The Gebhardts were surprised to see me, too. The dog's with them. The dog was too happy seeing me."

Joe didn't know what to do with his brother. He could understand him Sunday mornings, but not now. Yesterday Bill'd been home, too. Two accidents in a row. Hell.

"If you need any dough, pop the word."

"Is that why you came home?"

"You'll have me bawling. Cut it, kid. Take it for granted I'm home. I've a headache." Joe took off his overcoat. He didn't like it nohow. Bill's eyes were roving up and down the three rooms with the pathetic beastliness of a caged animal. Joe got scared. "I've been a lousy brother. I'm younger than you, but I should have spoken up like a man."

"What you blatting about? You've spoken too much as is." He puffed thick blue clouds of cigar smoke around him like an ambush. Staring intently, Joe felt his brother was disappearing. He seemed smaller than ever to Joe. Joe felt he'd been speaking to someone running away, hearing his voice getting louder as if attempting to reach someone far away. In that second he guessed something awful had happened. Bill was licking dirt, ready for a browbeating because he'd done something rotten, like a kid caught with a sling-shot near a smashed window. The blood pumped hot and surging into Joe's head. He turned around in panic as if the walls were bars. He thought: It's my fault, I'm so easily led, so spineless, I just let things drift, and what'll become of us? Then he grabbed hold of himself by the neck as it were, sitting down, speaking against whatever had happened, almost guessing what it was.

"This is what I want to say. I should've said it long ago. But I never saw you during the week. Only Sunday mornings for breakfast. I hated like hell to spoil our being together when we were together. I didn't want to argue. Nights before dropping off I'd think maybe I ought to wake you up in the morning, at six, and have it out. I never had the heart. You looked too dead."

"Get to it," said Bill.

"You're a racketeer. You're not a bookkeeper for any bootlegger as you told me yesterday. You've lots of dough. The clerks at Metz's are talking about the robberies on Ninth. You're in it, Bill." He paused, sweating. Bill was sweating too. They were brothers all right, reacting in the same blind way. Oh, how sorry he was!

"No use stalling any more. I'm in it." It hurt to hear it. It was no relief to hear it. It would've been better to have continued in the old way. He glanced about the flat…Cathy, Cathy telling the priest: Oh, reverend father, priest, pope, I been necking heavy with a guy Joe, kissing, and he's squeezing my tits; oh, priest, father, forgive me…This went through his head, obscene, like vague disappearing smoke. And there was Bill grinning without any fun, after the smoke lifted, grinning, his eyes hard and bright as a plotting beast's. Bill wasn't going gooey soft or thinking: *Crime don't pay.* Bill was working out a problem, hiding behind the cold wicked grin. "The milk's spilled," said Bill, "and we've got to get down to facts."

"What's happened, Bill?" Something had to be done. He leaned forward, so engrossed he appeared to know all about it.

"Before I tell you, I want you to listen. When I lost my job I tried to get another. I couldn't not in real estate or anything decent." He spoke sincerely as if he'd really tried endless months, rising at six every morning like an Alger hero hoping to save a fat plutocrat from being run over, tramping the streets, chin up, determined to land honest work. "I drifted. I'm mixed up with those holdups, but don't you worry. They're all temporary. I'll make a few thousand and quit. I'm cold-minded enough to do it. I'm in it like a business man, and for a short spell." His eyes were full of malice, proud, his voice a little hysterical.

"You're in trouble, Bill."

"It's nothing. Christ, the world's full of crooks, but some are called millionaires." Joe'd heard that baloney line before, of bankers being burglars; all of it was old stuff, except for Bill's grin, the clever mocking baleful grin that seemed to reiterate: It's all old stuff, sure enough, but I mean it. I'm the guy that means it and will get away with it. "Bill, you're in trouble."

"You're right, kid," he said wearily, not looking up. "You've got to get this straight. At dawn this morning Metz's store was broken into." He watched his brother turn into wax, the red leaving his cheeks, becoming a waxen figure with an open mouth and popping eyes. "They cut through the partition in the rear. I'm home to tip you off, to protect you."

"You shouldn't."

"It's done. Don't belly-ache."

"What'll we do?"

"That's better. Tomorrow when Metz finds his bank empty, it'll break. Metz is smart. We gotta be careful. He'll wonder how in hell anybody'd know he's got dough in his bank. Nine out of ten don't leave dough in their stores over Sunday. Night deposits or they carry it home. And Metz never leaves dough around. He must've been cracked to do it yesterday."

"What'll we do, Bill? Run away?"

"Hold your horses. Metz'll realize it was an inside job, that somebody blabbed the fact that that Sat night, of all the Saturdays in a year, he put dough in his store bank."

"You took a risk like that."

"It's done now." Oh, Christ, he was crazy too. He ought never've involved Joe. He was crazy. "I told you. I told you all about it yesterday. Didn't I? You knew about Metz from me. I told you." He looked like a preacher. Who was denying it? That was one way to be, Joe exclaimed. It isn't anything to steal. What would he do? He didn't want to go to jail.

"You're not going to any jail. Take it easy, kid. For Christ's sake, it's nothing. I'll help you."

"I wouldn't need help if you were decent."

"Sure," he said, listening to Joe dig up the ancient yesterday. "It's done. Forget it."

"You got your bastard nerve, you bastard. Why'd you do it, you damn bitch?"

"For the dough, you shouting idiot. Get hold of yourself, act like a man or you can go to hell." He glared as if Joe were to blame for everything. "Metz is insured. Think I'd hook him after he gave you a job?" (He was switching into a communist all of a sudden.) "The loser'll be a rich company. You got to keep a smart head on you. There'll be an investigation, but we're both safe. There's a chance one of the clerks saw him lock up his dough. But also a chance a customer saw him. You guys know nothing. You didn't tell a soul. Where were you last night?"

"At the Capitol."

"With Cathy of course?"

"Yes."

"Swell. Then what did you do?"

"Came home and hung around in her house until about two. Then I said good-night and went to bed. That's all."

"Your alibi's perfect."

"I don't need an alibi. I didn't do anything."

"Alibis never harm. Gebhardt'll vouch for you if it ever gets that far, which it won't. All you've got to do is tell the truth. This morning neither of us left before twelve." He grinned complacent as a cat. "The cops don't know the robbery was at dawn. All they know is that at ten this morning a guy—some kid we know—called up and said things looked fishy in the cheese store."

"What does that mean?"

"It means our alibis are tight. We were here at ten. Metz is wise at this second probably. He won't say much I don't think. The cops've probably advised him to watch you clerks tomorrow. Now, tonight you take Cathy out. Later I'll take the dog for a walk, bring him back, and pay a visit on the Stangers. We'll both have perfect alibis."

"It sounds good, but I don't know."

"What you leery of? It'll boil down to everyone thinking it plain dumb luck, with a coupla guys busting in accidental."

"They won't believe that."

"If they don't, what's the difference if they don't prove anything?" He glanced away from Joe, who was gasping as if he'd swum too far, his chest heaving, his face going greenish. "Tomorrow to all questions you just tell them the truth. It's easy. I'll see you tonight when I get back from the Stangers'. We'll rehearse again." Joe muttered as if his lungs were full of water, suddenly realizing what Bill had done. "You're a filthy crook. that's all you are, and you're bound to get into a peck of trouble even if you think you're wiser'n hell. You might get away this time, but you'll get caught sure as fate."

"There's nothing to worry about. The kids pulled off the job." He pressed the cigar stub in the tray. On Thursday the paint supply was due for a ride. He yawned at the window. Sunday abode peacefully in Leroy. But all he had to do was turn around and see Joe at war, his yellow head hanging, to see the death of youth and virginity. Hell, thought Bill, I've raped something in Joe. I always do in people. "Want dinner, Joe?"

"I'm not hungry. I'll make up a sandwich." He smiled. "Who are the kids you mentioned?"

Bill laughed. "They're little gents, that's all."

"I guess I'll wash up. I guess I'll get my sandwich later." It was almost eight and he didn't want to think of what he had to do tomorrow when he reported for work. His face was flushing, the skin hot on temples and cheekbones. He was punch-drunk. Bill's talk had had the effect of punches. Bill appeared to have discarded the entire affair like a shabby tie, as if tomorrow would never show up. He's acting calm for my sake, thought Joe.

"You have a good time with Cathy. Be normal. That shouldn't be hard. She's a neat little trick" he commented with an elder brother's leer.

"What's it to you?"

"Jesus, cut out the comedy. Want dough?"

"I got enough," Joe said sullenly. "I like Cathy, and your cracks don't go."

"Why let your liking prevent you from having a good time?" All these damn tenement dames were pie handled by a smart fellow. The poor sluts. Not a break in hell for them, all of them waiting to be knocked off. "Tell the Gebhardts I'm in with a headache."

"Aw right." He frowned at Bill, the bold laughing lips, this brother of his sprawling all over the place with a sense of being naked. Joe rammed on his hat. That God-damned swine hinting things about Cathy. What could you expect?

"Have a good time."

"Go to hell, you cheap crook." Down the gloomy stairs, he was thinking: Bill's a wolf. A wolf. Bill was a knife in his guts. The pain hurt. He was hopeless. Metz tomorrow. He'd see Metz. He swallowed his fear like another knife and knocked on the Gebhardt door.

He was glad when they were walking under the El. Inside her house, in the respectable light, with Mr. Gebhardt reading his *Zeitung*, the Sunday *American* folded on his lap, his wife in the kitchen, but not very busy, so that it was easy to imagine her resting soon and sewing, in the domesticity of the youngsters, smelling wholesome as carrots, he'd been forced to smile, to say words said by some being fatally associated with himself.

The two of them kept step like soldiers, almost of a height, both slim and vigorous. At night Greenwich was haunted, the El pillars towering high and almost black as the shadows, the closed shops and plants obtruding blank walls. The workers were all gone, but yet there was a threat of malicious people observing them from secret peep-holes.

Tomorrow wasn't a year off. Metz. Cheese day tomorrow. Forget. He had Cathy. Forget tomorrow. Cathy who'd been desire, the flesh of aching and youth, was sanctuary. He thought with the bromidic grandeur of a young man: Woman is everything to a man…He was rested, fenced in, guarded, magnifying her presumable love for him into a huge protective genie.

"Is Bill's headache bad?" she asked.

"Not so bad. It'll do him good to stay home one night."

She admired Bill for staying home with a headache. Bill was a stepper, and when Joe asked why she didn't forget about Bill, she wondered if he was jealous. Bill was a stepper, and fresh. Gee, he was fresh. What he'd done to her Saturday, the fresh thing. "Bill's still at that bookkeeping job?"

"And gets a raise every week."

"You're kidding."

"I haven't a tin belly, have I?" he said bitterly. She hadn't caught on. She belonged to him and also to the shadow so that she was his and not his. The darkness and solitude were everywhere. He gripped her, holding her tight, giving in to the loneliness inside of him, his youth flowing out. What could he hold to? He let loose, lonely as before. On this street of hallways crowded with ghosts, he didn't know what to say, taking her hand. The city too was taking her hand, and taking her hand was his life in the city these few months, the bitter winter mornings of rising early, the lonely days, the suspicions about Bill, the loveless grind with only the Gebhardts offering sympathy, only Cathy offering love. All this held on to her fingers and all this was voiceless, or, having voice, that voice the clangor of steel wheels, the sirens crying in the harbor.

That hugging a minute ago, outside a plate-glass window of copper appliances, was the real thing to both of them. Yes, sir, the real bona-fide thing. That was real love, thought Cathy with the bemused victory of a woman. For the first time she'd felt Joe was wanting something else besides her body. Wanting her body was grand, but real love was something else, real love had been the way he'd been a minute ago, wanting something else besides her body. Over and over she repeated this echo of her own making, now faint, almost out of hearing, her blood flooding up so that her skin tingled and she'd have loved to press every inch of her flesh to him; now loud and triumphant, Joe silent, his voice not bugling to her youth, stilled and at ease, sharpened to trivial details. Something else. Love. Sure. Love was grand. She loved him.

They got off at Ninth Avenue and Twenty-third. The towered area of London Terrace filled a square block. They hurried east towards the canopy of the Grand Opera House, announcing two features and six acts of vaudeville (only place in town where you could see the real old-fashioned vaudeville), all for forty cents. Joe bought tickets. The lobby was immense, marbled, hung with huge gilt mirrors and decorated with the heroic dubious bronzes of fifty years ago. They sat in old decaying seats, just dodging the edge of a pillar. It was 1932 and he'd see Metz in the morning.

When Joe left, Bill's face sagged. He didn't look so bright. He belonged to the flat. His face seemed to have too much flesh, his nose almost blobby, his lips thick, his forehead creasing suddenly like a curtain falling loose from a rigid support. He belonged to the flat—to the bedroom painted pea-soup green, the parlor with its few books, the kitchen with the combination sink wash-basin bathtub shower. His hopelessness belonged to the flat. His conscience like a sneered-at obscure relative suddenly popped up from round some mental corner. What a swell brother he was! Just swell. The Metz robbery proved his lousiness. Of all places to hook. Christ. But there wasn't a loop-hole. Not one. Didn't all fools think they never left loop-holes, clues? Fools were too hot in the pants, too near their crime to be truly observant. What if some damn bull would pick up one clue, two clues, a dozen? He turned the faucet on in the sink, watching the white jet splashing, the steady stream washing away all the clues and traces of a hundred crimes, playing around to give himself a holiday from thinking. He gulped two glasses of water, pacing up and down just as they all did, all the dopes and crooks. Walking up and down. Who? Me, the typical Me, the Me crook doing everything in the same old way, feeling remorse—oh, remorse, and fear—oh, fear. I pace the floor like a caged tiger, a caged rat's more like it…Holy Christ, how he'd kidded himself, thinking he was a brain guy because McMann said he was. Why'd McMann call him brain guy? Better be careful. Brain guy. What a damn laugh that was! He looked at himself in the dresser mirror with a feeling like nausea. How far away he was, as if he were staring at a photo taken long ago when he was a kid! His brown hair was getting dry, falling out. What a mug! And that mug was the cold analyst. He was the guy, the scientist, mind you, who took crime in his stride. Just look at those swellings under his eyes. Look at the brain guy and puke in your hat.

Starting from the inside corner of each eye, cutting down to the cheekbone, two heavy lines were graven. Inside the triangular areas the flesh was slightly discolored. A swell specimen. The brain guy. Like hell. What'd his phenagling get him? What had he, good Lord, what was the use of it, what was the profit? Some dough that was never enough, a taste for booze and whores. He stunk to hell. And now all he had to do was mix Joe up, the only person who cared for him. Wasn't that brainy? What a life! Madge? The nearest thing to love was a Madge who got laid all week for two bucks a throw, by any Greek, mick, wop. What did he have? A used hunk of tripe. He'd never pick up a couple grand. He'd die or get shoved in jail. His position was weak. As Joe had said, the avenue was talking. Wiberg, Soger, Petrucci, and now Metz. All of them socked when they'd been in the dough. His old clientele. He was the insider, and probably some smart bull was wise even at this moment, and wouldn't have to be so smart either. He put his feet on the table. Under the electric light his hair was reddish. He lit up another cigar, suddenly more comfortable, outside his own skin, laughing at himself. Why bellyache? Because he had nothing else to do. For the first time in months he was sitting on his behind, thinking up things to hurt himself with; not drinking or shooting pool or bullying with McMann or sleeping with Madge or on the way or coming home from all these time-killers. He was wide awake, he was alone. He puffed dreamily, remembering his old job, the first few times he'd smoked cigars. It was after a month or so with Stanger. That job was heaven with its easy dough. He remembered his first bet on a horse, on Amnesic it was. How in hell, when, where, how had he shaken down his first joint? He couldn't remember, but those pimps and toughs had shelled out regular. How I began, he thought with a sneaky admiration for himself; too much easy dough too easily got. You don't break habits.

Joe'd be all right. He pushed thought of Joe from him. What a life he'd had! Lousy to be out of work and Paddy sending him down to Pop; himself wandering around with that match-box. Some joke. But he'd got what he wanted out of Paddy just the same. And on Thursday there was the paint supply. My dear, he thought as if he were a charity worker, I've been so wrapped up. The world was spinning, the dumb goofy world with millions out of jobs, with headlines about depression, communism, Japan knocking off China, but he'd been so wrapped up. That was funnier than hell. One of these days he'd buy a newspaper and wipe something with it. What'd he care? He'd grab a few grand and quit. He better take the damn dog for an airing; then he'd call on the Stangers. If a smart bull checked up, that'd seem fishy. Home for the first time. Calling on Stanger. Doing this and doing that where he'd done neither before. An alibi was an alibi. Prove your body. That was all you needed. Bodies at certain places at certain hours. Nobody was interested checking up where your mind was, what you thought. The dog was growing like a son-of-a. What was it but a son-of-a-bitch? And that's what he was. He was not. Whatever you did in life inevitably dragged others along. If Joe had enough guts, he'd've cut loose from him. Not cutting loose showed Joe wasn't such an angel. Joe had taken his easy dough. Joe was just a punk.

The policeman on duty at the station house showed Metz into a private room. Metz thought the cop looked funny without his blue hat. Metz minded his own business, which meant walking in a fog, twisting his lips with his habitual idiotic grin, and rubbing his chin bashfully. The door slammed. He was all alone. They make me think they're important customers, he thought; funny people, cops. A round man in a double-breasted gray suit sat down at the flat desk. He wore his derby tilted far back on his head as if he'd come in from a game of pool. His fat cheeks were red, his eyes blue above a network of wrinkles. Not appearing to glance at him from behind his thick glasses, Metz realized he was one of those fellers. "My name's Hanrahan, Mr. Metz." He pointed a long nose at the shopkeeper, patting his belly, belching and complaining about a steak, his eyes flicking their bright blue points like little searchlights. His nose had many enlarged pores, his face was slightly greasy, with a jowl and double chin. Metz thought he was a greasy eater and a regular sneaky goneph.

"Yah, I'm here," said Metz.

Hanrahan had the cordiality of a third-rate politician. "You get what I'm going to tell you. I've the dope on your store, got it this morning when some egg called up and said things looked phony at the dairy store. Got any idea who called?"

"Me? Sundays I'm home. I live in Brooklyn."

"I know. The guy who phoned belonged to the mob holding up all those stores. See?"

"I hope so. I don't like coming down all the way here on the subway when it takes over an hour, and my wife she doesn't like it, Sunday being one day off."

"You took the Brighton, and that subway's strictly local on Sunday."

"Ain't it wonderful how you know?"

Hanrahan suddenly shot his jaw forward. "Why'n hell you make that crack? You know damn well that isn't knowing much. Don't play dumb with me. Don't you think I know that any feller that can work himself up into owning three large stores is a pretty shrewd article? Give me a little credit, Metz."

Metz grinned. "What you want? An inside job, ain't it? That's how you say? No one know about the money but me and the clerks."

"One of them is no good."

"All good boys, Mr. Hanrahan."

"Which one's a little bad?"

"I don't like to say it, but if anyone tip somebody off, maybe it's Joe."

"You're to keep him on. Get it. You're right. The holdup's dumb luck pulled off by some yeggs. Or an inside job. Your store's the fourth robbed in three months. Wiberg, Soger, Petrucci, and you. That's not dumb luck. You must help me, Metz. All these stores were taken when they had real money on the premises, payrolls and so on…Why in hell did you leave dough in your ashcan of a bank?"

"Oi a shame to be so dumb, but it was very good Saturday and some I took home, some I locked up."

"It boils down to some guy knowing all about you storekeepers and where your dough is kept. It's that easy. An insider's wise to your tricks. Insiders always get careless. They all slip. They know so much they think they can get away with murder."

"What you think?"

"This insider could've known about your dough only from one of the clerks. That's how we'll grab him."

Metz paled, deadly serious. He knew who the insider was, listening to Hanrahan expand needless detail. He had three clerks. One of them was a bad boy. Were the clerks all Jews, and who were they anyway? "Two is Jews, relatives of mine."

Hanrahan paled a little too. "Who's the goy, Metz?"

"Joe Trent. He's been on only a few months."

"How'd you take him on?"

"His brother's a friend of mine."

"What does he do? Does he work?"

"He used to work for Stanger's real-estate company. He is not working now. He used to collect all the stores. He collect Wiberg, and all them fellers robbed."

Hanrahan laughed harshly. "I wanted to hear you say it. I knew it without your help. I've been talking to Soger and Petrucci and Wiberg. 'How is it,' I says, 'you guys are held up when you're flushed? Ain't it funny? Don't it prove you told somebody, a friend, some good guy?' I got them to thinking. Wiberg admitted his wife knew and a cousin. Soger said only his clerk, who was also his son. Petrucci said his wife, two daughters, and about half of his ginny society knew how he ran his business. Oh, I had them using their heads, and without their suspecting it they pinned it on Bill Trent tight as hell. Why, of course, the rent-collector knew; not the new one, but the old one, a fine good fellow; too bad he lost his job. I'm crazy, Metz. Huh! Like hell I am, but I wanted you to tell it. You're smarter than the pack. Shall I third-degree your Jewish relatives or Joe Trent? Inside jobs are always easy. You always know what and where to look."

"Joe's a good honest kid."

"So's his brother. Why'd you hire Joe? He ain't a Jew. Why?"

"I got fellers not Jews working for me."

"All right. All right. You took on the kid. Bill Trent ain't so dumb, but they always slip. You took on a green kid because Bill says so when the town's full of experienced help."

"You know so much, why ask?"

"I've checked up on a few things. I wonder if this smart article got your rent reduced or what?"

"You should a Jew be."

"Maybe I am. You don't know why Billy boy got canned? Well, let it go. The point is, since his canning we've had four robberies among old tenants of his. Coincidence? Nope. You lost your dough like the rest when you had a pile of it. Is it coincidence or Billy boy?"

"He didn't make me hire Joe to steal from me. No."

"Why not?"

"It's no." As he'd listened to the detective, the abashed fake grin had disappeared. Now, dark, somber, he added: "I hate to hear. Bill a fine feller. His brother work hard and good."

"I still got plenty work. Not so easy pinning it on him. He worked smooth and fast. When Soger was stuck up they were chased by a copper in a cab, but they got away." He didn't mention he'd sent the word down to the stools with the regular mobs, but nothing had turned up. He had a hunch Bill wasn't in with a regular mob. Mobs weren't taking on outsiders. All they could do to keep themselves clicking. "You don't can Joe until you hear from me." He yawned, speaking again about the steak, vaguely intimating this was a social as well as a business visit. "So long. Don't forget."

"Good-by. You figure things pretty good."

"I'm good at pinochle too," said Hanrahan.

Bill read a magazine. The dog was sleeping in its box near the bed, three or four bones scattered on the floor where the dog had left them. The bones were the dog's treasures, and each day he cleverly hid them behind chairs and under the bed. Bill looked at the dachshundish body speckled black and white. That dog slept sound. His only worries were eating worries. That was his worry, too. Only he was greedier, a few grand greedier. Thursday's job ought to net a few pennies. It might be their real start and Duffy's end. McMann had said that the Metz break was half the battle. The kids is on the Metz job thought they were wonders, and if Thursday went off O.K., the kids'd be theirs.

Joe opened the door. The dog shot his groggy head up, his bright eyes watching. He sprang out of the box, leaping to Joe's hand, his tail like a fly-swatter. Joe sat down in his coat, taking the dog on his lap. The dog licked his ears. "Did you see Stanger?" he asked.

"No. That mutt can smell a key in a lock."

"You didn't see him?"

"How many times do you want me to say no?"

"Why not?"

"Joe the Sherlock. I thought too much of an alibi might look queer. I haven't seen Stanger since the holidays. Why call on him just the day Metz got hit? The Gebhardts saw me take the dog out, saw me make a face over my headache."

"Why've you got a headache today?" He put the dog in its box, patting its head and staring at his brother.

That was a hit. Best to laugh it off. "It'll be all right. It'll blow over."

"Maybe I ought to quit; that is, if I don't get sacked. He's treated me decent and I feel cheap."

"So that's what's eating you?"

"I'm quitting."

"You can't quit." He shouted, bitter, crafty: "Can't you realize that'd give everything away? Who gives up a job these days? Do you want the pair of us thrown in jail?"

"Hell," said Joe.

"You stubborn damn fool, want to squat in jail?"

Joe wanted to slam the swine. Things weren't so easily done. He suddenly caught on to the decorum, the routine necessary for successful criminals. They must act innocent. He was licked. "Find me another job. That'd be a good reason to quit."

"My eyes are open." He was sorry for the kid, averting his full glance, observing him covertly. "Want to go over tomorrow?"

"I'd like to die or run away."

"Cut that talk."

"Don't worry. I won't sneak out on you. I'm your brother. I'll look dumb and innocent for a hundred priests." (Cathy confessing to priests he put his hands here and there. Joe the accomplice, Bill the crook.) He laughed.

"Snap out of it."

"When Cathy asked me how you were making out I said you got a raise. Christ, that's funny."

"You're cracked. Don't tell that dame so much."

"Don't you order me. You can go to hell." They glared at each other like foreigners met for a common purpose, but hating each other's difference, thinking of tomorrow, hating. "I'm going to bed. It's still early bird for me."

"Maybe it'll do you good."

"Well, this was one Sunday we saw each other."

"Rest your bones." Poor Joe was beaten. He bit deep into his cigar butt, feeling the tobacco. Jesus, he thought, it's no good, it's just no good.

When Joe awoke. Monday morning to shut off the alarm, Bill herd the jangling for the first time in weeks, raising himself on elbow, squinting at Joe through one eye. "Hell, my right eye feels pussy. I left a slip on the dresser when you went to bed. It's my phone. You can reach me there afternoons, case you need me."

"Get back to sleep. I know what to do."

"Play mum, kid." The brothers looked steadily at each other in the icy cold room. Joe dressed swiftly, his head singing as if with fever. What'd Metz do? "Set the clock for eleven," Bill said.

Metz surveyed his three clerks. He himself hauled the bucket of water to the sidewalk. "O.K." He smiled insipidly, his eyes invisible behind the thick glare of his glasses, his black eyebrows lifting. They worked as always, sloshing the window, their raw wet hands scalded by the wind. Ninth Avenue was a meager town beneath the flat hopeless sky of January. Inside, the safe in the rear, high as Joe's chest, stood against the wall, "S. Metz, Cheeses & Dairy" engraved on it in gilt. The safe was closed, the jaws of the two clerks and the boss shut as firmly as the steel door. No one said anything. They just worked. Joe carried tubs of butter, later waiting on the customers, cutting cheese, making change, trying to act as if nothing had happened the day before. He felt punk, thinking of Cathy to help him forget.

He imagined the melancholy eyes of the clerks were staring at him when he wasn't noticing. They didn't call him Der Starker as often as they had. Only Metz, grinning affably, wearing his straw hat, seemed at all the same. Foxy Metz. All morning his head was singing. He listened for his heart. Did it beat faster? Concentrating on his work, cracking jokes with the ladies, hearing them compliment him for his looks, bored as if he were an old man and his beauty crumbled thirty years ago. He had no use for a woman. That's how he acted, hardly distinguishing between even the regular customers, blundering. He said: "Is that all, Mrs. Murphy?" when it should have been Mrs. Martin, saying Mrs. Skoularekes for Mrs. Skolpas. Each time he made an error, his head swelled to immense dimensions, his heart like a pounding hostile fist in him. Surely Metz had noticed, or one of the clerks next to him at counter. Each time he smiled at the surprised customer. "Why, Mrs. Martin, you didn't think I didn't know who you were? I thought I'd kid you along." And Mrs. Martin, a big Irishwoman with a peaked nose and the grim lips that somehow go with hefty Irish ladies, had smiled as if he were courting her. He was very handsome, fresh-colored, Amurrican down here on Ninth with the kike shopkeepers, the Greeks, the shanty micks, the ginzos and Dutchies. As for Skoularekes-Skolpas, he had whispered to the nearest clerk: "Christ, Murray, I can't get them Greek names straight." He didn't fool himself, however. He'd never made mistakes before. They must know it, pitying him as they put orders in brown bags.

He was a rat in a trap, a rat caught in a cheese store. His head was singing. The shelves crowded with canned goods, the clerks, Metz, all these known things were far from him, as if he were diving deep in water, gazing with strained eyes towards a lost and mysterious world. Things were so far away he knew he didn't belong. He was an outsider, the sharp precise outlines of human beings blurring as if he had the grippe. His head sang, and all the morning he listened to the sick song, wondering when the break'd come, hoping it'd be soon. They must know. They were playing with him like cats. That was it. Metz didn't say boo, watching him. Why didn't he send him to the market? The long free ride in the truck, the driver unable to spy on him because he'd be driving and keeping an eye peeled for cops and goofy drivers. That'd be swell. If only they sent him out! The pattern of their eyes, inimical, curious, the three pairs of eyes piercing him all over so there was no escape, worried him to death. They were waiting for him to monk up. He'd fool the bastards. He began to whistle, grinning at the fraudulent music issuing from his dry lips. He moistened his lips, but song wasn't in him.

Walking in the narrow space behind the counter, brushing against the secretive bodies of the clerks in passage, he thought he'd go bugs. They didn't goose him and he didn't goose them as he passed for a can of salmon for some customer. The customers dropped off. It was time to eat, the clerks forgathering in the rear, slicing cheese, smearing on butter, eating lunch in the usual panic, as Metz grinned, saying nothing, but seeming gabby anyhow with his smile and eyebrows and pantomimic hands. They talked of the trade, kidding Joe as if there'd been no robbery. He was frightened more than ever, suspecting they were doing their best to make him feel at home. His roll and cheese had no taste, a vague mush his teeth bit into until the bite was semifluid like a heavy syrup which he swallowed hatefully.

The sun slanted from high noon, the street outside was sunny, colored with the shawls of women and their wintry red cheeks. How long would it keep up? It wasn't fair. It was dirty cheap. Then Wiberg strolled into the store, and Metz waited on him. Wiberg hadn't come to buy, but to brag, the two clerks peering from him to Joe. Wiberg snorted how misery loves company, don't you know, hahaha; so Metz was stuck too, and Soger said it was Metz next like in a barber shop, and so he got his shampoo and schnozzle lifted. But Metz was lucky. He wasn't socked on the bean. Wiberg grinned, patiently demanding that Metz give him the story. "I couldn't get off till now. Sometimes I sell some dresses and then I know you busy. Hanrahan come here? He find out nothing. Already he speak to Soger and me and Petrucci. He knows to ask questions, but he finds nothink." There had been no one to stop the exuberant fat man. Metz grinned, baffled. Joe thought this time Metz was really dumb, without words. He watched the boss twist his lips from old habit, idiotic as ever, but licked, speechless. The clerks exclaimed, excited, what the hell had happened? Wiberg was kidding. And finally, like an awakening dreamer, Metz said: "What robbery?"

Wiberg's admiration was colossal. Metz said the boys didn't know till this very minute. Wiberg roared at the joker. "Everybody see the cops yesterday. The cop on the beat tell Soger. What a liar, the clerks don't know!" Metz insisted it was the truth. Hanrahan's case was ruined by this blabby Austrian. What could you expect from an Austrian Glitz. Well, sooner or later Joe must've known. He smiled at Joe shouting with the others. Oi, a shame. He'd known all morning Joe was in it. He was sorry. "Huh, Metz," cried Wiberg, "you sneak, you watch the boys; one of them is the goneph."

"Go home to your wife," said Metz.

"All right, I see you later." Joe almost dropped to the floor, his thighs leaning hard against the counter. He had the idea that Wiberg even while joking had snapped out of his fog, guessing Metz had a reason for hiding the robbery from the clerks. Wiberg, speaking the truth with blubbery good humor, the words lost forever, had pulled up, thinking: That's the reason. Metz is watching the boys. That's why he left so quickly. They were wise.

Metz rubbed his hands, folding them over the small bulge his belly made in the apron. "Yeh, them crooks. They bust open the safe yesterday. Why tell you boys? What's the use? And them cops know what? I tell them yesterday it's the racketeers, them hangouts." They all wished for a customer to come in, the clerks irritated and uneasy.

"A half pound salt butter," said a German lady. Joe sliced it out of the tub, dumping the yellow slab on a piece of paper.

"You wasting your time here, Joe," said the lady. "You should a job in the movies get."

"I will one of these days. The cheese business is slow." Other customers dropped in. Metz was sorry that later on he'd have to phone Hanrahan and inform the bull the beans was spilled and what was to be done? Joe wrapped up the package. Anyway, this was excitement, something doing. He had belly-ached about the sameness of his work, but this was something like. His eyes glinted. He felt a hot kinship with his brother, almost without regret. This was something.

CHAPTER SIXTEEN

Chewing a toothpick, Hanrahan marched into Stanger's office, pointing his nose at the girls. "The boss in?" He flashed his badge, holding it in his fat moist palm, continuing his stride. The girls whispered; the detective entered the last frosted window. The window said: PRIVATE, but those cops were corkers.

"How do?" said Hanrahan, unbuttoning his overcoat, dropping his bottom into a big leather chair. He slanted his derby further back on his wet brow. He seemed to have eaten a heavy dinner, smoking his cigar with the enjoyment of a man whose belly is full. He explained who he was. It was nothing important, but had Mr. Stanger heard of the recent robberies on Ninth? "Sure you have. I'm in charge. Do you know your firm collects rents from all four parties that've been stuck? That's coincidence. You must do a big collection."

"Are you implying anything?"

"Take it easy. We've been looking the clerks over at Metz's—two Jewish boys, Murray Hecker and Sam Rothbard, and a kid, Joe Trent." Stanger's pale eyes glared at the detective. "I can't say this interests me very much."

"That's funny. They're all your tenants. Maybe you want your firm to get a rep for being a jinx?" He breathed greasily as if bloated. "Hell, what a meal does to a man! My doc says if I don't cut out meats, my kidneys'll go bad. I'll be in the red. Ain't that funny?"

"What do you want me to do?"

"That's being sensible. I'm investigating the Metz clerks, as we think it may be an inside job. Maybe not. Therefore, just investigating, I found out Joe's a brother of a collector you had here some months ago. Nice boys, are they? Cooperation, Stanger, you bet. Wouldn't be nice if Soger and the rest complained to their landlords the agent's not co-operating."

"They're sons of my best friend. I let Bill go because business was getting rotten."

"Bill working?"

"I don't know."

"Don't they visit?"

"They're proud boys. I saw Bill for a few minutes during the holidays. I let them have a flat in a house of mine rent-free." (Oh, Poppa Trent, hear what I did for your sons, oh best friend!) "I believe that they avoid me because they're obligated."

"Is Bill working?"

"I said I don't know." Hanrahan stuck a fresh toothpick between his teeth. "I know why Bill was sacked."

Stanger blinked. "Really?"

"Really. A copper found out he was buddies with a pimp, proud boy though he is, a proud broth of a boy, as the Irish say. Maybe he had a racket shaking down pimps and fellers like that. He wouldn't be the first real-estate feller."

"You cops can't afford to talk."

"A Republican? Listen to me. The four stores robbed were collected by that proud feller."

"Are you implying he's mixed up with these robberies? I don't believe it." Stanger was affected, pallid, his nervous indigestion working up on him.

"I investigate. Don't get hot, mister. Maybe we'll see each other again. I just wanted you to know why you sacked him. See? I like to get the truth right off the bat. I believe in co-operation between real-estate agents and the law. Maybe I'm a sucker?"

"I've always co-operated with the police." Stanger wiped his brow. Ought he to dispossess Bill? What a nuisance! No use doing that. If they proved him guilty, that'd be different. If Bill were guilty, the law'd serve the dispossess and provide new quarters. He might be innocent.

"S'long. See you again, Stanger."

At a cigar store he contacted headquarters. He was informed Metz had phoned. He hung up, dropped another nickel in the slot, chewing on his frazzled toothpick. Metz said: "Gimme your number and I call you back tonight, Hannah." Hanrahan called off the number and hung up. There was a delay; then the phone rang. Metz was sorry to keep him waiting, but he'd sent Joe out to the market to get rid of him. Metz told how Wiberg had spilled the beans. What should he do, sack Joe?

"Nope," said Hanrahan. "I'll be in later to quiz the joint. S'long."

"Not in business hours."

"I'll come in at six. Seven?" He frowned, listening to protests. "Half past seven, then."

"Good-by, Hannah," said Metz.

Hanrahan laughed. The little Jew was funny. He hung up. Sure as God made apples, that Bill Trent was the boy.

Bill ran up from the pay booth in the hall. "How about a Hanrahan dick?" he said to McMann.

"What'sa matter, you see a ghost?"

"He's in charge."

"Who tole ya?"

"My kid brother over at Metz's. That guy Wiberg barged in and said Hanrahan's in charge. The kid says the phone rang late, and after that, Metz sent him down to the market. That's why he called me."

McMann heaved the *Daily Mirror* up in the air, celebrating. "You never tole me you had a kid brother workin' for Metz. You keep things close."

"Must I tell you everything?" He felt stronger than McMann, more resourceful. He wondered whether he was outgrowing McMann. "What sorta bull is

Hanrahan?"

"Honest. Honest dicks are smart. Smart 'cause they're honest. He ain't got a thing on us. Your brother's safe. What you wild for?"

"Do you know that a dick must know about me? All four joints were hooked when their bosses were in the dough. I collected all of them. It points to an insider. To me."

McMann laughed; he'd thought of that years ago.

"You never told me." That was because he kept things under his hat. Bill wasn't the only guy. Why worry? If Hanrahan couldn't prove anything, he was safe. Let him guess it was Bill. "Christ, that dick'n five others is wise I hock cars night'n day, wise I'm in this'n that. They knows it like I knows it. That ain't knowin' nothin'. Kin they do a damn? Naw. That means they knows nothin'. But after the paint supply holdup on Thursday, they'd lay off the stores until the stink died down.

"Maybe we shouldn't take the paint supply."

"Too late. Duffy's het up. It's the big chance. Hookin' Metz'n now the paint supply, and them kids'll eat outa our hands." He seemed happy, mentioning speaks uptown they'd tackle next. They'd go for real dough, borrowing Duffy's smartest kids, to lump some of the speaks above 110th. And gambling houses.

They had Joe between them, sitting in the room, blocking one from the other like a third person. Bill thought: I let it slip, I was so damn excited. What a brain guy! He listened as McMann explained how no cops'd bother them about speaks. They'd be safer than now. Bill laughed. The full tide was pulling out, the tide he'd created like God. Now the flux of events, the future he'd set ticking like a wound-up watch, dwarfed the creator. Out to sea, and God alone knew where…

Neither was very excited about clipping a speak. It was nothing. That was all. McMann picked up the tabloid, glancing up eagerly. "Here's where some ginzos had a clubba their own. That's swell. Hey, guy, we'll have a club any day now. Jesus. We'll spring the idea on the resta the kids. Schneck and Ray is nuts about it." Already he seemed to have sneaked control of the kids from Duffy, to have a clubhouse. Bill felt it'd all happened.

At seven-thirty Hanrahan edged into the dairy store, walking directly to the rear. He knew his way. He'd been in on Sunday. He shut the door and sat down on an empty tub. The clerks were busy with a scattering of customers, but Metz trailed the visitor, returning, waiting for the customers to go. "It's a detective'n wants to kibbitz you boys. Sam and Joe first. Then Murray." He implied it was a trifle, an interview formal and silly. Nobody laughed. "Take it easy," Hanrahan said to Sam and Joe. "I got a few routine questions. You're Sam Rothbard, and how in the devil could it be anything else?" He smiled at the clerks, the big blond one and the dark Jew. "Sit down. Find a comfy tub. Now, when you boys went home Saturday, did you tell anybody that Metz was sappy enough to leave dough in his bank? How dumb that was, boys! When you own your own cheese stores, let it be a lesson. Leaving dough after he knew of the stickups in the last two months. That's why there are so many robberies. Everybody is sappy. It's a sappy world, and fellows with special knowledge, special inside dope, some smart feller like that, can take advantage. We detectives like such theories such as insiders with dope. It makes it easier. A lot of us are kids. Now, did either of you boys tell about sap Metz to your families, to sweethearts when you had them out on dates and getting tired hugging, told them how sappy Metz was, to kill some time before getting wind up for the next session?" He paused, smiling, his plump red face gleaming under the suspended bulb, very jovial, just one pal with a coupla others. "Personally, neither of you two boys is in it, but when boys spill the word about sappy Metz thinking a cheese-box is the Bank of England, hell, boys, such news spreads to these smart guys. Tell anyone, Sam?"

"No, sir."

"How about you, Joe? Did you tell your parents or a sweetie?"

"My parents are dead."

"Too bad. How about a brother, sister, some kid brother or something?"

"I haven't much of a family. One brother. I didn't mention it to him or to anybody."

"Not even a sweetie? A big handsome kid like you."

"No one." His head was singing. Hanrahan was a liar, rubbing that finger on his oily nose, his blue eyes pretending they were sleepy or tired. Hanrahan didn't fool him, playing the dope like Metz.

"That's all, boys. Send the other clerk in: Maybe he was dumb enough to tell somebody." Metz said the jailbirds could go home. Joe and Sam returned to the back room, getting into their street clothes. "Sure you didn't tell your sweetie?" asked Hanrahan.

"I did not." Metz called good-night to him as if he were sorry for somebody. The night was warm. The next month might have been springtime and not February.

After supper Joe and Cathy strolled up to Seventh Avenue into the Village, walking sedately like long-established lovers, peeking into the shops, cute as Pekingese with their candleware and bath scarves and pewter. Cathy said he shouldn't worry, she had it straight. "Now, you know as much as me about the robbery," Joe said. "If that detective were to question you—"

"I'd say you never had much money. Suppose they dig up the cab-drivers, Joe?"

"Lucky we never pulled up front of your house." Fooling somebody—in this case Cathy's folks—always was handy for someone else. "I gave that bull what for."

"It was Bill's money went for the cabs." She stared at him as if to say: Bill's a crook, ain't he? It's Bill.

"You remember all I've said and don't tell a soul."

"Not even the priest," she promised religiously.

He had the most cockeyed feeling. Could you bet it? He was a priest, and Cathy was confessing to him. Tall, devout, her eyes shone at him. She was his private nun. He patted her arm. She was O.K. She loved him. She was grateful to him. He'd been in a sweat all day and now expanded with his power. Heck with the cops and Hanrahan. He wasn't scared. Every time he felt her body touch his own, he boomed with youth. His head sang, but differently than it had down at Metz's. He was listening fevered and exultant to his own blood and the love in his blood-stream. Her promise not to confess to the priest was the real thing. He was her religion. Thinking of the demands his religion, his love, would and must make…"What are you thinking of, Joe?" she said gently, proud to be helping him. It was like the girls in the movies protecting their lovers from the cops.

"I love you. Honest." It was miraculous to him that after all the Catholic youthhood of her, the candles, the choir boys, the priests intoning as she confessed to little sins, that she should stand before him so naked. He doubted his power, too Saxon, too American to really believe his love was the compensation and the cause. She wouldn't confess. She'd switched sides. Christ, it was because of him. Him alone. he arched his chest, appreciating who the devil he was. When he steered her past a truck or car, he did so with magnanimity, noting she'd accepted his estimate of himself, thought him grander than he dared to imagine.

He bragged toughly: "I guess you like me. Why not? Every dame's a woman. Even the black skirts of the nuns cover up flesh-and-blood bodies." He was combative, cocky, Protestant.

"You needn't speak like that, Joe. People ought to respect other people's religions." But there was no heat in her; she reminded him of her mother. Gee, she was a good-hearted kid and he ought not pick on her.

"How's high school? How you making out?" But he didn't listen when she itemized about her bookkeeping and Spanish, the commercial course that would train her for an office job. He was in love. He had her number. He could do anything he wanted with her. She was easy. And tomorrow there'd be Metz over again. Nothing to worry about. Hadn't Bill said there was nothing to be worried about? He respected Bill, admiring his brother like some white-collar reading of the deeds of Al Capone. Bill was a real man. Wouldn't be so bad to be like Bill.

On Thursday the paint-supply store was knocked off. It was a good profit. Duffy made money, but wasn't keen about it. Hanrahan thought: Another store collected by Billy boy. Damn Billy boy; didn't he think there were cops in town. Damn him. Billy boy was like a kid swiping apples…

CHAPTER SEVENTEEN

Bill and McMann entered the lobby of the hotel where Duffy lived. It was one of the newer hotels, a mass of clean brown stone put together when Coolidge was President. Duffy paid fourteen bucks a week for a room and bath that used to be twenty-eight. The immense lobby was a corner of old Siam or some such land where the green things are decorative and plenteous. Two murals faced each other vaguely, nice-colored, as Duffy said. Their processions of heroic figures, men and women obviously resident in a California-like climate, were undecided whether they were en route to a palace, a fiesta, to war or to peace, to tragedy or comedy; and the little people underneath in old Siam, talking in stealthy hotel groups, also seemed like mural folk, headed for other cities, engrossed in a hundred plots of sex, money, and crime, whose outcomes were also in doubt. They weren't mural folk, but guys like you'n me'n the nex' feller.

Two clerks gleamed like expensive wood at the desk. Bill and McMann strode through the flora inhabited by drummers, prostitutes, vice-presidents, women in their thirties on the make for young actors, Broadway boys in dope or numbers or racing, searching everywhere for Ray and Schneck. Three fags sat discreetly in an ambush of palm trees. A plumpish eye-glassed group of business men held a couch for the glory of textiles, one composite lewd eye out for passable stuff. And standing upright, as if they were on a corner, Ray and Blowhard Schneck were smoking. The two interested parties smiled at each other. Bill and McMann took the elevator. "They'll be right up. It's showdown, Bill." He removed his hat politely, nudging his hard hip and elbow against the side of a young woman, sniffing at her perfume. What a corker he is, thought Bill, always ready for anything, always with an eye peeled for life; hell, what a guy!

They got off. "Nice, huh?" said McMann.

"Haven't you some business, you punk?"

"That's business. She was soft as chicken. I'da liked to have plunked't to her." The long corridor, the numbered doors on either side, kept their footfalls silent. The walls seemed a hundred miles thick. "If it comes to a row it's nothin'. The dump's noise-proof, so the bums in one room can't hear nex' door with the lady nappin' with her mutt."

Bill nodded, his neck trembling, almost walking on tiptoe, the shivers rolling down his back like ice. He swallowed. McMann was the devil. That was an old and true thought. McMann was always leading him into danger, and now he was banging his blunt red paw against Duffy's privacy. "Come in," hollered Spat.

Like the representatives of two nations, the four men smiled at one another seriously. Duffy was wearing a purple gown, Broadway-splendid, his small naked feet in brown slippers. The trouser legs of maroon pyjamas were below the skirt. (Two to one his shirt's embroidered with a crest, thought Bill.) From this glory Duffy's thin face emerged with the desolate incongruity of an old hag in chic things. His eyes were hot and intense.

"Sit down, boys. Spat'll fix you a drink."

"We don't want any," said McMann, smiling. Spat and Bill, henchmen, paired off in a secondary feud. Spat patted his black hair, plastered down and immaculate; his suit of oxford gray was too tight for him, hugging his thighs and chest, and as he scowled, his hairy fists on his knees, he seemed in dark armor, an obscure black prince, medieval and remorseless.

"It's short'n to the point," said McMann. "We all made a lil money on Metz and on the paint supply. We gotta lay off awhile cause the dicks're smellin' around."

"Sure," said Duffy, waiting. "Why not?"

"Why the hell not?" said Spat.

"No use quittin', Duff. How about uptown on biz till things quiet down on Ninth?"

"Son-of-a-bitch, his district," snorted Spat.

"Sure. No one owns the west side, and even shysters like us kin make a play for some of the pickin's."

Spat's thick lips pressed into a thin white line. "Don't you be bitchin' at me." He sat tense, ready to hurl forward. Duffy waved a hand of truce. "Let it go," he commanded. What else did McMann have to say?

"Uptown, outa the west side. I wouldn' hijack speaks down here where we know the boys, but an uptown speak above a Hunerd'n Tenth, what you say?"

"Nix," said Duffy. "You're nuts. I ain't holding up speaks in the west side or out of it."

"You heard the boss," growled Spat.

McMann purred: "No one's talkin' to you, Spat. Shove your damn mug outa it. Get me. When I speak to you, I'll look your way."

"Who the hell do you think you are?"

"He's my uncle's aunt," said Bill.

"Let it go," said Duffy.

"Thanks, Duff," said McMann. "That gorilla of yourn's nuts." He grinned, insinuating everything was Spat's fault. He appeared to have no argument with Duffy. It was only Spat. Spat, not catching on at all, grew white. He didn't know what the hell to make of it. What was wrong with the boss? "Way I figure it, Duff, me'n Bill did you a favor with that paint supply, and Metz made a lil dough for ya. A lil dough for somea ya kids, showed your kids you were thinkin' of them, getting' work for them, not lettin' them down. Now, you oughta loan us some of the kids so me'n Bill can take a speak. Nothin' at all'n no harm coinin' some dough to pay for this swell room." He paused, his lean hard body treacherous as a cat's.

"It boils down to one thing. No use bunking about it. You want to get hold of my kids."

"Like hell, Duff. Who's tellin' you that? Spat? If it's him, then he's one prime bastard liar."

Spat groaned as if tied hand and foot, roaring out, tormented, like a baited beast. "I ain't been sayin' a thing, and you quit those names, McMann, or I'll slough you." His fists knotted, his breath left his distended nostrils too quickly. He had no support from Duffy, whose brown eyes in the dead pokerface were completely neutral. Spat wanted to fight, but the boss wasn't behind him. He quivered. Someone knocked at the door again. Duffy's Adam's apple rose and fell. "See who's there, spat," he said.

And after an interval, with names shouted back and forth, Ray and Schneck were admitted, Duffy swallowing.

"Just a lil call," said Schneck, wide-shouldered, ash-blond, pimpled. No other kid could lick him at in-fighting; with one hand bear-hugging an enemy he could whale the hell out of anybody. The other kid was whistling. Their call wasn't just dumb walking, thought Duffy, not dumb walking, their call meant McMann had been chiseling, and what was he to do? Did the kids want a snifter? Sure, they'd drink, why not?—gulping down the stuff. A pink color flushed Schneck's pale cheeks. Ray declared it was sweller'n swell. "I've been arguin' with Duff," said McMann genially, as if there'd been no hot blood, "that we've alla us made a lil dough and that we oughta go uptown'n knock off a speak with too much sugar. Not a joint down the west side, but outa the west side, some lousy ginzo speak—"

"Hey," shouted Spat, "I'm 'talian. Don't be wise."

"Who's wise? We mean the gink uptown. Chris' sake, quit belly-achin'."

"It's a swell idea," said Schneck.

"I'm against it," said Duffy. "Who wants trouble with an uptown bunch?"

"What trouble?" cried McMann. If you knocked off speaks, there'd be no cops to mess around, no damn Hanrahans for example. It was no trouble. None. He glanced at the kids standing behind everything he said. Didn't Duffy catch on? Duffy wasn't dumb. He was giving the guy a chance to crawl from under, to avoid a real showdown. He knew a way to help Duffy crawl. He'd blame Spat for Duffy's resistance. Damn the ginzo. "Hell, this Spat feller's been tippin' you wrong, Duff. It ain't no trouble, Duff. He's against it 'cause maybe the uptown speaks is run by wop cousins ahis and he's a wop."

Spat came out of his chair slowly like a man about to die, glaring desperately at Duffy. But Duffy was unmoved, fragile, small-boned in his purple dressing-gown, his brown eyes burning but anonymous. Spat glared at the kids, his thick red lips twisting pathetically as if to say: Hey, kids, you not letting me down, we knows each other…But the kids didn't recognize him, and neither did Duffy, these three glancing through him or over him. His lips squeezed again into a white line. he clenched his fists, lowered his thick courageous skull into his chest, and swaggered up to McMann. "You can't talk about me like that. You can't be calling me names." Duffy evaded. "That's neither here nor there. I'm against uptown hijacking." It was his final word.

McMann laughed as if it were a joke, not looking at Spat weaving in front of him madder than hell, his face black, looking a little silly because they were fighting out a bigger issue. "Jesus, Duff, you won't risk your hide. You'll be safe. Bill'n me and the kids'll do the real work. How about it, Ray, Schneck, you with us if Duff gives the word? Real dough, kids."

"You bet," said Ray. Schneck nodded.

"There you are, Duff. It's all set. You get your cut. We pull the job." He laughed brutally. "A cinch, ain't it?" He confronted Spat. "Now, you lousy bastard, you been fillin' up Duff with all sortsa bunk, sayin' we wanta steal his mob when we don't. Ain't we been givin' you'n Duff a cut on the paint and cheese stores? Sure. But justa same, you're a skunk, a double-crosser, with all kindsa bunk, you bastard wop."

Spat had been lowering his head and lifting it an odd inch or two as if it were on a chain. Now he choked, speechless, his eyes filling with blood. He knew he was being given a raw deal. They were using him for the goat, but just the same, McMann had gone too far. When Duff yelled: "Don't fight," his heart was cut in two by the treachery. He shot up his fist. McMann sprang back, shouting to the kids to keep off, he could handle the wop himself.

"Don't fight," cried Duffy, seeing Spat as himself. He noticed the kids fading back when McMann gave the order. He saw who was boss, for them two kids at least. Bill was keeping an eye on him. Duffy leaned back as if it were the Madison Square Garden.

McMann's left was jabbing away. Taller, faster than Spat, he flicked his clenched knuckles into the swarthy face. Spat rushed, head low, his eyes rolling up. McMann swiped him on the chin. Duffy groaned as Spat's head shot back; Spat was himself. He had no pity for Spat as Spat, but was sorry for the Spat who was Duffy. He, Duffy, was getting a licking. Ray put out his foot, and Spat stumbled, fighting to get his balance like a man slipping on ice. McMann's hard fists smashed twice. The blood ran from Spat's mouth. He retreated, dizzy before McMann's charge, backing up against the kids. McMann was on him. Schneck walloped him a nasty one in the ribs, propelling him forward into McMann. Spat seemed to be falling on his face, his knees angling, as McMann steadily pounded his head, ramming his fists into his eyes. Almost blinded, he retreated again. Schneck grinned, his hand clumping on Spat's shoulder, who, feeling the new menace, pivoted. McMann uppercut his chin. Schneck dug his big bony power into the kidney. Spat almost toppled, the fist tunneling deep into his belly, his insides bored through, dynamited with vicious power. Pushed forward again by the kids, staggering like a bar-fly, his eyes swollen, seeing Duffy and Bill wavering as dark, almost invisible shapes, and more distinct but also a shadow, McMann menacing, eternal, his fists shadows, but hurting as they landed. As his consciousness was battered out of him, the fists became shadows, almost not hurting, their impacts dull, without pain. He staggered weaker and weaker, some hidden mysterious courage battling for an ideal his dead-tired body had long forgotten. He lifted his arms and slipped to the floor. McMann had polished him off.

McMann peered down on Spat's bloody face, blinking at Duffy, who appeared bloodless, his Adam's apple rising up and down. Duffy saw his power, saw himself lying in a stricken heap. Spat was Duffy. Spat was himself and he was his own ghost. The real Duffy was Spat. Look what had happened to Spat. McMann wiped his face. He declared he had nothing against Spat, but it wasn't square for the guy to be shooting his trap off all the time, wasn't that so? Ray agreed. Schneck said a guy had to be fair or what was the use of it? "Yeh," said Duffy.

McMann poured himself a stiff drink, squirting in a little seltzer. "Hey, why'nt you wash Spat up?" The phone rang. Bill took off the receiver, remembering the cop who'd knocked at Paddy's flat so long ago. "Hello. Yeh? What do you mean a riot?" He put his hand over the mouthpiece. "The hotel says the neighbors've been complaining and to cut it out…Hello, if your walls were soundproof as you claim, there'd be no complaints."

"The brain guy," laughed McMann. Everybody grinned except Duffy. Why in hell didn't Mac quit that line? thought Bill. Gee, he was sick of it. Something tricky in that line about being a brain guy. He soaked a towel in the bathroom, bending over Spat. Suddenly loathing the brutality. Hell, it hadn't been a show. It was real. This was a man beaten to death almost. He washed the blood from Spat's nose and face. The towel became reddish. Spat's bleeding lips were cracked badly. He soaked the towel again as they all watched, bathing the eyes. Slowly Spat came to, peering between his bluish lids. "It hurts opening them," he said.

Poor Spat. He forced a drink of water between his lips. Spat coughed, choked, seemed to get a little better. He pushed Bill away. "Thanks," he mumbled. Bill helped him to Duffy's bed. Spat lay down.

"He took a pounding if a guy ever did," said Ray.

"His own fault," said McMann. Everybody agreed it was Spat's fault. No one said it wasn't.

After the visitors had gone, Duffy thought how McMann had framed him, stealing his kids. McMann had to be fixed. Now and then he called: "How you coming, Spat?" Finally Spat's groans got stronger. Spat was strong as a bull, thought Duff, staring at Spat sitting up in bed and fingering his swollen face. His eyes could hardly be seen. "Lucky the bastard didn't land one right on the eye, or I'd be blind as a bat," he said to the boss.

"How you feel?"

"You're a helluva swell boss." He returned from the bathroom, his hair dripping. "I look swell."

"Not my fault."

"My fault, maybe?"

"Didn't I say not to fight? That bastard's got Ray and Schneck bulldozed. It was a frame-up, plain as hell. He's out for the kids." He chucked his dressing-gown on a chair. Outside his gorgeous shell, he was skinny in pyjamas. He dressed swiftly, talking all the while.

"You let me down," said Spat, "you did."

"Could I help it with four of them? We got to spike McMann. You rest up, then round up all the kids you can find. Say, about seven tonight, to meet at the poolroom." Duffy gasped at Spat lingering. The beaten wop was himself. Duffy looked around as if maybe the Spat he used to command was hiding.

"Don't you rush me."

"Forget it, Spat. We'll fix him."

"You let me down."

"Too many, Spat. Gwan, get the kids."

When Spat was gone, Duffy felt sick. Spat mightn't ever come back. He had a good job as a numberbook and he didn't need Duffy. "Spat, too." he muttered. His face was pink in the cheeks as if from disease. He dressed, taking the elevator down to the lobby. On Eighth Avenue he darted into a drug store to make a call, dropping a nickel in the slot. In a steady voice he asked for police headquarters. A voice answered, stalling around, saying: "Will you hold the wire?" Duffy had a fear of a radio car. He said swiftly: "Tell Detective Hanrahan that the guys in the Ninth Avenue stickups are Red McMann and Bill Trent. The guys are McMann and Trent. Got it? He'll know." He hung up, walking outside. An apple-peddler clapped mittened hands, his box of red fruit waxy and artificial in the gray February light. They could trace that call. The booth Duffy had used was now occupied by a cloak-and-suiter insisting he was Simmy, yeh Simmy, she'd met him before, and could he come over?

At eight that night the proprietor of the pool parlor nodded at Duffy hurrying to the private room. "Who's that guy?" a customer asked. The prop had a reputation for being a clam. He said Duffy was a politician.

Right off the bat, Duffy didn't like the looks of things. The room was noisy, mischievous as a classroom of boys who didn't give a damn about teacher. They'd been bulling when Duffy marched in. They helloed him. None of the leaders were there, only a dozen or so of the crumbums and chiselers. Out of the twenty or thirty kids, six or seven counted. They weren't around. Spat was smoking a cigar, his battered face like a gargoyle's. The kids'd had a swell time kidding Spat, rubbing it in. Some fighter he was, the hell he was. You bunk inta door, huh Spat? Hey, Spat, who's been kissin' your puss? Hey, Spat, you thinking your mug's a beefsteak all carved up? Hey, Spat, better stick to numbers, numbers don't sock. Ha and haw and ho for Spat.

Duffy listened to them kidding around, waiting for their leaders to arrive. Ray was the first, lean, muscled, with a face like McMann's. Then Mike and husky Schneck, so wide it seemed as if a dozen inches had been cut off his height. "Hello, Duffy," said Ray smoothly. "Howya?"

"Fine, kid, how you coming?"

"Fine." Smoking to beat the band, the mob sat back for his spiel. Duffy choked inside. Ray and "Schneck had been lining them up. He was licked before he started. Mike McQuade had his hoofs on the table so they could all see he needed new soles. Babe's mouth was curved, wise-guying everybody without saying a word. Frisco whispered to Schneck and the Chisel. All these kids of his, none of them much over twenty, were sniffing around like a pack of wolves given a scent. "Give us the spiel," said Ray.

"You guys shut up and listen to me," began Duffy. "McMann and Bill've been trying to steer you wrong. This morning they asked me to lend them some of you kids to stick up a speak. I said no." They broke into voice, excited, commenting. Spat stared gloomily at Duffy. Louder than the rest, clowning to the crowd, Schneck was socking some invisible enemy. "Shut up. Shut up. I could've said yes, but I didn't want to get you fellers in trouble. I've known you a long time and it's nothing in my pocket to have some of you killed. McMann don't care."

"You're too conservative," shouted Ray.

Haw haw, listen to the big word, ain't Ray smart? Hey, Ray, you're smart. What collitch you go to? Conservative. Duffy grinned, thinking: Damn those hellcats, damn Schneck, damn Ray, they've made 'em daffy.

"You want a bullet in your hair, Ray?" asked Duffy.

"No such chance. McMann's a weasel. And we want dough. Looka the way he pulled off those jobs with the cheese store and paint supply. Slick ain't the word."

You bet they wanted dough. "We want dough," some kids hollered.

"McMann's got inside dope from Bill," said Schneck. "He's a weasel and so's Bill."

"What you driving at?" asked Duffy, avoiding Spat's smile.

"If McMann says we can take a speak, we can."

"You're crazy, Ray. where does he get this dope—this wonderful dope?"

"From Bill. Bill used to work for Stanger. He's got the ins and outs of a hundred stores."

"You've swallowed the hook. Bill's the brain guy? Bunk. Listen to me, Ray. Brain guy or no brain guy, he ain't keepin' you from dodging bullets."

The kids began to talk all at once. Mike exclaimed he was ready for anything. Christ sake, his shoes were full of holes, and every time it rained, his feet got wet. Christ sake, he wished he was in with McMann on the cheese store. It was soft for the guys in. Things were lousy when Ray and Schneck and a couple others were in and others were out. Ray bellowed that's just what McMann said. Why the hell should they starve? There was all Ninth to stick up when things cooled down. In the meanwhile a few uptown speaks could keep them in bread and butter. "McMann says we'll get a clubhouse and a chink to cook us grub. McMann's got guts. Let's take a chance with him."

They broke into voice, all the wild young voices. Duffy shivered like an old man caught up with in a dark place. Schneck was fight-talking a group, their heads lowered, glancing at Duffy now and then as if he were out of ear-shot. Duffy was licked. It was in the air. He was licked. The leaders were all tied up by Schneck and Ray. They were all for McMann. The holdups of the cheese and paint stores clinched things. They weren't saying it in so many words. It was in the air that McMann was a stronger and more profitable leader. Spat's licking proved something.

"Shut up," Duffy cried, his eyes burning little hells. "Get it straight. Me and Spat've been working and thinking for you." (Mike hollered to looka his shoes and the holes. Laughter.) "Yeh, working even if you don't appreciate it. Tell me how McMann and Bill ever met you. They came to me. They had jobs. I took them on because things were slow. Now these two eggs've gone cuckoo. They want to go in things that's bound to kill some of you."

"Me for that. A swell funeral with new shoes." They all laughed, the gang of wild boys, so intoxicated with their humor it was impossible for them to conceive death or calamity.

"And then," Ray said as if in rebuttal, as if he and Duffy were holding a debate the others didn't grasp, Duffy seconded by Spat, and Ray by Schneck, "McMann says after we get some dough from a coupla speaks, we'll rent a house, a whole house, a clubhouse for us guys where we can throw parties and sleep and knock off a dame if we wants, too."

In all the uproar they heard Duffy screaming: "Bunk, all bunk, and all of you falling for it."

"Like hell. Bill usta be in real estate. He says we can rent a house in some neighborhood for seventy-five to a hundred a month. Bill's got connections."

They couldn't get over this Spanish castle. Gee, it was just plain swell'n elegant. McMann's plans were the nuts. A clubhouse. Jumping Jesus, after hanging out on corners, in speaks and coffee-pots, and now a regular dive where a feller could drink his beer or play cards or lineup a dame. Jesus. Swarthy, frowning, his shoulders sloped, his face branded by the new power, the new enemy that had appeared against them, Spat looked at his boss. They were gaga over McMann. Showed what a little smearing could do. Ray and Schneck had sold them out. If Ray and Schneck had said: It's all the bunk…not one of them would've given a nickel for the clubhouse. Leaders. Damn them for bossing the bunch. Duffy thought: I've built up a mob for them bastards.

"All right," he said. "You want to take chances, take them. Go uptown. Don't say I didn't warn you. When you get plugged you'll remember Duffy warned you."

"No one's getting hurt," said Schneck. "Bill's got it planned."

"Who in hell is Bill, God Almighty?"

"He's a swell planner. And with McMann leading the stickups, boy, oh, boy, it's a cinch for a clubhouse." They gossiped again of that clubhouse, ignoring Duffy. Spat was out of it altogether. Hell, thought Duffy, McMann beat him up so the gang'd have a good laugh looking at him. He had his showdown. Maybe Hanrahan'd stop McMann and Bill. If not? The kids didn't give a damn about him. His guts soured at their excitement. He thought of murder, of some guy, say some dope, knocking off McMann. Some dope could fix the bastard with his crap about clubhouses. Duffy was cool inside, his mouth crisp as if from a mint drink. He sneered at the kids, that thought of his making him strong again. He said: "O.K., you kids. You wanta hold up a speak? Gwan. McMann'll see Ray and Schneck and fix it up. I'm out of it." They listened. "McMann wanted me'n Spat to split, but I won't touch it. If the stickup's pulled off, our share goes to the bunch, to the guys that won't be in on't. So Mike'll have shoes." He smiled at their laughter. Hell'n Maria. Jees. Holy Moses. That was swell of Duff. That was swell of the boss.

Ray and Schneck were silent. Schneck didn't catch on. Ray grinned in a nasty way as if to say: Hell, you ain't fooling me, Duff. McMann wouldn't've give you a lousy cent.

Duffy left, but Spat stayed behind. So Spat was trailing the mob. He'd have to fix McMann to win back control. The customers, outside, leaning on their sticks, were awed by Duffy. "Gee," said one of them, "that's the big shot." He chalked his cue enviously.

CHAPTER EIGHTEEN

It rained for many days, and the air was blue with chill. On the third morning Joe got up at six, dressing for work. Today'd be like all the others. Everyone'll make believe things are just the same. Oh, my God, why didn't something happen? He'd haul in tubs of butter like before, and everyone'd make believe things were the same. And they'd be watching, Sam and Murray and Metz, like three clever cats hoping he'd slip up. Joe lifted up the shade. The saturated light, ghostly, defeated, rolled in over Bill's sleeping face. Bill had it easy. Bill had it soft. He shook Bill's shoulder, pushing the dog to one side. Damn the mutt. Couldn't he wait with his kisses? Morning was morning to Spotty and he was always happy to be alive and see his friends alive. "Lay down, Spot. Cmon, boy. You'll get your breakfast." His hand was wet from the slobbering tongue. Bill's eyes were wide awake, as if he hadn't been sleeping worth a damn, rising out of sleep like Lazarus out of death with a comprehending knowledge. "Well," said Bill, "what is it?"

"I don't want to see all of them again. I don't want to return, Bill. All day, especially with no customers around, they'll be staring at me. I can't go back, Bill."

"You must. If you don't, it's a give-away." He averted his eyes from Joe's agonized face. It was as if a huge trap gripped both of them.

"Oh, Bill," he cried hopelessly, as if Bill were letting him down.

"You win. Go downstairs. Have Mrs. Gebhardt phone Metz you're sick and will be in tomorrow. We'll talk it over." He rolled over on his side like a prophet summoned from the grave for one last prophecy, returning to sleep again, the word spoken. Joe sighed in the dead used air of the bedroom. He opened the window to breathe the rainy air. The trucks weren't backing up to the warehouse yet, but he could imagine them, the horses lowering their meek heads. he turned on the faucet. Spotty attacked his hand, interfering with his washing up. Hell with fourteen hours of work. The hell with it. He was sick. Thank God, he was sick.

The Ninth Avenue Els rattled towards South Ferry. Glancing down to the street level, the laborers employed in the fruit and meat markets below Fourteenth Street saw the little gink; he was hot stuff that gink. Good for a laugh at seven every morning. Getting a laugh at seven was a stunt. The little dark man in a straw hat hopped out the dairy store in the pouring rain, shouting at two clerks sloshing his big window. That was funny.

When Joe failed to show up, Metz promptly thought: Oi it is him'n his brother, a shame, a verdamten shame. He couldn't say why it was such a shame except that two such fine educated boys with a good family…

Joe's absence had the effect of shoving him in a chair. Let that Hanrahan burn in hell. Detectives. American detectives. Why couldn't he work at his job without making peoples for rotten spies? He'd been a spy for a long time, spying on Joe. Phew. Metz had been born in Czarist Russia. He hadn't forgotten the elaborate spy system. He hated spies. His business was to sell cheese and butter, the best quality. Hanrahan's business was spywork. Helping the law was well and good. Every American must help the law, the law was such a baby, but where was it said in the Constitution for Americans to do spywork? The phone rang, and Mrs. Gebhardt, feeling the importance of the poor speaking to bosses, asked for Mr. Metz. She would like to say Joe was sick and said for her to call. Joe wouldn't be in today. He had the flu from the rain. He'd be in tomorrow. Metz exploded, doing what he wanted, his heart easier within him. "You tell Joe he's fired. I can't afforda sick people. I'm not sick. I send him what I owe him. What's the address?" When he went back to the counter, he was grinning, abashed. He'd over-shouted the woman. Poor woman. Always poor people. But he'd done Joe a favor. Let that cop do what he wanted without making him busy with spywork. He tapped his straw hat, winked at the clerks, who marched in wet and sulky, the rain spattering the window they'd just cleaned. "Hello," he said, "nice spring weather, ain't it?" Later he phoned the police, informing the person answering to have Hanrahan get in touch with him. Who was him? "Say Metz. He know."

Hanrahan burst out of the phone booth, cursing mildly as if too much violence'd harm the delicate balance of his digestive system. He bought a cigar from the clerk, sniffing at the premium coupons. "Counterfeit money." He put the cigar in his pocket. Standing outside, half in, half out of the rain, a kid begged for the coupons. Hanrahan handed them over, buttoning his overcoat tight over his paunch, chewing a toothpick. Men slopped past him for a pack of butts or three cigars for a dime or for wintergreen for smelly mouths, surprised at Hanrahan smoothly easing his clumsy bulk out of the way. He chewed his toothpick until the wood dissolved, the tiny mushy splinters in his gums and teeth, licking his tongue as if it were a swell morsel. The kid picked up some more coupons.

The rain didn't appear to be the soaking kind, but it did the trick, filling the depressions on the sidewalks with little pools. Everyone without rubbers was due to get his feet wet. No cooperation, thought Hanrahan philosophically. Metz couldn't wait for the kid to quit. Oh, no. Had to sack him himself because the kid said he was sick. Jesus. These foreigners and Yids never were good citizens. He pulled down his derby, thinking about Metz and the phony tipoff, not so phony either, that had been buzzed into headquarters about McMann and Bill being behind the robberies on Ninth. Bill was. McMann could be. Billy must be a corker to work in with a hound like Mac.

For lunch he ordered roast beef, arguing bitterly when he examined his portion. "Why in hell don't you serve better mashed? Potatoes are cheap as dirt with all them farmers starving."

Bill yawned awake. In the gloom, the red hair on his chest glinted dark and steely. He looked up at Joe as if he hadn't ever met him. Joe grinned, his hands restless so that they seemed grinning, his body trembling with mirth. "Mrs. Gebhardt phoned and guess what happened?"

"They made you chief cheese and raised your pay to a thousand a minute."

"Better than that. I'm canned. I'm canned."

"What?"

"Metz said for me never to show up. What luck!"

Bill wormed his feet into the step-shoes. At the sink he filled the cups of his palms with water, dousing his eyes, grunting between tastes of cool flavor as he washed his teeth. "Maybe it's not luck."

"Do you know how glad I am? Poor Mrs. Gebhardt took it hard."

"Why not? She's almost your mother-in-law."

"You picking on me again."

"Shut up." The fine teeth of his comb carved his hair into thin metallic strands. His eyes were very blue, the whites showing distinctly, dressing so swiftly Joe wondered what Bill was up to.

The flat was tight about him like a cheap uncomfortable garment. "I'm glad I'm fired."

"Ever since Hanrahan quizzed you, Metz has kept you on to spy on you." He knotted his tie. "Now they've found out what they want to know. You play sick. Get me, groan, complain, holler. Don't look so happy. You've got to convince Mrs. Gebhardt you're dying. Stay in. But don't worry. They haven't a thing on us, but playing safe never hurt anyone." He was gone, ignoring Joe's final shout about putting on rubbers.

It was a tedious day in the flat. There was no one to share his happiness with but the dog. He read a magazine and stared at the trucks. The iron gate in the printery rasped up. All day in the rain, men and horses and motors slaved at tasks remote to him. From the river the sirens and whistles were calling, crying, imploring like a mob of children's voices. They told tales of far rivers and forgotten ports. He was sad with listening, shivering, unable to forget Hanrahan, the crafty nose, the swollen cheeks. Where the hell were they going? Bill was steering for unknown harbors. Oh, Bill…Mrs. Gebhardt, her pale features seeming bleached in the pale light, dropped in to see how he was, sympathetic as he groaned and thanked her for the lemon and tea, refusing the aspirins. "One's plenty, thanks."

"You feel little better, Joe?" Each time she was so tearful he burst out for her not to worry about his job. It was slave work, fourteen hours a day for no money at all. Even if Metz worked just as hard, what was the use? The other clerks were saps to continue. At her third visit he said Bill might get him a job where he worked. She wasn't keen on the new job. He insisted she shouldn't tell Cathy. The flu was catchy.

The afternoon crawled away until he was a small boy again, actually feeling convalescent as if he'd been really sick. "How'd you know I was home?" he asked Cathy when she entered without knocking. It was simple, she said. Mom looked so sad she'd get it out of her. But he didn't look sick. She shut the door, smiling, dressed in a blue dress falling in neat folds. It was trimmed with a white collar and cuffs. In the dark blueness her neck and face were a lovely white, her eyes blue. He walked to her diffidently, his hands outstretched. Before either of them knew it, while she was still smiling like a little mother, their hands had met and he was kissing her. She pushed him away. The flat had been tidied earlier in the morning. The gas radiator was hot. The rain slanted and sang its song. They were sudden strangers who never before had met together on a week-day at this hour. Mom had been so worried she'd told her about Joe's job. Was it really so? Oh, it was awful. And was it true Bill was going to get him a job? What was wrong with that? What was wrong, as if he didn't know or had never seen Bill come in at any old hour and get up when he felt like it? What sort of job was that? Even millionaires had to go to work at ten or eleven.

"It's a better job than a bank president's." He scowled. "I shouldn't've let you kiss me."

She appraised him quickly. "You kissed me. Anyway, I never catch colds." He tugged her to his lap, shivering in the three empty rooms silent as accomplices, both of them frightened by the encouragement of the inanimate for all sorts of deeds, for murder and schemes and love. They thought of this, but not in this way. They thought: We are alone. The house was quiet. It was hard to imagine Cathy's mother downstairs or anybody in the flats. Her hands were icy; her blond hair brushed his lips. He tightened his arms, racked by this holiday in the flat, this temporary leavetaking from jobs and futures, kissing her neck and cheeks and eyelids with the tumbling madness of his youth.

She shuddered and they sat in silence a long time, dwelling together in their clasped bodies, content, wide-eyed. His lips wet through her thin dress. Pushing her from him, he thought of her slim body, soft and yielding. He got up. He didn't want to go too far. "Better go down. You don't want your mother getting wise?" She tidied up with the unconscious coquetry of a very young woman, kissed him on the lips, hurried downstairs. he listened to the sounds of her going until the house was without echo, truly sick, his body shaking, his brow hot to his hand. He was unable to read, thinking over and over again with a sad flagellation: I love her; I love her. He'd have to marry her, he wanted her too much.

After Hanrahan stepped into the rain. He visited a few pool parlors, drank a beer at several likely speaks, each time returning to the dark wet streets, the rain drizzling out of an ugly sky in which the tops of the buildings loomed distinct and sharp. He called on other places. His Chesterfield was soggy. He cursed the formal velvet collar that was no protection, thinking of big ulsters with collars high enough to protect the ears, collars that were collars, rising until they hit the lid of your derby. That was a coat. On Forty-second and Eighth the brown fort of the Franklin Savings Bank stood formidable. Behind it the smaller houses sheltered like town dwellings. It was misty, the ruby traffic eyes gleaming with an exact imperturbable beauty. Hanrahan turned down another sidestreet, the cars wheeling between the wet tenements. On the sidewalk an occasional pedestrian hurried by. Hanrahan grinned at the fellow behind the counter in a fake cigar store, pushing open yet another door. "All right, Mike," he called. "I know you're stepping on the button."

"Not me," said Mike. Hanrahan stepped inside the secret room, laughing like a good fellow. There was a bar, a mirror. At one of the tables McMann was drinking beer with a young fellow. Something like Joe, thought Hanrahan. A nice-looking fellow, and can he dress? Bill was wearing a gray suit, gray shirt with red stripe, and grayish-blue tie. It was all very neat and Wall-Streetish. Hanrahan joined them. "What you drinking, Red?"

"Beer."

"Three beers," said Hanrahan, tilting up his derby, opening his soaked coat. "I been looking ahead to this a long time, boys. What a day to be searching for one's pals! What a day! And you can't kick me out, boys. I've had my hands full finding you; not that I couldn't always pick you up, but it wasn't necessary…"

The bartender, fifty, his skull shaped hard, brought the beers. The sawdusty beer-smelling place, with one workman leaning on the bar (and confiding to the empty place where the bartender had been, how hard times were and how the district leader oughta get him a job), seemed like a nice clubroom where bulls and crooks could meet on a friendly basis. There were no jails and night courts here, no busted-in stores. Just a neutral nook where enemies could pal together in between normal hang-outs and professional duties.

"You're all wet, Hawkshaw," grinned McMann.

"I sweated finding you, but it ain't hard for a smart feller."

"Only fifty thousand speaks, and you know where to go."

"I blame near covered that many."

"Speaks go on forever," said Bill.

"No. Some day prohibition'll be dead, but even then we'll have speaks for guys who like it quiet. There always have been that kind of speak." His tiny blue eyes, above their finely wrinkled pouches, were so patently intelligent that Bill thought: He's a brain guy.

"The beer's not bad," said McMann.

"Most of your pals, Red, are sportier." He leered at McMann's shirt. "This must be Bill Trent."

"Sure he is; what you want with him?" Hanrahan puffed out his cheeks, wiping his lips and brows. "The other day a feller called up headquarters and said McMann and Bill Trent were in on the Ninth Avenue holdups." They all sat silent.

"Better trace that call," said McMann.

"Don't get sore. Probably just a crank. I'm just letting you hear what I heard." He toyed with his glass. "Don't speak much, do you, Bill?"

"I'm one of the silent kind."

"Yeh," said McMann.

"Your pal's got a sense of humor." Hanrahan appeared eager to argue any learned point. "No use pounding the streets when there's so much humor here." They smiled gently at one another. Bill observed the bartender polishing the bar. He listened to the blood pounding in his head. On the facts Hanrahan might suspect them, but could never convict. What the hell'd he have on them anyway? Suppose all the robberies were in stores he'd collected. He could shove the coincidence up his behind.

"I've always admired a sense of humor," said Hanrahan, "no matter who the proud owner. You take so many of Red's friends, nice fellows who show up for Sunday mass regular as saints. I like fellows like that with balance. A little religion ain't so bad. Am I right, Bill? Sure I am. What sense is there pounding the streets in this raw weather; the climate's changing in New York. Every season's more cockeyed. My feet are wetter'n hell. Hey, three more beers." The bartender placed the glasses down and trickled back to the bar. Hanrahan hardly paused. "I can't get over a sense of humor. That's why I stick to my job. One day a few weeks back I was passing down Eighth in the neighborhood of Twentieth when I see a coupla dames standing on the corner, nice builds. Then, some fellows pass by and one of them shoots his arm out faster than hell right up against her husband-catcher. Now that fellow had a sense of humor, a little raw and untrained, but he was all there. The dames were just bums with no drawers on. I holler out and they look me over. The funny fellow happens to be a certain chap I'm after. He spots me and runs. I chase him into a sidestreet. It's dark as hell, when I hear a gat cracking and some slugs whizzing past my face. I drag my gun out. What happened is neither here nor there. The point is, it shows you the sense of humor some boys have."

"The dames were probably sore at being cheated out of their four bucks," said Bill.

Hanrahan laughed as if that were the swellest yet, his round face quivering, his blue eyes beaming unhappily as if he realized that he couldn't fool anybody with sense with those eyes of his. He paused abruptly, idiotic. "A sense of humor's swell but sometimes, boys, and sometimes I put two and two together just for the joke of it. Now, you take those Ninth Avenue series, aren't they funny? Wiberg, Soger the pork man, Petrucci, the cheese fellow, the paint fellow, five shopkeepers mind you, not one, and all taken over by a real funny bird, a guy with humor. What a joke! All of them kicked in the pants when they had more money than was good for them laying around." He fidgeted, his belly pressed tight against the table edge. "Isn't that funny?"

"Coincidence," said Bill, "is funny as hell."

"I was about to remark that. It's funny." He accented the words unpleasantly. "What's even funnier is that the funny bird or birds have left no traces, none of those little belly laughs we fellers call clues."

"Birds fly," said McMann, his hard fists on the table, sitting very straight, his spine taut, his muscles tensed for a spring.

"I can stay here a week," laughed Hanrahan. "You birds should be at the Palace. What a pair!" They chuckled at him calling them birds. Birds. That was a laugh, as if they were the birds that had played such a riproaring joke on the storekeepers. Hanrahan winked at them. "These birds always flew the coop. Once they were chased. Once it wasn't so funny even if they made their getaway. Later combing the streets over which they'd flown, the cops found a stolen car. Soger and Wiberg tell me the birds were slim—"

"Just for a joke," said McMann, grimacing, "were they slim as us, them birds?"

"It looks as if some slim birds are the funniest blokes in New York. But one thing is especially funny. Wiberg, Soger, Petrucci, the paint guy, those four were stuck up. But Metz was burglarized. I wonder why."

"Why bother us?" said McMann.

"I want you to help me find those funny birds. I want to congratulate them personally for being so smart. I'll take the chance even though some funny birds, pigeons I think, drop things in your eye when you're not careful."

They were getting griped at Hanrahan, afraid of his laughter and small eyes. Hanrahan was a pain, not even bothering now to conceal his suspicions. Perhaps this was what the bull wanted, to dry them up, to drop vinegar in their mouths so that their faces were wry and not for laughing. They laughed, feeling stupid like men chuckling in a field with the lightning hitting all around. They were unable to speak much, the words refused to form, their throats and tongues dry and speechless, their saliva caking up. Damn the bastard. Why didn't he beat it?

Bill's head was stone, his thoughts petrified, his eyeballs hard from staring at Hanrahan, who from the very first minute had put his handcuffs on them. If there wasn't a good old law, he'd've dragged them to jail sure as fate. Why didn't he go? Either arrest them or let them alone. Bill was tired of being sported with by this fat greasy treacherous cat. He puffed thick smoke in front of him, a trick learned from Paddy, as if to screen Hanrahan from sight, hoping to irritate him, to cloud those midget eyes, hating the tedious sly humor of the man. Christ, if Hanrahan ever decided to third-degree Joe. Poor Joe. Harshly, Bill broke his mind from thought. Those roving pinpoint eyes, concentrative of Hanrahan's bulk and remorseless patience, might penetrate into his brain, right into the coiled gray matter, reading his thoughts. He vacated his mind of thought, so that it seemed a mirror without a future or a past, simply reflecting back the immediate present moment, duplicating Hanrahan.

"Ain't you got a home?" said McMann.

"One thing more, Red. It's funny for you and Bill to be buddies. What can you have in common? Why hurry me out when I like the company?"

"Hang around, but make it funny." McMann didn't smile.

"Maybe this'll make you laugh. I know why Billy boy was sacked. I know that between the time he lost his job and now, five robberies have taken place. How funny! Coincidence's funny as hell. I agree with Bill."

"I'm glad to hear it." He thought: Always uses "funny." Funny. Funny. Why? Funny is the hypnotic word, a wearing weary suggestive word. His voice spilled from his lips in liquid sounds. "Coincidences are damn funny."

"You said it. Funnier, even, when you stop to consider. Think of it. Five stores taken over by a guy with inside dope about all of them, a guy who knew or guessed when the five suckers'd have real dough. Couldn't be a relative. Nope. Imagine how funny it'd be for one guy to be related to Dutch Soger, to the wop Petrucci, to Wiberg and Metz, two Jews, to the French-Swiss mongrel who runs the paint shop. It's against biology, ain't it, Bill?"

"All funny stories are against somebody."

The solitary customer had left. The bartender with the commiserating brutal face was peering at the three at the table. He was among friends anyway, thought Bill; this was no jail. How easy it'd be to fix Hanrahan! But he'd probably be a tough bargain, and anyway it wasn't necessary to murder.

"No, boys, it couldn't be a relative, though that'd be a league of nations. But some feller was a cousin to all the private affairs of these storekeepers. This feller was related in more ways than blood. Maybe he was Bill, with Red, here, helping out?" He rose, putting on his damp overcoat, his big arms diving into the black armholes, never turning his smile away from them. "Wouldn't that be the funniest? Believe me, boys, I'm not so bad. You gave me such a good time I've no hard feelings. If I were Bill or Red, I'd say lay off. Honest, you fellers better lay off or you'll be killing some poor slob and burning for it. I'd lay off. Maybe I won't bother you if you behave. That's another joke, for all the time I'd be planning how to send you up. I'm a funny guy myself and like a joke, but certainly I wouldn't bother the avenue if I didn't want to burn…" He eased out of the door, his cheeks flushed, his eyes almost buried between their flabby lids, that fattened and rolled together when he laughed. It seemed as if he'd been with them a second or a year, implacable and vague as time. The young men wondered at his purposes, bewildered, stunned, thinking themselves forever lost. The time must come when he would get them. That was sure as fate.

"He's one of them funny bastards," said McMann. "What the hell's eatin' him to blame us? Christ. Two whiskies," he hollered, softening in his chair, his spine hitting the back of the seat, his legs relaxing, stretching enormously as if after an all-night session.

"He's a mean bastard."

"Hell with him. Circumstantial evidence in your hat. He ain't got a thing can stand up in court."

"Maybe he knows something he didn't say."

"Naw. Jus' tryin' to scare us." He leaned over, his voice steady and thoughtful, rehearsing the details of their next holdup. The uptown speak. Bill listened foggily. Hell with Hanrahan. Hanrahan or no Hanrahan there wasn't any stopping. The speak'd be safe. No cops. Only their own to deal with.

CHAPTER NINETEEN

The speakeasy was situated in a sidestreet between Broadway and Amsterdam Avenue. It was the middle reach of Manhattan, a neighborhood north of Central Park, south of Spanish Harlem. Here in a tenement block, with the street lamps shedding far-away circles of lonely light, Bill descended two cracked stone steps, rang a bell, showed his card, was admitted into the speak, the ironwork door clanging behind him. His heart didn't thud much. This surprised him. At ten o'clock he used the phone booth; behind the narrow pane of glass in the booth door, he seemed to be staring out on another dimension. The partition between two basement rooms had been knocked out. The speak was perhaps twenty feet long and fifteen wide, one of those hang-outs that existed even before prohibition, the bar near one wall, the ginzo barkeep filling the glasses. There were three tables. Two were occupied. A fat grubby man was drinking beer, reading a newspaper sedately as an old German in a stube. Three kids were laughing at the other table, with four beers each in their bellies, owning the world, now drinking whisky. God alone knew why. Everything was peaceful. It was time for the word. The operator connected him. Someone, it was Madge, was answering him from a drug store a mile away. "Hello," she said. "We're set. Are you?" "I'm settled for the night," he said. And that was all. Madge said for him to take it easy.

Bill laughed (he had had three whiskies at the bar, drinking them down in jig time and blabbing about the dame who'd jilted him. Holy hell, what a peach she was! "Gimme another shot. Maybe I'll get another date. Guess I will…" The barkeep had smiled, a low-built block with rotten teeth, but so wide and friendly a smile he appeared to have a good set anyhow. The men at the bar said nothing. One of them sniffing at the lousy drunk. The other guy, the fellow who answered the outside door, grimacing, a middle-aged Irishman with a hat worn straight on his head and looking like a cop…"Christ, she threw me down.") and laughed, obeying McMann's instructions to be noisy, laughing so they wouldn't perceive him as a quiet dog. (Only the guys holding their traps are remembered, McMann had said.) He imitated a guy with a bad jag on. Before he'd hung up the receiver he'd practically shouted: "How about a date, kid? You know where to meet me."

He staggered from the booth back to the bar. "I got a date with a peach. Meeting her in a minute. Gimme a shot." He drank, listening to his heart beating out the time, ticktocking like a machine. Nobody came in. What a swell way to build a reputation. The brain guy. He was nuts to let McMann talk him into taking chances. Showing off to convince the damn kids when they were convinced without any Nick the dare-devil stunts.

The fat man at the table swished over another page, one of those old men who take to drink because they can't fool around with the women any more and need some fun, hating to settle down. The three kids were arguing about a hockey match. The ginzo bawled out: "Say, you boids, shut up for Chris' sake, will ya?" The customers at the bar went off. Leaning heavily, Bill gazed into the opposite mirror. Down the end of the mirror, the Irishman's reflection was reading a newspaper, folded neatly on the bar, the brim of his hat low, his ears pointed for the doorbell. The ginzo yawned, mentioning to Bill with the incoherence of bartenders addressing dopey customers and guys shot under: "Yeah, women. Yeah, women they are. Yeah." He wiped the bar, fetched the kids four beers, one each, the extra one for the skinny braggart who could drink two to everybody else's one.

How long did it take for that car to come? He hated the idea of ordering another whisky. His head hurt. The stuff was lousy, lousier than hell. Again he belly-ached about his girl, obnoxious to himself. The kid who could drink two to everybody else's one was rushed into the toilet, where he puked, and brought back by his buddies like a conquering Caesar from the wars, the ginzo grinning, the fat old man to whom this was excitement and life and youth exclaiming like a philosopher that you shouldn't mix drinks. The Irishman looked up once, turned the next page of his paper as if he were the weariest bloke, sick of kids among other gripes. Just as things were settling down, the doorbell rang, everyone wide awake, the old man, the barkeep, the Irishman hurrying to answer, the kids laughing, the one who'd puked glaring with yellow eyes bathed in nausea and disillusionment. They're here, thought Bill. Christ. It was snappy once it started. But in the interval, the split second before the gang entered or the customer—it might be a customer—Bill's mind was one dark flash, unhuman and telepathic as a voice sent over a wire. He seemed to see Madge, whore Madge getting the call, she got the call, whore Madge hurrying out past showcases, syringes, a soda fountain, perfumes, kotex, hurrying to the car where McMann sat with the kids, McMann shooting down to the speak, when'll they come, what the hell, Hanrahan, it wasn't Hanrahan but the Irishman backing in, hands high above his head, retreating before a round steel eye pressed into his belly. McMann held the gun. Schneck and Mike heeling behind him.

"Get the hell up against the wall. Alla you. Snap it. Cmon, wop," cried McMann. The barkeep smiled, then his face fell into a grim angry mouth, popping out from behind the bar, joining the quaking old man. "Hands over your damn heads." The old man lifted his hands, gripping his paper. "Drop it."

In the silence Bill listened to the paper dropping. He stood next the old man, the bunch of them rounded up by Mike, lined up with the kids, the one who'd puked suddenly appearing ill again as if biting back another spasm. Schneck ducked behind the bar, pulling open the cash register, stuffing the bills into his pocket. Rolling out, he joined Mike. Both of them pointed squat guns. Schneck, his chin white as ice, but resolute, went through the pockets of the customers.

Two fives from the old man. Schneck dropped the silver to the floor, pocketing six bucks from the three kids. Their watches flashed a second and were gone. The ginzo surrendered a fat roll, a stickpin, a ring. Bill lost his wallet and watch, the Irishman a wallet, ring, and Colt revolver. The pockets of Schneck's overcoat were the common repository as property changed hands in a split second, the air hot and dead, the Irishman blanched and ferocious, the ginzo staring. As if opening his eyes, Bill suddenly realized what he'd known all along. All three stickup men were wearing black masks, McMann aiming his gun at the Irishman's belly, Mike, Schneck. "Alla you guys stay put or I'll bang your guts." McMann retreated like a phantom, walking backwards with his assistants as if they were a different breed of men. Schneck's shoulders filled the doorway, then Mike's; finally McMann like the last vanishing apparition in a dream was framed for all their hate to see, going out of sight. He was gone.

The fat man held his hands overhead, his face round and pale, his eyes excited at being young again for a second. The ginzo snarled: "Bastards." While all of them were rooted, reaching for heaven, the Irishman moved courageously, seeming swift because they were stones, peering out at the door, his body pressed to the wall. The car started up with a swift chugging. The Irishman rushed out, rushed in. "Clean gone. The tail-light off."

The skinny kid puked, gazing down at his own nausea. Christ, cried his friends, laughing a little. What a holdup and looka what the louse had done, looka the damn louse! The barkeep mopped up the mess, pouring a few drops of C.N. "You kids get goin'. N' forget it. You wouldn' sick the cops on us?"

"What about our dough?"

"My watch."

"Hell," said the barkeep, "you saw what they hooked on me. Between us two your Ingersoll's not much. Forget it'n see me tomorrow. Gimme a chance to square it. I'll make it up." They departed grumbling, grinning at the sick kid. The fat old man was a steady. They said nothing to him. He asked about his dough. "You no lose, mister, you know me long time." The old man said O.K. and left. The ginzo put the mop away. He and the Irishman surrounded Bill.

"Jeez," cried Bill. "Lose my girl. What a peach! Lose my dough and watch." He breathed his whisky breath at the hard faces to prove how drunk he was. "Jeez."

"We only seen you here a coupla times," said the Irishman. "How do we know you ain't in't?"

"Ain't in what?"

"You know what."

"You're crazy as hell." He stared at the ginzo's lips jutting out dark and red, at the Irishman's pale sweaty face, furrowed and crafty: "You seen 'em take my stuff. And what about the other guys?"

"We don't know you."

"Don't you pick on me. Hell with that. How about the fat guy, them puking kids?"

"They're nothin'. How about you?" The Irishman's body bulked between the door and Bill. "Who'd you phone?"

"My girl."

"You sure?"

"I can prove it. Here's the number. She always waits for my call in a drug store."

"I thought she kicked you out."

"This is another one."

The Irishman pulled out a nickel. "The boys left me something. Call that number. The women like you, huh?"

Bill laughed at the fear crawling in him, stepping into the booth, praying. He bit his tongue, trapped in that narrow space with their bodies crowding close. Lucky they had no guns. He'd once seen a knife kill a man up in Paddy's flat. He dropped the nickel, a voice answered. It was the drug-store man. The Irishman took the receiver, his body squeezing against Bill's. "Just to settle a bet, mister. O.K.? A frienda mine said he spoke to his girl in your drug store awhile ago. We think he's the bunk. How about it?" The drug-store man said about twenty minutes ago one of the phones had rung and a girl had answered. "What sorta girl, mister?" The drug-store man tittered. A very young girl, pretty, and he lost his bet, lots of girls and fellows used his place as a headquarters. They came out of the booth. "You got your damn nerve," said Bill. "It ain't my fault you got stuck up. First you rob your customers with stiff prices for lousy stuff and then you blame your hard luck on them. Howda I know you didn't fix this stick-up yourself?"

"Cmon," said the ginzo. "Times are hard and why give us trouble? Stickups do us no good among the trade." He smiled, his sleek clean-shaven skin stretched tautly across his oval face. "We'll feed you all the stuff you want. On the house until you figger we're square. Don'tcha blame us. We'd awondered about the pope himself if he was here."

Bill lifted up his collar. "That's a go. I had near ten bucks. Hell, I ain't got a cent for my date."

The Irishman tapped his arm. "I'm comin' along to see the dame. You won't mind, will ya?"

The ginzo laughed. "Course not. Why'n hell should he when he's gonna lap up all the stuff he wants?"

Anything to get out. "Come along, weisenheimer. See the dame, but I wouldn't come here again on a bet."

"O.K.," said the ginzo. "You don't want free stuff, you don't havta." Bill and the Irishman walked up the dark street. The wind was icy. Bill felt better. The mick had no gun. Even if Madge beat it, he could knock the guy over, at least he had a chance. Under the Neon sign of the drug store, inside the entrance, Madge was tapping her heels. Soon as she saw Bill she rushed out. "You keep me waiting, you stiff." The Irishman apologized. Guessed he was wrong. And it was free drinks. He retreated, murmuring vaguely about free drinks. Bill put his arm about Madge, kissing her.

"What the hell?" she said. He slapped her arm. "That was close," he said, patting her hand. Her face had been cold, a formal design with the lips painted darkly, surprise checked, her eyes deep with the color of it. "What was close?"

"The closest shave a fellow could have. Don't look back." He hurried her along down a sidestreet towards Broadway. Long rows of slummy apartment houses, dim lights in the vestibules, lit their path to the glare of the avenue. He whistled a cab. "Loan me a couple bucks till I get my cut tonight." The cab jerked forward. His hand cupped her knee.

"Sponging, huh?"

"I said you'd get it back."

"Hell." Her face was like a child's in the semi-dark. She was wearing a brown coat in which her legs seemed longer than ever. "What close shave?"

"That guy with me was from the speak. They guessed I'd tipped the guys off. Lucky Mac worked things out so carefully. Lucky I had a date with you. Lucky you spoke at the drug store."

"I was worried when the drug-store fellow told me about some guy wanting to settle a bet."

"If you'd a stood me up I'd've been forced to slough that investigating committee on his beak." The tires were zizzing him away from peril, the winter streets slipping by in big black squares, nameless and distant. He relaxed, his fingers on her cool naked thigh. He didn't kiss her, smoking his butt. Through the thin blue haze, his lips were apart. He might've been exclaiming: Oh, what a break!

"It's cold," she said, edging closer to him. She didn't get him at all. What the hell! It was all over with, he was out of it all right, what the hell was he moping for? She decided he was worrying about his share of the stickup. That was something she could get. She asked him about it. How much was his cut? He thought it ought to be pretty big. Damn right. He'd been close enough to real trouble for a good cut. He was soft in the brain to take the chance. Damn all hell. One of the kids could've been in the speak. Why him? He didn't expand the idea. He thought McMann was out to get rid of him, to get him in dutch, to get him killed. If McMann had been necessary to him in the beginning, he'd been necessary to McMann. But now they were blowing up big, the kids were practically their property; the burglary of Metz, the stickups of the paint supply and the speak, clinched it. They were shooting up with talk of a clubhouse. What the hell did McMann need him for? The hard red face of the bastard, the small red eyes never twinkling, never mad, but always cool and plotting. The damn devil. McMann didn't need him, and when a devil didn't need a guy…He wiped his brow, remembering the terror, the ginzo and the mick wedging him into the phone booth like a rat backed up against a wall by two cats, their breaths hot, their eyes hot with blood lust. He must've been punch-drunk not to have felt the terror of that, ringing the drug store, his life worth zero. Madge, her thigh against his own, thought she'd worked him up at last. He was shivering. She thrust her hand against his chest. Suddenly, out of fear and hatred, he smacked her across the face. She bolted back into her corner of the cab, glaring. "Cut it," he said.

"You bastard. What you mean slough' me?" She couldn't get him. A minute ago he was steaming up a lather and now he was an iceberg, sloughing her, the nervy bastard. He was a funny guy, damn him. A queer. A phony. A twist. Because he seemed strange, the whorish questing in her always seeking, without her even knowing it, the something in the male beast to cherish seemed fulfilled. He was happiness. The different guy, the swell guy. He was funny. Gee, she loved him even if he was a queer. sloughing her for nothing at all. Her eyes were moist. For the first time in months she felt a passion, a love, an emotion known when she'd lived out in Brooklyn and lined up for a guy she liked extra, getting nothing out of it but her pleasure. Now again, after the professional routine, the onslaughts of a thousand men built the same way, this passion swelled her breasts and lay between them like a rare flower. She breathed harshly, haunted by the quest, the search for happiness and a swell guy fulfilled, her lips hanging, her eyes larger and overwhelming her entirely like two huge misty pools from which in some mystic way her body flowered. She leaned towards him, forgiving as a beaten dog.

He was sorry he'd cracked her, puzzled at this yearning giving of her. What the hell was she acting for? She looked like a dope, a school kid. So that was it. Both of them misunderstood passion. She thought he was a funny bird, loving him because maybe he was the swell guy every dame dreamed of, the swell guy who was different, who had class, something. He thought she loved him because he was brutal. It was a cockeyed feeling, the reasons and the underlying emotions tangled up in one dark rose of love. The cab hurled along, its horn screeching. The streets were left behind like many yesterdays. They seemed to come to one another from across the city, each from some lonely place, no longer thinking or wondering why it was so.

She slipped him all her dough, sixteen bucks. He paid the hack, grabbed her arm, walking languidly against the wind, their thighs grazing. They registered at the desk of a small hotel in a sidestreet off Sixth Avenue. The street was full of restaurants, lobster joints, ginzo spaghetti houses. The three hotels in the block catered to fast-time crowds, small stone buildings that had known prime twenty years ago, even then decadent, as if somehow they could never be up to date. Grifters, racketeers and their molls, lived here. Bill had no baggage. He'd been here before, in this musty lobby with the boys scanning the form sheets. "I'll be back soon."

"Don't be long, honey," she said.

He glanced back at her from the door. She was standing at the end of the faded carpet, a little to the right of the desk and the impassive hotel clerk, a young ambitious man trying to uphold the grand tradition of hotel clerks in this joint, smartly dressed, polite as a diplomat; Bill's eyes swift across the lobby, the slick boys reading, two men heeling two doll-like dames, his impression was of something smooth as grease rubbed across the dank woods of the old hostelry. Madge smiled, her lips without any wild red. Lipstick was over his mouth. He took out his handkerchief as if signaling he'd be back soon. His stupid heart was beating and he thought of it with an old cynicism, stepping briskly. She was nuts about him because he'd slammed her. The secret of his success was a sock in the puss. Holy hell, just a caveman. But she was nuts about him. That was something among all his troubles. His head rang. The glitter of Broadway, like perfect teeth shining in the mouth of a diseased hag, dazzled him. He was awed by the city, this warren of six million lives, oh, little loves, little lives hoping, sweating towards the alluring promise of wealth and fame. Oh, to win, to come out ahead, to beat the racket. Christ, all he wanted was a few thousand. A fat chance with Hanrahan after him, with McMann and his sneaky brain-guy stratagems. Damn it, he ought to be glad someone, even a little bat like Madge, cared for him. She was his other self found again, his dark sensual self lost from flesh and returned in heart.

He hopped a cab, rubbing the handkerchief across his mouth. It stained red, the smudged color the blood of another time. Madge. Madge. He smoked furiously, aching to be with her, thinking of her legs, the cool thighs, the small young-girl breasts, with a new appreciation. She wasn't just a good piece any more. She was the world because she cared for a guy called Bill. Groggy, exultant, he paid the fare. The cab shot away, the tail-lamp a retreating sad eye. Twenty-third hid in the dark mist of February as if no soul lived in any of its houses.

McMann had been drinking with the kids, all of them surrounding the bottle of rye. The kids were celebrating, boisterous with success like a winning football team on Saturday night.

"Here's the brain guy." Schneck staggered over to Bill, his huge body like a wrestler's, his breath dark brown with whisky smell. He circled his shoulders fondly, his face pale and strong as a butcher boy's. "Want your cut, huh? We'll give ya a cut like the rabbi." Bill took the drink McMann offered. Mike declared he could kiss Bill. He thanked them for the compliments, nodding at Ray's buzzings. Ray looked more than ever like McMann's kid brother. Mike blabbed of the swell kicks he was going to buy. Three pairs of kicks at one clip, that was him all over, a sport. Their talk swung in low heavy circles. Schneck laughed, and in one triumphant voice all three kids were boasting of what a pipe the stickup was, what a swell guy McMann was, what a swell guy Bill was, of the best, both of them. This exultation of the mosquitoes filled his ears with irritation. This exultation was precisely what McMann wanted. Red devil with the real sting. Bill stared at the enigma of McMann, without comradeship, chilled, hostile, preparing. He told them of what had happened, his close shave.

He could've been dead as easy as hell if the coin hadn't come up lucky.

The liquor hadn't warmed McMann, his small reptilian head poised, the features built close to the bone. "What the hell, Bill. It was figured out O.K. Madge was there, wasn't she? You were covered. You were safe."

"I didn't like it. It was too damn close."

The kids clamored for him to forget it, to be a sport and forget it, riding him about Madge. Jesus, what a dandy life with a dame chipping in her love for nothing. Ray said heartily he'd been searching for a nice dame to keep him going, but he had no luck.

"You ain't got no personality," roared Schneck.

"I ain't got luck."

"No personality."

"Shut up, you guys." McMann handed Bill his wallet and watch. "The brain guy's here and we're splitting. Them customers were chiselers." Bill hated McMann and his young cubs, glancing away so McMann couldn't see his hate. McMann opened the table drawer, heaping the watches and rings near the bottle like an offering. "Somea the jew'lry'll gross cash. The Irishman and the wop had plenty. We got three hunerd in cash, two watches from the kids. Waltham'n Elgin. A swell watch and stickpin from the wop. A good ring from his pal. Not bad." He admired the large white diamond glinting in a circle of blue chips. He counted out twenty bucks, added the Waltham's octagon to the pile. "Mike's cut." The kids were watching quietly. They weren't so drunk now, with all that dough to sober them up. "You might get ten in hock, Mike." Mike took his share, dangling the octagon on its chain like a pleased child. "Thirty bucks'n the Elgin for Ray. Ray drove the car, that's why he gets more'n you guys. And thirty'n no watch for Schneck." The kids all had their share. There was two hundred left over, a watch, two rings, the stickpin. Who'd get them?

"I'm in a hurry," said Bill. "I've a date—"

"Hold your pants'n. Now, Duffy'n Spat don't havta get a cut. Did'n Duffy say his share was to go for the boys? Hell with'm." He gave the kids ten bucks more a man. "Two hunerd's left. The watch ought be good for forty in hock." He fingered the rings, squinting at the stones as if estimating how many carats, how many flaws, while they stared at him, the big shot turning jeweler easy as hell. "Them rings is a hunerd in hock. The stickpin's a carat. Say another hunerd. That's two-forty in jew'lry. Two hunerd in cash. Our pal's in a hurry to knock off Madge, an' we don' blame'm so here's a hunerd for'm and a hunerd for me." On the round table the platinum watch, the diamond rings, and the stickpin, resting on the crystal, were all that remained.

Everybody had had a square deal. The kids exclaimed damn right they were. Holy Moses, it was square. They hadn't seen so much dough in a million years. If it'd been Duffy's job, Duffy'd akept more'n two hundred between him and Spat. Here Mac and Bill, planning it all, working on the job and all, only taking two hundred. Everybody concentrated on the jewelry. What'd be done with that? McMann gulped another drink, grinning at Bill. "Me'n Bill've been thinkin! This jew'lry's worth two-forty about. That's plenty for a clubhouse. A reg'lar place. We can get a house somewhere for about a hunerd a month." The kids were speechless at this grandeur, shouting, laughing, important as hell. McMann promised them a future.

"What about Duff?' asked Ray.

"I'll give'm the car. It's a good car. I hocked it from a rich guy."

Schneck beamed. "A clubhouse, gee!"

"Two-forty's two months' rent. We're gonna be somebody. Don' you worry. Me'n Bill don' sleep. We're gonna make dough'n be big shots. Al stickin'll wear diamonds." He flashed the stickpin at the kids, intoning his fairy-tale. It was even money on it.

Bill put on his overcoat. McMann had the kids hypnotized with that clubhouse, the clubhouse palace. They were drinking goofily. Somebody in the world. McMann wasn't so dumb. They could rent a place for a hundred a month, a fifteen-footer on a side-street with three floors. That'd be one helluva palace. God alone knew what McMann was thinking in his bean. You couldn't guess from the words he spoke. "Give Madge the works for me," said McMann. "How's the ball of your feet? Say, when a brain guy gives a dame the works it's the works."

"You're funny as a crutch." This bag of his being a brain guy was n.g.

"Don't you be sassin' your buddies." He clowned.

"I'd like to boot your fanny for a week." Yes, kick him to death. That'd be fun. The kids might believe the spiel of brain guy, but the whole line stunk to him. Brain guy. So then you stuck this same brain guy in a hole as if brain guys were worth less than a nickel a dozen.

"Boot Madge's fanny. You'll like it better." McMann was a riot.

"Maybe you know from experience," said Bill, exasperated.

They laughed like crazy men as if he'd hit the truth. The hell with them. He was the goat. If anything went wrong he'd be the goat. Proof was putting the so-called brain in danger of having it shot out. So long, they hollered. The cab jammed brakes on, at his signal. He shivered in its interior, staring numbly at the city, black, repellent, a huge desert fantastically shaped in the image of a city of the dead. There was no life in the world but that in his body and in one other body. Stepping out of the corridor into her room, he guessed something was wrong. A bottle of gin on the dresser was half gone. In violent yellow pyjamas, conservative on her who was so slim, her breasts and hips outlined modestly, Madge greeted him too gaily. She should've been drunker if she'd had all that gin. Yet she was almost sober, strolling towards him as he slammed the door, like a soldier in her yellow pants. Somebody's been helping her put away that gin.

"Hello." He laughed. He was aware of his mind's coolness. Oh, he was smart. So smart that Hanrahan was gunning for him, and McMann doublecrossing him like the rat he was, and Joe in trouble. His wisdom was sour. She neared him. He smacked her cheek, his eyes disgusted. Damn her. Damn Hanrahan and McMann. Damn them all. He was like a corpse defeated by the purposes of other men, striking out against life. All life, all life's puppets were banded against him. God damn the lice. "You bitch. Turn my back and you lay for any guy at all."

"What the hell's eatin' you?" she yelled bitterly. "I don't get a bastard like you."

"But every bastard does." She was perplexed at her emotion, by his dark figure lowering in the room. She stared, rocked by a puzzlement that was lust as well as curiosity. She didn't know what to say or do. She couldn't get the fact of chastity to one man. What difference was it? The guy was gone, wasn't he? It was over. She only liked Bill. She pulled out three dollar bills from her pocketbook, offering them to him silently, her homage, her head obsequious as a slave's. There. That was proof she liked only him. He could have all her dough. She looked like an abandoned child, her thin face so high above the carpet. This face was pleading, alone in space, alone in the space of his thought, her deep childish eyes almost causing him to forget the body in pyjamas, the torso in yellow silk, her legs and thighs. He concentrated on thought of her face, ravishing it with his mind and soul, so that his body also quivered and was gone, and he was but a pair of eyes isolated in immensity, glaring at the last human, the last woman's face. He put the three dollars in his pocket. This was the action of a body forgotten, a body left on earth, obeying the earth's laws. "All right, Madge, let's forget it."

"How we gonna eat, honey?" she asked. Sure, she had to keep her job and he his. It was tough going, but what could they do?

"I got a hundred bucks. We're staying here until it's gone. Then you can go back to Paddy."

"It'll go like hot cakes. Once in a while. A coupla guys a day'd help keep us, Bill. That ain't much, an't's money."

"You ever lay for McMann?"

"Why not? He slipped me ten bucks once to lay for a coupla friends."

"Ray and Schneck? Or was one of them Mike?"

"I don't know their names, honey." The life of the elapsed months covered him. He was baffled by a huge mourning, sorry for her and himself. McMann's head and grim body took shape before him like an apparition. His life was in danger, he thought with a detached grief, as if that life had already been slain. No trusting McMann. The day'd come, must come, when it'd be showdown. He stared into her eyes and saw the time to come.

She pushed her body next to him. Was there anything wrong? She tried to comfort him, unbuttoning his vest. They clasped, but still he was black with the stupidity, the purposelessness of life. All he'd wanted was a few thousand. Was that wanting the world? It seemed that way. God, it was awful. They sat on the couch and he held her quiet the longest time, kissing the whore's cheeks, gently treating the body that'd just been mauled by a customer. By loving her so he was handling himself gently, raising himself up again to God's double, rebuilding the God in him. He was no better than she, and if she could become precious, he too must rise. He didn't' care what she thought. Perhaps she didn't think. He only saw her childish eyes, believing in him.

It was a new thrill for Madge. A new love. A new kick out of life. It was like her first memory of mass, the first purple wonder, the deep dark purple of something holy with fire. (As he gave the whore the sense of religion, his brother was negating it in Cathy.) He was her swell guy. Gee, she was lucky to have him. He was worth a million.

He took a drink of gin, sharing the glass. They went to bed, the aura of the strange minute vanishing from their passion. After, he'd fallen asleep. Later rousing himself to stare from one elbow's height at her sleeping faun body, he forgot altogether, pressing his body down, his mouth on her lips feeling a joy from God, but not like that other greater joy. His breath was foul from gin and the exhaling odors of the flesh. This love perspired. Their mouths were flat. It was the love of those who are to die.

CHAPTER TWENTY

Well, he had no job and that was swell for a time. No more slaving at Metz's. Every morning he toured New York, leaving the house around ten o'clock just as Bill'd be yawning over on his side for a second sleep. Not that it mattered when he left. There were entire days and nights when he never saw Bill, when Business kept him forty-eight hours and more in a stretch.

First stop was usually the Library on Fifth. Entering the huge high marble hush, slithering his feet along the stone floor, he'd take a seat in the magazine room. It was a poor man's club if there ever was one, bums, the seedy genteel, young men and women without a cent, would get their magazines at the counter and waste an hour or so. Joe noticed one fellow who always read the *Saturday Evening Post*, a nickel mag. What a sap when he could borrow such high-class, expensive mags as the *Cosmopolitan* or the *American Mercury*. Shabby Spaniards, shabby Englishmen, shabby Germans would read the literature of their native lands. Joe'd get a magazine, read for two or three hours, finishing one, then tiptoeing to the desk for another, handing his slip to the pale people behind the counter, who appeared to have other lives, but not happy ones.

He'd leave the club when his eyes hurt, zigzagging from avenue to avenue, from Park to Madison to Seventh, and then back again, exploring each little pool of life off the main rivers, playing sometimes he was dodging Hanrahan, dodging the cruel fate that must overtake the Last Of The Trents. He didn't have any doubt that Hanrahan'd get them both one day. He'd've liked to run away even if Bill said they were safe. There were no jobs and he didn't look for any. It was a city without work, although it seemed busy and prosperous. He'd tell Bill he'd searched high and low. In the beginning he'd sat around agencies, leaving the house at five in the morning. There was nothing. If he carried the paper in his pocket, the classified ads turned outwards, that was good enough. Mrs. Gebhardt knew he was faking, but she never said a thing to Joe outside of good-morning. He had a hunch the old lady was beginning to regard him as Bill's kid brother after all.

The walks were burials. Here, as if a thousand miles deep in the silence of the earth, stunned by the multitudes of the city among whom he walked like a ghost, he began to see with startled eyes the extent of the life of which he'd been but one stupid bug at Metz's, never dreaming the magnitude he crawled. He lost Hanrahan and his own life in this other life, striding Fifth, among its tribes of scarlet-lipped women, their fox terriers and limousines, jostled on Sixth, where the unemployed mobbed the agencies, crowding in front of the white cards scrawled with sucker jobs, adventuring in his own neighborhood, where the poorest Irish and German and Americans had dug themselves in against poverty like soldiers against an attack. He'd cut east and south into the ghettos of Avenues A, B, C, retreating north to Gramercy Park's green opulence. He slitted his eyes against the ever-flying dust of the city, dodging traffic, pausing a second on lower Eighth Avenue to witness a gypsy wedding party, greasy and smelling, exiting out of a store, the bride pale as a fish and dressed like a cheap Turkish princess, everyone piling into second-hand autos; or, pausing vaguely, dreaming on his city travels, the city of a million far-aways, he'd watch a peddler, or the pinhead at Hubert's Museum, or be one of an excited crowd with a woman hollering: He cut her head off, the police shoving everyone back, an ambulance on the curb like a vulture. The city opened its blinds to him on a dozen streets and avenues. He witnessed the terrible vision of millions of lives, millions living and dying in a few miles. He had no love for the town. One could not love the city. It was one of God's uglier creations, a dinosaur, a whale. And all the millions were shadows. He was bewildered, stopping at Union Square, by a Negro with Othello's head hurling heart and soul against capitalism, by the thousand screamers and exhorters addressing the shadow folk. The city was thronged with machines like animals, and people like animals with heads like horses or cows or wolves. Panhandlers accosted him for a cupacoffee. Couldn't they see he was broke? The city people were blind, shadows couldn't ever see.

Bill supplied him with cash, and around noon he'd duck in at a cafeteria and get a sandwich or a plate of spaghetti in a green-painted place on a sidestreet, the proprietor treating him as if he were a lord. Everybody was on the ragged edge, and all customers were millionaires. And all these days in early March would thunder into three o'clock, for the city respected one force, and that Time. No matter where he'd walked in early morning and afternoon, at three he'd be in the locale of the Washington Irving High School. The gongs ringing, the pretzel-sellers and candy-women, nearly all old squatty sexless creatures, competing for the nickels of the young girls. From the block-long school looking like an office building, the crowds of girls'd fill the afternoon with youth, with a feeling of fertility and potential motherhood. Some of them were rouged young ladies, but mostly they were awkward and loud as boys, their hard toughish bodies like boys', too fat or too skinny, like some gawky intermediate sex before womanhood. He'd be at the corner drug store, observing the city in another of its aspects, the city of a million young girls.

Taller and prettier than the majority, Cathy's pale face with blue eyes, her yellow hair edging the dark hat, waving her hand at his smiling progress, would appear in reality as well as in thought, her hair seeming yellower, her eyes bluer, his heart rising to some function of sight so that he saw with heart as well as eyes, his body pulsing, his vision losing steadfastness so that she moved towards him on rhythmic beating successive waves of emotion. He'd take her brief-case and they'd walk home in the warming weather, sitting in Union Square, busy with conversations never remembered, that were not to be remembered, careless, light, giddy, like the incredible somersaults of summer grasshoppers. All about them the city hummed and thousands passed with distressed faces. They were a union of two hemmed in by the grand empty visages of the city's banks and high buildings. Out of it all, they talked. Down among the gray glooms of lofts, they'd venture more happily towards Washington Square, with the kids playing and the Arch's gallant but meaningless barrier. Through narrow streets like veins running through pale masses of little lives, they'd gradually approach their own house. He'd say good-by in the hallway—this the only speech ever remembered during these March walking days.

Upstairs in his room, thought of her was chaotic. He seemed to have no idea of what she looked like or what he looked like himself, as if both of them were enthralled by the city and made into shadows like everyone else. He couldn't concentrate on eye color or lip movement. It seemed to him he was empty of gross hard life, light as air, unconfined as air, with but one thought, one idea, and that his love. This love was the sum of both their bodies and individualities. Their flesh shattered, mated in ecstasy, fleshless, wild. How could he tell how either looked or what they'd spoken of when his feeling for her was so voiceless, the shadow of another life? Good-by, Cathy. Good-by. Hell with that. He wanted to be with her, stay with her all the time. If he didn't say good-by, didn't float up to his room…Love meant union, the real union of bodies, just as they now felt that other giddier mental happiness. One was good as the other. His eyes began to flicker craftily like those of a man honestly in love and wondering how he can love the more.

McMann got rid of the stolen jewelry, hocking the rings and stickpin with certain fences. He sold the tickets and had about three hundred in cash. The watch he kept. They divided another hundred equally, smiling on lower Sixth Avenue in a neighborhood of French delicatessens and bleak spinsterlike houses. "The two hunerd's for the club. Right? Them kids don't hafta know every damn thing."

"You're a prize. You'd gyp your grandmother."

"So would you."

They grinned, their lips fixed with the mutual admiration of two outwitting a third party. It was eleven in the morning. The El curved at right angles, looping east. It was a gray morning; February had ended on a deathbed of immense gray clouds, March born gray as the mother month. They discussed a few of the houses they'd seen, knowing all the time which one both of them preferred. It was funny. They had the dough. The decision was easy and yet they argued, sharpening their teeth.

"You'll tell the kids it was my idea. I'm the brain guy. You've elected me." Bill grinned again as if to add: Whatever you're planning on doing, don't think I'm a fool falling blind.

"What's wrong with that?" His profile was all hard straight lines, the cigarette rigid in his lips. No guessing what a phiz like that thought. Bill regretted his wisecrack. He'd never learned to keep his trap shut.

"Nothing's wrong." His heart was weighty and dull before the danger. Here his body was keeping step, his body was safe so far, but there was no ease for him. McMann couldn't kid him forever. He knew the rat was waiting for the chance to get rid of him. For an infinite second McMann was ageless, neither old nor young, with the vague ageless eternity of a gun or a knife.

"You're drivin' at something, Bill."

"You know what it is, well as me. What do you mean by this brain-guy crap?" Oh, what a fool he was, an ass speaking out of turn, tipping McMann! His words were the vilest idiocies. His head must be softening up.

"You're nuts." His teeth showed in even rows out of his red face. It was childhood returning to Bill again. He grinned sickly. Here were the woods and himself in the role of Little-Red-Riding-Hood. "We gotta build each other up. You gotta make those kids think you're somebody."

They dropped the subject as if it were some common secret possession brought up out of a chest and put back again. They were too busy to bother much, examining the house. It was a three-story sixteen-footer on Sixteenth Street, situated in a block of tenements, the ash-cans and kids in two armies. Across the way was a butcher store. In a big cleared space on the corner the Socony Company sold oil. Eighth Avenue wasn't a hundred feet away and because of the gas-station their house was practically the corner. They received the key from an Armenian tailor who occupied the first floor, passing through the separate entrance to the upstairs. The two floors were exactly alike, two three-room flats in the front and the same number in the rear overlooking a yard with a clumsy shed and a small tree with gaunt branches like a thin beggar's arms. It was part of the works. "Some joint," said McMann, sniffing at the unused atmosphere of the wood and peeling paint. The floors were dusty and the former occupants had worn black silk dresses. "It'll need a good alteration." He said the landlord ought to take a month's rent, and then with the money left they could buy paints. The kids could clean and paint their clubhouse up.

"How do ya know he'll only take one month?"

"He'll take what he can get. If we sign a lease we ought to be good for two months' concession."

"Boy, we'll have a joint." He smiled blandly, his eyes glinting with a sense of might as if he were a baron or millionaire setting up an establishment. "Then a speak'll chip in, huh?"

They returned the key to the Armenian, a burly man with thick hair and a curved nose that made him appear Jewish. He stood in his undershirt above the pressing-machine, the pressed suits hanging like an army of apparitions behind him. "You take the house?"

"If we do, you're in luck," said McMann.

"All political clubs have lots of suits to press and clean for the members. Politicians are snappy," Bill said.

"And dresses maybe," laughed McMann.

"It won't be that kind of political club."

"I give you good service," said the Armenian with an effect of bowing.

"Me'n him," said McMann, "get a cut. Savvy? A nickel on each suit you press. We're the leaders at the club." The Armenian shook his head.

At the gas-station they glanced back at the house, whitewashed by the gas people on the side facing the avenue. "Why grab a nickel on a suit? It won't make you rich."

"Won't make ya poor. Anyway, it's the principle. All I wants is our stuff pressed free. Big shots are chiselers. You oughta get it, you're a brain guy." Bill did most of the talking at the real-estate office. The old feeling among the typewriters clicking out the February statements, pictures of buildings on the wall with certificates of membership on boards and taxpayer groups. They sat opposite a partially bald man with thin dry hands. His name was Gunther and he had the district charted in his head, every house, every loft. After palaver and mutual heeling, they shook hands. Gunther gave Bill a receipt for two months' rent. McMann counted out eighty dollars. It was a hard bargain, said Gunther. Eighty a month was twenty a week, less than twenty, as there are more than twenty-eight days a month. And the month's concession. Why didn't they consider a lease? Not that leases meant anything in these times. Bill declared he'd rather be a monthly tenant. Listen, begged Gunther; he was the agent and knew the details of the estate owning the property. It'd been empty over a year. If their club would sign a lease for two years he'd get the estate to clean and paint their floors from top to bottom. Wouldn't that be ideal for their organization?

"And you'd get a larger commission," grinned Bill. "What do you say to his proposition, president?" he asked McMann.

"Oke, secret'ry. The organization can use the dough that woulda gone for painting to buy furniture." They chuckled at the estate that was going to get the raw deal, and why not? It was rich as hell.

"It's a go, Gunther. We'll sign a lease for two years, but at seventy-five a month." There was a long debate, with the agent insisting they were ruining him, but finally it was settled. "As for cleaning and painting, that won't cost you much. I know these offices. Loads of carpenters and painters are working for what they can get these days. Union wages be damned." It was settled . They were to move in the first of April. "Now, president, hand Mr. Gunther a ten-spot for cigars." Gunther was hesitant. "Keep it. We want a decent paint job. We're a powerful club and maybe you'll want us to fix a ticket for you some time." They were paid up to June first. Gunther thanked them effusively. If it wasn't too much trouble, what was the official name of their organization? "Make the lease out to The Young Hamilton Democrats Club."

They said good-by. McMann thought it a swell name, and now that they were set they'd better divvy the dough left. They'd put a sum aside for furniture and food for the opening night. They'd have a swell party. They oughta go big. They didn't even havta knock off another speak. They were set, and the blow-out they were gonna have was gonna be a blow-out.

"Think Duffy'll like it?"

"The hell with him. If he makes a stink I'll slap the bastard down. The Young Hamilton Democrats Club. You thoughta it like nothin'. Can't kid me, you're a brain guy." They laughed like enemies who inevitably must come to blows.

"I wonder if Hamilton was a Democrat."

"He's a Democrat now." He sighed, almost sentimental. "We got a clubhouse. Yeh. Would you believe it? Me boss of a clubhouse, boss of a bunch kids. Would you believe it? I don't until I sees it with me own eyes. Holy Christ, me. Me?"

Duffy stood at his hotel window. Outside, the rain, confined between the defiles of the building, swept furiously. Spring is on the road, thought Duffy. Spring is almost here. His bathrobe was too viciously colored for this somber day. Below the gray sky the underneath city was dominated by rain, everything wet, blackish, misty. The city of hard contours and sun dazzling on windows had never been. Duffy retreated gratefully into the warmth of his room. He pulled on a pair of silk socks over his delicate ankles, sheathing them in what might have been their normal covering. He was fastidious, careful. Something had to be done about McMann. The clubhouse over on Sixteenth. Could you beat it? Ray had brought him an invitation to attend the gala opening night on April first. There'd be roast beef, beer, booze, cheese, women. McMann had to be stopped.

His mind presented the evidence like a district attorney. His kids had been used. McMann wanted all his kids. McMann had licked Spat and was easing him, Duffy, out. McMann was starting a clubhouse and would be boss. These deeds were crimes, and he had tolerated them although punishment was deserved and long overdue. He'd got Hanrahan after McMann, but you could never depend on bulls. Hanrahan might be letting McMann ride and haul him in when he was bigger, so Hanrahan'd get more credit. Duffy flung off his bathrobe. His meager body built in flat contours seemed impossible of violence, youthful, weak, almost pitiable. McMann had to be wiped out. That'd be only fair for the lumping he'd taken. His decision annoyed him as if he were some kindhearted judge compelled by law to be stern. How and when was the job to be pulled? Before the clubhouse opened. Sure. Before McMann pulled off another holdup, chiseling himself in deeper with the kids. Spat? Spat was too soft and respectable. He had a good job collecting policy slips and the nickels of the suckers. Spat wasn't the guy any more.

He buttoned his vest and his double-breasted blue jacket, more formidable, as if he'd got into armor, his shoulders wider. He belted his suede raincoat, lifting the collar high as if he intended walking five miles. Beyond the revolving door he marched under the canopy. The doorman whisked open the cab door. One drop of rain hit Duffy's nose. He breathed deep with an out-of-doors feeling. Soon he was indoors again, sitting down at the table in another hotel room. Three young men were playing pinochle. Duffy watched as if he were happy to be official kibitzer. The red queens and kings, the aces represented real dough. He blinked as the cards slid across the varnish and were molded into fans in each fist. Duffy drank, smoked a cigar, refused a second time to become a fourth, snorting the stakes were too high. Upon which the players, all under thirty, their eyes netted with the wrinkles of power and dissipation, murmured modestly. On a small pad one of them recorded the game's progress while the others observed carelessly but with their attentions wide awake. He wasn't scribbling figures just for nothing. It was the real dough. Duffy had endless patience, lingering so indefinitely that the keeper of the accounts caught on, glancing up every half-hour or so as if to wink: It's business, ain't it, Duff? Well, you wait and I'll be right with you. The cards slid out, the game seemed perpetual as the rain, the gamblers yawning, deploring the rotten weather. One of them had a date.

They exchanged checks. The game was over. The loser wrote out two checks for the winners. They left, smiling the smile of charm and affluence. Duffy stared at his host as if the game were still in progress, the cards gathered up by greedy fingers, the exhalations of breath, the slapping down of trumps.

"What's on your mind, Duff?" He was twenty-eight, his clothes the best money could buy, his nails and body immaculate with the lordliness of a peasant risen in the world. There were thousands exactly like him driving trucks, working in the building trades and subways, thick-shouldered, blue-eyed, with brash handsome faces and dirty fingernails.

"Nothing much."

They smiled. Carney'd been one of the winners. "How's things, Duff? You're lookin' swell."

"Not so bad. And you?"

"Not so bad."

"That's swell."

"You waited a long time. You must have important—"

"Nothing much."

"I thought it was important. Bet you were here two hours. Damn that lousy rain."

"I'd astayed anyway."

"Things are slow when you ain't playin'. I gotta play. No sittin' still for me. How's Spat and the kids?"

"Not so bad. I hear you boys are stepping."

"Not so bad with us. Listen, Duff, I never was the guy to stall. What d'ya want?"

"I was wondering to myself if some of your boys still do odd jobs? You're getting so big. Maybe some other mob's doing the small-fry stuff?"

"Fer instance, what small fry your kids ain't doin'?"

"One thing, my kids don't fool with guns much."

"That kinda job."

"If you don't handle it, le's forget it."

"I might do it for you as a strict favor, Duff, but that kinda stuff is small fry, just as you say."

"Didn't I say so? A guy comes to me and says: 'Duff, I'm willing to pay more than usual if you do a certain thing for me.' You see, that's how it is. I can't name this guy, but he's big and won't do it himself, although if I mention his name you'd be surprised. That big. But he don't want the job nohow and so I'm the in-between just to favor him."

"I see. How much he give you, jus' between us?"

"You'll be surprised. I got two-fifty with me. And two-fifty more when it's done."

"Five hunerd for a job like that?"

"It's a helluva lot. You can get it done for a hunerd anywhere."

"Though I don't do that kinda thing, Duff, as we got pretty big. I'd do it for you as a favor'n all, providin' I get two-fifty. I'll take your word on't."

"You don't botch it and we both make two-fifty."

"If I botch, money back. Nonea my boys'd bother. We're too big for that kinda stuff, but we got dopes allus hangin' round. Somea them are swell shots."

"What you getting now, Carney?"

"Seventy-five clear n every tin for the boys. You see why they don't like rough stuff. N' seventy-five's like nothin' at all."

"So it'll go through O.K.? It's a favor all around. Me doing it for the guy, and you for me."

"I know the feller to get spotted?"

"His name's McMann, a red-headed guy, usta drive a cab, running around with a kid called Bill."

"Don' know him."

"He's only peanuts."

"Five hunerd's a helluva lot for a peanut."

"The guy wants the job done's lousy with dough."

"Justa same, he's careless." Duffy took out two hundred-dollar notes, two twenties, and a ten. "Have it done the nex' few days. I want to get my money that's waiting."

Carney reached for the phone. He spoke a few minutes, grinning at his visitor like a salesman putting through an order. "A dope's comin' up. You point out this McMann to'm. He's a good worker and'll go to hell for a snifter." They sat around talking about things in general. Carney apologized why he was taking such a small fry on. It was peanuts and no money. He'd do things for a pal like Duff. They drank like two bad kids getting ready to do something bad. Duffy glanced over the rim of his glass at Carney boasting of how good he was in pinochle. He didn't count the cards like some of the guys, he just played hunches. If a guy was lucky, that was all he needed. Today didn't Duffy see him take over them experts? Experts stink. He shined goldenly, a man befriended by luck, his lips wide apart, his thick short nose also seeming to smile, the nostrils twisting up as his cheeks curved, proud, benevolent, a princeling doing favors for friends.

The newcomer made them both serious, a lean man with a wry apologetic mannerism. He was dead sober, sober and dead, without hope in his dope-fiend eyes. He was an Italian, but his voice belonged to no dialect. He was a living man's ghost without any allegiance, smiling uncannily at Carney with a ghoulish hope that he'd be granted hope again, would be given a return to life. To win life he'd do all things. His morality was honest; nothing is more precious than life; to attain it after death is godly. His face lowered and fanatic, he listened to his instructions like one to God's voice. "So long," said Duffy, leaving with the coke at his heels, who followed with the unquestioning obedience of a dog or black spirit.

For two days the coke spied on McMann. McMann was never alone. There'd be another guy with him, a handsome gink in a camel-hair coat, or else a couple kids. That McMann was never alone. It struck him as spitework, a nasty way of getting at him. As he glared through narrowed lids, McMann was the meanest guy alive, always going out of his way to hurt him. Why wasn't he alone? Everybody was alone once in awhile. Gradually after two days, McMann lost reality to him, who'd never been much of a person in the beginning, but now wasn't a person at all—merely something inanimate, tremendously immortal, like a natural manifestation, a mountain, a desert that the coke had to conquer like the ancient heroes of old before he could get what he desired most in life. Life itself, the snow of life.

He was dead sober. From some former existence, some memory distant as a former incarnation, he knotted his tie, dressed, loitered on Twenty-third. He carried a gat and a long knife. Both these weapons had also come down to him, an inheritance from another self. He didn't care for them, remotely knowing their use, trailing McMann from speak to hotel, seeing him walk with kids and women, but somehow with never the chance to use death, tempted to draw a bead on McMann in open daylight and then run for it like a beast who has struck. But he mustn't be caught. If he got caught, how'd he get the snow? He wandered eternities while other men ticked off the minutes and complained the days were speeding by like lightning and soon it'd be April, and spring around the corner.

He haunted the streets almost as invisible as a man can be, his face on his chest, his hollow light body attracting the gaze of no one. Not a woman, not a child looked at him to reaffirm his existence. At night he slept in a furnished room for which he paid three dollars a week. When the gnawing in his belly became a dull ache he got some doughnuts and coffee, not knowing or caring when the next meal'd be or where he'd eaten last.

He smoked one cigarette after another. McMann's continuance was evil and remorseless. Christ, what kinda guy was he? His mind was so misty there was no image in it but McMann's, and this a grotesque, a dream image with a huge red head, and arms and legs like stone branches, and all seeming of rock and earth, a red monstrous devil. And yet this mind decided something as quixotic as killing a devil, doing it somehow so that he could be given what he needed. There was no pity in him, but an entranced hate like a man fighting a river or a precipice or a dragon. During the next night, outside life, yet inhabiting a definite space, he stood across the doorway of the lodginghouse. He stood there because that was the most vital thing he could do, who had surrendered vitality and had nothing left but a dream and a lust for a dream. The month was March, and the spring winds were blowing. Blurs and shapes passed him. The street was quieter. The cordial shop did less business, its yellow glare shining through a window with edges painted orange. The coke stared. McMann and a woman walking. Like a beast he had no reason to look twice, hurrying into the corridor of McMann's house, hiding behind the stairs. The night light was on. It was still. He'd give it to McMann. This much he knew, planning no more, as a beast does not ponder whether claws or fangs will be used in an impending attack. The door opened, and McMann came in, the devil, huge, red, laughing until sound was everywhere, pushing the woman ahead of him as if she were a cow.

The coke rushed forward, his lips dropping spit like froth, hurrying with his perverted courage and desperation against his devil. McMann was the devil to him. His hand flashed long steel in the narrow passage. He darted his sting. McMann swiftly, light-footed, swerved aside, half-pushing the girl before him, gripping the coke's knife-holding wrist, springing in counter-attack as the woman cried once, the blade in her arm, piercing the furry sleeve of her coat as if in an animal's hide. Falling against the corridor wall, her face blanched, she stared at McMann smashing once, twice, thrice, his knee kicking up hard like another fist into the attacker's belly. McMann urged: "Up to my flat. Get up." She obeyed because the blood was still inside and she couldn't see it. McMann slipped the knife into his pocket, lugging the light body up the stairs. Not a head had appeared. It was a furnished rooming-house populated by whores, thugs, easy folk, wastrels. Cries and screams were a commonplace, and every week somebody called up the police about the racket going on.

McMann dropped the attacker on the floor. His face flushed pink, flushed white, as he contemplated the little man sprawling on his rug. He kicked out once and said as if to someone very near him: "Quit cryin'. It's only in the arm. Shut up."

She flopped to the bed in her fur coat, one hand gentling the place where the blade had entered. Over and over again in words pale and lifeless as her face she repeated: "You pushed me inta it."

"Chris' sake, it was blind actin'. Honest to God, I wasn't thinkin' at all when that bastard poked his knife. I didn' know what I was doin'." He lit a cigarette, pushed it between her pallid lips. She puffed slowly like a big bloodless mechanical doll. He poured her a shot of gin, forcing her to drink. All the time the coke lay on his face, his head on one arm as if he were grieving at his failure.

She felt better, the drink like a man's hand against her belly, but inside of her, warm, intimate. "Get a doctor."

He helped her off with the fur coat. The sleeve of her thin dress was red with blood. The knife had slashed the fleshy part of her upper arm, missing the biceps. He wiped the coke's knife on a towel and slit open the sleeve. The girl didn't glance at the wound, puffing steadily as McMann swathed it with handkerchiefs. He brought back a small bottle of iodine from his bathroom. He had used the iodine for corns. "It'll burn like hell," she said.

"Quit belly-achin'. You're lucky it's only a scratch." He pulled off the handkerchiefs and spilled the iodine on the wound. The long knife had gone deep. The iodine spread all over her arm, running down the white skin in little coppery rivers. She fainted.

"Poor Madge," he said. He soaked a towel and placed it on her head, bandaging up the wound tightly. She was completely out. The blood seeped through. Christ, he'd make it right for her, fix up the coat and buy a new dress. Christ, looka the blood. He tied several new handkerchiefs about the wound, but still it bled, carrying the antiseptic stain away in a red flow. He'd havta call a doctor. He tightened a handkerchief above the wound, inserting a fork, which he moved around and around like a clock-hand. He looped another handkerchief about the fork, tying it opposite the street. She'd be all right. Her heart was beating O.K. Jesus, her breasts were small. He yanked down twenty bright ties from his rack binding the coke's feet together with seven or eight, cross-binding with another batch. He fastened the coke's hands behind his back, heaving him over as if he were a turtle, stuffing a handkerchief into the mouth until the thin cheeks bulged with a horrible sense of being fat. That gag'd hold. He raised his fist, gazing at it a second as if it were a hammer, and then smashed the unconscious face a few times as if working out a sculptural problem, pounding the fist into the stomach. That'd keep the bastard. he dragged the body out of the living-room into the bedroom, pushing it into a closet. He slammed the door, returning to Madge. The knife he put in a drawer. Now he could go downstairs and phone a doctor. he searched in his pockets and tugged out quarters and dimes. No nickel. She had many nickels in her pocketbook. All chippies had plenty nickels. He unlocked the door, hurrying downstairs to the phone booth under the stairs. This doc oughta come right over; only a lil shyster fresh outa the hospital and with no practice.

He watched the blood stain and restain the handkerchiefs until the doctor knocked, a young man of thirty with a black mustache and a sallow complexion that seemed competently medical. His popping eyes twinkled as if to say: This is the little patient. Madge didn't say anything.

"Hello, Doc," said McMann, slipping him two fives.

"Hello, McMann. An accident. How unfortunate!"

"Yeah, she was slicin' bread. Snap on't, she's fainted again."

The doctor had already opened his black bag, his hairy hands skillful as an old hag's. He stripped off the handkerchiefs, surveying the wound, and then set to work with cotton, adhesive, gauze, sterilizing it, stopping the flow of blood, rapidly bandaging the wound so there was no sight of red, the bandaging neat as a bracelet. His hands had been gentle. "Now, young lady, you're all right now. I'm right in the neighborhood and you see me tomorrow morning. Before eleven."

"O.K.," said McMann. "I'll give her the address and she'll be round." He smiled grandly as a baron. The doctor was gone. McMann smoked with the air of one who's done a good day's work, treating himself to a drink. "You see, it was nothin'. Your arm'll be dandy in a few days."

"Hell, it's gonna be in the way."

"Way of what?" He laughed, guessing. "Hell, they don' shell out for no arms."

"Gimme a drink. I shouldn' come with you. I don' like you. I like Bill. He knows how to treat a girl. I mighta been killed." It was her first lengthy reproach, her triangular face pallid, her eyes seeming black in the light, her lips scarlet and sensual, prominent in her pallor. Two small pimples were near the corner of her mouth. She told him to ring Paddy to send a girl over. She was going pronto and get some sleep. She looked at him, smiling faintly as he threatened she was to keep it under her hat about the guy in the closet. Sure, she would, she cut her arm cutting bread; the louse stabbing her up, he could go to hell far as she cared.

"You can tell Paddy we were at a party and some ginzo got nuts with booze and run wild before we could smack him down Get me. You're gonna get a dress and fixed coat outa it, so keep shut." Downstairs again, he switched on the light above the phone, then rang up.

After the call they smoked. Who'd Paddy send? It was a fat bond, Jackie. She gave the customers a motherly sympathy and a strong thrusting of Amazonian hips. Jackie was sorry as hell, her round face crinkling, particularly about the nose and mouth like a bull pup's. She got Madge in her coat. McMann slammed the cab door, Jackie shouting: "You damn men, can't even protect a gal. Now, don't you worry, Madge. You'll be O.K."

McMann hurried upstairs, locking the door. It was a lucky break. That bastard had come close. He'd square it with Madge. Now, who the hell was behind the coke? He was a coke, he'd noticed that when he was smacking his jaw. The pouches under the eyes. It was a coke, and who'd sent him? Bill? Naw. It was only one guy, only one guy, and why kid himself? He'd known it the second the killer had slashed at them in the corridor. The guy behind it was Spat'n Duffy. He thought of them as one guy, a corporation of crime, his feet on the table, his face impassive, abstract, as if considering an astronomical problem. Spat was a muscle man. Spat'd been licked. If Spat was sore he'd acome after him himself. Spat carried a gat and if he'd awanted him bad enough he'd abeen got. McMann felt his stomach turn inside out. So guys might be after him. It wasn't Spat. It was Duffy. Duffy was a fag, a bitch of a man. Duffy had hired the coke. Yeh.

First thing, he thought, I'll slip Spat some dough. Spat had to be on his side. Spat was dumb as hell, but he'd foller a dollar anywhere. Couldn't afford guys like Spat after him. He dragged out the coke from the closet, yanking down the bedroom shades. He slapped the guy's cheeks, slopping water on his face. He removed the gag and poured whisky down his throat. The coke opened his eyes, moving feebly.

"The dame you cut's dyin' in the hospital." The coke's eyes had become black with fear, not fear of death primarily, but fear of a banishment to a somewhere without snow. "Yeah?"

"I got you'n her upstairs. The ambulance took her away."

"Don't bunk me." He rolled his tongue about in the dry cavern of his mouth. The handkerchief had absorbed all the moisture.

"Who put you on my tail?"

"Nobody." McMann slapped him. "It was Duffy."

"I never hearda Duffy."

"You're a liar."

The coke writhed, moaning. He'd spoiled the job, there'd be no snow, nothing. What tough luck! His eyes bulged, he chewed at his lips, raving: "Damn ya for spitin' a poor man. Spitework. Jesus Christ, you're too hard on a poor man."

"Who sent you after me? You tell me and I'll turn you loose and get you some dope."

The bound man's eyes gleamed. He had no faith in McMann, but still he hoped, still his eyes yearned to believe. "You're a lousy liar."

"Want me to turn you over to the cops? They'll put you away without dope. They'll cure you, you bastard."

The coke glared at McMann like a victim at his inquisitor. He begged mercy, pity, his eyes starting, his teeth showing as if he were being seared with hot irons, tortured too foully. Jailed without snow. Jesus. He cursed, the sounds coming from his throat in another speech, not human, an animal tongue as if he were a beast, a crow with split tongue who had learned to make certain sounds men used. Then sharply, his eyes cunning, as if remembering the time when he'd been a man, he spoke with man's reason. "Fat chance you handing me to the cops. Not you."

"Right," said McMann. "If you don' speak up who put ya on my tail, I'll fix ya meself."

"Go ahead," he snarled. Death was the same as prison. There'd be snow in neither place. What'd he care?

McMann wrenched one arm until the bone almost cracked. He let go. The coke was shouting too loudly, his mouth open, shrieking his pain. "I'll cut ya into small hunks if you don' tell me. Was it Duffy? Who sent ya? Who sent ya?" He stuffed the mouth with the handkerchief. "Holler your head off. No one'll hear ya. Gwan. Holler." He flung the coke on his face, the thin hands resting on the small of the back, held together by bright maroon, green, and blue striped ties. There was a bulge on the hip. McMann pulled out the gun. Crazy not to have gone through the bastard before. He searched him swiftly. Nothing else. "You gonna tell me who it is? Ain't it Duffy? Duffy?" He snapped the bullets out of the gat, holding it like a hammer. "Shake your head for yes if you're gonna tell." The head was motionless. He smacked the butt down on the elbow. The body was in agony. "Shake your bastard head if you're gonna tell." Without pausing, the butt landed on the elbow the second time. He slammed it on the buttock, feeling the hip bone. He tossed the body on its back, the coke's corpselike face deep red. Torrents of blood had roared into the head, the body donating all its blood to the head so that the tongue might shout out: Enough. "You ain't hollering," grinned McMann. The coke was mute as a fish, no longer a man, but a tongueless creation compelled to suffering in silence. "Who was it? I'll quit foolin' and bang your damn eyes out." He lifted the gun butt, the head rolling from side to side. McMann yanked the gag loose. The coke couldn't speak. The veins in his neck were choked with blood, thick as cords. McMann gave him a shot of booze. "So it was Duffy?" Who'n hell was Duffy? His boss was Carney. He whispered it was Duffy.

"You'll get the snow I promised," growled McMann. "You'll get it in hell." His lips were fleshless, two stiff hard wrinkles, two white scars. He tapped the butt down on the coke's skull. It was nicely judged. The coke was still alive, paralyzed, voiceless, unconscious, his eyes shut. McMann untied him, flinging the ties on the floor. He put gloves on his hands, unlocked the door. A radio was hooting, there were several parties on, drunken voices bellowing. McMann shoved the knife into his overcoat pocket, thinking of the parties, men in shorts getting woozed up. He shoved the hat on the coke's head, lifting him upwards, his arm under the armpits. The coke looked like a guy staggering home from a party. As if in a dream, like a drunk almost completely out, the coke dragged his feet. McMann helped him downstairs. They looked like two drunks, McMann grinning falsely, his pal scraping along. On the midnight street the stores were closed, the apartments and furnished-room joints blank and desolate as if everyone were indoors and about to go to bed. He called a cab.

McMann said to the hack, "Short haul, buddy. I wanna take me pal home. Lives in Twenty-foist, Eight'n Ninth."

They sped towards the avenue, the Bickford's on the corner like a genial night spider enticing the stray homing flies. The cabbie pulled up, making change. He stared at the tail-light dimming into a small red dot, laughing as if his pal were troublesome, helping him into the hallway. Through the glass panel on the heavy vestibule door, the stairs led up to unknown lives. McMann propped the coke against the wall. He took the knife out and thrust it into the unseen heart. The coke dropped, sprawling like a drunk. He placed the knife under the body. In the darkness, the corpse was sleeping. He hot-footed it back to his apartment and cleaned the place up. Time to check out even if he was safe. He filled two valises, cramming in his property. He didn't own much, the three extra suits the only big items. Ninety outa hundred, when the cops found the coke, the papers writing up the story of so-and-so murdered in a hallway, the hack wouldn't say a word even if he remembered his short haul. This was the weak spot. The hack might talk even though most of them minded their business. Nothing like playing safe when a guy was coming up in the world, with a clubhouse and all. Nothing to worry about. The doc'd keep shut. In his house hardly anyone lived under his right name. They knew him as Smith. Let 'em sue Smith. Screw them. Damn the red hair.

He hired a room on Ninety-second Street. The clerk yawned and McMann was out five bucks for it. He'd look around later. He went to sleep. It was over with. So it was Duffy. The coke said it was. It was plain that Duffy had to be fixed early in the morning before the papers could tip him off. Duffy wasn't wise yet. Duffy was a late riser. That was gonna be Duffy's hard luck.

CHAPTER TWENTY-ONE

McMann awoke a few minutes after seven, some mysterious and urgent alarm ringing in his bowels. He dressed, gulped down a cup of coffee in a cafeteria, boarded the downtown elevated. In the inner pocket of his navy-blue overcoat the coke's gun, with its empty chamber, was like an iron wart on his body. His hands were unprotected, the gloves folded up. He chewed a toothpick, seemed like a business man, calm, factual, mapping out the activities of the day. At Christopher he got off. It wasn't eight yet. A bunch of roughly clothed workers piled around him on the way to the machinery plants and welding companies. Bill's name wasn't on any letter-box. He rang the Super's bell, chewing his toothpick, the letter-boxes gleaming golden in the vestibule.

"What can I do for you?" asked Mrs. Gebhardt.

He was looking for a feller Trent, Bill. She didn't care for the stone face, the red eyes peering out at her between fringes red-blond in a stray beam of sun. "Bill Trent lives here," she said. Of course he did. He was a friend of his, they were in business together. Where did he live? It was important. Third floor front. He thanked her, chasing upstairs. She stared at Bill's first visitor. There was no answer when he knocked. He rapped loudly. A sleepy young fellow with tousled yellow hair informed him through the slanted door that Bill was sleeping. He pushed past the boy. Joe snapped awake. Thank God it wasn't a bull. McMann at least didn't seem like one. The visitor was shaking Bill's shoulder. Bill yawned at the red face, so wide awake it seemed he'd been flung bodily from consciousness to an almost frenzied alertness. "What the hell you doing here?" he cried, staring from his brother to McMann, from sanity to nightmare. He choked, bitterly frightened. "Never you mind. It's important or I'da never comed. Get dressed, willya?"

Bill was bewildered at McMann in his place. Distrust caused his head to ring. Never had McMann seemed more like a tempting devil to him, the foul creation that would eventually destroy him. He slipped his feet into the step-shoes. What more did McMann know about him without letting on? He washed his teeth. He'd known McMann for months and knew nothing about him. McMann's suddenly genial voice was speeching to Joe: "Me, I'm an early bird. You look like Bill. Same build'n looks'n both late risers." Bill shut the tap. McMann had crawled everywhere. He'd never make a couple grand. Hanrahan or McMann'd be his finish. Christ, now was the time to quit, the last chance, the very last chance. He had a hunch he shouldn't go with McMann. It must turn out rotten. McMann never before had been to Leroy. He mustn't go. Sure as fate something rotten was up. He pivoted around with the swiftness of a prisoner glancing at his captor as if to surprise some thought in the smooth hard face, some idea of what had brought him. He saw nothing but the bitter enigma of the devil's own face, promising the world and promising nothing. Christ, you couldn't even kill a devil like that. McMann calmed down the dog in jig time, socking the pup playfully. The dog was licking his hand.

His heart beat, his hands trembled, but he put a cagy knot in his necktie. By hell, he was getting tough. Time to decide, the events and thoughts of the elapsed months resolving into an invitation, a note to which one must answer yes or no. "It's damn important to bring you here so early. You like to sleep late as well as the next. How'd you find out where I lived? Stanger tell you? Who?" His words clipped from his lips with stiff edges and hard corners. There was no warmth in him, not even the heat of fear. Stretching up through his flesh, gripping his eyeballs frozen hard, a coldness that was another self concentrated on the visitor.

"It jus' had to be tended to. It's for your own good."

Bill guessed he was lying. How far can you trust a liar? Maybe this was to be the finish of himself, a scheme to wipe him. McMann wouldn't excite suspicion that way. His brother was silent and youthful in his pyjamas. Joe studied him from the distance of their two minds thinking their different thoughts. His brother's lips moved, his eyes said a definite thing, and that thing was: Don't go, stay here, don't go, for God's sake.

He was completely dressed. "I've half a mind to stay here."

"I don't get you." And he, too spoke silently, as if saying: We're partners, aren't we? And not go when I call for you, for Christ's sake?...

"I'll be back later, Joe. Need any dough?"

McMann offered his wallet. "I'll loan ya some if you need any."

"No, I've got enough."

"Keep the mutt quiet," said Bill, realizing he owned a barking wild dog, and the dog's name was Spotty. It seemed to have created itself out of thin air like a devil's dog. Again his brother, strong, yellow-haired, innocent as an archangel, seemed to plead with him. He thought: I may be leaving all that's good and there'll be no more chance or hope for me. Shutting the door, he followed his guide. The red hair shone beneath the felt down to the nape. The flights had never been so long. It was a descent into hell. McMann said how some bastard had almost killed him. Yeah, a guy with a knife and gat. Fool's luck he was here today. The street swung its heavy stone at Bill, gasping. Yeh, it was no fooling. He'd almost been spotted, but he'd dragged the coke bastard bitch to his room, and the coke said it was Duffy sent him. Duffy had paid him and some other mugs to put them on the spot. Now, maybe, Bill guessed why he'd bust into his joint so early, getting him up from his beauty nap. Bill thought: And these are my feet climbing the metal stairs to Christopher El station as they have so many times before, and there is the El roaring. McMann's voice thrummed, elaborated, thrummed again of the danger, of Duffy, danger, danger.

"Where we going, McMann?"

"Don't ya know?"

"Maybe I don't want to."

"We're returning Duff's call." They sat side by side, their knees touching. Sure he meant it; if he didn't mean it, they might as well lay down and die. They were practically alone in the car. it was going on to nine and the traffic was going downtown to work. "I fixed the coke," said McMann simply.

"You expect to fix Duffy?"

"Duffy gets up late. He'll be home."

Bill looked as though he was going to rise and hop off the El. There was no getting off. There were no stations where one could. "Count me out, I'm not killing anybody."

"You'd rather get killed." Christ, if he didn't want to puke! So he didn't want to get mixed up. Wasn't he mixed up at Paddy's? That was different, said Bill. Like the hell it was; maybe he'd like that coke poking a knife a foot long at him. His bewildered mind rolled over and over, the wheels of thought grinding and flashing like the steel wheels of the El, progressing to one thought, one destination. "What happened to the coke?"

"I give him back his knife."

"You did—"

"I got an idea to give Duffy back his gat."

"I'm out."

"You mean you're yeller." He frowned. "You dumb bastard. It's Duffy or us. He's been to bat, it's our turn. You wanta die? We've grabbed his kids. He's sore."

"I don't want any blood on my hands. Give'm the damn kids back."

"You can't welsh. He's out to wipe us. He'll do it unless we wipe him." The train stopped. It was Fiftieth and Ninth Avenue. Farther east in the Broadway sector Duffy had a suite. They legged down the long bright morning blocks. "You sap," cried McMann, "thinkin' I'd kill a guy. What for? Who wantsa burn? I gotta proposition to make Duff, and this is the time. He can't double-cross us. No, sir."

"You're a liar," Bill said heavily, hypnotized by McMann's will, matching stride for stride. What should he do? Still time to welsh, to backscuttle? Still time to fade into the crowds. There flowed the bright vague faces gleaming like coins in the sun, the thousands of them. Broadway shone under blue sky, spring was nearing. April Fool's Day. Soon, soon, the clubhouse'd open. The dust flew and time was leaving him stranded on this hard marble moment. Always time to begin over, time to begin, not to heel along like a fool, time to get out of murder, let time's washing wave drag him out to life again.

"Here's the facts straight. Duffy's after us. Honest to Christ he is. Almost got me last night. Ya can't hide. You'll be got no matter where ya go. Run from town. Sure. You'll be safe, and what'll you do? Starve. Here we got a good biz, a livin'n all. Wanta chuck it back to Duffy? Gwan. But not me. I sweated too long to swipe his kids, and jus' with the big dough near, I ain't nuts."

Isolated in a dream, he followed McMann into the lobby, and they rode in the elevator to the tenth floor. Two things he recalled. He hadn't any breakfast, and Duffy lived on the eighth. While he watched, McMann, in a corner, loaded the gun. If anybody'd ask, well, they'd got off at the tenth. It was a gun. Yes. They walked down two flights. The hotel was still asleep, the only things alive the sunbeams searing through the windows hot and yellow. Bill bit his thumb. McMann never looked back, engrossed in his mission, careless of Bill, or seeming so. He thought: I want Duffy murdered; that's why I'm heeling along; no use making believe I want Duffy to live. I want him murdered so we can be through with him and because I want my life to be safe. I do not want to be attacked like McMann. He shivered. Life, the good sweet life, oh, life, he'd hold on to it even if other lives must go. For yourself. Watch, guard yourself, no one else will. The thoughts fermented out of his hesitation. He debated as the thoughts circled his head in the imminent aura of that doing morning, like drunken things on wings. His body was host to many disputing beings, walking drunken as if he were striding down some nebulous stairway of dream on queer missions, inevitable, sadistic. His head whirled and it wasn't fresh morning but late night, his brain sick from wildness, now, suddenly lucid, or regretful, by turns melancholy, exalted, mournful, stolid. And all these moods knew one union, the walking forward of the body containing them.

McMann's fist knocked on Duffy's door, so bright, calm, reassuring, that he felt he was in the hands of a trustworthy guide. Sullen, sleepy, Duffy answered: "Who the hell?"

"Telegram" said McMann. "Telegram for Mr. Duffy."

Bill wallowed in inane admiration. McMann was the enchanter, producing the necessary magics for each crisis. Oh, he could be trusted. You fool, he thought, you're another heel like Spat. And then he was hurrying in and McMann had shut the door, Duffy, horrified, retreating before them. McMann turned the key in the lock. "Don't holler, duff. The walls' soundproof, ain't they?" He gripped the collar of the purple gown, holding the splendor of the cloth and the miserable man in it.

"What the hell you want?" cried Duffy, trying to smile. He'd forgotten long ago. Even when happy he never smiled, and this terrified contorting of his lips seemed a memory from childhood, pathetic, wistful, begging.

"Jus' to say hello."

"What you want?" said Duffy.

"Nex' time don' open doors like that. Ya didn' think I'd be after ya so quick." He scowled at the false smile, and the more his face wrinkled blood-red with hate, the more Duffy smiled as if that were his one mechanical reaction. "Sit down," pleaded Duffy. "Sit down, Bill. Let's talk it over like reg'lar guys." And he squirmed within the silken shroud of his dressing-gown, writhing against the wall, careful even now not to move against McMann, his eyes dark and remote from the slanting sunlight. His ankles were small as a girl's, he wasn't very strong.

It was soundproof construction sure enough. On three sides, the rooms to right and left and from beyond the corridor, they heard no sound, seeming as if there could never be sound of rescue. Only through the open window, on the fourth, precipice side, was there a voice, the low voice of the city, the sound of traffic, the sound of human lives in narrow spaces, the voice of a god seeing all, never interfering. To this voice the three men listened gravely.

"I'm not sittin' down," said McMann. "Your mouth stinks. You ain't washed it." He called to Bill. "Get the gat in the inside pocket." Duffy's mouth widened to holler. McMann uppercut him. Duffy moaned, not screaming. Bill fumbled, the three together in a stricken fatal knot, and there was the gun in his hand, holding onto it while Duffy glared blind with unbelief. McMann socked him twice, Duffy's knees sagged. He couldn't holler much.

"Hell," cried Bill, tormented, "what you gonna do? Hell, Red, what the hell? You aren't dragging me into this. I won't help. Damn. I'll kill you first."

"Want the rat to kill ya, you dumb bastard? You wanta die? Christ, you wanta die?"

No, to live. Life. He dropped the gun on the chair, disowning McMann and everything connected with him.

"You're crazy," cried Duffy, his thin hands resting on the clenched red fist. "You're tipped wrong. Bill, don't let'm."

"Soundproof walls. Shut up. Radio'n all. Bill, some jazz. Loud. Duff's gonna be harda hearin'. N' shut the winders." There was no voice now, not even the city's. There was no music, but an aggressive personality bellowed something political. How like the time, the time at Paddy's, how like; time repeats itself, does history and time. Nobody listened to the speaker the dial had ushered in, whipping harsh, warlike, chanting like a medicine man in a croaking tongue.

Duffy lunged at McMann, who, gripping the lapels of the robe like an envelope in which he'd captured a pallid bug, smacked his free fist into Duffy's face. "No rough-house," he muttered. Duffy was breathing hard, a man who'd lost a bitter fight, the sweat on his brow, his lungs empty of air.

"You're going to kill an innocent man. Honest, Bill, I don't know why he's picking on me. Why?"

McMann hurled him against the wall. "Don't know about a dopey ginzo with a knife and gat? The ginzo knows you. Duffy sent him round. Never hearda the bastard wop, did ya?"

"I never did."

"You bastard liar."

"No. No. I ain't. Christ's sake, Bill. Bill, Bill, you ain't gonna let him. Bill." Bill glanced away, the drift of unreality of dream lifting from about him. The room was a hotel room, not a vision. He stared the stark horrible truth in the face. They were killers. Duffy was nix. McMann, implacable, wolfish. Duffy the image of fear, coughing and coughing. He thought: Is he coughing to get my sympathy? Duffy's eyes weren't human, nor the eyes of a beast in a trap, nor the eyes of anything living, but the glassy orbs of a corpse with a strange cold haunting light of their own, the meat of his face pickled and creased in the acid of fear. Bill swallowed, a pity for himself almost bursting his heart. He was here at the death of a human. Christ, he didn't want blood on his hands. "Mac," he mumbled, "how ya know it's him?"

"The coke told me. What would a coke come after me? Cokes got nothin' against me. This bastard."

"No, no." His voice was weak as if he'd lost interest defending himself, speaking out of habit, twisting, his hands shaking. He opened his throat to shout. McMann's free hand leeched tight to this throat and yet he seemed to shout, as the radio speaker blared big words and little words. The blare spoke for Duffy. For a second they listened to the sound of the speaker as if to the voice of a second god, co-equal to the city. The radio spoke of what concerned it, not giving a damn for any of them, or for the fact that a man was about to be murdered. Bill bleated: "Don't be hasty, Red," realizing he was speaking above the radio like a man shouting against the sea roar. Even if his voice sounded listless, his was shouting. The blood flooded his veins. He saw clearer, as if he'd been bled, weak in body, but stronger in sight.

"Gimme the gat." His fingers dug into Duffy's throat like grapnels as if he'd tear the heart out of voice.

Slowly Bill picked up the pistol, obeying McMann, who was as godly or evil as the radio or the city noise shut out behind the window. He didn't look at Duffy. His ears banged with sound, with the high-climbing city's voice of brick and steel, the sound of the machines clicking out, lives and machines that were unlives, with fury of words and foreign tongues, with the power of the unknown radio speaker. In this din, his own heart missed a beat, hammering into consciousness so that he heard his heart, his inner self beating. McMann dominated all the sounds. "Dumb bastard. Want'm to live?" McMann's voice was the saddest of all, the most human, for none of the other voices were of any interest. The city didn't care nor the radio nor Bill's own blind heart. He surrendered the gun. One sound more. Duffy lay on the floor, a mean persistent thing to be avoided. His gaze lowered, and now it filled his gaze, and his eyes were with tears. Duffy lay on his face, the purple gown spread about him aspirant like wings.

The radio clamored. Its voice of the dead speaking unintelligibly of matters the living had no concern for. McMann put on his gloves, carefully rubbing barrel and hilt with a handkerchief, then placing the pistol near Duffy's hand. He whispered very respectably: "Let's beat it, huh?" Bill admired his decorum in the presence of the dead.

They went up two flights, buzzed for the lift. The lobby was full of living folk, the streets so crowded death seemed the biggest rarity. Bill thought:

McMann's a ghost, a magician, someone you can't harm. As in all their crimes, they appeared to be wearing invisible rings. Nobody ever saw them, nobody was the wiser.

"The kids is ourn," said McMann.

"If I didn't hand you the gun?"

"Why not? Don't I know I kin depend on ya?"

It was exciting from a gangster movie into bright sunlight. He felt sorry for Duffy. Good God, Duffy wasn't Cagney or Robinson or Raft. Christ, Duffy had been real, Duffy wouldn't ever come to life like the movie fellows when the film was over. "What'd you do with the coke?"

"I tolya, him, I give back his knife. Duff got his gun. I don' feel so hot. Too much excitement. I've gotta get drunk this minute. Come 'long."

"I suppose so. I feel sorry, yeah, sorry, I feel punchdrunk, groggy, sick, I don't know how I feel."

McMann grimaced. "Quit bitchin! Think I had a grand time? Le's get soused'n forget it."

"Sure," said Bill. "I meant I was going to say I was sorry for the both of us. For you and me, not for them."

"I don't make you outa all."

CHAPTER TWENTY-TWO

Joe dressed rapidly after his brother left with McMann. No wonder Bill was the way he was, pals with such an egg. The hell with them. He couldn't be worrying about his brother. He had no effect on him. After breakfast he left the house. March was burning itself out in sun, the sky a blue promise, the wind the one force remembering winter, a little harsh and chilly. He spent an hour at the Library, idling up Fifth to Central Park. He opened his coat to the wind, repeatedly wiping a slight sweat from his upper lip. The world was on the move, no time for lagging steps. He was alive, he was in love. The Park was empty.

There was no getting away from it. He was in love with Cathy. He wanted her, and why not? She was only a woman like everybody else. He had had dreams at night, warm before-dropping asleep images of Cathy being courted by him man-fashion. But why feel so paralyzing stifling hot today? Why this day with Bill running off God alone knew where? There was a crisis in his brother's affairs, he might be in danger, and yet he didn't really give a damn. He'd tried his best, failing, and now reverting to the stone basis of his being, the passion slowly accreted in the months. There was a crisis in his body. The flesh and youth of him were demanding. No use waiting. Gazing on the women passing by, their trim legs, the coats tight about their bodies, he was battered again by the beastly fecundity in him that didn't give a damn about anything, wanting only to slake itself. Oh, to be lying down with Cathy on a June shore! Cathy, I love you.

All that wandering morning in the city, with his halts at the Library, at a cafeteria for a bite, conjured up his fever. Was it him, Joe Trent, approaching the desk at a hotel and asking for a room? He didn't focus the clerk, just knew it was somebody in charge. He paid in advance, took his key, and visited his room, brooding among the whiteness of linen. Downstairs he memorized the room number in case he should lose the key, jamming the key in his inner jacket pocket and stuffing a handkerchief on top of it.

"Let's go for a long walk," he said to Cathy at three o'clock.

"It's a beautiful day."

"And I know somebody beautiful, too," he said, his voice humorless. In silence they strolled away from the multitudes of girls, green and dapper as frogs. "Getting on to April. The hell with it. I'm not stalling around. I got a room today at a hotel so we can go up there and talk. To talk," he repeated swiftly, as if the trees in Gramercy Park were a forest about him. He stepped gingerly. Her hip touched his own. He listened to the song of these things. Hip and arm spoke grandly.

"We can't go up," said Cathy. She didn't blush, but her words seemed to be all red and white.

For God's sake, he preached, didn't she love him? He wanted her alone. It was natural. They came out on Fifth and Twenty-third, winding through Madison Square, and their way that morning was all parked and green to the eye. Northwards to Forty-second, and the sense of brown trees accompanied them. What they said was forgotten and they were hearkening to the voices in their bodies, the city voice muted down to one inconsolate cry of longing. The tremendous phallic gleam of the Empire State caught their visions and they glanced skywards saying how big it was, jostled by people pausing for the traffic lights. At Fifty-ninth, north again was the endless country of Central Park. Their conversation had a summer hum. "I love you," he said; "do you love me?" "I love you," she said, "but it isn't right." He'd make it right. Why, how could he? He knew how. Let her wait and see. (St. Patrick's Cathedral had given him an idea—not a nice idea, but he meant it right.)

"How can you make it right?" she said.

"Gee, you're set. Don't you love me? If you do you'll see. Just hold your horses." Then, excited he led her up the cathedral steps, under the central doorway into an immense hush of darkness, folding and draping their bodies so that they were part of the hush. "I brought you here for a reason. You're Cath'lic. This is a Cath'lic church. I want to say I love you and will you marry me? I want you to." They hadn't been inside a minute, and yet the hush followed them. Breathing deep of cool air didn't help that funny feeling of God spying down and saying: O.K., Joe, it's a go, you're man and wife. This feeling wasn't part of his idea. On Fifth the whole idea seemed plain dopey. Her face was averted, but he swaggered, stepping briskly like a man fetching a slave home from market. He loved her. That was plenty. If he loved her he wouldn't harm her, would he? The world flashed before him in hard gleaming color, enameled by his emotion. The avenue was thick yellow sun. Diamond points of light glittered from autos. The sky waved down between the rows of buildings like a blue flag. Thank God the loneliness was over, the crucifixion of the time before three o'clock. The long walk uptown belonged to another period, to the emptiness before the cathedral. He owned a new mind and body that hadn't existed ten minutes ago.

When they were alone in the room, they were shy as newlyweds, standing far apart, smiling down at the city. She wore her hat and coat, waiting for him to act, to do, to be the man. He knew it, idling, hearing time ticking into agony. Now that he had her here, the warm visions and lusts he'd counted on had stayed behind, not entering the room. He was solitary, a young fellow with no merry sensual company urging him on. Love? Hugging? Why was she silent? Her yellow hair, silky above her pale forehead, had no prettiness for him. Looking into her eyes he was more helpless than ever. They were just eyes. Animals had eyes. Men had eyes. He fastened his glance on her listless virginal arms, her pink lips, and it seemed strange that he had dreamed such a dream of this thin girl with the narrow hips and the silence of a hunted rabbit. His words and her answers were both stupid. Was this how lovers talked? It couldn't be. They were two suspicious animals, contemplating each other because they were in one cage. This wasn't love. This wasn't anything.

Seeing him this way, his arms strapped to his body, his mouth gagged, she felt pity. "Why you so goofy, Joe?"

"Hell, you're goofy yourself." Her eyes were softer. He hated her pity, remembering something at Metz's…All these slum girls were the same, all of them were, the same, the same, ready to flop over soon they got outa diapers, diapers, and a guy outa pants, pants, outa pants. He thought this memory, but without believing it. Pity. It was pity in her, and nothing else.

"I want you to know," he began tediously, "that I love you and will marry you some day like I said back in the church." And after speaking to his conscience, reassuring God it was on the up-and-up, he hugged her with the formality of a kid with his number one official sweetheart, his neck twisted, his head stiff as if repelled by her nearness.

"Not so hard," she said. "You're strong."

He smiled like an idiot, relaxing his grip, sitting down and pulling her onto his lap. What a sap he was! His insides broke free from tautness. He was himself again. "I'm crazy and you're the reason." He was masterful, home again with the knowledge gained from piling on sluttish maids. He kissed all the area of her face, for this lingered in his mind as part of the ritual. Inside of him the deep flame of quiet, gentle, intense, overwhelmed the tricks. He forgot all he'd learned of the art and the way, holding her tight to him on the chair as one would a valuable possession. They were two children in the first greenest gladtime of love. They had no harm for each other.

She was so sweet and vague, so little the woman or piece of tail, he remembered she was virgin. He said seriously: "You're just a kid. You can guess what I mean. I can't love you the way I want. We must wait or else. Gee, it's hard to say. I've got to love you slowly, by degrees. I don't want to hurt you all at once." She was blushing, helpless as if he'd beaten her. He had sounded brutal and now asked if she understood. He wouldn't hurt her. He loved her too much, but he had to love her. He had to.

The blood receded in her, she seemed sick from blushing, diseased with the irregular burstings of blood in her head, but when she answered, she was practical as a woman in love or a woman in passion. "Where'll we go? I love you, Joe. I do."

"I'll take a room by the week."

"What of the money?"

"You do love me." They kissed in a tense second that broke down in its duration the churchly scruples of all her childhood and youth.

Later in the afternoon McMann and Bill, stewed to the gills, hopped a cab for McMann's new diggings, stopping en route for ginger ale and a carton of ice. McMann dug the booze from one of the valises. They were alone in a strange room, their faces flaming, their hands trembling. McMann's eyes were so bloodshot they seemed wounded. He was very confidential. "Tha's how it goes. Yesterday'n today I bops two guys. Me. I killt two guys. Can ya beat it? That steppin' or ain't it? Naw'n I don' like it. But them or us. Think I liked that Duffy rat's mug, the yeller bastard. Your fault when ya gets down to't."

"Get down on it yourself."

"I ain't no damn fag. It's your fault I killt—"

"My fault!" yelled Bill; "how'n hell you get that way?"

McMann peered drunkenly above the rim of his glass, the low square brow of forehead beneath his red hair wrinkling. "I was nothin' till you blowed round with your dope."

"Then what you bitching?"

"I ain't bitchin'."

"What the hell you call bitching if you ain't?"

"Paddy usta say to me you're a smart sonufabitch." He grinned fondly, inveigled towards a feeling of auld lang syne. "The first time I saw ya. At Paddy's."

"And you fetched down a guy in a trunk." They laughed like two old men recalling a childhood memory, pleased that they both remembered, sighing, their whisky breaths filling the room.

"Jeez, yeh. It's plain no-good." He complained so dully Bill was sorry. "It ain't fair. N.G. What a lousy life! Two ginks dead. Not my fault, it ain't. Faulta lousy life. Looka," he exclaimed. "My ole man ain't worse'n the rest, nor me old lady, but they're plain stinkin' Irish, sockin' me when they had nothin' on. Out in the gutter with the other kids, that's me, learnin' to drive by hockin' cars, jumpin' into one after 'nother. Lotsa saps never shut off their motors. When we got jammed up I run away. I learn every damn thing that way. Myself. Myself. Not one bastard to help me." He refilled his glass, his small clever head perched on his neck, swaying gently as he talked. "Tha's too bad," said Bill. Injustice in the world, you could bet on it. A lot of injustice directed against them. It wasn't fair, with the world ganging against their drunkenness. His insides were heated. The room was humid as if summer were outside, yet his cool mind held guard. He didn't trust McMann even when he spoke of his kid days, never done before even under liquor. Why now? Christ, McMann could drink a barrel and not feel it. Why was he blabbing all the bunko about kid days. He thought: I'm sitting here with a murderer, he's killed two men in a day and a half. He is feeling me out. He is pulling a fast one. Maybe I am to be killed.

Bill consoled himself drunkenly. Why, he was an accessory to Duffy's murder. He'd handed over the gat. (Why in hell had he done it?) And as McMann mumbled about his kid days, Bill's streak of sanity like a lightning fought itself clear of the thundery cloudy darkness of the booze. The few months, the few yesterdays. All in a life. He was in dutch with guys wanting him. Hanrahan,

Duffy, McMann, sat morbidly at his funeral, the death of his former life, staring at his new life sweeping along. Murder. Oh, Christ, Hanrahan the bull, the kids, the stickups, Metz, Joe and Cathy, the clubhouse. This compacted past was creating a future even while he breathed and sprawled in a strange room.

He caught the tag end of a sentence. "Reform school. Nex' stop for me and whatta hell. Too smart for them lunkheads and they knew it, an' hiding us done no good. I hacked, was in odd jobs for ginks like Paddy, a lil pimpin', boozerunnin', but nothin' much—"

"Your parents dead like mine?" asked Bill, patriotically sad.

"What the hell you got 'gainst my parents?"

"Not a damn thing."

"Shut up. The ole lady wasn't a bad un."

Bill wanted him to speak about his folk for no reason at all. What'd he care? Far behind the haze of drink in which his body was etherized, he felt he didn't trust McMann, McMann had no parents, had been born like a devil without them, a devil sent to lead him into hell. Drugged, inert as he was, this flicker of thought was shocking him, his conscience laboring against the red McMann who wasn't a human, whose thoughts were hidden, whom he distrusted. What was he thinking of, what did he mean to do, and who but a fool could trust this gab of childhood and old ladies?

"April first isn't far off and we need dough to fix the clubhouse proper." McMann stated they ought to see Spat and give the bozo a chance, Spat was a numberbook with connections. And they needed dough. Sure. Wasn't he figuring on a joint in Harlem and figuring bigger jobs, like ferinstance, how about a kidnapping of some big shot's kid, sure, why not? Lots of mugs in booze and numbers with kids they could grab for ransom, sure, why not, big dough in one lump…Bill was dazed with a sense of I-told-you-so, as if one astute segment of him were boasting to another, more naïve Bill. Double damn right. Always McMann led further on, further into hell. Even now with the cursed devil sentimental about childhood he had but to say the word of God, the word *dough*, and the devil was ready for something else. McMann was leaning on his elbows. He declared what they needed was a ransom job. They had the kids, and it was easy. Bill filled the glasses. Kidnapping paid well if you got away with it. He wouldn't put a thing past McMann. "I bet you got the details ready."

"You have," said McMann; "ain't you the brain?" He laughed for a long time at this perpetually funny joke.

"You plastered it on me for good?"

"Why not?"

"Anything goes twisty and I'll be the goat."

"If you know the answers, why ask 'em?" He was staring at Bill's face every other second, glancing away amused, as if the joke were still there.

"That's it," cried Bill, infuriated. "Just careful. I'm goat for the slip-up. I don't blame you." Life taught the lesson, the survival of the most cunning. What a damn fool he was to speak so seriously! He smiled. "Hell with it. Tomorrow's another day."

"Down the hatch." McMann grinned, his bony head nodding from side to side, the high skull-cap coming straight down to the eye-ridge, where, deeply sunk, the reddish eyes glinted, the only live things in his face. Just like Duffy's, thought Bill. And Duffy had to go. It was them or Duffy…McMann's cheek-bones, jaw, slitted mouth, were impassive and brutal, not from choice, but from creation. What could such a man think? So had life cut him forth from the womb, made him what he was, a civilized beast obeying the principles of a jungle society. Climb the ladder. The drink was strong and amiable in Bill, pounding him on the shoulder, drawing the men together as if it were the mutual crony. He was sorry for McMann, his head tumblesaulting so that it was impossible to say whether he, Bill Trent, was being sorry or some other groggy Bill. "Life runs on like a river," he orated, boozily philosophic. "You follow the river. Looka me. Good family. Education. A good job. And I'm a wolf. Looka me. Terrible. A crook, a murderer. Don't you think I'm not spoiling my brother. I see it. Bad enough I ruin myself, but I'm taking him with me. I see it. I'm not a fool altogether. He should never have come to me. Getting him a job, I shouldn't have caused him to lose it. He spends my dirty money and he'll come to no good with me. What can I do? I can't back out. I don't want to back out. I'm not a bad fellow, but I got to have dough."

"Tha's the way it goes," said McMann with profound acquiescence. "Two killin's on me hands. What'd the priest say, huh? I don' go to priests even if they're clams. I trust nobody, not one livin' guy." He smiled, asking approval for his code. The city in which they sat had never been built. They needed one another that second in the softening of their souls, using one another as priest, holding this mutual confessional in a strange place. Beyond the window the city gripped the earth with a fist of stone, the squared pyramided city of the millions. They were lonely.

"Looka me," cried Bill, driving nail after nail into his cross, "Months since I've been with respectable people. This what I live for? Living and eating with gangsters and whores?"

"Everybody's a lousy whiner," said McMann. "What's the use? So what? You oughta be glad you'd a fat time of it for so many years. Hell, you had a fat time, so what you bitchin' for?"

Bill hated him, happy his face was fiery, his eyes turning on drunken orbits. McMann couldn't see his hate. He was afraid of him. Even now he might be reading the hate behind his eyes. If it'd suit him, I'd be the next after Duffy. He was sorry. It would've been better if they'd been real friends. Now suppose he grabbed a knife and stabbed it into McMann as one would into a wild beast. Why wait to be slashed? That'd be a real brain guy. You let the head decide what was best. He glanced up as if he'd been away a week. The tempter, satanic, formidable. Oh, McMann. McMann wasn't human. He was so gifted. He could destroy him when he was utterly lost. McMann had compelled him to be an accessory to murder. What next? Kidnapper, pimp, dope-peddler? How low, Jesus Christ? Forgive me, not my fault. McMann's, the bastard devil. He'll make a murderer out of me yet…knife. He drank and his heart plotted. If he killed him, there'd be an end to everything. He'd be able to quit. Not too late. He thought murder, concealing his devil's blood lust. It was a lie. He wouldn't quit. Quitting didn't put dough in your pocket. He needed dough. "Sometimes I'd like to kill you, Red."

"Me, too." His eyes glared as if he were happy to confess his mind. They smiled at the truth spoken, like brothers united by a single ambition. "Have a drink. You're a good guy even as I says to Paddy when we hooked up."

"It's a long time. Every day the future shows bigger."

"Dog eat dog. They don't eat us, we eat them. I don't eat you, you eat me. The way it goes. A dinner party, a big feed, tha's all."

"The big feed." He laughed. "That's funny."

"An' it tastes good."

"But some dogs are buddies like you'n me." He heeled McMann, lounging in the easy chair near the window, mapping out his relation to McMann like a mathematician. He allowed for time. McMann was unarmed. But he could drop hand in pocket and snap out a five-inch blade by pressing a little button. He'd be on Mac in a jiffy. Not ten feet separated them. There was no convenient chair for McMann to swing. He had the knife, he'd get the first punch in. He casually brushed his hand against his pocket. The knife filled the pocket. The button on top of the bone sheath faced the rear of the room. It wasn't murder in his thought but the exhilarated acting-out of a simple equation involving length and time, McMann the completion of all formulas. He wasn't even surprised he should finally come to murder. It had to come. You accepted life as it was. Better for him to be armed at the showdown than McMann. McMann hadn't needed him for a long time. McMann destroyed what was of no use. What was the use being a brain guy if you didn't act on it?

Glass in hand, McMann staggered towards the table where the bottles of whisky and ginger ale stood. Bill thought: I'm going to kill a drunk. It didn't occur to him he was drunk, too, his mind finishing up the last decisions and moves in a chess game begun long ago. He allowed for the glass McMann'd heave at him. Getting up with his glass, he circled the table which had become a possible barricade, a pawn obstructing his victory. His hand dived in his pocket. The knife was out, the button clicking, five inches springing from his fist. He lunged it forward deep into McMann's side. The glassful of whisky into which McMann had been pouring ginger ale dropped to the carpet. McMann silently grabbed one of the bottles, his red eyes amazed, angry. Blood gushed. The knife was out. "You coke," cried McMann. Bill felt it freed from the sheath of flesh, tightening his fingers into McMann's neck so no more words could come. Face to face almost, their drunken bitter breaths mingling, he plunged the knife with a continuation of motion and the first attack, remorseless, ultimately successful, into McMann's heart, who, choking, fell forward upon his attacker like a lover, a drunk surrendering himself to the care of a bosom pal. The bottle, gripped, eddied from his slack fingers, rolling across the table. Stopped by the whisky bottle, the ginger ale ran out from the narrow neck as if it too had been murdered.

Bill lowered the body to the floor. McMann lay as Duffy. It was strange to see in the one day the *killer* equal to the victim. Bill thought: I can't make it look like suicide, not with that extra stab in the side. He took McMann's gloves out of his overcoat, wiping the blade and throwing it into the basket. With another handkerchief he rubbed the glasses and bottles free from fingerprints. The ginger-ale bottle he set up on its bottom as one assists a drunk to his feet. No sitting up for Mac. There were no clues. Even a fingerprint'd mean nothing. He wasn't fingerprinted, even though he might be. There were no clues. Still wearing McMann's gloves, he hung on the outer door-knob: "Not To Be Disturbed." Hotels these days provided for everything. The corridor was empty. He'd grown to expect emptiness and a lack of witnesses whenever he pulled a job off. He was lucky.

He was elated. It was a joyous thing to consider that so tough a bird could be wiped out in a second. Showed how equal people were after all. His heaving breath stank of whisky. He walked downstairs. It was all over. He hadn't stepped into McMann's shoes, but he wore his gloves. there were things to be done. He stripped the gloves from his hands, holding them stylishly in one fist, then dropping them in the gutter. He boarded the Broadway subway, soothed by the yellow gross files of faces. In that light, in that mutual linkage of lives for an indifferent second, he felt at home. it was more transient than a railroad trip. Nobody took the slightest interest in anyone else, not even a pair of legs to magnetize the males, nothing but a drab group in a long swaying car traveling through a dank diseased smell, which held blue and white lights and sudden stops where they got off and came on with no significance or hope. It was the ideal sanctuary for a murderer. When the train stopped at Times Square, he hurried off. In a cafeteria he ordered a sandwich and a cup of coffee. The cafeteria was almost as lonely as the subway. Again the colossal anonymous face of the city leered over his shoulder, vague, questing. In this white gleam of tiled walls with people eating in hats and coats as if come in by accident, as if deliberately refusing to enjoy what they ate, one was a hermit among the other solitaries, monks worshipping the city's face, which was really the composite of its worshippers. It was self-idolatry and hideous. But here he was free and alone.

He had to get started. He had an idea. He was the brain guy. Let the brain help him. McMann was away, gone somewhere, anywhere, say to Yonkers to plan a stickup. He'd be there a few days. The brain was in charge. He was in charge. Sure. Right. No kick there. He'd see to everything. What of Duffy?

What of Duffy dead? He and McMann had complete control of the kids. McMann was dead. Who was to know? He was boss. Must rivet himself as boss. Strike when the iron's hot. He needed help. McMann said to give Spat a chance. Spat must be won over. He must solve these problems or scram the hell out. Go where and do what? He smiled. Hell, he'd stick. He was proud of his loyalty to something vague and idealistic, sipping his coffee, knowing where McMann had slipped. Knowing where with such an autocracy of knowledge he loved himself. McMann'd been too careful. Too careful. If he hadn't invented the brain-guy dodge, he'd still be alive. McMann had been so careful he had to thrash Spat. Didn't pay to be too careful. Look at McMann the fool. Forget the fool. He had to clinch control, to work Spat. Boss.

The cashier, a Jew with glasses, eased his surgical hands in the drawer of the cash register. There was a lot of money in the drawer. Bill's mind moved indolently as if only lesser matters occupied it. A code'd been killed . Duffy. McMann. How remote these things were. Out of sight, out of mind. Like hell. Maybe he was drunk, but he walked straight. His watch said it was ten after eleven. Christ knew where Spat was. He'd have to see him in the morning. If anyone got rough he knew how to fix them. No use sleeping home. Let Joe worry. He took a room at a hotel and slept immediately. He was absolutely worn out. His mind knew he had to find Spat. Where was spat? He knew where Duffy and McMann were to the exact inch. He was sorry for Duffy. Maybe it hadn't been really necessary to kill Duffy.

Come to think of it, Hanrahan might be curious about McMann being killed…

Awaking, he stared at the sun's shafts as if to comment: Here you are again, right on the dot. He used his finger as a toothbrush, rubbing it across his teeth, careful not to scratch his gums. McMann'd gone away. That's how he thought of yesterday. McMann'd gone away. It was sad. Who did he have left in the cursed city? He was lonely, no friends, no nobody. His brother and maybe Madge, that was all among the multitudes. If Hanrahan bothered him about McMann, well, he didn't know a damn…

He thought simply as if it were a bright idea, an inspiration: Do you know you're a murderer? No, he thought, grinning foolishly. Yes, he answered, laughing at the repartee. Where was remorse? He wouldn't kill a fly. He thought with superb justification: I wouldn't kill a little fly. McMann's death was business. Business didn't have a damn to do with extra-business hours when even the flies were safe. All murderers looked in mirrors and he might as well. It was an old trick. Was that him? He was shocked as if someone were fooling around. It was him, the same Bill. He was disgusted, beating it out for coffee, whistling in a melancholy way like a jilted fellow.

He ate heartily, then walked down Eighth. Spring was at least half-way round the corner even if prosperity hadn't yet showed an inch of its schnob. The sky was soft, the wind mild, it was what is known as a great day to be alive. The yellow bitter stone faces of the mob welcomes spring, but with no acknowledgment. It was a secret between the coming season and each individual. A fat man smiled shabbily, a slim girl held her head higher into the annual delusion of the warming sun. Ah, life would be better for everybody in the spring. They would prosper, know love. Bill, striding among them, also gazed towards the dazzling sky. Perhaps it was for him? Perhaps something good was waiting. Perhaps in a short time he'd have enough dough to leave New York to settle somewhere in a decent life. His teeth snapped tight. He felt a cavity in his lower jaw. It hurt like hell. He smiled like a fifteen-dollar-a-week white-collar spurring himself on to the rainbow's end of thirty bucks every damn week in the year, plus a month's vacation. His future was charted; Spat was the first future hour.

It was almost one before he found Spat. He'd dropped in at pool parlors and speaks, but Spat had already collected the betting slips. What a job! All you did was collect numbers and the nickels bet on them, paying out five hundred to one when some sap won. What a respectable racket! If a lousy bull picked you up, you phoned the boss, the bull'd get fifty bucks, and that'd be that. If you got hauled to a judge, it was a few days in stir. And yet this dope Spat wasn't satisfied, had to better himself in life. Maybe he was working towards a stake so he could retire and raise chickens.

Bill laughed wildly. Was that the way conscience played its tricks on him? Spat was coming out of a saloon on Tenth Avenue, wiping his lips. He was dressed in sporty gray and seemed beefier than ever.

They both stopped, two enemies met at last. "I been searching for you, Spat. First I got some dough for you from the last job."

"McMann givin' me dough? Nuts."

"I'm giving it to you." He smiled at the dark sullen face as if to remind Spat of the time McMann had licked him and he'd washed his bloody mug…

Spat grinned. "Le's have a beer." They went inside. It'd been a saloon in the old days, the woodwork, the mirrors, preserving a sense of handlebar mustaches and fighters like Sullivan and Corbett. They drank beer.

"Let's sit down," said Bill. The place was almost empty. "You don't get it because you think McMann's chief cheese."

"Who is? You?" He laughed.

"I'm his partner."

"And the brain guy."

Bill scanned him carefully. Spat wasn't kidding. His glib face betrayed no knowledge of Duffy. Didn't he read the tabloids? McMann's death might even be in the papers already. He wondered how much Spat knew. "I'm the brain guy, but I didn't dope out your pounding. That was McMann's idea."

"Yeah?" He twisted his glass. "Mebbe so."

"No maybe about it." He stared into the black eyes, hard, hostile. "If I had a thing against you I wouldn't've helped you after that fight."

"I thank ya." He smiled maliciously.

"McMann beat you up because he was aiming to get control of the kids. Beating you up was poking Duffy." (Still Spat was pokerface.) "It let Duffy save his face while banging yours. Now you know why you were lumped. McMann's got control of the kids. We're holding a party at the clubhouse. You're invited."

"Duffy won't be there. Why should I?"

"It wouldn't look right for Duffy to come. He's through. Duffy's through. What you care? He let you down." They stared across the plate of pretzels. He thought: Spat's wise.

"You and McMann are funny guys."

"In what way?" His eyes flashed, he tightened his fists, a recklessness in all his bones, stripped down to hardness. "Maybe you were lucky coming off with a licking. Lickings aren't the worse things." He could lick the world if he had a mind to. His heart whispered: You're McMann now. He was McMann as if, with the death, the qualities of Red had become part of his body.

"The hell with it," said Spat despondently. "The papers are full with Duffy found killt. Poor Duff. Shot to hell."

"He ain't the only one. Another guy was found stabbed in a doorway over Chelsea."

Spat gripped the table with both hands, leaning forward all dark eyes, so near Bill noticed the coarse hairs in his nostrils. "Clip 'em, Spat."

"Clip what?"

"The hair in your beak. That might give you some brains. Duffy and that other fellow were mixed together, in case you don't know it." Spat was tapping his beer glass, the beer was flat. "McMann's in Yonkers." Hadn't a chambermaid removed the Not To Be Disturbed sign on the knob? "McMann's out there on business."

Spat shivered. "I don' like the whole business. Poor Duff."

"That's what I told them. What the hell good would it be to wipe Spat, I said."

"You ain't scarin' me any."

"That's what Duffy said."

"Christ, why wipe me?" He blew his nose. He was used to Duffy's murder, but now to hear another guy'd been finished, it wasn't so hot.

"You're O.K. I want you in. I like you."

Spat trembled more than ever. "I don' get it."

"You ever wonder why I mixed with lil stinkers like you'n Duffy and McMann?"

"Me? I knows nottin'."

"I'm from a big guy. I got orders to get hold of a bunch of kids. That's why I was sent down. That's why I was called the brain guy. So I got McMann to help. Duffy was out for McMann. He got sloughed with that other guy. You can't act up like that when big guys are behind a feller. And McMann ain't in Yonkers. I got it over the phone." Spat appeared like a kid watching a magician. "McMann tried to cut loose from the big guy. He'd wiped out Duffy and that other guy on Mac's say-so. Now, McMann was thinking he'd be independent, he had the kids sewed up. Well, it ain't in the papers, but you'll read about it. McMann's dead." He enjoyed Spat's amazement, the enemy eyes losing harshness. He was a god predicting the future. "You'll be reading how McMann was fixed in some hotel right here in town. The big guy told me he was watching me night and day. If I did as I was told, everything'd be O.K. I'm a brain guy, I listen to guys bigger'n me."

"I'm outa it."

"Like hell, Spat. It's too late."

"What the hell you mean?" Frightened, he forgot the glass in his hand, his lips parched with another thirst.

"I'm looking for you for a reason. When I heard McMann was wiped I said how about you as assistant. They said O.K." He winked kindly at the terrified book, at the striped green tie and yawning jaws.

"I'm outa it."

Bill spoke dreamily, his heart floating in the current of his power, the current roaring in his body. He pulled out his wallet and handed Spat two tens. "Those guys got loads of kale. They're free with it. Don't be a sucker."

"I'm makin' plenty runnin' numbers. Hell with it."

"You can use small change. You damn fool, get it in your bean. In two days and a half, Duffy, the other guy, McMann are wiped. Come in. You'll be treated square if you're on the square. Big things are ahead. Real dough."

"Yeah, a stinkin' clubhouse off Eight."

"You dumb bastard, you stunk around with Duffy when you didn't have any hole." He glared sternly. "Maybe it's a stinking clubhouse, but it gets things done. One way or other you'll be leaving this man's town. You were Duffy's pal and we gotta know how you stand. If you don't come in, we know. I'm tipping you straight, you dumb bastard. You're mixed with Duffy. Why let you off? Only on my say-so that you'd come in and behave…

Spat shook his big head from side to side as if trying to get something out of it. He wet his lips, leaning on his fists. "What am I gonna do?"

"Take the twenty and listen to me. You'll be in the dough. Keep your job with the numbers but here's a chance for easy side-money."

"I got no break," said Spat. He put the money in his pocket as if it was cigar-store coupons, stiff in his chair as if pinned to it.

He was trapped by a bull story, a lousy lie, the best trap in the world. Bill smiled. "I need a guy to take McMann's place. I got a hunch I can trust you. Now, you pass the word among the kids to meet at the poolroom tonight. I want to talk to them. We'll begin clean."

"O.K.," said Spat, rising. He stared at the table as if he had left something behind. There was nothing. "S'long. Around ten tonight? O.K. I'll be seein' ya."

They parted. Bill admired himself for that bull story. He was a bull artist. The way he'd got round Stanger, Paddy, McMann, Spat. Hanrahan, though, was a tougher egg. Could Spat be trusted? He felt so strong, so cocksure, he didn't give a damn. If he lived or died, what of it? It didn't mean a damn. He wasn't excited, his life was mean, lonely. The only beautiful picture in it was the long dream of power. Ten o'clock…He wondered about Joe. With some sleight-of-hand trick he placed Joe out of sight, plunking him down beyond the horizon with that future of his. He phoned Madge, the people in the drug store drinking sodas and eating lettuce and tomatoes. Madge seemed reluctant to meet him. "What's wrong?" he said. "You meet me at Fiftieth and Ninth front of the A. & P. or you can go to hell." He hung up. He flipped his nickel, heads or tails? Let's hope it's tails. He laughed.

His thoughts walked with him, the remorses, the doubts, the terrors encancering heart and brain. On these light streets hewn in gray stone out of the year's dying, sunlight flowing between in beneficent rivers, he went with the crowd of memories. He'd killed a man. He. No one but himself. Bill Squattamellon Percy Macaroni Whathaveyou Trent. With these hands, this lunge of body, he had killed. This brain had plotted and consummated. It was hard to believe. It was entirely a matter for belief. Not him. Somebody else.

Madge smiled. Her face was pretty with the exception of a few skin roughages the nightly Zonite had not eradicated. They went north-east to Broadway. She was brisk, normal, at ease. Suddenly he wanted to shock her, with the morbid impulse of a kid scaring his mother late at night. "Things've been happening to your pals."

"Paddy's sore as hell you haulin' me out."

"He can go to hell."

"He says I'm getting' to be charity cherry."

"You sorry?"

"Nope."

He squeezed her arm. "Listen. McMann's been fixed."

She lowered her head like a devout Catholic passing a church. "Killed?"

"Twice as dead as hell." He heard the word *hell* deep within him like an angelus: Hell hell hell…He suggested they go up to his room, McMann's death fading into a sex deadlock. She refused as if she were a dilly-dallyin virgin. Paddy's holler and why now? "I'll be waiting. The number's 453." Minutes later she knocked. He called: "Come in with the ice water."

It was a hot joke. he helped her out of her coat, kissing her neck. The winter's sun slanted pale rays of another spring. Life was moving to another awakening. Despite themselves, spring was in their blood and they were listening for the voice of the new year to cry out like that of another sleeping beauty. Her arm was bandaged.

"What's that?" A kiss, she said. Like hell it was. If it ain't a disease what could it be? How'd she get hurt? "It's a burn." "You're a liar."

"I got cut accidental at a party."

"White a knife?"

"So what?"

"So what. Just as McMann'd say it. So what. I can't get rid of the bastard. Maybe McMann did it."

"What the hell if he did?"

He slapped her. So that was it. Well, let her spill it. She blurted the details of that night. He thought the red devil was at every turning of his life. That McMann was his own tissue and had been and done unto Madge as his flesh. He was confused at the duality of their lives. They were brothers, and the murder was as evil as the slaying of Abel. He was aghast, superstitious. "You're not sore?" she asked. "I give it away to a million guys; maybe as well be a buddy of your'n." She smiled, female and logical.

He quibbled over the morality of the situation. "But he didn't pay you like the rest." It was ethical and consistent with their love if she got paid. It was false to do it for nothing, for the love of it.

"He paid me."

He let the lie be, for McMann was dead and there could be a courtesy for a dead man. McMann pay? Like hell. McMann'd never pay. McMann was like himself, his brother.

"It's all over. He's been taken for a fall. I'm boss. You're my girl till get tired of your face. If I pull down enough dough you'll quit Paddy. I'll buy you from him." He spoke wearily of a future opulent and dangerous. "You tell Paddy I'll see'm tonight. The clubhouse is opening soon and I want him to supply the dames. They'll get paid well."

"For April Fool's Day? Ain't it?"

"Maybe you wouldn't've cracked that? Maybe, but I don't think so. Oh, you little fool."

"Go to hell, you're too snotty."

"That's why you love me."

What'd she do if he were spotted? She'd do nothing, go back to work, look for another guy. He'd do the same if she were dead. He was proud as Lucifer of their self-sufficiency…

Afterwards, returning to Leroy, he felt like a tourist coming back again to old streets with valises in both hands pasted with foreign labels.

"Hello," said Joe.

"Hello," said Bill, with a death between them. He patted the dog, incredulous to be remembered, he'd been away so long; what memories beasts had!

"How's it going to end, now, with that red-headed guy chasing you early in the morning? God's sake, why don't you quit?"

"I'd like to work."

"What do you do all day?" Bill persisted as if he was fresh from Siam or Australia and was quizzing old friends. "You must do something. Yes, a handsome kid." (Just like Hanrahan, thought Joe.) "How about Cathy?"

"I see some of her. What you driving at?"

"You like her, kid, don't you?"

"Aw, cut it." He was red to the eyes, his hands, his forehead up to the yellow shock his hair rooted in red.

"I wish you luck. That's what we all need in life."

"Are you sick? You're talking groggy."

"Both of you young and goodlooking. Why not?" His manner was comparative, like a traveler's noting the likeness between love in Siam and in the home town. "My dough's running low, but I'll have more later. Take this fiver. "Gwan." He moved to the door despite Joe's pleading, not even listening to the names of the words, so that it seemed one big sound spouting at him, low, monotonous. Behind the voice Joe's mouth was open, his teeth set in even pearly lines. "Sorry, I got a date to address a political organization. Your brother's becoming a big shot. Good-by."

"More dirty money," shouted Joe at the closing door. He grinned. Whatever Bill was, he was a sport. Thinking of Cathy, the sweet limbs of virgins, new fruit, new creation, so that loving them was like dreamy sleeping under springtime apple trees in the scent of beginning. He hummed to himself. A scent as if of apple blossoms rose in the flat.

After supper he was happy to pluck her from her parents. They went up to the hotel room. Bill's money was needed to pay for it, you bet it was. It wasn't her who walked with him. She was still afraid, a girl child with blushing face. The one who came was the ghost of her not yet materialized, the woman who was to be, was becoming with each step down the lengthy hotel corridor. Inside he was alone with a woman, the virgin child shivering and crouching at the door, the virgin child the ghost. The reality was a woman whose hands he took, her body moving towards him without compulsion, as if there were a mechanism in both of them that could only function when they were together. He was hearing the roar in his head like wheels turning, the movements of heavy ominous things. The machinery was spinning. Like the memory of a good summer, the scent of their youths lingered, mingling.

He kissed her slowly, both of them burrowing deep into passion like two woodchucks hiding from winter. Digging deep, the world was left high on top, a surface world where there were families, priests, brothers, problems, the agonies and compunctions. But here there was only warmth of the earth and the dense pressure of their bodies packing them together. Distant from outside contact, they made love, fondling like savages, endlessly innocent of time until, in passion spent, he stared down at her naked body with sobering eyes. Seeing him stare at her, suddenly aware of time, with time in his stare, she covered herself up, no longer innocent.

They listened to the city. Through the lowered shades they felt the weight of a million eyes, and all sight belonged to priests, mothers, censorious persons. "It's a sin," she moaned. "I'm no good."

"The thousandth time you've said it. Nothing wrong in my loving you, is there?" He gripped her close, his lips in hard oval kisses like little mouths declaiming: Of course there's nothing wrong, Cathy.

CHAPTER TWENTY-THREE

These were the last days before April, and April was the name of the spring, the awakening, and the days thawed into nothingness and there was night, and then the nights were gone and another was nearer spring…

The kids hadn't said a word in dissent at the meeting. Holy Christ, McMann spotted. Tough. The word leaked out. They considered the fact of Duffy and McMann wiped out in so short a space, right after one another. Who was left? That's what counted. The clubhouse counted. Bill and Spat were buddies. So what? The kids didn't give a damn about the killings. They were the results of some godly battle out of their understanding. What they wanted was leaders. And dough. It looked like they were set for bigger things. The clubhouse was going to open on the dot. Jobs were scheduled soon after. Bill was smart. Didn't even McMann usta call him brain guy? And Spat was a good muscle if there ever was. O.K.

Ray and Schneck were sorry about McMann because Spat mightn't like them much. But Spat wasn't the big cheese. You could see it with both eyes shut. Bill was the gink to heel. Bill said every guy was due for a break. Ray and Schneck listened at the meeting, and once Bill looked at them, talking to them the most, even with the words meant for the crowd. Ray and Schneck said that meant somepun. It was oke. If things didn't work out so hot, they could quit. Not a thing was lost.

Everybody felt fine when the meeting was over. It had gone off the nuts. Everybody had a hunch there'd be tons of easy kale. Hell, and they'd hardly noticed that Bill. He usta be quiet with McMann around. But them quiet guys. Hell. They noticed him plenty. He was O.K. Any guy to fix Duffy and McMann was some guy, hadda be O.K.

The meeting was over and the last days of March like the final waters of a flood tide carried all the torrents in its wild course.

Busy with plans, the clubhouse, Bill was always aware of that heart of his ticking out the story, recapitulant, all the long story since he'd lost his job and become a brain guy. Tick tock, telling the story of McMann and the robberies, the murders, tick tock the past, April first, the club, telling the tales of March and April and May, all the months to come as if time had no hold on his heart. Greater than time it told the story of the days to come, ticked the prophecies in a strange dour tongue. What would it be? A fool to worry about the future. If McMann had foreseen his murder, if he'd foreseen blood on his hands…Hell with the future. Hanrahan might clip him, or Spat, or Ray, or some new leader led at the moment. Or he might be lucky and make dough. A decent sum, three thousand, say, enough to quit on, go west, south, anywhere. The clubhouse was prepared. He ate and slept with Madge…

He wasn't surprised Joe looked sick. His world was in crisis, and Joe was part of it. He, Bill, was the world, and when he was stricken, all felt the impact. Joe glanced up from slicing the grapefruit. "I'm in trouble, Bill. I got Cathy in trouble. She says her mother's getting wise. She wants to run away. She don't want to hurt them."

Bill laughed. "We spread hope and goodwill wherever we go." And he smiled sadly at the clean seducer before him, his brother Joe. He himself was the seducer above all, not Joe. "How long's it been going on? My eyes've been shut."

"It's done. What shall I do?"

Bill was sorry for the Gebhardts, sighing, sympathy cold in his heart. All he could do was act the outer shell, nodding his head. "Why don't you marry her? She's a good kid. She might do you some good."

"That's a joke. You saying that. Christ." He stared at Bill as Bill remembered he used to stare at McMann.

"Why not?" McMann was in him now. The tempters never died, passing from body to body. McMann lived. "Want to ruin her life? If you don't give her a break she'll hit the gutter. How the hell do you think they keep up the whore supply in town?" "I was thinking of living with her—that is, if you don't mind. You see, I love her."

"Why not marry her, Joe?"

"Who the hell wants to marry?" he said bitterly. "I'm your real brother, Bill."

Bill's heart thumped miserably, the shell of sympathy radiating inwards, warming the core of his heart. A sadness spoke to him. No use kidding himself. He'd ruined his brother, murdered a life. "I'm not arguing. I'm not keeping you and any mistress. You marry the kid. You love her. Marry her and I'll help you out until you get a job."

"I want a job. I'm sick hanging around this damn town living on you. Get me any job." He laughed suddenly. "Where you work."

"Where I work?"

"I'm being polite."

Maybe Spat could get Joe a route, have Joe collect numbers. That was respectable, almost. "I'll see what I'll do. Will you marry her?"

"We'll see," said Joe, grinning like his brother so that they looked like a mirrored reflection of each other.

Bill laughed softly. "It beats me why you asked me for advice when you're so set." And that was over, passing into the swirl of those last days, and there was this to be done and that to be done, their lives floating chips on the river of his purpose. He was the river and held all of them, floating himself on time's huger torrent. Every day it was nearer April.

Life was grand. Life was elegant. It goes on. that was the swell thing about it. It never sits down on its pants to ask: Who am I? What am I doing? It just goes on, and I'm a hunk of life. I'm not Bill. I'm not a guy, I'm just a miscellaneous blind hunk of life, and what the hell if I am? When I get five thousand I'll quit and become Bill again, not a hunk of life. But now I'm a blind hunk, and one harvest's in for good or bad, and on Fool's Day I'll be planting another harvest, and here's hoping to Christ it nets me big dough.

CHAPTER TWENTY-FOUR

For an hour the Armenian tailor who occupied the ground floor of the Young Hamilton Democrats Club, had looked up from his pressing-machine at the young Democrats trooping up to their headquarters. To his experience they were a little young for citizens, but maybe the Young covered that. They were eighteen, nineteen, and in their early twenties, exactly alike, slim, hard-faced, kidding around. They'd be damn particular about clothes, and the Armenian figured how much there'd be in it for him. Plenty bad bets in that crowd, sure to be some who'd cheat a poor man out of his just pay.

Upstairs the two floors of the club presented the spiffy exhilating flash of newness. The light buff paint was fresh, the floors shellacked. Each of the floors had been prepared for Hamiltonian democracy. A few chairs, a lounge, kegs of beer. It was a very political sight. The kids who'd been awed in the beginning at their importance (although joking to beat the band as if they had a clubhouse on every block) began to shout: "Swell," "This is what's what," and otherwise applaud the arrangements. The dirty mouths among them got busy.

Jesus, it was swell. On the second floor it was extra swell. One of the flats had been fitted up as an office with a plain desk for Bill. A regular office, big-time in the bargain. The other flat had two beds, the younger kids wiggling their wrists in the sign language that meant: Plenty kife, hey, kid? The world-lier exclaiming: "Looka them hot bastards." Downstairs rushed the mob, maybe thirty guys gathering around Bill and Spat, who appeared as if they were on soapboxes ready to spiel them. Hooray! Speech. Speech.

"Speech, Bill," cried Schneck from the window, his wide body in a blue serge suit, his fat Germanic face seeming without a neck. Near him, Ray's sharp eyes met Bill's. He spotted the two of them, smiling at the young grinning, shouting crowd, thinking: There's the trouble to come.

"This is the first meeting of our new club," he said. "No business'll be discussed tonight. But in a coupla days there'll be work for those who wants it." They roared. "This club's backed by some big shots. You'll be in soft if you follow orders. There's beer and hard stuff. Go to it. Later we'll have some dancers for those that like them." They yelled, the eager groups of young men, their faces downy, crisp as spring leaves, their bodies straight up and down with hardly any hip. They began to circulate among the rooms, some meandering into the rear flats, others staying where they were. They slumped in the new chairs, filling the fresh-painted rooms with smoke. What kinda club was it without plenty smoke, huh? In the dense blueness they drank beer and spat at the brass spittoons on little rubber mats covered with sand. Some gink turned on the radio, and between bellows and wisecracks the radio played dance music.

The kid called Mike returned with a huge leg of roast beef. Another kid like an assistant chef lugged big loaves of sliced sandwich bread. Mike dropped the roast on the table, the wolves packing in, begging like kids for an apple core: "Don' forget me, Mike."

"I'm a pal, Mike." Mike cut off hunks of beef. They grabbed the slices, gulping beer. Jesus, it was a swell party. Another kid brought in a dozen quarts of gin and rye. The shouts were jubilant; what a party, what style, classy as anything! Nobody cared where the gifts were from. In their brains there was a vague idea that the beef, the booze, emanated from some kind of god, some overbeing known as the big guy. They accepted the gifts and were grateful.

A kid puked; a wild cannibal cry banging against the walls. They coulda mobilized him, cursing the puke for a son-of-a-bitch. Where the hell did he get that stuff, stinking up the new clubhouse? They concentrated on the sissy, made him clean up his filth.

This was only the start, the party was pepping up. They cracked dirty jokes, the one of the wise philosophical parrot whose throat was cut and then thrown into the toilet…They ragged about the dames they'd knocked off and the dames ready to be fixed. Kids circulated along the staircases from one flat to another with the boozy swelldom of plutocrats on a spree in sumptuous quarters. They cheered, tottering from one room to another, happy, laughing, fighting with other guys sprawling up like ghosts. They ganged to the second floor and squatted on the stairs, and after songs and explorations, returned to the first flat, where the grub and drinks were dispensed. On the second floor, in the flat with the beds, a bunch got steamed up and were going to lizzy up one of the younger kids who had a girl's complexion. They'da fixed his wagon, only some bozo remembered that the office was on that floor, and Bill'n Spat might be around.

The first hour or so Spat and Bill wound in and out among the kids. They were slapped on the back and asked to drink, the kids genial as politicians and the sons of Irishmen. Spat and Bill grinned like wardheelers, easing out to the next gang with their cheery cry: Got enough to eat and drink?

Spat and Bill shut the door behind them in the office. Bill swung his feet on the desk. A few minutes later Ray, Schneck, McQuade, the Chisel, marched in uneasy as applicants for a job. None of them were very drunk. It was the meeting of a war staff that might be torn by dissension. Bill said that they were the natural leaders, that's what they were and they knew it; when they said anything, the other kids opened their ears. He glanced from thin malicious Ray, whose face was memorable of McMann, to Schneck smoking like a burgher. The Chisel was a little runt with a big crop of hair immediately differentiating him from the other, close-cropped kids, he wasn't saying a thing, smiling as if to assure the others he was listening. McQuade nodded, a toughened-up chorus boy in looks. It was a silence of secret thoughts. Was Spat with him? Who gave a damn? Caught by his own story, he was believing in the story of the higher-ups of whom he was the appointed instrument.

"Wonder McMann ain't here at his own party," said Ray.

Bill slapped him hard and viciously. Ray jumped up and sat down. "McMann ain't coming to parties, Ray."

"Maybe I had it comin'?"

"You damn well did." They banded against Ray, even his buddy Schneck, wolves against Ray because he was wounded and nobody had any use for the wounded.

"Once and for all," said Bill. "Christ, as if Ray didn't know it, the bastard wise-guy, McMann's wiped. We were the leaders. And Duffy's gone and a coupla others you guys don't know about. Wiped because they tried to bust loose from guys bigger than them. Spat and me's here because we take orders. The big guys who rented this house, who're supplying the eats and drinks, are tough to fool around with. McMann and Duffy were wise-guys."

"I had it comin'," said Ray.

They were leery in the office because the symbol of force, the flame of sudden death, was in Bill. He was boss and they listened respectfully because boss meant power. It was Bill now and Spat with him. It'd been Duffy and McMann yesterday. And tomorrow they'd be on their knees before somebody else.

"That's all," said Bill. "I don't need none of you, but I figured I'd start with you four, give you guys the first break. In a week we work. Dough for workers, and something else for the lice. Now scram, there's a party here tonight."

They scattered among the flats, glad the meeting was over. Hell with tomorrow. The Chisel began drinking with Mike McQuade; Ray and Schneck formed another coalition. They herded together. Only Spat and Bill were powerful enough to venture their own ways, joking, acting as if they were a mob in themselves.

Bill pulled down the shade in one of the rear flats. The bare yard with its lonely tree calmed him. "You boys, keep it down. The neighbors might get sore." A kid pushed a bottle at him and he drank. "The women'll be here soon, so you guys keep it down." They cheered, the swaying drunken hands walling him in. He walked out, the bunch staring after him as if he were the colors of a parade. He stepped along the corridor, his hand sliding on the banister. He made the round of his kingdoms, getting groggy himself. There's McMann here tonight, but they call him Ray. McMann's ghost is Ray. Ray is Ray. We're McMann's children, and this bastard Ray is a son. I know he's a son, that's all to it...His drunken positiveness struck him as an instinctive wisdom. Ray and McMann, with the same stone courage. Schneck was a big tough egg and could be made to toe the line. Not Ray. The Chisel was a slimy little skunk whispering in everybody's ears. McQuade? Spat? Hell with my buddies. I don't need be feared. Ask Spat for a job for Joe? Joe the policy book...He took another drink, mournfully walking out on a bunch jabbering at his heels like apparitions he had created and could never be rid of. Joe must marry Cathy. Yes u'no.

Oh, my God, give me a rest. "Say, you kids," he bellowed, "I told ya to keep the noise down."

He was getting tangled with all the millions of rooms he'd been in, the millions of corridors connecting them, reasoning out his troubles. Tell you what, Bill, he said to himself, numbers are accuracy and how many troubles you got…Things to a brother's life had been done, spoiled a brother he had, maybe Cathy'd make him decent if he married her…Hanrahan, you fat bull…blond, strong like the mamma and marriage?... Hanrahan, McMann; oh, you wait a minute, Hanrahan'll be number eight-one… McMann's dead and here with his pal, me is his pal, hello, McMann old boy. How the hell're you? (He searched in the blue smoke which was the graveyard of a thousand rising ghosts. Schneck was telling a dirty story to a fellow, himself, he was laughing.) Hello, McMann, how are you? I don't feel sorry I bopped you. Have you anything against me? You have not, you must be proud of me, that's why you sent your little boy Ray to watch me…

"I wish the women'd come," said Schneck. Hahaha. Laughs. A glass of rye tilting.

"What women?" said Bill. "hell, they'll be right up." He moved with dignity, engrossed in his game of numbers. To the toilet to take a leak and there he noticed some dope'd already decorated the fresh-painted buff wall with a dirty mural, sketching in a fat woman, the important parts shaded, and with witty slogans above and below. Number one, two, three…Hanrahan, lousy mick snooper. Wise to me, want to get me on the holdups on Ninth, come after me about McMann, why the hell aren't you interested in me and the McMann murder, don't you think I know a little about it? What'd you do, McMann? I wish I had your brain wrapped up in a hanky to advise me…Joe and Cathy, I got to fix that and be careful of Hanrahan, and run the club and get jobs and kidnap Rockefeller's daughter and get plenty dimes and then I quit…He staggered out of the lavatory.

The kids had gathered outside the flats like boarders piling out at word of Fire, and down below coming up were five women, Madge leading a quartet. "Back, alla you," growled Bill. "Keep the racket down, you damn mugs." The five women smiled, ding-donging their hells like bells. "Hello, Bill," said Madge. "Hell," he said. The kids whispered that was Bill's dame, snickering, yeh, that dame there, and what he sees in her, the bunch of bones, but nice eyes and legs, and she ain't skinny, she's slender, guy, she's slender, guy. They admired him more than ever with a dame like her nuts about him. "Thirty guys here about," said Bill. "You four babes gotta make love to seven eight guys a head. God damn it, no racket. You get twenty bucks apiece from me. If the kids wants extras they'll pay it." He glanced at the four dames, plump, thirty, wide built, ideal for lineups. Madge'd done a good job, got the right kind. While they watched, he yanked out his wallet and paid out the money. "None of you guys swiping this or I'll kill you. You, Ray, Schneck, Mike, Chisel, you four fellers take charge, count out your sides." He laughed in the turmoil, the scent of women, the smoke, all the boozy beery atmosphere like a hell about him. "You four take care of the dames, see everyone gets a fair break." He winked at Spat, and Spat smiled back. Bill thought: If I show him dough he'll be my man. He went to the office with Madge, shouting for Spat to keep the racket down. He switched on the light and shut the door. In the rear there was a brown couch.

"Holy Christ, ever see anything like it, those four palooks like monitors, so serious? Christ."

"I wonder how much cut Paddy'll take?"

"Forget it." He took her hands. "How easy to bop a man off, but they're scared of me so far. Work. I've got to find work to keep 'em quiet. If I get by, you'll be in the dough."

"You're kinda wild, honey."

"Naw, only drunk."

She seemed older smoking her cigarette. "Them dames oughta be glad with them nice kids, no greasers and no tellin' what else they make. What a riot! You been feedin' 'em booze in trucks, it sounds."

He thought of Joe. He had built his house well. Joe would marry Cathy and work for Spat. Cathy would help save Joe. The kids loved each other. He snickered. Madge stared at him. Madge didn't know what a master builder he was. He knew. In a hundred years they'd all be dead. The hell with it. So Joe wouldn't be a respectable clerk, wouldn't lead a sissy life. That was his doing. Good Christ, always the weak must follow the strong. He put thought of Joe away from him. Hell with it. He had work to get for the kids. He needed his brain to think of that and of Hanrahan. How would he end up? Who cared? He felt careless of everything. He had one regret. He said to her: "Only McMann isn't here."

"Forget him."

"I'll give a reward for his killer." He thought: My brother Joe.

"Cut it, Bill, you got me leery, you're so pale, you look bad."

"Just a lil drunk. Me and Spat got to run that pack of tigers, and the bull's wise." His eyes shone, the whites glaring an abandoned power, his thoughts leaping out of the office into which he'd sneaked like an animal to a den. He was alone with his body and her body, but his thoughts were in the world. His thoughts were with Joe and Hanrahan and the jobs to be pulled and the five grand or five trillion to be made. Hell, but he was also alone with their two bodies, and when she walked to him, her hips swaying, he rubbed his eyes to be sure. She put her arms about his neck. His body seized her body, but only his body. His thoughts were out in the world, and it was only a game of bodies, his thoughts with the time not yet come, fixed on the hour-hands not yet passed across the face of his life. Oh, blessed God, I cannot forget my brother or Hanrahan or the things I must do. It was only a body for Madge to love and that's why she loved him, hoping to get all of him, and hoping, therefore loving…The grand sweeping world, oh, the world, his life not yet begun, the tomorrows for seedings and harvestings, and what seedings and harvestings he now knew.

He looked at the bandage on her arm, and even in this secret hide-away where his body rested, McMann had come to put the bandage there.

THE END

PLUNDER

BY BENJAMIN APPEL

For Fred

CHAPTER ONE

One thought ate at him—to break out of the stockade somehow and return to Manila. Not for a minute could he forget that sweet money town where even the back alleys were paved with the folding stuff.

Late at night in the womanless stockade when the other GI prisoners tossed in their sleep, dreaming happy or grotesque dreams about the women of the liberated city, the little Filipino and Chinese girls spicy as ginger, the Spanish mestizas and White Russky blondes, he lay awake methodically working out the details of the scheme that was sure to make him rich, if he ever got back to Manila. It was a perfect scheme because it was the perfect swindle; the blue-sky deal that all the awols turned operators were always chasing after with greedy fingers.

His name was Joe Trent but even the stockade guards called him Joe the Lawyer. Maybe because of the latrine rumor that he was a busted officer. In any case, schemes were written all over his hard blond face, his blue eyes like two lenses focused on one thing only: money. That was the kind of lawyer he was, a graduate of larceny, a specialist in soft deals. After the Battle of Manila, in February 1945, he'd awoled himself out of the Army to stick up his shingle over a place known as the Five Sisters. The sisters weren't sisters but pom-pom girls, the sweethearts of any GI with ten pesos. His partner was a mestizo by the name of Tommy Cruz. With an army of liberation loose in all the streets of Manila, with no more battles to win and the only action in a bed or at a bar, business had been fine. But his good luck cracked up in a gambling joint off Avenida Rizal, where the MP raiders refused to be bought off by the crap-shooting awols.

How in hell was he going to break out of the stockade? Joe asked himself. This stockade up in the rice country at Fernando was tighter than an iron box. A few escapees, it was said, had paid their way out, but he didn't have a single peso stashed away anywhere. The pesos, he thought grimly. It was always the pesos! The pesos to cure the itchy palm of a stockade guard. The pesos he hoped to make in Manila. Always the pesos! O.K., he told himself; he had to figure up a pile of phony pesos and pass them off as the real thing. There were always guys so greedy they'd fall for the counterfeit. By and large, you never could go wrong appealing to what was low down in human nature. Joe the Lawyer had decided that long ago.

The prisoner they all called Blacky had no loot stashed away either. Blacky had awoled himself out of the Army to take up the trade of armed robbery in Manila. "You were a lone wolf," Joe explained to Blacky. "A lone wolf might— he just might—have some money stashed away. There's a top kick here, Murdock, who'll go to hell in a wheel chair if you give him a smell of money. The money you haven't got—"

Their shadows followed them as they darted from wall to wall. Nobody else in the stockade seemed to be awake; the barracks, long midnight blocks, were silent in the starlight. Sergeant Murdock was in the lead, Joe the Lawyer and Blacky right behind him.

Blacky wasn't thinking now of the deal that had bought the Sergeant. All Blacky could think of was that a miracle was happening and maybe it would come off and they'd get to Manila.

The Sergeant crossed to a shed. The prisoners followed him, flattened against the shed wall, staring at the row of seven or eight trucks and jeeps lined up under the white blazing stars.

The Sergeant whispered, "That's the truck. Second from the end. She's gonna pull out in twenty minutes. Sam's driving. He knows you'll be on, but he don't wanna know, get me? Don't say nothin' to him. The guard with Sam don't know about you."

Blacky was afraid somebody would overhear Murdock and they'd all be hauled in. He blinked at the second truck from the end, biting his lips. Twenty minutes, Murdock had said. Why didn't that bastard of a sergeant stop talking!

"We got it all straight between us?" the Sergeant asked them anxiously.

"Sarge, you worry too much," Joe answered him.

"You better start worrying! I'll be in Friday to collect my money."

"Sure! Liberators' Café, twenty-one hundred hours."

"You better be there!"

"Where the hell else would we be, Sarge?"

"With the ten thousand pesos."

"Sure, Sarge. And we'll have that party at the Five Sisters. All the pom-pom girls you want."

There was a second of silence. Then almost regretfully Murdock whispered, "Aw, get goin'. See you Friday!" He watched the two prisoners steal out of the wall's sheltering shadow, targets in the light. Then they were gone and the empty night held only the jeeps and trucks.

The prisoners had crawled into the second truck from the end, shutting the truck doors and inching their way deep into a no man's land of stacked boxes. Blacky felt as if he'd climbed into some huge box himself and pulled the lid down. A coffin lid. His heart thudded loudly in his ears. "Joe," he whispered.

"Shut up! No telling when Sam gets here!"

Blacky was silent. He waited patiently as he had learned to wait in the stockade, and time, for Blacky, became the endless minute that only prisoners and fugitives know about.

Ten minutes, maybe fifteen, maybe thirty minutes ticked off before Blacky started at the sound of approaching footsteps. He heard voices. Then the motor started up and the truck rolled forward, braking to a stop almost instantly. They had come to the stockade gates.

The truck driver shouted, "Open up, jerk!"

The soldier at the gates drawled up at the guard sitting next to the truck driver, "If I was you, I'd take that forty-five out of my holster."

"Don't have to!"

"No? You can draw faster'n that fuggen Lone Ranger? Those black-market hijackers'll jump you and you'll wake up dead!"

"Goddamn jerks at Quartermaster!" the truck driver cursed. "Ball up everything! Load me up with soap, and the pigheaded C.O. has to shoot the whole goddamn load back! Get hijacked for a load of goddamn soap! C'mon, let's blow!"

Listening from inside the truck, Blacky picked out the voice of Sam, the truck driver. Murdock must have promised Sam a slice of that ten thousand pesos, the ten thousand they didn't have, the ten thousand Joe the Lawyer had used as bait. Blacky grinned to himself. Things would work out, he thought; things had to work out when a guy like Joe was doing the headwork. When the truck lurched forward, Blacky pressed his lips against Joe's ear. "I'm hitting the sack, O.K.?"

"O.K."

Blacky closed his eyes to the tune of the tires singing on the road, the motor humming. He wondered vaguely what the deal was in Manila. Joe hadn't ever spelled it out exactly. All Blacky knew was that it was in the pom-pom racket, which suited him fine. He couldn't imagine anything better.

Blacky slept. It was the sleep of a man who knows he's in good hands.

He awoke to the grip of Joe's fingers on his shoulder. Their truck wasn't moving and Blacky listened to what seemed to him all the running motors of all the trucks in the world. "Check point," Joe whispered. Blacky breathed deeply. They'd made the fifty miles south to Manila! Their truck shifted into gear, creeping along slowly as if through a tunnel of roaring motors. Blacky could almost see the long traffic line of weapon carriers and jeeps and trucks, the bright yellow headlights, the MP's at the check point waving their electrically lit batons that always reminded him of jeweled sticks. Manila! He gulped, thinking of the city he'd dreamed about in the stockade. The great big city of Manila, greeting him now in a screeching of brakes and a honking of horns, a raw chorus that also held the voices of the pom-pom girls at the Five Sisters, whom he hoped to be seeing this night.

They passed through the check point. Faster their truck rolled into the downtown city. The first voices lifted faintly to weave into a solid web of sound. GI's on the crowded sidewalks, brawling, laughing, hollering, with now and then the clear light voice of a woman. Inside the speeding truck, Blacky's fingers tightened as if he were clutching at all the unseen women out there in the Manila night.

Then the web of sound began to unravel. Blacky guessed that their truck had left the big streets, Avenida Rizal or Quezon Boulevard. There was a load of soap on this truck and they must be headed for the depots on the water front.

When the truck slowed, the truck driver's voice, louder than natural, tipped off his passengers. "Something's loose. I'm gonna stop and see." The truck driver climbed down, walking toward the rear of his truck. It was dark on the water front, the piers fingering out into Manila Bay like shadowy dead-end streets, the lights of the anchored ships dabbing yellow and red streaks on the black silken water. "Be with you in a minute," the truck driver yelled to the guard as he stared at the two escapees.

They had jumped out of the truck, and they moved into the shadows. The driver got back in and started up the motor.

Blacky had wanted to run, but Joe grabbed his elbow. The smell of sea water and rotting wood filled their lungs, and floating in the night air too was the stink of bloated corpses, excrement, and gasoline. It lingered on, this last faint haunting reminder of the Battle of Manila. Once Blacky turned around. The truck's taillights were diminishing by the second. There before his eyes, the stockade rolled out of his life.

"God Almighty," Blacky murmured gratefully, "Joe, we're in Manila!"

They had come back to Manila, all right, to the fireburned jungle sprouted by the war in all the streets where once people had lived. The brilliant tropic stars shone down whitely on black jagged walls and staircases leading nowhere, on the depots and warehouses, newly built by the Army, like a beachhead established on the edge of a stone and rubble wilderness whose huge dark flowers were of twisted iron.

But the two escapees hurrying in silence along the ruined streets were absorbed by other Manilas. Joe looked inward at the Manila of easy money. His first move would be to sell his scheme to Tommy Cruz, his old partner, Joe was thinking. As for Blacky, he was thinking of the Manila that was a pom-pom house.

"Where the hell are we?" he asked Joe.

"San Nicolas part of town. We want Zaragoza Street. Then Rizal."

Blacky sighed. "All I want is one of those Five Sisters you've been telling me about."

"They're nothing to the women we'll have, Blacky! This idea of mine's a million-peso idea! Wait till you hear it, Blacky. This is what—"

"Some other time," Blacky protested.

"No, you should have the picture now."

"Only picture I want to see now is a girl's!" Blacky laughed. "How're those Five Sisters?"

"They're GI bags."

"They sound beautiful to me. Lead me to 'em!"

Blacky and Joe hiked east into streets where the houses hadn't all been leveled. Soft candlelight gleamed a lonely yellow from the few flats where Filipinos were still awake. If his legs didn't drop off, Blacky thought, he'd be taking a load off his feet in that Five Sisters joint. There was the start of a little pom-pom song, Blacky thought. A load off his feet and a load off his arms

Pom-pom songs were a specialty of Blacky's ever since training camp in the States. He got a bang out of inventing rhymes. There was a romantic streak in Blacky MacIntyre. In Australia he had tried to play a banjo, but his blunt powerful fingers, as he said himself, were made to handle one-inch rope rather than banjo strings. He was superstitious, too, and in New Guinea he had sworn he could feel when the Jap bullets were marked with the D of Death and when they buzzed by harmless as flies.

"Hey, Joe!" Blacky exclaimed. "That must be Rizal Street now!"

Before them was a winding alley, but they could both hear Avenida Rizal even if they couldn't see the broad avenue. Somewhere on the other side of the night was a steady hum of traffic, a low rumble at first like a faraway surf, then louder, louder. They turned the corner and gaped as if blindfolds had dropped from their eyes, feeling as if they'd stepped out of the sleeping city into a city where no one ever slept. At the end of a second alley, Avenida Rizal shone like an electric diamond. From the headlights of the trucks and jeeps pouring north and south, a made-in-America daylight glittered.

"Wow!" Blacky cried.

"Jerks back home'll have to pay heavy for the gas of this man's army!"

"Man alive, Joe!"

"There goes the ninth war loan, in case you don't know it."

"Looks like heaven to me, Joe. I just want to plant my lil feet on Rizal again!"

On Avenida Rizal, the clock had stopped forever on that magic midnight hour when there was still plenty of time for another bottle of whisky or a girl. GI's, their peaked jockey caps tilted on their heads, shuffled up and down the sidewalks as if celebrating a perpetual block party, smoking big cigars and chewing on hot dogs bought from the curb peddlers. Drunken GI's vomited in the gutters and carousing GI's looped along, tagged by barefooted brown kids who seemed to have no place else to go, drawn by the noise and lights like little human moths. Yet some of the Filipino kids were businessmen. "Pom-pom for you, soljer," they cried in shrill voices. "Good pom-pom for soljer!" And the MP's walked by in bored pairs that even an occasional revolver shot in some dark and twisting alley didn't disturb. Souvenir-buying GI's carried Batangas knives and bolos, and a soggy corporal broke into a trot, waving a small Rising Sun flag.

The voices of America, south and north, drawl and twang, competed with the monotonous single voice of the roaring traffic. The headlights of the khaki-colored trucks lit up the corrugated iron roofs of the new stores erected on the sites of the old buildings, pulverized by shell fire and carted away. The prewar and occupation-time avenue was gone forever to make room for this honky-tonk promenade where all the cash customers were GI's.

Blacky and Joe peered in at the *panciterías* or restaurants, the curio stores, the bars, the night clubs open on the sidewalks. Inside, GI's were dancing with the Filipino hostesses to the jazz music they were so homesick for. Nothing had changed, Blacky thought, from the time he'd been on the prowl in Manila four months ago. There were the same GI's, the same little brown girls and mestizas, but now there was electricity in the night clubs. He stared at the dancing women and felt the blood thickening in his veins.

They sidestepped a drunk and Joe sneered, "The Japs've gone, the jerks've come!"

Blacky stared at Joe as if he'd never seen him before. He was a big blond man, Joe the Lawyer, a shade under six feet. Blacky himself was a shade over six, an inch and a half over. The guy had everything, Blacky thought, build and brains and good looks, with his thick blond hair, his blue eyes and Hollywood nose. Blacky was aware that his own hair was thinning, although he was seven or eight years younger than Joe. As for looks? He was average, his mouth a little too wide, his nose a little too long. Brains? He couldn't have wangled Murdock in a million years. "You're thirty-four or -five and I'm twenty-six," Blacky said gropingly. "I look as old as you. I guess everything slides off you, Joe. Yeah, that must be it."

"What are you talking about, anyway?"

"What I mean is you take everything in your stride. You couldn't be a jerk if you wanted to."

"No? When I think how I wasted my time running a lil pom-pom place when I could've been making real dough! Aw, the hell with it. What's under the bridge is under. Let's find that Five Sisters place. You want a girl and I want to see Tommy Cruz."

"Don't you want a girl?"

"Sure, but it's business before pleasure, peckerhead!"

The Five Sisters wasn't too different from a dozen other places that Blacky had known both as a soldier and as an awol. It was located on the ground floor of a two-story house in a dark alley where homeless kids waited for GI coins and the starlight twinkled from the broken glass of whisky bottles. They entered what might have been a *panciteria*, except that the main course wasn't served up front. At the wire-legged tables GI's were feeding their faces under a smoke cloud made out of their own cigarettes. At the counter in the rear a Filipino girl in a tight red dress sliced bread for sandwiches. In the wall behind her there was a window open into the kitchen. "She must be new,"Joe said, sitting down at an empty table.

"New or old, I'd like it. Hey, sister!" Blacky called, no longer thinking about what made Joe tick. No use thinking, anyway. It was all a snafu and the miracle had happened. He was out of the stockade, in a pom-pom house! That was enough to think about. "Hey, sister!"

The girl in the red dress walked over to their table, a menu in her fingers.

She smiled at the two big soldiers. Blacky stooped and ran his hand up her bare leg. Gracefully, like a dancer, she stepped away. Blacky grinned happily. "Sister, I've been dreaming of doing that for a long time. Thanks! Which one of the five sisters're you?"

"You behave!" the girl in the red dress said in Spanish-accented English. Her face was almost plump for a Filipino, and she wore red coral earrings.

"What's your name?" Blacky leaned back in his chair, observing the curve of her breasts with that same grin on his lips.

"Franny. You behave!"

Joe was squinting at the electric bulbs hanging from the ceiling on long dangling wires. "You had candles when I was here last, Franny."

"Electric," Franny said proudly.

"Is Maria here?"

"Maria go away."

"Sisa, Bella?"

"All go away. You know Bella? You come before?"

Blacky laughed. "Hell with Bella. Who you got now, Franny?"

"Teresita and Rosalina, Adeline and Lucy." She turned, her eyes shifting to a green-curtained doorway in the rear. Two GI's emerged from behind the curtain; two GI's arose from their table.

"Where's Tommy Cruz?" Joe asked Franny.

"He is home."

"I have to see him right away. He's a friend of mine. You get me a piece of paper and a pencil. I'll write Tommy a note and you get somebody to take it to him, O.K.? I have to see him right away."

"Tomorrow you see him, no?"

Blacky wasn't listening to them. His dark, thin face was flushed and the names of the pom-pom girls, Teresita, Rosalina, Adeline, Lucy, repeated themselves in his mind. Teresita, Rosalina, Adeline, Lucy.... His eyes moved up and down Franny's body, stripping her of that tight red dress. He could almost see the pom-pom rooms behind the green curtain, the four sisters on their cots, four Frannys, four brown girls with big black eyes and little breasts, Teresita, Rosalina, Adeline, Lucy....

"Will you get me some paper and a pencil?" Joe said to Franny, a smile that was as hard and metallic as twisted wire on his lips. His hand shot out, catching Franny by her wrist. He tightened his grip.

"I bring! I bring!" she promised him, and he let her go. Rubbing at her wrist, she stared at him. Then she hurried to the counter. A GI in horn-rimmed glasses waved at her, teetered to his feet, and announced, "Gonna make a speech. Speech 'bout the best dame I ever had."

"You were a lil rough on Franny," Blacky said to Joe.

"Rough? That's what they cry for." Restlessly he picked up the menu, reading it. "That Tommy Cruz certainly made some changes. Listen to this." He began to read to Blacky:

"'Five Sisters Place. Open Whole Day and Whole Night Service. Enjoy Romantical Entertainment. Never put off until tomorrow what you can eat, take, and drink today and tonight. Cure your aching Heart. Give Vigor to your undying love and awaken your sleepy heads.'"

"Pretty corny," Blacky agreed, "but it packs them in. Joe, how about fixing me a lil credit now?"

"Take it easy," Joe said. "We don't want trouble." He consulted the menu. "Prices are coming down. Fried chicken's six pesos, Coke's two pesos. Coffee's fifty centavos We'll have to hustle before they ship everybody home."

"Hustle me a lil credit, Lawyer!" Blacky said, getting to his feet.

"Sit down, jerk."

Blacky headed straight for the green curtain. A swish and he was behind it, a long, dimly lit corridor lined with five or six doors and painted in almost as many colors: the salvaged doors of the bombed city, bought in the black market. Some fitted perfectly, but at the bases of others there were broad gaps filled with light from the rooms. Blacky could hear voices, male and female. He trembled as he breathed in the smell of talcum powder, sweat, disinfectant, and cheap perfume. He reached for the knob of the nearest door. "Hola!" somebody cried at him. A mestizo whom he hadn't noticed, sitting inside a doorway at the end of the corridor, stood up. He was short and wide, and his shirt, open at the collar, showed a brown meaty neck.

"I'm next!" Blacky smiled when the mestizo neared him. "Franny said for me to go in."

"Six pesos! T'ree dol-lar!" The mestizo held out his hand.

"All taken care of. My buddy's taken care of it."

"No, no, Joe."

"Joe's right. Victory Joe, he takes care of every damn thing! Look here, Pedro-"

"My name, he is not Pedro, and you drunk!"

Blacky blew his breath into the mestizo's face. "See, I haven't got a drop of whisky in me. I'll wait here and you go ask Franny yourself."

As soon as the mestizo went through the curtain, Blacky opened the nearest door. An angry GI shouted him out. Grinning, Blacky tried the next door and ducked a shoe. On his third try, he was offered a drink by the GI inside. "No, thanks, buddy," Blacky said. "What I want's that pom-pom special!" In the next room, the girl was alone.

Blacky went inside as if sleepwalking, as if he'd seen this room and this girl before, many times before, in his stockade dreams—a room not much larger than a big closet, the plaster walls dingy, with a gray fly-eating lizard on the far wall to one side of a crooked mirror. There was a bamboo table under the mirror, a pitcher of water, a couple of towels; and sitting on the army cot, as if she'd been patiently waiting for him and nobody else, was a girl in a bright-flowered kimono. She was the phantom of his dreams. He walked over to her, his eyes on her small oval face. She had the tiny nose of the women of the country, and her child-sized lips were stretched in a meaningless smile. On her flat brown cheek, Blacky noticed a long whitish scar, the kind of scar a man might expect to see on an older pom-pom girl, but this one was very young, eighteen or nineteen. "Which sister are you, kid?" he asked, sitting down next to her on the cot.

"You are big man, no?" she said, tilting her head to look up into his dark, gaunt face.

Blacky listened to the cot groaning under his weight. "A noise made in heaven!" he said, curving his arm about her waist. "What's your name?"

"Lucy."

"How'd you get an American name like Lucy, kid?"

"My boy friend Conway, he give me. You know Conway?"

"Sure, everybody knows Conway. Kilroy's first cousin."

"You give me snow job," she said in the GI slang she'd picked up from her customers.

He patted her belly. "That jerk Conway left a kid like you!"

"*Hang gnang* Pier Seven."

He laughed, for he knew the meaning of this expression used by the girls of Manila, this combination of the native Tagalog words and the English: *Hang gnang* Pier Seven—It is love until Pier Seven. "I'm going to stay here, Lucy, and make love to you. Never going home."

And that was no lie, Blacky thought fleetingly.

Home was a place for a GI, but not for a two-time awol like himself. For him the welcome mat was waiting outside the stockade. Reserved for him was a bunk on a prison ship, a cell in an Army clink. Home? It was a laugh. Even if he could walk into a replacement depot like any other GI and hike up the gangplant of a trooper, singing the repple-depple blues, there wouldn't be much sense going home. For he really had no home, and no home town. Not since the day in New Guinea with the jungle rains pouring and his sister's black-edged letter in his hands. Home was his mother, and his mother was dead and buried two years now, and Beaver Dam, Wisconsin, was only the name of another town. Big maples shaded Front Street in Beaver Dam. Eighty-acre and hundred-sixty-acre farms of Germans and Poles and old-time settlers surrounded the tiny spot of neon light that was Beaver Dam on a Saturday, when the farmers took their families to the Odeon movie and crowded into his father's hardware store to talk about the latest price on cheese and hogs as they picked up some tools or a keg of nails. But his father had died and his sister's husband, Pete, ran the store, and it was no fun living in Pete's house, and less fun for his old mother. Blacky was eighteen when he graduated from high school to go to work in the town's stove factory. He had rented a little apartment for himself and his mother. He was a big, powerful boy then, with a thick black shock of hair, and he had never traveled farther than Milwaukee when the events of December 7, 1941, sent him westward across the continent and the Pacific with a million other small-town boys and big-town boys.

And now his home was any room that had a smiling girl in it, and whether the smile was real or fake wasn't too important any more.

He helped this little brown girl out of her kimono. He lowered his head to her small breasts. He felt her hands in his hair. "Forget that goddamn Conway!" he said, laughing wildly and happily. "Any guy who'd leave a girl like you, kid, isn't worth a damn."

"I cannot forget," the girl said coquettishly. "Conway, he say he go to church with me Christmas."

"I'll take you, kid."

"Yes?" She smiled.

Her voice reached him from far away as if muffled by the sound of his thick roaring blood. To hell with Conway, to hell with Sergeant Murdock, due on Friday, and the MP's due any day. To hell with Joe and his deal, whatever it was. He looked at Lucy on the cot and staggered toward her like a drunk, like a man walking in his dreams. He embraced her, breathing in the soapy perfumed smell of the shampoo she had used in her hair, and suddenly he seemed to be falling. Falling from an immense height, down, down, down into her yielding softness, into all the stockade dreams come true at last....

The gray lizard on the wall darted out its inconceivably fast tongue at a fly.

CHAPTER TWO

The corridor pimp, his eyes slitted, had rushed through the green curtain complaining to Franny. Joe listened to their furious Tagalog-Spanish. That Blacky was too much of a lone wolf, he thought angrily. He'd have to whip the big bastard into line.

"Six pesos, t'ree dol-lar!" the mestizo demanded as he and Franny hurried to Joe's table, while at all the other tables, the GI's waited joyfuly for a riot to spice the night.

But there was no riot. Joe held up the piece of paper and pencil Franny had fetched him. "Tommy'll straighten out everything when he gets here," he promised them blandly. "Tommy Cruz owes me two thousand pesos, Franny. Figure it out yourself. At six pesos a throw, my buddy could stay in there until Christmas. Right, Franny?" That two thousand pesos was printed on the same invisible paper as the ten thousand promised to Sergeant Murdock. "O.K., Franny?"

He could see with half an eye that it wasn't O.K. But at least he'd silenced their squawk for the six lousy pesos. But O.K.? Never. They had met too many other GI's whose only cash was on deposit on their tongues. What confused them was the note he was writing to Tommy Cruz. Joe smiled up at the silent girl watching him like a policewoman. "Get me some chow, Franny, and tell your boy friend to stop beefing. Two thousand pesos is a lot of pesos. A lot of pesos!"

The GI's, praying for a riot, abandoned all hope now. Some of them were waiting to cure their "acking Hearts," as advised by the menu. Others were eating swiftly, as if they still were on the conveyor belt that had rolled them in and out of the rooms behind the green curtain.

"Beer, Franny!" a GI shouted. "Three beers!"

Franny spoke to the mestizo, who walked toward the curtain. Franny returned to her counter and Joe smiled. He could chalk up this round, too. There was nothing like the big lie! It had paid off with Murdock and with Franny. The big lie! Fraud and misrepresentation, Joe thought gleefully; they were as good as pesos in the bank. He finished writing his note; he snapped his fingers at Franny. "Get me one of those kids outside to take it to Tommy Cruz, and where in hell's my chow?"

Franny mockingly patted her plump bottom.

Joe's blue eyes gleamed. "Not before I eat. Bring me some fried chicken, Franny. Better make it two portions and a pot of coffee and some cigarettes."

"I bring you this!" With her brown thumb and forefinger she made a zero.

He plunged his rigid forefinger into the zero. "And I'll give you this, but first I have to eat! Goddamn, I got two thousand pesos coming to me out of this hole. You want me to tell Tommy Cruz how dumb you are? You haven't the brains to run this place! Two thousand pesos and I can't get a lil lousy chow! Here, get this off to Tommy Cruz!" He gave her the folded sheet of paper.

He watched her walk to the door, and her hips in the tight red dress reminded him that Blacky was getting his while he had to fix it up with a roomful of goddamn flips. When Franny came in from the alley he shouted, "Franny, that chow!"

She shrugged wearily. "O.K.," she said. "You bad man."

What was bad in a chippy's dictionary? Joe wondered smiling to himself. Maybe she was smarter than he thought. Maybe she had a hunch he was going to do Tommy Cruz no good. Right now he needed Tommy Cruz. But once things started rolling, he was paying off that sunavabitch. The odds were a hundred to one that Tommy had celebrated like crazy when the MP's had picked him up.

Joe was smoking one of the cigarettes Franny had given him with his fried chicken when a fair-skinned man in a white sharkskin suit and white silk shirt, a fine buntal Panama on his head, walked into the place.

"Ah, Joe," the newcomer said, sitting down at Joe's table and taking off his Panama. With the Panama on his head, shadowing his eyes, he could have been a white man. But no white man had eyes so slanted, so narrow. Tommy Cruz was one of those men who seem to belong to no definite nationality. He had a Filipino name but he wasn't Filipino. His eyes were Japanese or Chinese, his skin was a pale white, his features small and neat and international.

The mestizo smiled at the American. "I am hap-py to see you, Joe," he said. His English was good, with only a slight accent. Tommy spoke four or five languages with only a slight accent. In the Manila of pom-pom houses and Tondo thieves, they said that Tommy's father had been a half-breed Russky married to a Chinese woman in Shanghai. But no gossip-loving pickpocket or pimp knew how or when Tommy Cruz had come to the Philippines. Some said he had served Japanese Intelligence until liberation had forced him to tear the rising sun from his lapel and replace it with the stars and stripes.

Joe said not a word, smiling his greeting and remembering how he'd convinced Tommy they could open a big place like the Five Sisters. That was three, four months ago, and now the sunavabitch was wearing silk and sharkskin. "Looks as if you're making a peso, Tommy."

"I make, yes."

"Let's go somewhere and talk. I got some ideas for some more pesos, Tommy."

"Yes?"

"First, you better tell Franny my buddy's O.K. I pulled into town with this guy. He's locked himself in with one of your pom-pom girls. I had to give Franny a snow job about you owing me two thousand pesos." Joe laughed. "You don't owe me a thing," he added quickly.

They went over to Franny. She was wiping the counter nervously with a dingy gray cloth. Joe reached across the counter and pinched her hard. She cried out and he said grimly, "That's for all your griping, Franny. Tommy, I'll be with you in a minute. I'll tell my buddy he can stay all night. O.K.?" Tommy Cruz nodded and Joe hurried behind the green curtain. He parleyed with the corridor pimp. "Don't bother me! You don't believe me, Tommy Cruz is out there! Lose yourself! Where the hell's my buddy?" The man gestured at the last door. Joe opened it, and stared. "Blacky, I'm going with Tommy. You stay here. I'll pick you up, you lucky bastid! You never had it so good!"

Five minutes later they were driving north in Tommy's jeep. "I don't talk about a big deal except over a table," Joe said to Tommy's feelers. "Hell, this town's changed."

The jeep's headlights lit up the Manila he had known, the city half crushed to death in the arms of the liberators, kissed by fire, and ravished by war. Palm trees without crowns thrust upward from a scorched earth still littered with fire-fused glass. But the headlights also spotted the stores on Rizal bulging with goods. "Where'd you steal the jeep, Tommy?"

"I buy from Army Motor Pool," Tommy Cruz answered him calmly.

"That means some dispatcher's got himself a soft deal." He felt a strange satisfaction, as if he himself were profiting from the black market in jeeps. God Almighty, this town was ripe for the picking, Joe thought. He had an image of Manila—a city like an old tired Filipino woman, her pockets full of American gold, trudging down a ruined street where the operators were lurking.

He wasn't surprised when Tommy Cruz stopped in front of a two-story house in a respectable street that had escaped the war. Fat and smug in the night, the houses were nearly all dark. "Jeeps and a regular palace," Joe commented bitterly. "Yeah, stockade's the wrong screwen place to make a peso!" They walked into the *sala*, or living room. Tommy switched on the light. The paneled walls of bronze-like *nara* wood gleamed. There were an American-style couch and chairs, and, near a draped window, an old-fashioned roll-top office desk and a typewriter. Joe nodded at the business furniture. "You must have three or four places like the Five Sisters," he guessed enviously.

Tommy Cruz only smiled. He walked to a lacquer cabinet and brought a bottle of whisky and two glasses to the long mahogany table in the middle of the *sala*. "Stateside whisky, Joe."

"When I met you, you were drinking rotgut spiked with gasoline."

They sat down and Tommy poured the whisky into the glasses. They were big glasses, holding about three jiggers each.

"Here's to forty places like the Five Sisters!" Joe toasted. They drank. Joe smacked his lips and poured the second round. "Stateside whisky, huh, and maybe a Stateside woman upstairs? I haven't had a woman in so long I'm rusted."

"Ah, you have tough luck, Joe."

"The hell with it. It's all under the bridge." He grinned. "Who've you got upstairs? Do I know her, Tommy?"

"No. She is Japanese girl."

"What's her name?"

"Hanoco."

They killed the second round and Joe said, "These glasses're real hookers. A bottle's not safe with 'em around. Tommy, I didn't come here to drink up your booze. I've got a deal for you. A deal in pom-pom!"

Up in the stockade he had rehearsed this scene a dozen times, deciding on every word like a con man preparing his pitch. But one stage prop had been missing in the stockade: the bottle of Stateside whisky. Missing too was the backdrop: the city of Manila with its feel of money in the air and women to help a man spend it hand over fist. He was drunk on the two stiff shots of good whisky, and he was just as drunk on the city. He had mixed his drinks, Joe the Lawyer had. Stateside whisky plus the sparkling wine of greed was an overpowering combination.

His eyes were bulging and the words he'd planned so carefully tumbled out with the maudlin vehemence of a drunkard. "Protection money! That's my deal. To get you and me into the pom-pom protection money!"

"Yes?" Tommy said warily.

"What's a pom-pom house afraid of? The MP's! Right? An MP officer paralyzes 'em. Right?"

"So?" Tommy Cruz answered so quietly he might have been a bank clerk.

"So I said to myself, Joe, if you could get to be buddies with an MP officer you could hold the bastid over every pom-pom house in Manila. You could be on the collecting and not the paying end of the protection money."

Tommy Cruz stared at him. "You and the MP officer? You, buddies?" His words were soft, as if coated with the slime of his disgust. He laughed and his laugh too was soft and slimy. "The stockade make you crazy!"

For a second Joe almost sobered. He realized he'd given Tommy the story backside forward. Then his blond face flushed. Who was this sunavabitch to laugh at him! "Yeah, I'm crazy! You sit there and say I'm crazy. If it wasn't for me, where the hell would you be? An alley hustler, not much better than the kids yelling pom-pom at the GI's. Listen to me, Tommy, before you yell crazy. Me, yeah, me! A lousy escapee, an awol! Who am I to be buddies with the MP brass? You're right, Tommy, only you're not right. There's a way to become buddies with an MP officer. There's always a way!" He paused for a split second. "All you have to do is become an officer yourself!"

"You become officer?"

"I put on an officer's uniform! Simple? So goddamn simple any jerk could've thought of it, only they never do. That's what makes it a perfect deal. It's simple, a natural. With every goddamn pom-pom house paying protection to somebody higher up, we become the guys higher up!"

"*Dios!*" the mestizo exclaimed. "It is good, Joe. Good!"

"Goddamn right it's good! For a hundred pesos I buy a major's uniform. Suntans, MacArthur shirts. The gold oak leaves. The whole works. I put it on and I'm no longer an awol. I'm a major in the Air Force, and my buddy's a captain! Nobody checks on the Air Force. They're always flying in and out, and an Air Force major who likes a good time ought to hit it off with an MP officer who likes Stateside whisky and a piece of pom-pom on a rainy night. That's where you come in, Tommy. We have a party. You ask a couple of big pom-pom boys. We want them to see for themselves who your friends are—MP brass and me, Major Fenton, and my buddy, Captain Hurley! I've even got the names picked out. Nothing like a stockade for solid thinking. That's who your friends are. The brass with MP protection to sell! And the first guys we sell are the big pom-pom boys at the party you give. See, we'll need their organization, their support. We've got to have 'em, and the rest's easy. We make a partnership. We all sit down and figure out how to sell our protection. Good, huh? It's perfect!" he gloated. He refilled their glasses, lifted his own, and toasted, "To Operation Pom-Pom!"

"Yes, yes," Tommy Cruz echoed him eagerly.

They drank and Joe slapped his empty glass down, his eyes bloodshot, his head reeling. "Gotta hustle fast. The GI's are having their last fling. By Christmas, most of 'em'll be home and the lil pom-pom houses'll be dead broke. Gotta protect 'em now! Now, Tommy, when the boom's on! That's what this pompom is! A gold boom!" he cried in the high-pitched voice of a fanatic. He was mad that second, mad with the madness of a conniver who finally sees his pet scheme moving out of his coiled brain into the real world.

He grabbed for the bottle, poured more whisky, drank greedily. "To Operation Pom-Pom, Tommy!"

"To Operation Pom-Pom, yes." Tommy spoke with the fastidious care of a man who knows he's getting very drunk. "I will ask Dimang and Johnny Yen Lee to the party, yes? Dimang has twenty, perhaps thirty pom-pom houses. Johnny Yen Lee has perhaps fifty houses—I think more."

Joe nodded. His head was spinning. He squinted at the bottle on the table. It was empty and Tommy was leaning his heavy head on one elbow. A few more drinks and Tommy would be a dead pigeon and what was to stop him from going upstairs to Tommy's Japanese doll? Why the hell should Blacky be in that soft velvet, and Tommy, everybody except him?

Joe staggered over to the lacquer cabinet, returned with an unopened bottle. He fumbled at the seal. Again he filled their glasses. "Fraud and perjury, Tommy!" he shouted. "That's our slogan. That's the way to get rich. We'll be screwen millionaires, Tommy! You build me up to Dimang and that Chinaman what's his name. Dimang I heard of. A big wheel. Pom-pom and fence. Say he's biggest jewl'ry fence in the whole screwen town. You build me up to Dimang, Tommy! I'm a big wheel, you tell'm. Major Fenton, with connections to the biggest brass. Fraud and perjury, Tommy!"

Tommy giggled and pillowed his head on both hands. Joe poured more whisky into Tommy's glass. "Have a lil drink," he invited him. A few more and Tommy'd be under the table and he'd sneak out of the goddamn *sala* up to the Japanese doll.

Drowsily, Tommy drank half of his glass. The glass dropped from his fingers and the whisky spilled. Tommy crossed his elbows on the wet table, his sleeves in the whisky.

Joe blinked at the sleeping man. His bloodshot eyes shifted to the sala's sliding doors. He thought of the woman upstairs in her bed, a cherry blossom of a Japanee. "Damn!" Joe groaned. He couldn't chance it. She might yell, squawk the next day, blackmail him, queer his deal with Tommy. He'd get even, Joe promised himself insanely. He'd have that Jap girl if it was the last thing he did on this earth, but not tonight, not tonight....

He picked up the bottle and took a long drink. Disjointed and fragmentary schemes to seduce the woman whom he'd never seen, whom he hated because he could not have her this minute, whirled through his brain. They hadn't called him Joe the Lawyer for nothing.

CHAPTER THREE

He opened his heavy eyes on the morning. A hangover made of little wheels was spinning furiously inside his head. He realized that he'd blacked out on the floor of the *sala* like any blind fool of a GI in an alley. He was the prize jerk to louse himself up with whisky when he had a million things to do.

Joe staggered over to the sliding doors. A Filipino in a brown pajama-like servant's uniform, who had been waiting patiently for the *americano* to wake up, bowed his small sleek head. Joe sent him for Tommy Cruz. A half hour later he was breakfasting with Tommy in the *sala*. The servant in brown brought them orange juice and mango, a platter of scrambled eggs, and a pot of coffee. Joe wanted only coffee, but the mestizo ate hungrily. The little wheels in Joe's head lost momentum with his second cup of coffee. The sunavabitch, Joe thought, had an appetite. Damn him! He'd be hungry too if he'd passed out in a woman's arms. That second, Joe hated the clean-shaven woman-satisfied look of Tommy Cruz. "Who carried you upstairs? Your girl, what's her name again?" He smiled. The hate behind his smile was like fire on his lips.

"Hanoco," Tommy Cruz said. His smile was neat, like his features. In his dark blue robe and slippers he could have been another Manila businessman. Hanoco, Joe thought viciously. Sweet or sour, ugly or flat-chested, he was going to get to Hanoco one of these days. "First thing we have to do, Tommy, is get uniforms for me and my buddy. That's your job, Tommy. He's bigger than me by a coupla inches. What we want's a major's uniform and a captain's and all the brass that goes with 'em."

When Tommy Cruz left the house, Joe explored the lacquer cabinet. He found a box of cigars, the native-made Alhambras, worth a peso apiece. Tommy was doing all right, Joe thought. He took a cigar, sat down wearily on the couch, and lit up. First thing, the uniforms, Joe rehearsed to himself. Then he and Blacky would run over to the replacement depot, the reppledepple out on Dewey Boulevard, for dog tags and identification papers. They'd need a lit-tle smear money. That's where Tommy'd come in. Then they'd be ready to pro-mote some MP officer. Operation Pom-Pom wasn't worth a cracked centavo if he didn't produce police brass for Tommy Cruz and his big pom-pom boys.

Joe arose from the couch, crossed the *sala* to the business corner with its roll-top desk and typewriter. He inserted a sheet in the machine and pecked out the names and ranks of two officers. Major John Richard Fenton, Captain William Hurley. From escapees to Major Fenton and Captain Hurley in twen-ty-four hours was fast work, Joe complimented himself. He puffed on his cigar, admiring his flair for minute detail. Even the phony middle name, Richard, had been planned in the stockade. He wondered how Blacky'd take to the William Hurley. He'd told Blacky next to nothing in the stockade. No point in it, when Murdock might have double-crossed them, or the break might have misfired. And last night the big bastid had been too pom-pom crazy to listen.

Joe's eyes slanted to the sliding doors and he thought of Hanoco. Was she awake? Combing her hair? Tommy Cruz must have mentioned his sleeping downstairs in the *sala*. Joe blew out a mouthful of the rich blue cigar smoke. It curled gracefully toward the ceiling, tracing the soft curves of the Japanese girl's body....

Tommy Cruz was carrying a straw suitcase when he returned to the house; inside the suitcase were two officers' uniforms he'd bought on Avenida Rizal. Tommy reached into the pocket of his white coat jacket and placed an assortment of Army insignia on the table: the gold oak leaves of a major, the silver bars of a captain, the insignia of the Air Force. "Swell," Joe said, and he explained about Blacky. "He's going to get the surprise of his life when he sees those silver bars. Don't you tip him off, Tommy. Blacky's a good guy, but kind of dumb." Joe winked as if he and Tommy were in a private conspiracy of their own, thinking cynically that it always paid off to make everybody feel he was your brother. "I guess you better bring Blacky here now, Tommy."

Joe saluted Blacky and Tommy Cruz as they came inside the sala. Blacky stared speechlessly. There before his astonished eyes stood an Air Force major in fresh suntans, his MacArthur shirt open at the neck and showing a snowy T shirt underneath. Joe had shaved and showered; he was as immaculate and shiny as the oak leaves pinned to his collar.

"When you see an officer, you salute!" Joe snapped as if he were the real genuine brass.

Tommy Cruz grinned. "Major, tonight we meet my house, yes?"

"Wait a minute, Tommy!" Joe turned from Blacky and pointed down at his stockade boots. "We'll have to buy officers' shoes. That's money. We'll have to smear a lil at the repple depple for dogtags. You'll have to loan me five hundred pesos. And I'll have to borrow your jeep."

"No! Not my jeep!"

"The brass doesn't travel on shoe leather in this town. They ride, Tommy. Look, we have to do this right or not at all."

Shaking his head, the mestizo pulled out a thick alligator-skin wallet and counted out the money. He sighed but surrendered his jeep key. "Good-by," he said to both of them leaving. "You want something, you ask my servant, Juan."

"Hey, big strong silent type," Joe laughed at Blacky. "Say hello anyway."

Blacky muttered incoherently.

"Stop acting as if a truck's rolled over your head. I tried to give you the picture last night. All the picture you wanted was a dame. Wish I could say the same."

"That uniform! What's the idea?"

"What's always the idea?" Joe retrieved Tommy Cruz's five hundred pesos from his pocket. Smiling, he waved the bills. "That's the idea! The folding stuff!

Listen. I'll give you the picture quick, Blacky."

When Joe finished explaining to Blacky about Operation Pom-Pom, he added, "It's a natural, if I say so myself. Now go clean up, Blacky. The bathroom's upstairs. Your uniform's in that suitcase."

But it wasn't that simple. Somehow Blacky felt as if all the officers he'd known and hated had caught up with him somehow, and the phony major was their latest representative. "You go to hell!" Blacky shouted, jumping from his chair.

"Goddamn, if I didn't have a hunch you'd yell! Blacky, didn't I try to give you the picture last night?"

"Now you tell me—"

"You'da thought me stir crazy if I'd said a thing about it in the stockade."

"To hell with it. You're not crazy wearing that fuggen uniform? A major! Brass gives the orders and the soldier jumps! That's you, and you can go to hell! I'm not gonna be no captain! I'm just a fuggen GI—and glad of it."

"You're no GI, you dope. You're an awol."

"Yeah!" Blacky screamed at him. "An awol who hates the brass, who went awol on account of 'em!"

Joe smiled. A second ago he had been angry, contemptuous. But there was no sense in a yelling match with Blacky. They had too much to do. He'd take care of Blacky a little later on. Blacky and Hanoco both. "Blacky," Joe said softly. "Will you calm down? Calm down, will you?"

"To hell with you!"

"You can afford to gripe after I fixed you up with an all-night shack job." Joe smiled. "What a buddy!"

"What do you want me for when you got this guy Cruz?"

"How can a guy be buddies with that kind?" Joe almost whispered, as if he were afraid the servant, Juan, might be eavesdropping. Joe spat at the shiny floor. "Blacky, listen! I don't blame you for griping, honest. But what do you want to do? It's up to you, Blacky. You can walk out of here and go back to armed robbery or you can stick with me. Hell, we'll be round-shouldered from the pesos in our pockets. That girl you had last night—Hell, Blacky, we'll have the cream! Spanish mestizas, Russky blondes!" His eyes were blue and intense and hypnotic on the sullen dark face.

Blacky thought of Lucy at the Five Sisters. He thought of Tommy Cruz, who was behind Joe to the tune of five hundred pesos and his jeep. He rubbed at his stubbly black-whiskered chin. "O.K. But goddamn it, Joe, you could've let me in on it gradual."

Captain William Hurley sat next to Major John Richard Fenton, who was driving Tommy Cruz's jeep. From under the wheels the dust flew. They were on a narrow street lined with rows of squatter huts made of blackened wood and salvaged corrugated iron. A Filipino woman glanced after the jeep of the two American officers. Then she walked to her hut and picked up a stick with a wired-on beer can. The top of the beer can had been pushed into place and punctured with nail holes. With her homemade watering tool, the woman patiently wetted down the flying dust.

On Avenida Rizal, the dust floated in a yellow haze through which the GI traffic of weapon carriers and trucks rolled endlessly. On the crowded sidewalks, footloose soldiers hoofed along, now and then stopping to window-shop. "Rizal was nothing three, four months ago," Joe remarked to Blacky. "Now it's all stores. Everybody's cutting himself in on the GI's peso." They passed a *haba haba* or burlesque, where GI's were buying tickets at a booth flanked by two huge paintings of naked girls. Above the truck motors, a barker shouted, "Get your tickets for the Atom Bomb Follies! Get your tickets, boys! There'll be a hot time in Berlin when the Brooklyn boys begin!"

"Hear that?" Blacky said. "Means we still haven't licked the krauts."

"All the kraut I give a damn about is that green folding kraut."

Behind them in the yellow dust the barker was spieling, "See the dancing girls, boys, and last but not least our special pinup for Uncle Sam's gallant fighters, the Goddess of *Haba haba*!"

"Blacky, if we could collect just one centavo of every peso spent on this Rizal, we could retire!"

"You're money crazy."

Joe grinned at him. "You call that crazy?"

"Only yesterday we're biting our nails waiting for Murdock, and just listen to you! What're we doing about Murdock?" Blacky asked anxiously.

"Nothing."

"What do you mean, nothing? He'll be at the Liberators' Café Friday! That's day after tomorrow."

"We've got other things to worry about now."

"But—"

"But hell! One detail at a time."

"He'll come for the ten thousand, Joe! You going to borrow it from Tommy Cruz?"

"Will you let me worry about Murdock? He's my headache."

"We could've forgotten all about him if we'd stayed lost, but we have to be officers! Going to the replacement depot!"

"Quit griping for a change. Here. Have an Alhambra on Tommy Cruz."

"Murdock knows about Tommy Cruz and the Five Sisters."

"Will you shut up? Shut up!"

"Officers," Blacky muttered, staring down at his knife-edged suntans. Blacky shuddered. "Suppose the MP's stop us?"

"We forgot our dog tags. Worst comes to worst, we've got five hundred pesos to play with."

"Riding around in the open, we're sure to bump into guys we know."

"Nobody's looking at your mug, Blacky. Use your eyes! You'll see the GI's out there have stopped saluting the brass. They're not looking at the brass and the brass aren't looking at the GI's. The big show is over. All they got on their mind is a piece of pom-pom before they get shipped out. That goes for everybody. Goddamn it, tonight I'm getting mine!"

"We could go to the Five Sisters," Blacky suggested.

"GI pom-pom's out for us."

"So you're telling me who I can have!" Blacky flared.

Joe whistled patiently. Then he said, "Blacky, we're officers, right? How can we get on a GI line of dogfaces?"

Ahead of them was the Army-built Santa Cruz Bridge across the Pasig River; the Japanese had blown up all four stone bridges that once had joined the northern and southern halves of Manila. Three GI trucks and a jitney bus packed with Filipinos were crawling behind a two-wheel horse-drawn calesa that the GI's called "Manila taxicabs." "They ought to send that nag to the butcher!" Joe cursed as he inched the jeep out on the bridge.

Below, on the brown muddy river, uprooted water lilies floated downstream to the sea. Blacky wondered what was going to happen to him. As if it made any difference. Maybe he ought to just ride along like those water lilies below and let Joe do all the thinking.

Time had passed like the water lilies.

New Guinea was a hundred years ago. Even the Philippines fighting was moving away fast. It was all over and nobody gave a damn. Blacky thought of how bright and red the blood of the wounded had shone on the streets, before the dust had faded it. There had been a lot of wounded, a lot of good guys killed in the fighting south of the Pasig. Mortars and booby traps and a guy smoking one butt after another while behind the advance the burning Escolta and Avenida Rizal lit up the northern sky.

Joe swung off the bridge, driving by the smashed Legislature with its leaning, bulging walls, as if concrete had been turned into rubber and inflated. Blacky said, "Joe, you were in the fighting here, weren't you?

"Huh?" Joe said. "Yeah, don't remind me."

When they reached broad Dewey Boulevard bordering Manila Bay, he stepped on the gas. The water gleamed like a great blue mirror between the peninsulas of Cavite and Bataan. Far out in the bay the island of Corregidor was a dim blue pollywog on the horizon.

Blacky looked across at Joe. The repple depple wasn't worrying Joe one single bit. The jeep raced up Dewey. MP's in white helmets stood on guard outside the bullet-chipped residence of the governor general, where the Japanese commander Yamashita, the Tiger of Singapore, was being tried for his life. But under that huge vaulting sky the war seemed unreal, the MP's like toy soldiers. Blacky glanced at his captain's bars and felt that he was dreaming. Maybe that's all life was—one big dream with stockades and pom-pom houses jumbled together without any meaning.

The replacement depot loomed up ahead of them, a dusty encampment facing the blue bay. "Blacky," Joe said in a low, charged voice, "one thing you want to remember is this: We got five hundred pesos on us, and when you've got money to buy your way, there's nothing to worry about."

He drove into the replacement depot, parking behind a Quonset. Side by side, they walked to the main building, to be saluted by the GI outside the door. Blacky blinked. He felt taller than his six feet one and a half. A mile taller. Inside, the rows of desks seemed to float before his eyes, the deskmen scribbling or typing or looking busy multiplying into a paperwork army.

Joe paused at a desk where a jowly corporal was stamping a pile of papers. He questioned the corporal, who answered him politely. Joe stepped from the corporal's desk, Blacky tagging him, over to a thin noncom who glanced up from his typewriter. "Sergeant," Joe said, "Major Duplay said you could help us out."

"Major Duplay, sir? Do you know Major Duplay, sir?"

Blacky looked at the floor. He couldn't believe this would work.

"Sergeant, I don't want to know anybody or see anybody," Joe was saying. "Not in Manila, anyway. This is no town to trust anybody. Captain Hurley, here, and myself, we were at a party, Sergeant, if you know what I mean. And we were taken but I mean taken."

Blacky listened to that man-to-man voice with its cozy hint that when it came to a hot party, the sergeant and the major were two of a kind. For the first time Blacky looked at the sergeant. He was grinning a little.

"The sooner we get shipped out, Sergeant, the happier we'll be. I hear the boys are beginning to go home fast now."

"Yes, sir. Those big cargo ships are coming in all the time and they're leaving with the boys crowded to the anchor housings. Twenty-six thousand slated to go this month, and half ought to make it."

"Wish I was with them, Sergeant. Goddamn jeep girls we were with took everything. Uniforms, wallets, dog tags. Lucky we didn't wake up in an alley with our throats cut. Right, Hurley?"

Blacky started. Hurley was him. "Right," he muttered.

"We didn't have a stitch left, Sarge. Borrowed what we're wearing. But we couldn't borrow shoes. We're heading for the PX over the Manila Hotel soon as you help us out." He unbottoned his pocket and pulled out the sheet of paper he'd typed on Tommy Cruz's machine.

"That's kind of short, sir."

"It's all here, Sarge. Names, rank, all the dope. Now if you can get it fixed up in the next hour, Sarge, we'd appreciate it.

"Look, Sarge. I'm one soldier who appreciates a favor in this man's army. I want you to know that. Live and let live's my motto." He was talking so low now that Blacky could scarcely hear him. "When I think of the dough this man's army blows on pom-pom and rotgut and the lousy pay a man gets—Live and let live, Sarge. You help us out and we won't forget you."

"Yes, sir," the sergeant assented eagerly. "You come back in two hours, Major—"

"Major Fenton."

"Yes, sir, Major Fenton. Two hours."

They walked out of the replacement depot, climbed into their jeep. Out on the blue bay the sun lay like another sea, suspended in the sky, yellow and hot. "We'll get an envelope somewhere," Joe grinned, "and paper it with a lil folding stuff for our pal Sarge." They drove off.

At a red-tiled hotel in the stylish Pasay section of Manila, Joe parked, leaving Blacky in the jeep. He returned with an envelope. "Two twenty-peso bills ought to be enough for good old Sarge. We ought to pick up some decent shoes now. But hell, we've got plenty of time. Let's see what's coming into Fliptown, Captain."

They cruised along Dewey. There were stretches here where the occupiers had resisted the liberators street by street, house by house, floor by floor, room by room. The Luneta, the park on Manila Bay, was a scorched brown prairie, the site now of a GI township of tents.

It was a city of tents or else it was a city of refugee huts slapped together with corrugated iron and bamboo and old wood and burlap. And the colors of both the GI and the Filipino cities were iron rust and stone gray and the dark green of the shield-shaped banana trees that hadn't been mowed down by shell fire. And it was always a city of dust. Dust covered the naked brown bottoms of the little babies playing among the huts. Dust filtered down through the wrecked stone arches where the sidewalk peddlers sold GI shirts and K rations. Dust lifted in lazy clouds at the Port Area, where the trucks rumbled out on the piers and the winches hoisted great wooden boxes out of the ships' holds.

The war and the peace, the past and the future, were spelled out on the water front in letters made of ships. The freighters and cargo ships were America. Sunk in the shallow water was Japan, the hulls and masts of the Mikado's scuttled destroyers lifting out of the blue water at crazy angles. And far out in the harbor the Filipinos glided by, fragile and graceful, in the native outriggers with their red and white sails and green sails bellying in the breeze. And Joe's shrewd eyes took it all in.

Stevedores swarmed on the even-numbered piers in the north harbor and on the odd-numbered piers in the south harbor. Gangs of Filipinos unloaded the American ships, while the American trucks carried the American goods to the Army-built warehouses and depots. Joe had been unusually silent, but now he exclaimed, "This town hasn't got a pot to pee in or a window to throw it out of or a target to aim it at, and just look at that stuff, Blacky!"

"So what?" Blacky shrugged.

"So what, he says. While you and me were stuck in that goddamn stockade, look what the hell's been happening! Blacky, don't you see it? The black market must be booming a mile a minute! God Almighty, this town's a paradise!"

John Richard Fenton and Captain William Hurley returned to the replacement depot. Their dog tags and identification papers were ready for them. The Major casually placed the envelope containing the forty pesos on the sergeant's desk. Back in their jeep, the Major said to the Captain, "Now we'll get some decent shoes." They sped down Dewey Boulevard to the Manila Hotel. In the PX, a GI waited on them, opening up cardboard boxes and taking out pairs of shoes. They bought a pair each and also stocked up, at the Major's suggestion, on extra MacArthur shirts, trousers, shorts, and socks. With their purchases, they strolled out into the hotel's palm lobby, where lieutenants and captains were reading papers and magazines or talking in groups; the Manila Hotel had been taken over by the Army for its officers. "I'll get us a room," the Major said to the Captain.

Ten minutes later, they looked at each other in a room on the fourth floor. Joe was grinning, but Blacky gritted his teeth. He flopped down on one of the single beds. "I haven't got your nerve! A room in the middle of all this damn brass!"

Joe stepped over to the second bed, testing the mattress. "You never had it so good." He winked at Blacky. "Come on, Hurley, We've got things to do over some MP battalion."

Blacky crossed his arms across his face. "I'm beat, Joe."

"Come on, jerkeroo. If we don't promote some MP brass hat, we might as well dump these uniforms and hide out in the Tondo."

"Haven't we done enough for one day? Tomorrow I'm with you." Blacky sat upright, his dark brown eyes pleading.

Joe shook his head. "Blacky, I want to explain something to you once and for all. We haven't any time to goof around in. You heard what the sarge said over at the repple depple? The GI's're going fast. What's going to happen to all the pom-pom houses? They'll go broke. They'll be giving away a piece of pom-pom free with every Coke in another month! Don't you see the picture, Blacky? We have to protect 'em before they go broke."

"Speaking of pom-pom," Blacky said eagerly, "what you need's some fun, Joe. The jeep girls'll be coming out on Dewey toward evening and Tommy Cruz expects to see you tonight. You might get tied up. Now's the time—"

"You're taking awful good care of me." Joe grinned.

"I'm taking care of myself," Blacky admitted. "You give me the shakes. What you need's a girl. Joe, the first time—Joe, it's out of this world."

Joe's face flushed. He ran his hand through his thick blond hair and licked at his lips. "O.K., you've sold me. We'll wash up, get some chow, and go get it."

When Joe stepped out of the bathroom, a towel around his middle, he said, "No hot water! We'll have to complain to the Pentagon."

Blacky went into the bathroom. He showered, soaping himself and letting the water sluice the suds off. Dripping wet, he walked to the mirror. He stared at himself. He was just a GI again, Blacky thought. No uniform, no bars, just a GI. He picked up the soap and wrote across the mirror: KILROY WAS HERE.

God knew how many times he had written that same slogan. Kilroy had been in New Guinea, and he'd come ashore in the Philippines in brand-new landing craft, and if he was somebody like Blacky MacIntyre, the only thing he liked about the Army was the guys he got to know, the other Kilroys, some of whom had fallen in their own disemboweled guts on the burning streets of Manila. Well, the war was over and the days in Australia, where he'd marched to the cheers of the girls, wearing the old-style flat helmet of the year 1942, were gone. And the boy who had learned to be a fair salute-dodger in New Guinea and an expert salute-dodger in the Philippines was unable to settle down to the saluting and the proper uniforms of Manila at peace. So he'd walked over the hill and used a .45 to pick up some pesos. They had caught him, and he'd escaped, and here he was in the Manila Hotel with lieutenants and captains by the hundreds on the floors above and below. God Almighty, it was one hell of a place for Blacky MacIntyre to be in—and a hell of a place for Kilroy. And the guy who'd done it was Joe. Joe the Lawyer, who maybe or maybe not was a busted officer.

Blacky stepped out of the bathroom and looked at Joe, wearing shorts and stretched out on his bed, an Alhambra cigar in his mouth. "Hey, Joe, were you ever an officer?" he blurted.

"Stop reading the comics!"

"Were you?"

"Even if I was, which I wasn't, what the hell's the difference?"

"A guy's naturally curious about his buddy. What's your home town?"

"Easton, Pa.," Joe said. "And New York, the Hotel Astor."

"That's where all the wise guys come from!"

"That's right, hillbilly." Joe puffed steadily on his cigar. He rarely thought of his life in the States. When he did, it unrolled like a story in a book he wasn't especially interested in: the depression years in New York, the jobs that paid peanuts, the furnished rooms no larger than closets. He had learned early that you had to look out for yourself and to hell with the rest of the pack. It was a look-out-for-yourself rat race. He'd learned enough to connect himself in a couple of small-time racket jobs, but when his luck went bad, he'd joined the Navy. He'd been in Cavite on December 7. There was nothing left but surrender to the Japs or turn guerrilla, like the soldiers escaping from Bataan and the mining engineers who'd lost their mines. In the Usaffe guerrilla forces led by American officers he had become an officer and been busted because he'd looked out for himself a little too carefully. When MacArthur landed at Leyte he was just a GI again in the khaki of a private, first class.

"Blacky, let me tell you something," Joe said, his face impassive, the face of a man who had no past. "A guy's got just so much brains in his head, and no sense throwing it away on what's under the bridge. You and me, we've started from scratch. All that counts is how we make out."

"You can't blame me for being curious, Joe."

"No, I don't blame you. But take my advice. What's under the bridge isn't worth talking about. Right now all I'm thinking of is a woman. Come on, let's go."

CHAPTER FOUR

Through the windshield of the jeep, the yellow speck on the edge of Dewey
Boulevard blew up into a yellow stick, into a girl in a yellow dress. "There's
your jeep girl," Blacky said. He was driving. "What do you say, Joe?"

"We'll look her over."

The jeep pulled up alongside the girl in the yellow dress. She smiled at them,
the bay like a vast dark blue frame behind her, the sky another vast frame of
pink and mauve and burning red. She was neither a girl nor quite a woman,
her long black hair brushed away from a thin hollow-cheeked face, her slender brown legs bare, her feet in the bright red and green wooden clogs many
of the Filipino women wore. At that hour, with the sun poised on the horizon,
she seemed very small. Joe's eyes moved up her legs to the tiny waist and budding small breasts. "Waiting for me?" he said to the jeep girl.

"I wait for you, Major," she agreed in good English.

"Want a ride?"

She walked slowly and languidly over to the jeep, a child imitating the movement of some screen actress.

"Señorita!" Joe exclaimed with a smiling sarcasm that only Blacky perceived.
"How much do you think you're worth, señorita?"

"Major, I am poor."

"Yeah, you have an old mother and sixteen kid sisters," Joe said. "O.K., how
much?"

"Twenty pesos, Major."

He got out of the jeep and jerked his thumb at the rear. "Let's go, señorita."

"Pay me now, Major."

He nodded at the Army traffic sweeping up and down Dewey Boulevard.
GI's in a passing truck whistled and shouted. "A major can't be seen paying for
pom-pom in broad daylight. Somebody'll tell the general." His voice was low
and mocking. "You wouldn't want somebody to tell the general, señorita."

"You give me snow job?" she asked suspiciously.

Blacky grinned at them as the sinking sun flamed on the western water and
the new colors streaked the sky.

Without a word Joe climbed into the rear of the jeep. He unbottoned his rear
trousers pocket. His fingers fastened on his wad of pesos and he showed them
to the girl. She walked closer to the jeep. He pulled off two twenty-peso bills.
"Want them?"

But she wouldn't get into the jeep with him until she had the bills in her
hand. "You are nice!" she said happily, folding the bills and slipping them into
her bag. It was a heavy yellow cotton bag, decorated with a red floral design.

As she sat down next to Joe, he said, "What's forty pesos, señorita! Drive,

Blacky! What's forty pesos with the black market?"

"The black market!" the girl echoed him, her large eyes eloquent.

"Bet you paid plenty for this dress," he said, his hand darting to her small breast.

"No, no, Major!"

"O.K., señorita." He grinned. "Don't get upset. How much?"

"For dress?"

"For dress."

"Twenty-five pesos, Major."

"What'd you pay for the clogs?"

"Ten pesos, Major."

"What's forty pesos for a piece of pom-pom? Black-market pom-pom! Right, señorita?"

She laughed and he stared at her lips. They were painted a bright red and her teeth were small and white, unlike the gold-toothed mouths of most of the pom-pom girls he'd known, or the black-toothed mouths, stained by the juice of the betel nuts that the peasant girls chewed in the provinces, the girls of the rice paddies when he'd been a guerrilla.

He placed his hand on her knee. She wriggled a little but she let his hand stay. Out on the bay, the sun was sinking below the surface like the giant golden helmet of a sea diver going down into the waters. Blacky drove on in silence. It was Joe's night.

Now twilight was beginning to fade, the tropical and furious twilight. The sun was gone and the twilight was going like a fast breath and the earth was darkening with the first white stars outlined palely in the sky. Blacky switched on his headlights.

"Señorita," Joe said, "let's have a lil action." He circled her waist. "I gave you forty pesos. You gonna give me five pesos' worth of love?"

"No, no, I love you very good, Major."

"Damn right! Blacky, pull over when you get to an empty stretch of beach." His hands were all over her, and when the jeep parked and Blacky called to him, Joe felt as if he were still in movement, moving down the speedway of his veins and arteries.

Joe and the jeep girl descended to a narrow sandy beach; high above their heads the stars shone white and splendid, while on Dewey Boulevard the headlights streaked the night.

"Strip!" Joe said to the girl.

"No, no," she cried. "I lift the dress, Major. I lift."

"For forty pesos, you strip!"

She obeyed. He stared at her slender body, a shape of darkness. He went to her, embraced her, and they sank down on the sand.

After a while she tried to rise, but he dragged her down, his hands around her. "Where you going? I paid you forty pesos."

"I go now, Major," she said, and there was a whimper in her voice.

He knew then she must be really new at this racket. Somehow that angered him. "You'll go when I tell you!" He pulled her to him, his fingers tightening, hard and relentless. The girl whimpered again. He slapped her across the lips. She sniffled. He hated her for crying, this little make-believe woman. He leaned over her, and suddenly he seemed to see another shape, the naked shape of the unseen Hanoco, Tommy Cruz's woman. His arms went about her.

At last they returned to the jeep, the headlights of the traffic on Dewey stabbing into their eyes. Blacky was impatient. "Hey, Joe, how about me?"

Joe didn't answer Blacky. "I'll give you more pesos," he said to the girl. "I've got a hundred-peso bill. You give me the forty pesos I gave you and I'll give you a hundred pesos for me and my friend. O.K., señorita?"

"One hundred pesos!" she exclaimed.

"Yeah, for me and my friend. Blacky, put on your lights a second so we can see something." The lights shone yellow. Joe unbottoned his rear pocket, took out his wad. He held up the hundred-peso bill. Quickly the girl opened her bag and fished out the two twenties. Joe snatched them from her fingers, pocketing the twenties and the hundred-peso bill.

"No, no," the girl cried hysterically. "Major, no, no!"

"She's just a kid!" Black said angrily.

"Shut up and start that jeep."

"Joe, you can't roll a kid like that!"

The girl rushed at Joe, screaming. He punched her in the belly. The girl sagged, dropped to the ground. Joe jumped into the jeep. "Drive, damn you!"

"Joe, for God's sake!"

"Drive, I said! That dough's better in our pocket than in that tramp's!"

CHAPTER FIVE

Morning, another crazy morning, Blacky thought as they drove out of the MP compound in Tommy Cruz's jeep. It seemed to Blacky that he was caught in a dream where he was always on the move but bound for nowhere. His heart was beating so fast that the faces on the sidewalks blurred and he saw no individuals, only the brown face of Manila. Between the blue glare of the sky and the yellow glare of the streets, these Filipinos had the sinister aspect of a crowd of strangers in a dream—for who could believe that only a few minutes ago, they'd been with the commanding officer of the 14th MP Battalion Headquarters? He was a bristling redheaded major, and he had listened politely and coldly to Joe's line in his office among the smashed buildings of the Ateneo, the Jesuit university, while outside in the roofless auditorium, now an MP target range, some officer was practicing with his .45. The explosive plunk of the bullets had sounded unreal to Blacky. It was all unreal, because they were unreal, their uniforms, their dog tags. They were dream characters with dream names in a dream city where the Filipinos on the streets eternally held handkerchiefs over their mouths against the dust of the unending Army traffic, a nightmare that would end only when he awoke in the stockade.

Blacky pushed a cigarette between his parched lips. He glanced out at the houses baking in the heat, the passersby walking on the side where the shadow of the houses made a cool lane. Two Filipino women were carrying bamboo baskets, and in the shimmering light they might have been the jeep girl in the yellow dress and Lucy of the Five Sisters, but that couldn't be; it was only because all the women of the country were brown and small and fragile. He remembered that on Tuesday he'd slept with Lucy. That same Tuesday he'd been in the stockade, and here it was Thursday with the MP's saluting them, even though the MP Major had cold-shouldered Joe.

"Joe," Blacky said unsteadily, "let's get rid of these uniforms."

"Hell, that redheaded sunavabitch isn't the only MP brass hat in town."

"Joe, there's a big silk house I know on Quezon Boulevard. We could stick it up. There's twenty, thirty thousand pesos there. We could buy passage on one of those Swede freighters to Shanghai. Hell, Joe, if we got a break we could even buy passage home!" Home—that was a dream, too, because he had no home with his mother dead, but it suddenly became precious because he had said the word "home" in a land of strangers.

"When did you cook up that lil idea?"

Blacky winced at the contemptuous voice. "Last night. I couldn't sleep thinking of the brass around us."

"You'll get used to it."

"Joe, you can't get away with this officer racket!"

"You think it's easier getting away with a dumb stickup? That's you all over. You're a hot shot once your blood's up, but when it comes to talking to some bastid with a lil tin on his collar—"

"O.K., I'm the hot bastid and you're the cold one!"

"We make a good team." Joe grinned.

"Have it any way you want. I haven't got your nerve. Your kind of nerve."

"Blacky, listen to me!"

"What about Murdock? My God, Joe, we've got to get rid of these damn uniforms! They're a jinx!"

"What we're going to do is go to Bilibid."

Bilibid! The word was like a club across Blacky's spine. Bilibid, the central prison of Manila! He'd been locked up in Bilibid forty-eight hours before being sent to the stockade.

"I should've gone there right away," he heard a voice saying; he was numb and the voice was far away and at the same time roaring in his ears, although Joe was speaking quietly. "No percentage going to another MP battalion. Don't make out, you're done. Bilibid's loaded with police brass and we're sure to hit the mark we want."

The Manila dust rose from under their wheels, a dust smelling of the Philippine earth and the gasoline burned by the countless American vehicles, acrid and pungent and heady like some strange perfume. And out of a hazy dust cloud, the high yellow walls of Bilibid wavered before Blacky's fascinated eyes. Then steadied into solid yellow stone, spiked with even taller watchtowers. Blacky wondered which of those towers was the one he'd seen from his cell. Cell 17, he remembered, and he would never forget the wooden floor, the cot with its mosquito netting, the iron bars running from the floor to the ceiling, and the watchtower another iron bar down the middle of the sky.

"Yeah, we should've started right here," Joe said to Blacky when they parked on Azcarraga Street, the walls of Bilibid on the other side. "Come on, there's nothing to worry about, Blacky."

And maybe there wasn't, Blacky thought when they passed the smartly saluting guards at the entrance.

He followed Joe into a big cool building, the Administration Building. A Filipino in suntans with official papers in his brown fingers hurried by them. Maybe that same Filipino, Blacky thought, feeling as if a hot rod had plunged up into his head, had once carried the papers of Prisoner Blacky MacIntyre. But hadn't Joe said there was nothing to worry about? Nothing. Leave it to Major Fenton, good old Major Fenton.

Silently, asking no questions, Blacky followed Joe up a broad flight of stairs. Two other uniforms marched downstairs, two lieutenants, who nodded in friendly fashion at the man in the captain's uniform and the man in the major's uniform. Blacky trailed Joe into a large office on the second floor and he heard Joe call over a Filipino clerk and talk to him. The clerk conducted them to a desk where a stocky lieutenant with a big clefted chin was sorting through some papers. Blacky listened with a dreamy kind of wonder as Joe spieled out the same line he had used on the redheaded MP major. "My father was a police officer in the States, Lieutenant, and I'm kind of curious about the police setup here in Manila, in Bilibid. That is, if you're not busy." The lieutenant smiled and offered to show them around. He introduced himself; his name was Murphy.

Joe nodded at Blacky. "Hurley here's part Irish, Lieutenant. My name's Fenton, and maybe I've got some shamrock in me somewhere." They all laughed.

Murphy led them into an office where the walls were covered with maps of Manila. "This map is a map of the black market," Murphy said. "Those little black pins stuck in there, they indicate where black-market arrests have been made. Captain Williams is a good man. He gets them!" Blacky looked dutifully at the glossy black heads of the pins as Murphy continued. "There was a bad black market the last year of the Jap occupation that we've inherited. The Filipinos called it the buy and sell. It's almost as bad now. Too many GI's can't resist an easy dollar. A few months ago it was mostly small stuff. Cartons of cigarettes, K rations. But now with the goods pouring in—" Murphy shook his head and moved over to another map dotted with red pins. "Every pin you see here indicates where a murder's been committed. You notice the pins are thickest in the water-front sections of town. Lieutenant Swensen heads up our homicide squad." There was a map of traffic accidents and a map of armed-robbery arrests and a map of prostitution arrests. "If we didn't have good detectives, men like Swensen and Williams and Ide, conditions would be much worse. The whole town's boiling!" Murphy said as they walked upstairs. "The political situation doesn't help any. There's bad feeling, of course, between the guerrillas and the collaborators. The Huks are stirring up trouble on the water front, trying to get the longshoremen to go out on strike."

They crossed the compound to the fingerprint bureau and chemical lab; they visited the morgue, where two cadavers lay on long slabs; they peeked in at the lie-detector room. "I wish I had more time," Murphy said finally, consulting his wrist watch. "The old death house here is interesting. The Japs kept it working overtime. On one wall there are about three thousand small blood marks. We think the Jap executioner dipped his finger into the blood of the guerrillas he finished off. Tallied them on the wall. Nice feller."

When Murphy left them outside the Administration Building, Joe said to Blacky, "That ninety-day wonder was a big help. Let's go."

"Where?"

"You're the big strong silent type, but I thought at least you hear things. Where? We're going to see Swensen or this Williams or maybe Ide."

Swensen was out on duty; Williams was in conference. "Ide's next," Joe said.

They were directed to an L-shaped building where Filipino stenos and typists sat at the desks up front. If the Americans in the rear hadn't been in uniform, Blacky might have imagined himself in a business office. Joe smiled at a Filipino girl. "I'm Major Fenton and I want to see Lieutenant Ide." She led them to a desk in the rear. The officer at the desk nodded. His sharp gray eyes were set in one of those pale, meager faces that seem a size too small. As if aware of his plain looks, First Lieutenant Ide had grown a narrow blondish mustache. His uniform was custom-made, but it hung awkwardly on his bony frame.

"Lieutenant Ide, I'm Major Fenton," Joe said. "This is Captain Hurley. As I explained to Lieutenant Murphy a while ago, my father used to be a police officer in the States. That's why I'm curious about Bilibid."

"That so? Do you know Lieutenant Murphy, Major?"

"Hope we're not breaking into your work, Lieutenant," Joe said, sitting down without being invited. "Murphy was nice enough to tour us around Bilibid. But I wanted to see you especially because I think you're the man I've a message for from Tokyo."

Blacky stood there listening. It was the same line, the same message from Tokyo that had failed at 14th MP Headquarters. The guy was a born con man, Blacky thought nervously. Joe had a triple-plated brass front; he was an expert at using names picked out of the air to break the ice. At the replacement depot he had been a "friend" of Major Duplay; at Bilibid a "friend" of Lieutenant Murphy. He had been handicapped at the 14th MP's, with no names to spout.

"A message for me?" Lieutenant Ide asked, interested. "Who from?"

"Hyland or Ryland or Ryan, something like that, I don't remember exactly. Air Force, like us."

"Hyland? Ryan, did you say?"

"Something like that, but he had your name right. Said you were at Bilibid, and I made up my mind when I got to Manila, to Bilibid, that I'd see you, Lieutenant Ide. For one reason, because my father used to be a police officer. He'll be curious when I get home." He reached for the cigars in his pocket and offered one to Blacky, who accepted. Ide thanked him but said he smoked only cigarettes. Joe lit his own cigar and said expansively, "They're Alhambras, the best cigars in the world. You ought to try 'em while you're in Manila, Ide. To get back to Tokyo—" Joe laughed. "I'll have to tell you. This maybe won't make any sense. We were at a party. There were some geishas this Hyland or Ryland knew."

Blacky, watching Ide's face, perceived a brightness in the gray eyes missing a few seconds ago. Leave it to Joe the Lawyer, Blacky thought with relief. He understood now that Joe played percentages. The redheaded major hadn't bit, but somebody else would, sooner or later. Maybe Ide.

"Anyway," Joe was saying, "your friend said to look you up. He said you liked a good time yourself." Joe checked himself as if embarrassed. "Excuse me, but that's how it was. He had your name, even if I haven't got his."

Lieutenant Ide smiled faintly. "I can't think of anybody with that name I know in Tokyo. Ryland? I knew a Rogers."

"No, I'm sure it wasn't Rogers. Well, anything can happen in the Army, I've always said."

"That's true," Lieutenant Ide agreed.

"He might even show up with his geishas in Manila tomorrow. Leave it to the Air Force," he joked. "It'd be O.K. with me! It's a profession with geishas, an art, not like the pom-pom girls here. Well, so long, Lieutenant. We'll see you sometime when you're not busy."

When they were in the jeep again Joe said to Blacky, "Ide's our man!"

"Just because he was friendly?"

"I'll drop in on him in a day or so, have a drink with him. Ten to one he'll come to a pom-pom party if I ask him."

"How can you be so sure?"

"What's a guy like that got back home? Some tomato for a wife? He's no different from the GI's. This is his last fling. He'll come to a party when I ask him. We're not strangers any more, with all that geisha yack-yack between us." Grinning and exultant, he pounded Blacky on the shoulders. "It's working out like I figured it, Blacky. Every detail! That's all there is in anything, the details! One detail at a time, Blacky, and before you know it we'll be round-shouldered from the pesos we'll be carrying." Joe stepped on the gas. "Hell, come on! I know where they're giving jeeps away."

"Goddamn it, what're you up to now?"

"Tommy Cruz bought this jeep at the Eighth Motor Pool. Last night when I was drinking myself stupid on his Stateside booze I asked Tommy who sold it to him. Some guy name of Kroll. Sergeant Kroll. He's the motor dispatcher over at the Eighth."

"Joe, you're pushing your luck too far."

"It's not luck. A robber like you operates on luck. I operate on information, pal. On the lil facts you let slip by under that Indian nose. One fact at a time," Joe bragged. "One detail at a time." He twisted his wheel sharply, pivoting around a *calesa* pulled by a little gray horse. "They ought to keep those buggies off the streets!"

Joe frowned. Sergeant Kroll had reminded him of Sergeant Murdock. He'd better figure out what to do about Murdock. Murdock was showing up tomorrow night at the Liberators' Café. What was he going to do? He hadn't wasted any brain waves on Murdock, but now, what about Murdock? If Murdock hadn't known about the Five Sisters, he could have let him hold the bag. Joe's white teeth bit viciously into his cigar. That was the weak spot, the Five Sisters. They had to meet Murdock or the sunavabitch would run to the MP's. The Five Sisters would hook in Tommy Cruz, and Tommy Cruz would hook in nobody else but Major Fenton and Captain Hurley.

Joe was a perfect driver, and he was driving now almost by instinct. Ten thousand pesos! Even if he could borrow the dough, it would be wasted. Murdock would want more. Joe stared through the windshield at the yellow sun like a thick glue binding the slow-walking Filipinos on the sidewalks. And the detail for Friday night shaped itself inexorably in his brain: murder. He glanced sideways at Blacky, deciding he couldn't talk to Blacky, not today. Blacky was fine for a stickup, but no good when it came to any cold-turkey propositions. He'd tell him tomorrow.

Joe sighed. He stopped thinking of Murdock to concentrate on the sergeant whose name was Kroll.

The Eighth Motor Pool, south of the Pasig River, was surrounded by a wire mesh fence. Behind the wire mesh, jeeps and staff cars gleamed in the sun, the trucks lined up in rows. The Major and the Captain parked outside the wire mesh and walked to the entrance, where an MP was sitting in the shade of a little wooden hut. The MP lounged out into the sun and saluted the two officers. "Take it easy," the Major said genially. "The war's over. I want to see the dispatcher, Sergeant Kroll."

"One minute, sir. Hey, Bill!" he yelled into the hut. A second MP stepped out, putting on his black helmet with "MP" painted in white letters. He led the two officers to a long garage open at one end and smelling of gasoline and grease. Inside, seven or eight GI mechanics were working on repairs and lubrication jobs; GI chauffeurs polished the staff cars of their colonels and generals.

"Kroll!" the MP called. "Hey, Sergeant Kroll!"

A noncom with a round freckled face turned from a gossiping group.

"The Major wantsa see you, Jake," the MP said.

"I want to talk to you, Kroll." The Major smiled. "Nothing important. A private matter."

"This way, Major," Kroll said. They crossed the sunlit yard to a Quonset and went inside. The Major parked himself on a stool. He smiled again.

"Quite a few jeeps are going awol out of this motor pool, Sergeant!"

"What's that got to do with me, sir?" Kroll demanded. "You're Air Force, Major," he added, as if to say: It's none of your damned business.

"That's right, I'm not from the MP's or Bilibid. I've got no right questioning you, Sergeant, but maybe I have a right. Can I use your phone, Sergeant?"

"Go ahead, sir."

The major picked up the phone. "Operator, I want Bilibid Prison. I want Lieutenant Ide." He smiled at the dispatcher, who glanced at him calmly. That Kroll was a cool customer, Joe thought. The freckles helped give his crook's mug an honest look. Maybe, Joe speculated vaguely, he might even do a little business one of these days with Kid Freckles. A voice buzzed in the receiver. "Lieutenant Ide?" Joe said. "Hello. This is Major Fenton. John Fenton. I didn't mean to call you so soon, right after our chat, but I'd appreciate some information about this jeep-stealing racket." He spoke for a long time with Ide, as if he were really an Army detective disguised as Air Force. When he hung up, he said to Kroll, "Lieutenant Ide over at Bilibid's a good friend of mine, Sarge. It's up to you, Sarge, if you want to be friends. What we want's no big deal.

Hurley here and I would appreciate having a jeep assigned to us while we're stationed in Manila. It's a damn big town, Sarge, and a jeep'd be convenient. Think it over, Sarge."

Afterward, driving from the Motor Pool in Tommy Cruz's jeep, Joe said, "Ten to one we'll have our own jeep." He continued thoughtfully, "Kid Freckles got himself a nice racket. Once we have a lil spare time we ought to look into it."

"Joe, you won't listen, but spreading yourself so thin—"

"We're not going to spread ourself! Kid Freckles'll do all the spreading. Hell, Blacky, if we can protect pom-pom houses, we can protect black-market babies like Kroll. He's only a lousy sergeant. He could use a lil brass to protect him!"

"Aren't you gettin' ahead of yourself? Protecting what pom-pom houses? You don't even know if this Ide—" He stopped talking. He could see that Joe wasn't listening to him.

"We'll work both side of the street," Joe was murmuring as if to himself, a happy smile on his lips.

CHAPTER SIX

In GI suntans again, Joe and Blacky walked into the Liberators' Café on Quezon Boulevard an hour ahead of their appointment with Murdock. The place was a noise box. GI's sat drinking at every table or danced with the Filipino hostesses on a crowded floor no bigger than a five-peso note. Four Filipino musicians wearing red berets and perched on a high wooden platform knocked out their version of Stateside jazz.

"I have not see you in long time," a hostess in a green evening dress greeted Joe and Blacky, although their faces were strange to her. She led them to an empty table. "Whisky soda, boys? Highball? Singapore Sling?" she asked when they were seated, smiling ingratiatingly. She had a wide mouth and her skin in the glaring light was like coffee with too much cream poured into it.

"Bring us a couple Tom Collins," Joe said, and he glanced at Blacky's big dark face. It showed about as much emotion as a plate of Spam. There wasn't a give-away wrinkle on the smooth forehead, the steady lips. But Blacky's eyes were shifting and darting about.

"Blacky," Joe said.

"Yeah?"

"All you have to do is drive the jeep."

"I know."

"So look alive, will you? Goddamn it, Blacky, there's nothing else we can do. Even if we had the ten thousand, he'd want ten the next week."

The hostess in the green dress brought over their two Tom Collinses and a third one for herself. As she sat down between them, Joe snatched up her glass and tasted it. "You could drink a dozen of these and still stay sober!" he told her. "Goddamn thing's just water from the Pasig."

"We have fun," she laughed. "I am better not drunk for fun."

"Everybody's screwen the GI," Joe said. "And the bastid deserves it for being such a jerk!" He opened his wallet, pulled out a peso bill, and shoved it between the girl's breasts. "Get the hell outa here!"

She retrieved the money, carefully smoothing out the bill and smiling at the blond soldier as if she hadn't made up her mind whether she liked him or not. "My name Isabella. Isabella—you do not forget?"

"A shape like yours I'll never forget. Beat it, monkey!"

The girl's black eyes wavered at his hard contemptuous stare. She shrugged her bare brown shoulders and left their table.

Joe watched her go across the floor. A GI asked her to dance. They maneuvered a space for themselves on the floor and danced without moving as the band walloped out the hot brassy rhythm of "Tiger Rag."

"You ought to feel good here," Joe said to Blacky, who was silently sipping at his Tom Collins.

"O.K., I'll bite. Why?"

"You're a GI like all the GI's."

"What do you want?" Blacky said sullenly. "What do you want?"

"What do you mean, what I want?"

"Just that! I'm here! What in hell more do you want?"

"Now, that's a question we don't have to go into tonight." Joe grinned. That Blacky had something there, he thought. What more did he want from Blacky? A hundred-per-cent yes man? No. There was more of a bang beating Blacky into line, just as there was with a woman who tried to keep you off. Bit by bit, you put the pressure on, watched them squirming, trying to break free, but they couldn't break free, they could never really break free.

They were on their third Tom Collins when Joe spotted Sergeant Murdock coming in from the street. "He's here," Joe said, getting up from the table and walking through the smoke clouds to where Murdock was standing.

"My old pal!" Murdock smiled tightly. He was almost half a head shorter than Joe, his short powerful arms hanging loosely at his sides. Stocky and squat, Murdock looked more like a cook than a stockade top kick.

"Hi, Sarge. Let's have a drink."

"Buying drinks, huh? When I think how up at the stockade—"

"What do you want to think about that for, Sarge? We'll have a drink and go over to the Five Sisters."

"You got my dough?"

"Sure. Let's have a drink." Joe looped his arm around Murdock's fat shoulders. Stepping over the legs of the drinking and shouting GI's at the smoke-wreathed tables, they joined Blacky.

"Look who's here!" Murdock sneered. "The pride of the black hole of Calcutta himself!"

"It's Old Home Week, Sarge," Joe said, "and everybody's going to be happy. Park yourself, Sarge. We've got a girl over at the Five Sisters who'll make you forget all your troubles."

"I got no troubles. Other way round."

"What do you want to drink, Sarge?"

"Whisky, straight. Hey, you, Blacky. Lose your tongue to the cats in Manila?"

"So long as he didn't lose anything else," Joe laughed. He clicked his fingers for a hostess. A brown girl in a blue dress trimmed with rhinestones walked to their table. "Better have a double shot of whisky, Sarge, and catch up with us."

"I've caught up with you." Murdock's little eyes disappeared between their lids. The Sergeant seemed to be swelling with a rage that in a second would lift him out of his chair and start him running to the street, yelling for the MP's. It was as if he'd forgotten all about his ten thousand pesos and the promise of unlimited pom-pom at the Five Sisters.

For once Joe the Lawyer was unable to speak. The brawly café, with its loud-mouthed GI's and four-piece band and patient hostesses, was whirling into a black and silent spot.

"Sarge," Joe heard Blacky saying, "how're my buddies in your clink?"

Joe listened to Blacky gratefully. Murdock had made Blacky hit back.

"Here Sarge's caught up with a deal and he's griping!" Joe exclaimed. "No wonder nobody likes a sergeant!"

As for the hostess in the blue dress, she was bored. The GI's argued too much, the GI's fought too much, the GI's drank too much, the GI's did everything too much.

"Aw, I'd like to put you away for ten years!" Murdock retorted.

"Until you do, how about a double whisky?" Joe smiled. "A double whisky for Sarge and two Tom Collinses for us and nothing for you, sweetheart!" He slapped the hostess on her buttocks, winking at Murdock. "The doll we've got for you, Sarge, is outa this world! But I know you, Sarge," he went on, his voice shuttling between a leer and a sneer. "No doll can beat ten thousand pesos. Right, Sarge? Ten thousand pesos, five thousand bucks American!" He was watching Murdock's face. Murdock was as full of poison as a rattlesnake, but as greedy as a guy who hadn't eaten for two days. "Ten thousand pesos!" Joe repeated deliberately, and watched the greed swallow up the poison. He guessed what was burning a hole in Murdock's heart. Here they were, two stockade birds who could put their clutch on ten thousand pesos. "A soljer has to think of his old age," he said, his eyes two blue pin points stabbing into Murdock's face. He was getting a big bang out of this clown. By God, he'd have this clown panting with joy at the idea of the ten thousand pesos in easy money! "You'll be going home soon. Be washing dishes somewhere or punching a time clock somewhere. Right, Sarge? And ten thousand pesos'll be mighty handy for your old age." But there'd be no old age for Sarge. The sunavabitch was going to die like a soldier, all right, with his boots on....

The hostess brought their drinks. "Beat it, sweetheart," Joe said. "You haven't got enough for Sarge, here."

Murdock picked up his double whisky. "You talk too damn much. Too damn wise!"

"Blame the good Lord for that, Sarge. Some He made wise and some He made like you and Blacky."

Murdock turned to Blacky. "Joe the Lawyer! I wouldn't trust that bastid with a crock of—"

Joe laughed. "You're a smart guy, Sarge!"

Murdock rested his glass on the edge of his lips as if on a shelf, and then he poured the liquor down.

"Feel better?" Joe asked, grinning and leaning his head on one elbow.

"Only when I get my money."

"The night's young, Sarge."

"Skip that! I want my money!"

Joe signaled the row of hostesses. A tiny girl with the brown skin of a Filipino and the slanted eyes of a Chinese came over to them. "One double whisky, sweetheart, and nothing for you! Sarge, the night's young. We're gonna have us a party."

"First, I want my money!"

"Look what one double shot does to a man!" Joe exclaimed. "It's enough to make me give up drinking."

Blacky lit another cigarette. He'd been chain-smoking all night; the ash tray on the table was overflowing with his cigarette stubs. The slant-eyed hostess set down the double whisky, jutting out her breasts and hoping to be invited to join them.

"You go find yourself a tape measure," Joe told her. "And when you find it, you go measure the girls in this place, and when you find a size thirty-six you let us know."

Murdock drank his second double shot of whisky. "Joe, you're too wise. I'll tell you somethin', you're one of the few bastids in the stockade I got no use for. I like mosta the guys like Blacky here. My duty's my duty and there's nothin' personal," he confided vaguely.

Joe smirked. "Me? You don't like me, Sarge?"

"I want my money. That's all I care about you."

"You'd be rolled if I showed a roll that size here, Sarge."

"You'd be the first to roll me!"

"After what you done for us?"

"What I done for you's right," Murdock snorted. "When I think how four days ago you couldn't buy a glass of beer, and here you're buying double whiskys and talking about ten thousand pesos!" His little eyes glittered wildly and he pounded the table. "That's a whole lot of money!"

Sarge had had only two drinks, but he was drunk, Joe thought. Loony drunk, as he himself had been drunk with Tommy Cruz his first night in Manila. Drunk on more than whisky, drunk on the thought of easy money.

Isabella, the hostess in the green evening dress, wandered over to their table, the lipstick on her mouth smeared awry by some drunken kissing GI. Joe shooed her away, explaining to Murdock, "We don't bother with no used-up pom-pom, Sarge. We've got the stuff for you, Sarge. A kid who was a virgin only last week," he invented. "She's only fourteen, Sarge. A Japanese cherry blossom."

"Who broke it? You?"

"No. Blacky's getting her oiled up for you, Sarge. Right, Blacky?" Joe grinned at Blacky, sitting stiff and straight as if he had a rifle strapped against his shoulders. Out on the dance floor the GI's danced with the little hostesses while at the tables they poured whisky and gin and beer down their eternally dry throats. "Just a good time," Joe remarked hypocritically. "That's all a man wants in this goddamn life, a good time and a lil money, and you're going to have both tonight, Sarge." And there was only the grin on his lips, bitter and mocking, to chalk up the lie against the words.

"Don't think I come tonight like I don't know what I'm doin', Lawyer!" Murdock declared abruptly, with a grin that was almost an exact copy of Joe's.

"Oh, you know what you're doing," Joe assured him.

"Damn right, I know what I'm doin'! Ten thousand pesos is money!" Murdock said, his mouth crafty as a company moneylender's. He lurched to his feet. "Let's get the hell outa here. Let's go someplace where I can collect my money."

"Sure thing," Joe agreed. "We'll go to the Five Sisters."

They walked out to the sidewalk, where soldiers paraded up and down, their faces spotlighted in the bright lights, the street kids tagging after them. "Joe, chewingk gom," the beggar kids singsonged, while the salesmen kids offered, "My seester, Joe. Nice pom-pom, Joe, my seester."

Murdock roared. Waving at the kids, he shouted, "Everybody knows you, Joe! You must be a big wheel here in Manila! Where we goin', big wheel?"

"To my jeep."

"Look who's got a jeep!" Murdock cried, astonished.

"You don't expect us to hoof it, do you, Sarge?"

Blacky took the wheel. Murdock climbed in next to him and Joe got in the rear. They drove past the Golden Gate Café, the New York Eats, all the honky-tonk places, christened in honor of the liberators; a boulevard dedicated not to America so much as to the dollars of America. A huge, crudely lettered sign proclaimed: OLD SPECIAL WISKEY. REFREECH YOURSELF WITH BUKANAN.

In the rear seat, Joe rubbed at his temples with his fingers. He let his shoulders sag, his muscles go limp. For a second he was only aware of the breeze on his forehead and cheeks. Then Joe lit a cigarette. He felt better after the self-imposed interval of relaxation—a trick he'd learned as a guerrilla in the Zambales Mountains north of Manila. His muscles tensed now as he smoked. He pushed the toe of his shoe along the floor of the jeep until he felt metal. He reached down. His fingers tightened on a flat iron bar. He released the bar now that he knew exactly where it was. Everything was planned, every detail. The bar to slug Murdock with; the knife in his pocket to cut Murdock's throat.

Blacky, despite being practically deaf and dumb all night, was following instructions. He had cut into a side street, away from the night clubs and crowds on Quezon. Their headlights tunneled into dark streets where only candles and kerosene lamps glowed in the windows. Between the sidewalks, shallow pools of water gleamed; it had rained in the afternoon and the sewers on this street were blocked.

"If we hit a shell hole, we'll all go swimming," Joe said.

Murdock peered out at the water through which the jeep was moving hub-deep. "Where the hell're we goin'? Give me my money!" he said suddenly, as if the sight of the water had quickened his instincts.

"Can't you wait until the Five Sisters, Sarge?" Joe laughed. "You'll forget about money when you see this dish, Sarge. Fourteen years old, Sarge, and all woman. In Tokyo she'd've been a geisha girl."

Late as it was, their headlights picked out a Filipino, his trousers rolled up, wading through the water and holding his shoes in one hand. The Filipino had left a *pancitería* on the corner. "Let's eat in there!" Murdock demanded. He would have been unable to explain why he felt he had to get out of the jeep. Maybe it was the water, reminding him of the bottomless seas his convoy had crossed, the ships blacked-out phantoms on an ocean as indifferent as death.

"We'll eat at the Five Sisters, Sarge."

"I wanna eat here! Blacky, stop! This is my party! Blacky, stop!"

Blacky slowed, swishing through the water to the curb.

"Keep going, Blacky," Joe ordered.

"I wanna eat here! Stop!" Murdock grabbed at the wheel. "Stop!"

Blacky stopped.

They entered the *pancitería*. A Chinese cashier was dozing inside the door. The place was almost empty, but even here, distant from the main thorough-fares, the few customers were GI's. Three soldiers were eating at a table near a potted plant; two others with two Filipino girls were smoking over their cof-fees. The three GI's, jaws champing on their food, watched the women in silence.

"This joint's dead," Joe said disgustedly. "Let's go to the Five Sisters, Sarge. They fry a chicken there that's a *chicken*!"

"Big deal!" Murdock retorted. "They fry a chicken everywhere!"

A Chinese waiter in a black jacket fetched them menus when they sat down. "I'm hungry," Murdock announced.

"Have an American dinner and have a *comida china* too, Sarge." Joe smiled. "You want to eat hearty. Nothing like a good feed beforehand."

They ordered American dinners and Joe reached for the catsup bottle. He read the label: "Victory Catsup." Everything was victory, he thought savagely. Victory catsup, victory girls, victory pesos for a fat sunavabitch called Mur-dock. He felt like smashing the bottle across Murdock's face and another bot-tle across Blacky's. "Aren't you eating your soup, buddy?" he asked Blacky.

"I don't like soup," Blacky muttered. It seemed Blacky didn't like the fillet, either, or the fried chicken sauté à la Maryland. He only nibbled at his portion and Murdock asked Blacky if he could finish it up. Blacky nodded. Murdock speared Blacky's chicken.

Outside the *pancitería*, a night-owl jeep swooshed by now and then. The Chi-nese cashier dozed. The whole town was sleeping, Joe thought; and Murdock would be sleeping soon, too, in a sack whose strings would never again be opened in this lifetime.

Apparently the hot food had relaxed Murdock, for when they were finished, walking out to the jeep, he started asking questions about the cherry blossom at the Five Sisters. They piled into the jeep again, Joe in the rear, Murdock and Blacky up front. Blacky stepped on the gas. "You're a lucky man, Sarge," Joe said. "But if anybody deserves a girl like that, it's you. We'd still be in that screwen stockade! Nothin's too good for you, I say." And he picked up the iron bar and balanced it across his knee. "Wait'll you see this lil cherry blossom we got lined up for you, no beat-up piece of pom-pom every soldier in town's had."

As he reeled the words off like a professional pimp, Blacky drove the jeep deep into the narrow midnight streets, the headlights probing like knives of light into the shell holes pitting the gutters.

"Don't you ever talk, Blacky?" Murdock asked. "All night you've been clammed up."

"Joe does the talking," Blacky said slowly.

"Blacky's the big silent type," Joe hastened to say. "Only talks when he sees a girl." Joe stared about him, into the heavy darkness, and then, as if the darkness had pulled a trigger in him, he lifted the iron bar and smashed it down on Murdock's head. He heard the thud of iron on bone and he heard Blacky gasp. And then, sighing, spent at last, finally, after waiting for this moment the whole living night, Joe gaped at Murdock's head rolling forward as if the iron bar had unhinged the head from the neck and spine. "Turn right," he said to Blacky.

"My God, Joe—"

"Shut up! Turn right! We want a busted part of town. Try this corner." He kept on directing Blacky until they drove down a street of fire-gutted walls, stars glimmering where once roofs had blocked out the sky.

They had come to a nameless street where only the two of them seemed to be awake or alive. The Battle of Manila had raged here and stormed on, leaving a few walls and the quiet and eternal stars. "Put your lights out," Joe ordered. And now the only light was starlight. "Stop, Blacky."

Joe jumped out of the jeep and walked close to Murdock, slumped in the front seat. He emptied Murdock's pockets: wallet, dog tags, papers, coins. He tugged a ring off a fat finger. Blacky sat at the wheel as if he'd been hit by that iron bar himself. Joe pocketed Murdock's possessions, and when he was done, he dragged the Sergeant out to the sidewalk, his muscles straining under the weight. "Keep an eye out!" he warned Blacky, and dragged the body to a broken wall. Overhead, the starry heaven stretched like a ceiling over all the roofless houses; the Southern Cross blazed in white splendor. Without shifting his eyes from the body, as if afraid Murdock might spring to his feet any second, Joe reached into his pocket for his knife. He pulled open the big blade and the peaceful starlight shone on the steel. Gritting his teeth, Joe slashed Murdock's throat.

CHAPTER SEVEN

Between the Friday of Murdock's death and the Wednesday of the party for Lieutenant Ide, Blacky was always reaching for a drink. He was drunk when he walked into Tommy Cruz's house on Wednesday night with Joe and Lieutenant Phil Ide. The two other guests were a thin Filipino called Dimang and an old Chinaman with a face like a soft mango by the name of Johnny Yen Lee. Blacky eased away from the handshaking and picked up a Martini from a tray on the table in the *sala*. Sipping at the Martini, Blacky glanced at Tommy Cruz and his guests. As might have been expected, the big talk was coming out of Joe. Good old Major Fenton, Blacky thought with a drunken bitterness. The ranking officer tonight. The ranking bastard. Good old Major Fenton and good old Lieutenant Ide and good old Captain Hurley, don't leave him out, he's a good guy, too. They were all good guys. As for good old Sergeant Murdock, he was under the bridge, to use a favorite expression of good old Major Fenton's.

Blacky killed the Martini. Juan, the servant, offered him another, as if he had glided out of the thick cigar smoke, or maybe it was the cigarette smoke at the Liberators' Café. Blacky squinted at the cozy little circle at the far end of the *sala*, Major Fenton and Lieutenant Ide in their uniforms, Tommy Cruz and Dimang in white sharkskin, the Chinaman in a brown business suit. Importers—that was how good old Major Fenton had introduced Dimang and Johnny Yen Lee to Phil Ide, Blacky remembered. Good old Major Fenton, with every detail planned. Major Fenton had a brain that was all details and deals.

"Captain Hulley."

Blacky peered through a Martini haze at Johnny Yen Lee, waving his small hand. Blacky walked over. He towered above the Chinaman.

"Be sociable," Joe smiled, and to Dimang he said, "My father was a police officer in the States. That's why I'm interested in the police problem in Manila."

Blacky wanted to laugh, but the impulse backed up in his throat.

"We only have a hundred radio cars," Phil Ide was saying, "for a city of over a million! Law enforcement's almost impossible. A Filipino policeman gets a hundred pesos a month. Think of that! A hundred pesos a month, when a pack of cigarettes costs three or four pesos!"

"It is a bad condition," Dimang agreed, as if he made his money selling rosaries instead of pom-pom.

"Bad, ve'y bad," Johnny Yen Lee echoed.

"We will have dinner, no?" Tommy Cruz smiled, a smile that promised other things besides dinner. The six men sat down at the white-covered table in the dining room. Juan and a second Filipino served the first course, abalone from California.

"We will have the shark-fin soup and the bird nest," Tommy Cruz proudly announced to Phil Ide. "They are the dif'rence between the good Chinese dinner and the excellent. The bird nest can be soup," Tommy Cruz went on. "Can be dessert. We sweeten for the dessert."

The servants removed the abalone plates and brought a huge bowl of meats in deep reddish gravy; they served the course and poured a pale red tangy wine into the waiting glasses. Blacky drank thirstily. He picked up a fork and speared a morsel of meat on his plate and suddenly remembered Murdock with the fried chicken sauté à la Maryland. The hell with Murdock, Blacky thought. Murdock must be on a slab in Bilibid.

But he couldn't eat. He reached for his wineglass.

The servants kept bringing new courses, shark-fin soup, shrimps in lobster sauce, but only when the table was cleared and they all sat smoking, torpid and heavy, did Joe speak of women. Casually, puffing on his Alhambra cigar, he said to Ide, "What we need's a workout, Phil. A lil pom-pom. Any objections? 'When in Rome, do in the Romans'—that's what I say. Tommy's asked a few girls after dinner."

"Fo' me, no. Ol' mans!" Johnny Yen Lee sighed.

"We'll date him a *binabae*," Joe declared. "Phil, tell 'em about the headache the *binabaes* are at Bilibid."

Bilibid! Blacky thought. The magic word, the key word for Johnny Yen Lee and Dimang and Tommy Cruz, too.

"You can't do a thing with the *binabaes*, the homos," Phil Ide said in a low voice. "When they're taken into Bilibid, they're dressed as women. Legally you can't arrest them for prostitution, because they're men anatomically. It's a problem. Do we put them in the female cell block, where they might behave as men, or in the male block, where they might decide to be women? Can we legally cut their hair? Some wear their hair as long as a woman's."

"Tommy, what've you got for us, *binabaes* or the real stuff?" Joe interrupted Phil, grinning.

"Real stuff! For you, Major Fenton and Captain Hurley, I have ask Spanish girls. I have ask Spanish girl for Dimang. For Lieutenant Ide I have ask a Japanese girl, because Major Fenton, he say you like Japanese geisha, Lieutenant Ide. Her name is Kao."

"Kao," Phil Ide said, his pale gray eyes brightening.

"She is dancer, Lieutenant. Not geisha girl. We have no geisha girls in Manila. She is dancer, very good, very beautiful. You like to see her dance?"

"Why, of course," Ide said eagerly.

They all got up from the table and walked into the *sala*. Tommy Cruz excused himself. The servants pulled the easy chairs into a row, pushed the big table against the wall. Juan put out all the lights except for one dim lamp, and in the theatrical darkness Tommy Cruz's guests seated themselves. Blacky glanced down the row of shadowy profiles, flat-nosed Johnny Yen Lee, dark Dimang, and, at the end, the big-chinned American faces of Joe and Phil Ide.

Tommy Cruz returned. "Kao is ready," he said to his guests, and a second later a draped woman entered the room and faced the audience. In the yellow-tinged shadow her teeth gleamed, her slanted Japanese eyes two dark holes in a mask. The long silken sheet about her shoulders, covering her body, rustled faintly. She turned around. One second she had been covered, wrapped in silk. Now she was nude. She stood there, faceless, her black hair falling between her shoulders, her waist narrow and slender and curving delicately into her broad hips and firm buttocks. For another second she stood still, and then, as music sounded from the dining room, her shoulders swayed. This music was Oriental, intricate and formal as the design on a Chinese jewel box, and to the music she danced. Her arms rose from her sides, long and slow and seemingly boneless, like snakes. All her upper body was dancing now, but the lower half of her body, her hips and her legs, might have been carven ivory. The arms moved a heartbeat faster and her fingers could be seen separating one from the other, and they too seemed curiously boneless, like ten little snakes crawling out of the long snakelike arms. Arms, fingers, shoulders, neck, all were undulating in the dance. But her lower body remained ivory, not flesh. Then suddenly her hips came to life, then were still again. A tremor swift as a shadow moved across her buttocks and Kao whirled around so fast that what had been a faceless figurine was now a woman with a face and breasts and thighs. She stood there, her eyes closed, not a muscle quivering, motionless, and then the sleeper's eyes opened and she rotated her heavy hips like a drunken slut, dancing not to the sinuous Oriental music, but as if to American jazz, to the raucous shake-it, break-it music of the burlesques. Kao's hips rolled wildly, pushing forward as if she'd lost control of them, as if she could never stop.

From his chair Lieutenant Ide sprang up and ran to her.

"She's yours, Phil!" Joe called. "Take her upstairs."

Operation Pom-Pom had changed from a stockade pipe dream into a going business. The day after the Ide party, the Major and the Captain met with Tommy Cruz, Dimang, and Johnny Yen Lee. The Major outlined his ideas. Dimang and Yen Lee promised to bring in lists of the small pom-pom operators. Within the week, the word was on its way; protection. In the curtained alley rooms between Quezon and Rizal, in the shacks clustering around the four bridges over the Pasig, in the wine-and-women joints, Dimang's Filipino gangsters, with their Spanish flair for exaggeration, spelled out the word in one way while Johnny Yen Lee's Chinese spelled it out in another, but it was always the same word: protection.

"There are American officers in Bilibid," the Filipinos said to the little pimps who smelled of their own cheap wine, "who are the good friends of Tommy Cruz and Dimang. These Americans are the friends of the American colonels in charge. They will protect you."

The Chinese, with their mainland tradition of key money, said, "The American officers will protect you from the Military Police. Is it not true that such protection is a treasure from heaven? It is cheap and desirable to buy."

In the first week more than fifty pom-pom houses agreed with the bringers of the word. The Major and the Captain, consulting Tommy Cruz and the others, discussed the holdouts. The holdouts were raided. Phil Ide, living now with the Japanese dancer Kao, his expenses taken care of by the partners, proved reliable. The Major had the Lieutenant on a leash of flesh. The holdouts dwindled and a second word traveled up and down the pom-pom alleys, so that even in the Binondo and Quipo sections of town, and north to the Tondo and Santa Cruz, the little women peddlers were all whispering of the Big Ones. Yes, truly, Tommy Cruz and Dimang and Johnny Yen Lee were the friends of the Americano officers! The little peddlers cursed the Big Ones and decided to pay this new tax levied from above. And for the few who remained stubborn there was the final treatment of knife and bullet. Tommy Cruz had a friend, a Filipino called Manuel Pangamban, on whose chest was tattooed, "My Destiny Is to Be Thief" (in the Manila underworld these tattooed slogans were very common), and Manuel Pangamban directed this end of the new pom-pom syndicate. The fifty pom-pom houses paying protection shot up to eighty, to a hundred and nine.

Everybody was satisfied except the Major. "We're doing O.K.," the Major confided to the Captain, "but time's passing. The guys are being shipped out. We can't wait for the rest of these bastids to make up their minds to play ball." The Major could figure, scheme, connive, but he couldn't control time. Time was the frame in which even he was forced to operate.

The Major began each morning by reading "The Daily Pacifican," the GI newspaper, as a broker reads the stock page. "Four thousand GI's left on the Admiral Benson," he read to the Captain as they breakfasted together at the Manila Hotel officers' mess. "Figure it out yourself. Figure it conservative. Say only three thousand out of that four thousand were good for, say, once a week. Figure it conservative. Three thousand guys at an average of six pesos apiece. That's eighteen thousand pesos, nine thousand American bucks, pulled out of the pom-pom market. And the Admiral Bensons's only one goddamn ship! In a couple of months this town's going to be dead."

But the pom-pom protection money rolled in. The Major and the Captain rented a suite of three rooms at the Hotel Cosmos on Avenida Rizal, where they could entertain their women. They frequented the best night clubs, the Chateau, Old Mansion, Ciro's, Jimmy's. The Major insisted on only one taboo: no gambling. And as they drove from one expensive place to another in the jeep supplied by Sergeant Kroll, only the Captain had eyes to see the GI's lined up a half mile, waiting for their beer rations on the broken streets of Manila, where the shack-and-hut people had created a new architecture. For the Major's eyes were concentrated, as always, on one thing only: money. The pom-pom money wouldn't last forever, the Major was thinking; the only sure money was in the black market—in the buy and sell. The GI's were moving out of the repple depples in truck convoys bound for the ships home, but for the Filipinos there was no other port on the horizon but Manila. Junk-heap Manila, rags-and-patches Manila, hole-in-the-belly Manila. Buy-and-sell Manila.

CHAPTER EIGHT

A breeze blew along Azcarraga Street. In the whirling yellow dust the tele-graph posts down the middle of the gutter looked like ships' masts whose stripped sails were tumbling across the sky in white patches of cloud. As if carried on that dusty breeze, the jeep braked to a stop outside a garage with a huge red and white sign:

SOLANO BROTHERS
DOCTORS TO MOTER CARS

Joe honked his horn until a Filipino mechanic came from under the sign. With grease-stained fingers, the mechanic pushed a cigarette between his lips, lighting it with a windproof Navy lighter.

"How much for five gallons of gas?" Joe asked, his hands on the jeep wheel. Next to him, Blacky listened with the foreboding he could never get used to moving towards his heart, to rest there as lightly as Joe's tanned strong hands on the wheel of this courtesy jeep out of the Eighth Motor Pool.

"You buy?" the mechanic spoke directly to the American Major.

"No, I just want to know what you're asking for gas."

"I bring boss," the mechanic offered.

"I don't want the boss. Can't you tell me how much five gallons of gas costs?"

The mechanic only smiled. It was the smile of the Manila buy and sell.

"Suppose I was a Filipino with a jeep and wanted to buy five gallons?"

The mechanic laughed at the thought of this blond, blue-eyed *americano* as a Filipino.

"How much is five gallons of gas for a Filipino?" Joe persisted, and with those same blue hundred-per-cent American eyes, he seemed to drill the question into the mechanic's skull.

"Forty pesos," the mechanic answered slowly. Then the buy-and-sell smile was on his lips again, a smile that seemed to say that everything could be had for a price.

But Joe was already shifting into gear. "Forty pesos, twenty bucks!" he exclaimed to the silent Blacky. "Our lil pal Kroll's got himself a gold mine!"

"We're doing O.K.," Blacky ventured to suggest.

"Blacky, you're so damned lazy you could be a flip yourself."

Blacky's eyelids fluttered but he said nothing, for there was nothing a man could say to his C.O. Once in the *sala* of Tommy Cruz's house, when his captain's uniform had still been unworn, he had dared to tell Joe off. But that was a long time ago. He'd put the uniform on, and the silver captain's bars, among other things, were like silver bands strapped across his mouth. Silver bands in a silver lockup whose cells Blacky had to admit to himself, were all plush-lined. The food was the best that money could buy, the whisky was Stateside, and at the Hotel Cosmos there was never a shortage of women. That was just the trouble. He'd never had it so good. If only he could put his mind on some shelf and become a soldier for the duration. A soldier in a captain's uniform was all his new C.O. wanted from him; a good soldier, like some obedient muscle flexing on command.

"With Phil Ide in a glass case, the big job's done," Joe was saying thoughtfully, as if to himself. "Operation Pom-Pom's on its own. The rest is organization. Goddamn it, I've meant to see that Kroll conniver before this!" And talking out loud, rehearsing his bagful of tricks, he let Blacky know exactly what his procedure would be. "I'll start off easy, but if the conniver acts tough, I'll tell him straight out I've got the proof on the jeep he sold to Tommy Cruz. If he still toughs it out, I'll pick up his phone and call Phil at Bilibid. We'll see how much pressure he'll take. The jeeps that guy's dumped on the buy and sell! The gasoline! Forty pesos for five gallons!"

That, of course, was the unforgivable crime in Joe's books. The forty pesos for five gallons that somebody else, Sergeant Kroll specifically, was collecting.

They drove to the Eighth Motor Pool, and when they left, Sergeant Kroll's face was so pale his freckles seemed painted on. Later, at the Army and Navy Club bar, Joe said, "We'll drop in on Kid Freckles again when his blood pressure's down and ask him to a party. A lil more pressure and he'll be glad we're protecting him." And Blacky nodded dutifully even as the foreboding, stronger now, gripped his heart. Three Army and Navy rye highballs weren't enough to warm him, for he felt there was a limit to pushing people around. A limit somewhere, sometime.

The party was at Tommy Cruz's house. Joe, his arm around the Sergeant's shoulders, introduced Kroll to three Spanish mestizas, Conchita, María, and Serafina, and to the Japanese girl Hanoco. Hanoco was more beautiful than Joe had thought. Tall and blond in his crisp uniform, joking and smiling, Joe had elected himself the life of the party. "Wine, women, and song, like the gag goes! Right, Sarge? And these are women, you've got to admit!" He glanced at the foolish smile on Kroll's face and thought that Kid Freckles was a real soldier. Kroll was sitting over a gold mine in his motor pool, but when it came to pompom, he was probably a solid six-peso man. "You stick with me, Sarge," Joe said, "and you'll get to know the classiest dames in this town." He winked, sizing up the women. The three mestizas in their evening gowns might have been a chorus, all of them black-haired and black-eyed, with dark lush faces, as if they'd been manufactured like dolls in the same factory. Only their names and their dresses were different, Joe thought. María, in a red dress, was Kroll's date. Conchita, in black, was his own girl, while Serafina, in yellow, belonged to Blacky. Serafina and Blacky walked to the table, where Juan was mixing the evening's first cocktails. Joe's eyes followed Blacky's broad khaki shoulders for an instant. That boy was becoming a regular boozemaster, he reflected idly.

"Maybe we all ought to have a drink," he suggested, his eyes shifting to Hanoco. He wouldn't mind swapping Conchita and Serafina and María for one night with Hanoco, Joe thought, and he smiled a big blue-eyed smile at Tommy Cruz. "Tommy only drinks Stateside liquor. Right, Tommy?" They all went to the bar, Hanoco and Tommy Cruz a step or two behind Conchita and Joe. But he could still see Hanoco as if she'd been cut into his brain in everlasting lines and colors, the round face with the pink cheeks and pink lips, a face like some vividly colored porcelain, her eyes glowing between her slanted lids like pieces of black steel, her hair combed away from her forehead, the blackest hair in the world, blacker somehow than the Spanish mestizas', her body in her evening dress hidden rather than revealed, but not enough for him to forget the curves of her breasts. He heard Conchita chattering, but no word registered now. No deal in blackmarket gasoline agitated the restless brain. The blood was pounding in his head. How was he going to get Hanoco? How could he work it without Tommy's coming for him with a knife?

The deal with Kroll was clinched at the Antelope Restaurant in the Pasay. Here, as soft Basque music played for lunching businessmen and lunching black-marketeers alike, Joe described the dishes he'd ordered to Sergeant Kroll. He acted as if he'd cooked them himself.

His mouth full of *arroz valenciana*, Kroll agreed to supply five hundred gallons of gasoline every week. Joe mentioned a garage in the Tondo that Tommy Cruz had already arranged to have handle the Eighth Motor Pool's gasoline. Blacky listened. He only listened. When their coffees and brandies were served, he lit an Alhambra cigar—the Captain was a straight Alhambra man these days—and smoked in luxurious if uneasy silence.

The gasoline was only a beginning, although Kroll didn't know that. After the first delivery, Joe, with Blacky for a witness, sketched in a few more details of Kroll's future for Kroll's information. "Sarge, no reason why we can't handle some staff cars. I've looked into it, Sarge. The motor numbers can be changed with dies, the cars repainted in two-tone shades, the Army finish chromeplated. A car like that ought to be worth seven or eight thousand pesos in the buy and sell. There's nothing to it. Tommy Cruz knows a lawyer, one of these flip *abogados*, who'll fix us affidavits proving they were bought from American officers running for Bataan."

Only a beginning. And not only for Sergeant Kroll. An immense greed was burning in the heart of the synthetic major. Gasoline, tires, automobile parts—what didn't the town have? Among the rubble-filled lots of the liberated city there were other motor pools besides Sergeant Kroll's. There were QM depots roofed by the blue blazing sky and walled in by barbed wire. Out on Calle General Luna, acres of tires, of all sizes, were piled up like gigantic doughnuts, while on Mabini Street the fenced-in boxes of automobile parts looked like a toy city made of blocks. A blind man could see that there just weren't enough warehouses to hold all the stuff coming in from America.

The ships silhouetted in the north and south harbors represented floating warehouses to Joe. He would drive along the piers with Blacky, nervously glancing at that sharp-eyed face, parking the jeep for a few minutes to watch the LST's scooting between the sunken Japanese destroyers like boats in an amusement park. Above the water, the Japanese superstructures jutted in rusty islands that day by day were being cut to pieces by the Seabees to make more space for the incoming cargo ships. More space for more ships for more stuff for more pesos! And here they were nibbling around, Joe would think despairingly as they rolled along the water front.

One afternoon Joe said to Blacky, "We've got a date with Dimang."

Out in the stylish Pasay, they sat with Salvador Dimang in the garden behind his big house. They sat under a fan-shaped tree as the sinking sun ignited the reddish golden flowers. "We're doing all right in pom-pom," Joe began, "but that's small, Salvador. The people in Manila need every damn thing the ships're bringing in. I've been investigating, Salvador. Between the pier and the depot is no man's land! Forty, fifty thousand dollars in every truck! What's to stop a truck driver from driving his load where we want him to drive it? Give a truck driver a couple thousand pesos and you're in business."

"No, I do not like that." Dimang shook his long brown head. "It is the Army on the pier and in the depot, and I do not like to go against the Army," he added emphatically, and in this walled Pasay garden he looked as law-abiding and respectable as any other citizen of Manila.

Joe stared at him, regretting that he hadn't approached Tommy Cruz. But Tommy Cruz was in on the Kroll deals. That was enough for Tommy Cruz for a while, Joe calculated. "O.K., let's forget the water front. What I'm after mainly is how do we get into the buy and sell? You ought to have some ideas, some connections."

"I have a cousin who buys lumber from the Army sawmill on Cavite," Dimang said slowly. "I do not like to go against the Army," he reminded himself. He had his principles, this pom-pom dealer and jewelry fence. "It is bad to go against the Army."

"This cousin of yours," Joe interrupted him. "Suppose we see him tomorrow? Maybe there's something in it."

"I do not like to go against the Army."

"Who's going against the Army? We're going to work *with* the Army, Dimang. Lumber sounds good to me. Far as I can see, this town needs lumber more than it needs pom-pom," Joe laughed.

"I do not like to go against the Army!"

"The hell with it!" Joe snapped. "Maybe Johnny Yen Lee has some ideas. They say the Chinese have better heads for business, anyway, than the Filipinos."

"No, no," Dimang protested. "Major Fenton, you mistake me. We will go to my cousin."

The Major had his principles, too, and one of them was that you could never go wrong appealing to the larceny in everybody's heart.

The sign above the lumberyard proclaimed in three-foot yellow letters:

DIMANG LUMBER INC.
100% PILIPINAS CORPORATION

They went inside the office and met Dimang's cousin. Pedro Dimang was a short, thickset man with smooth brown skin. Salvador Dimang explained to him that Major Fenton and Captain Hurley had money to invest, and perhaps it might be in the lumber buy and sell. Pedro Dimang led them out into the yard, where piles of fresh-cut boards shone in the sun.

"This is red lauan," Pedro Dimang said. "I sell for seven hundred pesos for one thousand board feet. It is eighty pesos before war. This is white lauan, six hundred fifty pesos. Before war, sixty-nine pesos. This is apitong, seven hundred pesos. It is seventy-three pesos before war."

And in that dusty yard with the air filled with the sweetness of the tropical woods, the refugee shacks of the city flashed like a dazzling vision across Joe's mind.

"How big is the building boom, anyway?" he asked the lumberman.

Pedro Dimang smiled. "There is not sufficient lumber, Major Fenton. Before war we cut more than nine hundred million board feet. Today we cut only thirty-five million board feet. We have not enough, for there is not enough sawmills. We have thirty-eight sawmills near Manila but only eight sawmills cut for civilian use."

"The other thirty cut for the Army?"

Pedro Dimang shrugged. "Yes. We must buy from the Army sawmill or we do not have lumber."

"I know. Your cousin said you buy from an Army sawmill on Cavite. What do you pay for this red lauan?"

"Three hundred pesos for one thousand board feet. Sometimes four hundred pesos. *Tawad-tawad*, Major Fenton."

"What does that mean?"

Pedro Dimang smiled. "It means to make the bargain. The GI's want me to pay four hundred and fifty pesos. I say I give you two hundred pesos. *Tawad-tawad*."

"Could you handle the whole cut from this Cavite sawmill at a straight three hundred pesos per thousand?"

The lumberman stared at him, astonished. His black eyes sought the thin wrinkled face of his tall cousin, who said, "Major Fenton and Captain Hurley, they have the connection, Pedro. The big connection."

"Pedro," Joe said briskly, "you can keep that sign of yours, all that hundred-per-cent Pilipinas stuff. But from now on you've got two *americano* partners and one new Filipino partner, your cousin Salvador here. Now where is this sawmill on Cavite, exactly?"

They returned to their jeep, without Dimang, and drove down the long narrow street. Filipino boy scouts wearing bright blue and red handkerchiefs paraded around the corner. Joe honked at the troop. A rooster strutted out of an alley to an overturned garbage pail and a boy ran from a house banging on two empty K-ration cans as he cheered the boy scouts. Joe, the dust winging behind him, curved out onto broad Quezon Boulevard, where only the Quiapo Cathedral and the Times movie towered over the low-lying rows of jerry-built stores, the sun glittering like molten steel on the corrugated iron roofs. On the plaza, the street sweepers lazily shoveled the droppings of the *calesa* horses into their dump cans, shining like gold in the fierce light. Joe wiped his sweating face. "Figure the percentages, Blacky. Thirty-five million board feet against nine hundred million before the war, with the Army controlling thirty out of the thirty-eight sawmills. There's a fortune in this lumber!"

"I don't know, Joe, about these Filipinos—the two Dimangs. Kroll's O.K., but I have a feeling those two Dimangs'd sell you out in a minute."

"Not as long as we show 'em a peso profit. That goes for a flip or an *americano*. For anybody! You stick with me, Blacky," he exclaimed, "and we'll be lighting our cigars with hundred-peso bills!"

"Unless we get the old hot foot."

"If we make out on Cavite, we'll give those lil mestizas of ours the old hot foot!" He thought of Conchita and Serafina. "I'd swap the pair of 'em for Hanoco."

"Tommy Cruz's girl?"

"How many Hanocos do you know, jerk? What I'd give for that dame!"

"You're kidding."

"Kidding? I've never told you how I feel about her, but I wanted her before I saw her."

"You what?"

"Sounds goofy," Joe admitted with a wry laugh. "Remember when we pulled into Manila and you shacked up at the Five Sisters? I didn't see Hanoco that night, but Tommy told me about her. I knew she was upstairs, and I wanted her. I'm sick of Conchita. What d'you say we swap tonight, Blacky?"

"No!"

Joe glanced at him and laughed. "No," he mimicked. "You're a stinker, Blacky. What's a shack job among buddies?"

"The hell with you!"

Joe roared. "You're not falling in love with lil Serafina, are you?"

"No, but I've got kinda used to her."

"And kinda used to the bottle. You want to taper off, buddy."

Blacky flushed. "I'll drink as much as I damn please!"

"Too much booze is poison. It's like gambling. The MP's wouldn't've caught up with me if I hadn't been crazy on the gambling."

"I'll drink as much—"

"Cool off," Joe advised him calmly. "Cool off, bud."

They crossed the Pasig River to Dewey Boulevard, the shining eastern sea on their right, and to the south the peninsula of Cavite, a long emerald-green arm in the sea blue. Army trucks crowded with GI's and their Filipino girls passed them, bound for the downtown city. Joe stepped on the gas and they sped along the Manila South Road. Nipa huts on stilts bordered the beaches. Banana trees, heavy with green spiky fruit, grew in clumps, and the feathery-topped bamboos creaked mournfully in the sea breeze. Ahead, on the road, three open trucks packed with peasants and bright with flags and hand-lettered signs rolled toward them. The truck caravan sped by and the peasants waved and smiled and lifted their Tagalog signs at the *americanos*.

"Huks—Reds," Joe said grimly.

"Where they going with all those signs?"

"Don't you read nothing in the 'Pacifican' but the comics, Blacky? The papers've been full of them. Last few weeks they've been coming into town from all the provinces with their goddamn petitions. Parading into Malacanan Palace to see the President, the Red bastids! They've been after the longshoremen to go out on strike."

"Yeah?"

"What they want's a revolution. That's what they wanted when they were fighting the Japs, and that's what they want now—a goddamn monkey revolution!"

"What're you so hot about 'em for?"

"I fought the bastids when I was a guerrilla."

"You've never said much about that, Joe."

"Why the hell should I? It's over now."

They heard the whirring saw before they bumped around a bend to see the rotating blade slicing into a clamped log, faster than a table knife into cheese. Logs, piled like matchsticks, and six or seven GI's stripped to the waist appeared through the jeep windshield. "What a racket!" Joe grinned. "Cutting board for Uncle Sam a coupla days a week and the rest of the week and every night for the buy and sell! Blacky, bet you they could use a lil protection."

They pulled into the clearing, to a yellow hill of sawdust, and stepped from the jeep, clean and neat in their suntans. "Who's in charge?" Joe asked the sweaty, staring loggers.

A GI with a jockey cap on his red hair walked over to the Major and the Captain.

"You in charge?" Joe asked, sizing up the GI's square reddish-tan face with the skin peeling from the blunt, short nose. Two dark brown eyes peered out cockily.

"Yeah," said the redhead. "I'm in charge."

He had left off the "sir," but Joe only smiled. "Come along with us. We want to talk with you."

"About what?"

Joe bent over to the heap of sawdust. He stooped, picked up a handful, and tossed it into the air. "About this!" he said to the redhead and the silent crew of loggers. "About this, *sir!*" he added ironically.

Without a word the redhead motioned for them to follow him. They strolled up a narrow path under the green sighing branches. Joe peered up at the leaves. "Red lauan! White lauan! Apitong! Is that why it's so relaxing here, Red?"

The redhead turned to face them. "What do you want?"

"This army's sure gone to hell," Joe remarked to Blacky, "when you get guys like this guy here who's forgotten how to talk to an officer!" He advanced a step toward the redhead. "That's because you're not a soldier, Red, so much as a sunavabitch selling board to the black market!"

"That's the story you hear everywhere," the redhead said quietly. "Everywhere. Everybody's selling to—"

"I happened to hear it from Pedro Dimang in Manila. Want to hear some more? Listen, you wise sunavabitch! What's to stop Pedro Dimang from bringing that lil story you hear everywhere to Bilibid, to the MP's? The story you hear everywhere, but which happens to be true in your case, how he's paying three hundred to four hundred pesos a thousand for Army lumber. You're one lucky boy it's O.K. with us for you to keep on cutting. Cut twenty-four hours a day if you want! But all your board'll go to Dimang from now on. He'll pay you a flat three hundred pesos a thousand for everything you cut, red lauan or white, good quality or bad. You don't lose a thing. You'll get your price and you'll be protected with only one flip to sell to instead of a dozen!"

The redhead pulled out a wad of chewing tobacco. Blinking at the officers, he bit into the wad, but when he had a chunk off, his jaws moved sluggishly, as if half paralyzed. He was like a man chewing tobacco in a slowmotion movie.

And Joe said in a friendly voice now, "I guess you can't smoke here, Red, with all this timber around."

CHAPTER NINE

When they returned from Cavite, they met Conchita and Serafina and dined at Jimmy's night club. Later they danced on the lawn under the swaying Japanese lanterns, the breeze from the bay like a third dancer hugging the dresses of the women. Toward two o'clock, back in the living room of the suite at the Hotel Cosmos, Joe suggested with no preliminary at all, "A lil variety, boys and girls! What d'you say? Serafina, you come with me and Conchita'll take care of the Captain."

"Nothing doing!" Blacky shouted.

"No!" Serafina said. "No!"

"You are drunk!" Conchita accused her unfaithful lover.

Joe circled Serafina's waist and kissed the girl on her ear.

"She's my girl!" Blacky cried.

Joe turned, the corners of his lips lifting in a false cat smile. "Why should she play around with a captain when she can have a major?" And his eyes, as false as his smile, shifted to Serafina, his fingers rippling along the soft flesh sheathing her slender waist. "Right, Serafina?" And whether the mestiza was attracted by his handsome blondness or by the oak leaves pinned to his shirt, Blacky would never be able to guess.

Serafina laughed, a harlot's laugh, which, like an open pocket, can hold any man. That laugh echoed in Blacky's head as he watched the door close behind the pair.

"Hell with both of 'em, Conchita," he muttered sourly.

Conchita's black eyes were staring right through him at the closed door as if the treacherous lovers were traced on the wood.

She was jealous, and when Blacky thought of how easily Serafina had given in, the little knives scraping at his nerves fused into one hot point probing into what had passed for his pride and manhood. "The hell with 'em!" he said.

"I love him," Conchita said in a voice that was a little too rich, a little too dramatic. In this room with the bamboo furniture, the mestiza was playing out a part written long ago when the first white man in the Orient had sent away his brown-skinned or yellow-skinned mistress. Conchita seemed to have forgotten that she was only a high-class pom-pom girl. "I love Major Fenton," she declared passionately and almost virtuously.

Blacky didn't know whether to laugh or to curse. "Conchita, don't snow me," he pleaded. "You don't love that sunavabitch. Let's hit the sack, baby."

"I love Major—"

"Major, hell!" he interrupted, jeering. "You rank-crazy too?"

"I love—"

Blacky's dark hairy fists knotted and the woman recoiled from him. "I'm not gonna hit you, don't worry. You're not worth it." He glared at Conchita and remembered Lucy at the Five Sisters. There was a real woman, a real GI woman full of sweet loving, not like these mestiza tramps. But he couldn't go to Lucy. Orders from Major Fenton. God Almighty, he'd had enough orders.

He flung Joe's door wide open. "You can have Conchita, too! I'm going out."

Blacky was not only angry, he was frightened. This was the first time the muscle had mutinied against the brain. He changed into a shirt without bars or Air Force insignia and went out into the Manila night.

Lucy was wearing what could have been the same flowered kimono she had worn when he had first seen her at the Five Sisters. But as Blacky stared at the small brown face with the whitish scar on one cheek, time slowed for him and his heart eased. For in this room with the unmoving gray tropical lizards frozen on the walls, he wasn't Captain Hurley spinning like a crazy top from the nonstop hand of Joe the Lawyer, alias Major Fenton, but plain Blacky Mac-Intyre, GI.

Blacky was drunk, double and triply drunk on the spirits that come in the bottle with the label "Awol."

"Remember me, Lucy?" He smiled at the girl.

"Yes," she said, obediently as any child.

"Like hell you do! I'm Conway, your old boy friend Conway. *Hang gnang* Pier Seven."

The pom-pom girl studied him with large black eyes. She brushed away a wisp of hair from her forehead with a tiny hand and smiled. "You go *hang gnang* Pier Seven?"

"Not when I've paid Franny out there for the whole night." He frowned. Franny had remembered him, even if Lucy hadn't. Good old Franny, who might tell Tommy Cruz, who in turn might joke some night about the captain who liked to sleep with GI pom-pom girls. To hell with Franny and Tommy Cruz and Major Fenton. "Come here, baby. I want to look you over."

Lucy walked to him. She walked slowly, because he was a GI who had bought the night. She even tried to remember this huge black-haired GI, but a whole platoon of GI's, all big and dark of hair, was marching across her memory.

Blacky grinned, he patted her small bottom and sat down in the only chair. He slapped his knee, and obediently she lowered herself onto his lap.

"What is your name?" she asked, and pinched his chin ever so gently, as she'd pinched the chins of so many other nameless soldiers.

"Conway."

"No," she laughed. "You are not Conway."

"How do you like Kilroy?"

"Kilroy?"

"Conway's cousin. Everybody's cousin, that's who he is, Lucy. And he's got a helluva thirst. Franny's bringing us a bottle of whisky. You like whisky?"

She held up her hand and with her thumb and forefinger measured out how much she liked whisky. Blacky looked critically at the inch of space between her fingers. "You're not Conway's girl friend, sister! That bastid could drink."

When the bottle arrived, he poured two stiff drinks. Glasses in their hands, they sat cozily together on the cot. Lucy's thin brown neck tilted and half the whisky in her glass slid down her throat.

"You're Conway's girl friend, all right," he amended gravely. "Where'd you learn to drink like a fish?" And he answered his own question. "Just a lil GI girl who likes her whisky." Blacky drank, grimaced. It was GI whisky, all right, out of some cellar still, blended with dynamite. He finished what was in his glass, bounced up from the cot, crossed to the dresser and treated himself to a second hooker.

Lucy laughed tipsily and ambled over to the dresser, wrenching open the top drawer, and tipsily she turned to him, a photograph in her hand. "This Conway," she said, giving him the photo. Blacky took it. He glared blearily at a GI with a big-chinned face standing in front of a tent. Inscribed on the tent were Conway's parting words: With my undying love. We'll go to church Christmas but if you're not faithful to me it's all off.

"You weren't kidding about Conway and church Christmas," Blacky said. "How many GI's you hand that story to, baby?"

"Only GI I like!"

She smiled and held up an empty glass for him to refill. After he had put the bottle back on the dresser he stood before her. He bent down and kissed her on the mouth, and then he spread her kimono wide and time spilled out of his consciousness like the whisky out of his glass and they were together on the cot, a big white man and a little brown girl no longer knowing whiteness or brownness, lost in the black velvety midnight land without boundaries where all the world's lovers go....

And again he was at the dresser, the whisky bottle in his hand. "You don't remember me." He laughed happily. "You don't remember me, kid, but you're gonna remember me!"

"You are Kilroy."

"Kilroy," he agreed, lowering his bulk to the cot. "Thas who I am. A goddamn GI. Thas why I love you, baby. You're a GI woman." He kissed her. She was the first woman he'd had after the break from the stockade. The first and the best, he thought drunkenly. The first was always the best. The first was good luck. Like Joe was bad luck. "I'm gonna spend all my time here, Lucy baby. Why don't you put out the light?"

He watched her walk from the cot to the dangling light cord. His eyes lifted from her little buttocks to the white dazzling bulb. He could still see it when the room went dark and she pattered back to the cot.

Who the hell was he kidding with all this GI baloney? He wasn't a GI and he wouldn't be able to come back to the Five Sisters. Not worth the risk. "Lucy," he whispered, "think you could ever meet me someplace else?"

"You want to be my boy friend?"

"Yeah. You could meet me on Rizal someplace and we'll see a movie or something. O.K.?"

"O.K."

"How can I meet you?"

"You come here, no?"

"No, I don't wanna do that."

"You want to be my boy friend?"

"Yeah, I said so, for God's sake! Where can I write you to meet me? Where besides here?"

"My mother has room in house in Tondo."

"Don't forget to give me her address. You work every night?"

"No. Tuesday night my holiday."

"I'll write you and we'll meet some Tuesday night, O.K.?"

"You be my boy friend, yes?"

He kissed her and stroked her face as he'd done before. Maybe because he couldn't see her scarred cheek in the dark. Maybe because he was sorry for her or sorry for himself. His fingers glided gently across the scar. They were both scarred: Lucy, who had once been in love with Juan Esteban, a Philippine scout buried on Bataan, and Blacky MacIntyre, once of Beaver Dam, Wisconsin. Scarred, wounded, maybe even destroyed, the pom-pom girl and the awol soldier.

CHAPTER TEN

"Sarge, our deal in gasoline's going to look like small beans next to the deal I've got lined up now."

Blacky stared at Joe, who was smiling at Sergeant Kroll.

"I've been waiting for the go-ahead," Joe was saying, his eyes shining as he smacked one fist into the palm of his hand. "This is the blue-sky deal, Sarge!"

The sergeants were different but the deal was always a blue-sky deal, Blacky reflected grimly. Ask Sergeant Murdock about how to pick up an easy ten thousand pesos. Or ask redheaded Sergeant Mallinson on Cavite, who was selling his lumber at a straight three hundred pesos a thousand board feet. They were all just a bunch of sergeants to the demon salesman sporting a major's uniform. Murdock and Mallinson and Kroll. And Phil Ide, too, who foolishly thought he was a lieutenant, and Tommy Cruz and Johnny Yen Lee and Salvador Dimang and Pedro Dimang, and last and maybe least none other than Sergeant-Captain Hurley.

Kroll was arguing that he was pretty busy. Joe, puffing on a cigar, waited for Kroll to finish. He was a picture of politeness, and Kroll, who didn't really know him, was no doubt thinking that Joe was listening to him. Blacky felt sorry for the freckle-faced sergeant.

"You're right, Sarge," Joe agreed when Kroll stopped talking. "You're right and you're wrong. I've been waiting for my friends higher up to give me the go-ahead, and now I've got it," he declared earnestly, as if he hadn't invented this little detail about the "go-ahead" between one breath and the next. "Sarge, there're fifteen piers down the harbor. Between the pier and the depot is no man's land. That's where we can score. Shut up, Sarge! I listened to you, so you listen to me. You know and I know there're plenty truck drivers who wouldn't mind making an extra peso. What're you shaking your head for, Sarge? The protection I've got goes to the top brass in this town, so stop shaking your damn head! We're going to find out the depots the trucks're consigned to. Pay off the checkers at the depot. Pay off the drivers. Some of those trucks carry twenty, thirty thousand bucks in stuff. That's worth ten thousand on the buy and sell at the least. Between the pier and the depot is where we can score. Stop shaking your damn head, will you, or I'll take it off for you!"

In the next few days Kroll began contacting truck drivers and checkers. Joe said to Blacky, "We can take it easy until Kroll's set. Anyway, this business before pleasure is a lot of craperoo. Business *and* pleasure, that's our new motto!" So there were more parties, more faces; Salvador Dimang and his mistress, Espanita; Pedro Dimang, the lumberman, and Filemón Victorio, an actor friend of Pedro's who had appeared in a dozen Filipino-made movies. And girls—always more girls. But one Tuesday Blacky met Lucy. Only Lucy could open the gates of the gilded stockade commanded by Major Fenton.

The Major's water-front heisting ring was ready now. Sergeant Kroll had greased all the stretched-out hands on the piers and in the depots. And like any properly lubricated machine, this one hummed smoothly. Their truck drivers diverted K rations, sheets, pillowcases, medical supplies to places lined up by Pedro Dimang. "Let Salvador Dimang suffer." The Major grinned at the Captain. "He doesn't like going against the Army? We won't make him. Let him suffer!" They lost money in electric blasting caps; the fishermen who used dynamite wouldn't buy the electric cap. But nearly all their other deals were profitable. In this city where the headlights of their bribed truck drivers shone on piles of rusty scrap iron changed by night and shadow into huge flower-like masses, the demand for made-in-the-U.S.A. goods was insatiable.

The Major decided they had to have an office. "This doing business out of a jeep doesn't make sense." They rented space on the Escolta, the main business street in Manila. "If you have a front, you might as well have a good front," the Major said, like an oracle. The Japanese demolition squads had wrecked about every second office building on the Escolta and rentals were expensive. Their twelve-by-eighteen-foot office on the fifth floor of the Rutledge Building cost them five hundred pesos a month, plus three thousand pesos in key money. The Spanish manager had only smiled at the Major's efforts to whittle down the key money. "There is no business today, Major Fenton, without the *pabagsak*." *Pabagsak* was Tagalog for key money. It was a *pabagsak* town, a *tawad-tawad* town, and only Blacky had any misgivings.

"This damn office puts us right out in the open," he complained one morning, gloomily staring at the new desks and files and the new black letters on their door. "Investment Company," he read off sourly. "Where'd you get that one, Joe? Joe, no kidding—we've been lucky, but how far can you push your luck?"

"I don't operate on luck, jerk."

"Sure, sure," Blacky appeased him. But when he glanced at the legend on the door, he felt as if Joe had dipped his little finger into the sign painter's inkpot to dab a little black mark on his heart. God! he thought. They were going too damn fast with pom-pom and gasoline and lumber, and all the stuff heisted on the water front, and now this damn office. Maybe the wise thing would be to heel out. And hide in the alleys? That wasn't for him any more. But passage to Shanghai, to home? And end up in more alleys? No, not for him.

The black letters on the door whirled, spelling another name, a girl's name. Blacky swallowed, his heart raced. If Joe could rent himself an office, why couldn't he rent himself a hideaway?

All that morning he nursed the thought and felt a strength entering him. A hideaway with Lucy. With Lucy! He'd pull a fast one on Joe, the king of fast ones. On Joe, who'd been against the Five Sisters. Joe, his C.O., drawing up a list of places off limits. By God, he'd keep her off limits, private stuff for himself, one woman Joe wouldn't ever put his hands on. Lucy, who was a straight GI girl and no fancy two-timing mestiza like Serafina. A secret hideaway for the day when he'd have to dump his captain's uniform and kiss Joe good-by.

Blacky rented a small house on María Clara Street out in Santa Mesa Heights for three hundred pesos a month. It was in a neighborhood far to the north of the honky-tonk soldiers' city, west of the Del Norte Cemetery with its countless crosses and stone Gabriels and near the Chinese cemetery, where the men of the Golden Rule lay quietly with no stone angels to blow trumpets for them. "Lucy, baby," he said to her when she moved into the house on María Clara Street, "you mustn't ever see Franny or anybody from the Five Sisters. You're through with all of 'em! If I catch you fooling with a GI or a Filipino, out you go!" But he didn't have to threaten Lucy. The little brown girl was overwhelmed by her new position. All her life had been spent in small rooms; her cubicle at the Five Sisters was large compared to the crowded hole she'd known as a child in the Tondo. To Lucy, the house on María Clara was like a Taft Avenue mansion in the Pasay. Built of salvaged wood, with a corrugated iron roof that leaked, with only one stone wall and the red-tiled floor surviving the war and the liberation, the little house had three rooms. *Three* rooms! Blacky gave her two thousand pesos to furnish the *sala*, the kitchen, and the bedroom. And when he stealthily visited her, perched huge and silent on the seat of a horse-drawn *calesa*, listening to the clip-clop of the horse's hoofs and glancing moodily into the dim interiors of the houses in the night, the windows lit by candlelight and kerosene and coconut-oil lamps, he could almost forget that Lucy's last address had been the Five Sisters.

When she timidly asked him after a week or so if her old mother could sleep in the kitchen, he said yes. The request pleased him. He thought it proved Lucy wasn't a hundred per cent pom-pom. He could trust her, maybe, since she was getting a good deal. For that's all life was—a mixture of good deals and bad deals, mostly bad. A buy and sell where there was always a buyer and a seller. And always a price. A price for everything. For Sergeant Murdock and for Lieutenant Ide. A price to be collected one day in the buy and sell run by the Collector some men called God and other men called fate and Blacky called luck.

Meanwhile Lucy was a good deal for the black-haired soldier whose face was hammered hard and thin by war. All the fat living hadn't softened his jutting jaws or filled his hollow cheeks. These days Blacky felt a contentment he hadn't known since his boyhood in Beaver Dam when he'd lived with his old mother; a sense of protection, not only by a set of walls, but by protection of another person's heart. He was sheltered now in the heart of a Manila pom-pom girl.

The heart was scarred, as was the face; a six-peso scar paid for by too many GI's. For six pesos she had welcomed all her ten-minute lovers, knowing there was no permanence to any of them, as there was no permanence to the GI who finally had admitted his name was Bill. But there was the house, solid and strong, and she loved the house with the deep love of any street waif for a place of her own, loving Bill too, for he had given her this beautiful house that she would remember when he was gone, when all her lovers were gone, their faces dimming and merging and vanishing and leaving only the indestructible profile of the house on María Clara Street.

CHAPTER ELEVEN

These days it was a different Blacky, all right. Joe wondered sometimes, especially in the early morning when they drove to the Rutledge Building like any other pair of legitimate businessmen in the jeep maintained by Sergeant Kroll. Joe liked piloting the jeep, polished up like a diamond and mounted on four brand new tires. In the cool of the morning he would speculate about a Blacky who hardly ever beefed. Not so long ago, Blacky had been a regular flock of worry birds, but now he was letting the world go by.

Joe asked Blacky no questions. He knew when to keep his mouth shut. Besides, with the mornings allotted to the buy and sell, the afternoons to pom-pom, he had too many other details to think about. With the water-front heisting ring in operation, there were possibilities of really hitting big money. These days, Joe seemed to have forgotten his motto of business and pleasure. Nights, he was seeing one woman mostly, an American girl named Janet. "There's a limit to playing around," he admitted to Blacky. "One doll's enough to take care of. I've got too many other things on my mind." What he had on his mind, of course, was the obsessive image of his truest love: the deal with the blue-sky eyes and the breasts made of wadded peso notes.

The big money was on the loose in this town. Sooner or later, he'd catch up with it, Joe swore to himself. In the meantime, he was like a lover chasing a woman and getting no closer than a whiff of her perfume. Every morning in the Rutledge lobby he would purchase an armful of Manila newspapers, the Chronicle and Manila Times and Herald and Free Press.

When he sat at his desk in his office, reading the business news—of a powerful new Filipino syndicate formed to bid on Army and Navy surplus, or of the Philippine government's latest program to curb the black market and control prices, or of the American Commercial Agency's blast against irresponsible elements circulating rumors that Army and Navy surplus was not being released fast enough—he would feel as if he were a spectator in some immense arena whose lucky contestants fought for a prize he couldn't compete for: the billion in Army and Navy surplus. Here he was heisting a few truckloads when millions of dollars were lying in the ships and in the warehouses.

One morning, after reading an account in the Chronicle of the expected arrival of one thousand tons of refined sugar in the holds of the Reuben Jones, Marine Runner, and Southern Cross, Joe tossed his newspaper aside and said, "Blacky, ever think how we've been fooling around with too damn many things for our own good?"

"That so?"

"Come on, let's see what's the price on sugar."

"Sure," Blacky agreed, smiling amiably.

"That all you have to say? No curiosity?"

"Let's go." Blacky smiled at him. "I'm with you, bud."

Joe smiled, too. This Blacky had sweetened up, Joe thought. When he had a little more time, he'd look into it. Into Blacky, into Hanoco.... What he needed was a little more time, Joe promised himself.

They drove to the Quiapo Mercado, or market, and parked the jeep on a side street, the sun a yellow blaze in the sky. "We could've phoned," Blacky said, wiping his sweaty face.

"You're lazy. I like to see things for myself."

"Like when we went to Cavite?"

"That's right. I get a bang out of the stuff I'm in," Joe said. "It can be red lauan or a brown woman."

They entered the Mercado, the shadow under the tent-shaped corrugated roof sliding across their flushed faces. "Sugar, *azúcar*?" Joe inquired of the Filipino housewives buying eggplants and coconut and the huge white daikon radishes. "*Azúcar*?" They smiled, the brown-faced little women, and indicated the direction. But Joe and Blacky ended up among the meat stalls. Red chunks of beef hung on hooks. The head of a carabao on a butcher's block stared at them with strangely lifelike eyes. "*Azúcar*?" Joe asked the butcher, who was stripped to the waist, his straw hat streaked with blood.

The butcher waved behind him.

"Thanks," Joe said. "Come on, Blacky. Goddamn it, don't you ever say anything?"

"You once said I was the big silent type." Blacky grinned.

"What makes you so damn silent lately?" Joe darted the question and immediately blunted its point. "Hot as hell here. The goddamn flies!"

The flies buzzed everywhere as Filipino men and women haggled with the stallkeepers and children ran underfoot. The two Americans blundered from the meat into the fish stalls, walking gingerly so as not to spot their immaculate suntans. Mudfish wiggled in great woven bamboo baskets, and through the open wall in the rear Blacky looked at the Pasig River flowing by, the uprooted water lilies in floating clumps. He could see GI's hoofing across Santa Cruz bridge and he wondered how it would feel to be a GI again. Blacky grinned to himself as he remembered the house on María Clara Street where a little brown girl who had learned her slang from the GI's was always waiting for him.

At last they located the sugar stalls. "How much?" Joe asked the Chinese stallkeeper. "*Azúcar*—how much?"

"Peso foh leighty," the Chinaman said slowly, wiping his cheeks with a cloth.

"Four pesos eighty a kilo?"

"Yes, Majoh."

Out on the hot street again, Joe said as if to himself, "They're paying four pesos eighty centavos a kilo. That's two dollars and forty cents in American cash."

"What's a kilo weigh, Joe?"

"Two and a fifth pounds. The flips're paying more'n a dollar a pound for sugar! A dollar a pound, Blacky, and there's going to be a thousand tons of sugar sitting out in the harbor in a couple of days! One thousand tons! That's two million pounds! Two million dollars in sugar!"

That day Joe skipped the pom-pom business. Like a greedy market fly himself, he buzzed about on what he was already calling "a big sugar deal." Sergeant Kroll was instructed to find out when the first of the sugar cargo could be expected to hit the piers. Pedro Dimang promised to get storage space in the suburbs of the city for fifty tons of sugar. After they left the lumberman's office Joe said to Blacky, "Pedro can't handle this by himself. Maybe we ought to see his cousin Salvador. No, let him suffer a lil more. We'll see Johnny Yen Lee and Tommy Cruz. Hell with Tommy, too! We'll give Manuel Pangamban a taste of sugar," and he smiled at Blacky cunningly. "That's what you always want to do, pal. Give 'em all a taste and let 'em all suffer. The switcheroo, pal. The big switcheroo!"

Blacky was grateful then for the house on María Clara Street. For Joe was less a man than an adding machine; all of them were numbers to be manipulated and combined. Tommy Cruz plus Kroll added up to pesos in the gasoline buy and sell; the two Dimangs plus Mallinson added up to lumber pesos; and now Kroll plus Pedro Dimang plus Johnny Yen Lee plus Manuel Pangamban were to be added up in the sugar buy and sell. Fifty tons of sugar! One hundred thousand pounds of sugar worth one hundred thousand dollars in the markets!

The day the Reuben Jones, Marine Runner, and Southern Cross anchored in the harbor, Joe raced down to the water front with Blacky next to him in the jeep. Out on the blue water, in the holds of the silhouetted ships were his sugar dollars. "Goddamn!" Joe groaned. "If we only had storage space for more'n fifty tons!"

A week passed and the sugar cargo hadn't moved an inch closer to the piers. For in the city a controversy was raging between the American Commercial Agency and the Philippine government agencies over how the sugar was to be distributed. In the *mercados* the price of sugar stayed up in the same vaulting sky that was like some blue and immense and empty bowl over the sugar fleet from America. The Chinese stallkeepers shook their heads when the housewives cackled and the Filipino merchants blamed the situation on the war.

"Our lousy luck!" Joe cursed as he lunched with Blacky. "That damn sugar's going to stay out there until the paper army decides who gets what. The Filipino relief administration say they want half the sugar stock to sell at the controlled price of a peso twenty a kilo. Isn't that a phony? What they're not printing in the papers is that the bastids want to grab half the sugar. Five hundred tons! And sell it on the black market! Controlled price my controlled foot!

Then you have the American Commercial Agency saying they want to sell the whole thousand tons to the prewar sugar importers. Our lousy luck! Just when we're set to move fifty tons! We'd've made at least fifty grand on the deal!"

CHAPTER TWELVE

On a Wednesday morning, the longshoremen went out on strike. The MP's marched in. The Port Area became too hot a place to work, even for the black marketeers and the buy and sell boys. MP's with Tommy guns and carbines patrolled the water front as soldiers turned longshoremen snafued all the fifteen piers in the north and south harbors, piling boxes and crates in crazy mountains. The picketing longshoremen laughed at the amateurs even as they waved their signs of protest. In English and Spanish, in Tagalog and Visayan, their signs declared that two pesos fifty-five centavos for a day's work was not enough for a man and his family. The crazy mountains grew higher. The Port Area looked like a place swept by a hurricane with boxes, trucks, and winches seemingly dropped out of the sky. Only a dribblet of goods was moving out of the hundred thousand tons of struck cargo. "The rats!" Joe muttered, crouching over the wheel of his jeep. "They ought to shoot the Red rats!"

Two days after the longshoremen struck, the railroad workers left their jobs. And then the cement workers and tobacco workers. From the provinces, the peasants sent truckloads of food to the strikers and delegations to Malacanan Palace. All over the strike-bound city, rumors circulated as in the occupation years via the telegraph of lips. President Osmena was in favor of the strike; President Osmena opposed the strike. The Army intended to settle the strike; the Army would never settle the strike. "It's a goddamn revolution!" Joe raged. At least twice a day he visited the Port Area, staring furiously at the longshoremen's picket line, at the MP's beyond the longshoremen, a double chain of men barring him from the piers. His glittering eyes would lift from the man-made chaos to the serene harbor where the Reuben Jones and Marine Runner and Southern Cross lay calmly at anchor in another world. Staring at the three sugar ships, he felt the frenzy of frustration, as if the longshoremen and the MP's had somehow conspired together against him, their picket lines and police lines criss-crossed like strands of barbed wire.

He felt like screaming, felt like killing. Blacky's recommendation, a good drunk, was no medicine for him. Whisky couldn't make him forget the sugar fleet from America or disperse the brown-faced men with the placards. His girl Janet no longer amused him; he'd explored all her possibilities, and when she slept he lay awake. He remembered one sleepless night a woman with the blackest hair in the world.

A picket marched tirelessly about her, a single solitary picket—Tommy Cruz.

Smoking, he stared at the moonlit windows, remembering how he'd been meaning to get to Hanoco for a long, long time....

The next morning in their office he said to Blacky, "I can't sleep account of that damn Hanoco!"

"Hanoco!" Blacky scoffed. He had his feet up on his desk and now his heels tap-danced derisively. "I used to believe all that stuff you told me about Hanoco, but you don't give a damn about her. She's not easy, that's why you think you want her. Who you kidding?"

A strange candid grin touched Joe's lips. "You're getting smart hanging around me," he conceded grudgingly.

"Not smart enough."

"She's not easy, like you said, and when I get to thinking how to get my shoes under her bed, I can almost forget those ships. Goddamn those Reds!" he groaned. "That lil cherry blossom now, I could make her if I worked it out right."

Blacky looked at him. "You forgetting Tommy knows we came to this town out of a stockade?"

"No, but there's always a way."

"Don't be so wise! They live together, don't they, like regular man and wife? Tommy'd—"

"Tommy Cruz," Joe said softly. "That's not his name. He's as much Filipino as you are. What's his reason for giving himself a flip name? There were a lot of stories in the beginning on how he collaborated with the Japs."

Blacky wiped his sweaty forehead with the back of his hand. "Forget it! So he's a collaborator and you're an awol. That makes us even."

"Phil could dig up what Bilibid's got on Tommy."

"For God's sake, Joe, forget it!"

"Even if there isn't a thing, I could say there is."

"And what'll he say about us? Two awols!" Blacky said hoarsely, his feet on the desk crashing down to the floor.

"He's not giving us away."

"You fool around with Hanoco and he'll run amok like those crazy Moros."

"Maybe, maybe not. There's always a way. All you have to do is work out the details."

"What's the matter with Janet?" Blacky decided to try a new angle.

"You can have Janet."

"What about Serafina?"

"I've had enough of her."

"There's Phil's girl, Kao. She's Japanese."

"Buddy, as a bird dog you're not so hot."

Blacky glared at him. "I'm no bird dog! I'm just trying to stop you from wrecking everything. Think you're so damn wise, think you can always put the squeeze on everybody and get away with it—hell, you're gonna have yourself an explosion one of these days."

"Me? Not me, buddy. You, maybe, but not me." And he smirked with self-satisfaction.

"You stay away from Hanoco!" Blacky shouted.

"I need a lil excitement." Joe grinned at him.

"How about one of those Russky blondes?"

"You're getting interesting, buddy. You know any?"

"No, but I heard of this blonde who runs the twenty-one game at the Chateau."

"You've been gambling!" Joe accused him. "What'd I say about no gambling?"

"Who the hell's been gambling?" Blacky cried, outraged. "I just heard of this Russky from Pedro Dimang. He's been trying to make her."

"Trying?"

"He's bought her things, but all she lets him do is take her to lunch once in a while. Pedro says she's the best-looking woman in Manila."

"That's because she's a blonde in a brown town," Joe observed. "For my money there's nobody like Hanoco."

"Why don't you look this blonde over?"

"Hey, you, you're a pretty good bird dog. Maybe we will one of these nights."

The sixth day of the strike ended with no settlement in sight. Joe, accompanied by Blacky, drove out to the sawmill on Cavite; he suggested to Sergeant Mallinson that they pay the GI loggers a bonus to increase the cut. The promoter in Joe had supplanted the griper. As he said, "Griping won't put a peso in our pocket." He consulted with Sergeant Kroll, too, on a scheme to buy up the guards at a depot where tires were stacked by the thousand. The strike had rubbed a new and dazzling shine on every illegal peso for the illegal major who believed so wholeheartedly in details. He even turned his mind to the decreasing pom-pom business. The trouble there was that the customers were shipping out. Whenever Joe happened to see a GI truck convoy traveling their last Philippine miles to the piers and the troop ships, he'd think: Some more damn houses'll go bankrupt. The fewer the houses, the smaller the take in protection money.

One afternoon he invited Salvador Dimang and Tommy Cruz to his office. "I didn't ask Johnny Yen Lee," he said, smiling vaguely, and let it go at that for a while—the gentlest of hints. Tommy Cruz offered an Alhambra cigar to Blacky, who thanked the mestizo and explained he had a boxful in his desk. "The GI's are going home in droves," Joe said. "In a couple of months there won't be enough left to keep one pom-pom girl busy. Anybody here doing any thinking about what we ought to do?"

"We cannot keep the GI's in Manila." Dimang picked at his long sad chin. "It is bad condition."

"What is to think?" Tommy Cruz said as he joined the mourner's chorus.

Hanoco had walked off with that gook's brains, Joe thought, and felt the contempt in him sharpen into envy. For suddenly, out of nowhere, the Japanese girl was in that office. "What is to think?" he mimicked Tommy Cruz. "I should've asked Johnny Yen Lee. The Chinese have the best heads for business."

"You can't trust the Chinese," Blacky said, coming in on his cue; Joe had rehearsed this little act with him before the others had arrived.

"I don't trust the Chinese, either," Joe said, like some Filipino rabble-rouser. "But we can't just sit here and watch the GI's go. There just isn't enough dough in it for any of us."

"You are right," Salvador Dimang agreed. Tommy Cruz nodded.

Joe was studying their faces intently. He could read that pair of peso-snatchers like a page in some book: the con man's primer, where the D stood for divide and the R for rule. There were two counts at least against Johnny Yen Lee as far as both Dimang and Tommy Cruz were concerned. First, Johnny Yen Lee was a Chinese. Second, there really wasn't enough pom-pom dough these days. Maybe the second came first.

"Sure I'm right, but what can we do?" Joe said.

The pupils of Tommy's slanted Oriental eyes gleamed, two bright enigmatic beads between his white-skinned lids. Salvador Dimang muttered, "The Chinese." But neither of them dared say what they both wanted to say - that there was one partner too many.

Joe had led them on, and now, reversing himself, with a faint smile of the purest pleasure on his lips, he said, "We need Johnny more than ever." They stared at him, confused. Joe smiled at them. "Why put the screws on one Chinaman when we can put the screws on every Chinaman in the city? That's why we need Johnny. To go see the Chinese pom-pom houses, every damn Chinese pom-pom house. He can get them to pay in more every week."

"The Chinese pom-pom house?" Tommy repeated.

"It's very simple. We convince Johnny and he convinces the rest. We tell him what's in all the papers, all this talk about cleaning up the city. We tell him the pressure's going to be put on the Chinks. He'll believe us. There isn't a Chink in town who doesn't believe everybody's out to get him."

Tommy Cruz glanced swiftly at Salvador Dimang. The eyes of the two men shone like the eyes of hungry wolves.

Joe knew exactly what they were feeling. His own eyes shifted to Tommy Cruz, and for some reason he felt he had come a little nearer to Hanoco.

"This night's good as any," Blacky insisted in the suite at the Hotel Cosmos. "You're not seeing Janet, and I'm not doing nothing. Come on, let's go the Chateau. What've you got to lose?"

Forty minutes later they were parked in the Chateau's parking lot. They strolled toward the night club from under the red and blue electric bulbs strung over the rows of limousines, staff cars, and jeeps. The Chateau was a two-story mansion built before the war by a millionaire Filipino rice *hacendero*. His paintings still hung in the foyer, somber religious canvases whose only vivid color was the red blood of their martyrs. In all their visits to the Chateau, Joe and Blacky had never really looked at those paintings, always attracted, as they were now, by the music and the faces in the huge *sala*. The faces were always pink because the light in the *sala* glowed out of innumerable pink lamps fastened into the paneled walls; in the main room of the Chateau, the patrons, whether American or Filipino or Chinese, had no distinct nationality.

Joe and Blacky climbed a flight of mahogany stairs to the second floor, and here the illumination was a diffused and radiant yellow. Joe nodded at the closed doors. "O.K., guy who's never been here, where now?"

Blacky stopped walking. "You're a fourteen-carat rat!"

"As long as I'm called a rat I know I've got money and not a hole in the sock," Joe answered him cheerfully. "So you've never been here, never seen this Russky?"

"No, you suspicious bastid!"

Joe patted him lightly on the shoulder. "I trust everybody, pal. Everybody when they're dead." The thought ticked in him that maybe Blacky wasn't so dumb after all. He'd never said a word before about seeing Pedro. Maybe, Joe reflected, Blacky was playing around with both the Dimangs. Maybe it would-n't be a bad idea to get Manuel Pangamban to tail Blacky.... "Let's go, buddy," Joe said. "Which door's ours?"

"Pedro said the third door from the left."

When Blacky knocked, the third door opened a few inches and a thin Spaniard with a cigarette plastered to his lips looked out at them. "I'm a friend of Pedro Dimang," Blacky explained. The Spaniard nodded and admitted them into a foyer. "Yes, señores," the Spaniard murmured blandly, and unlocked another door. They stepped into a room painted the palest of blues, lit up with an intense white light that held the players at the roulette, dice, and twenty-one tables in a common public glare. Nothing was secret in this room, yet everything was secret. The room was too bright, yet Blacky felt the shadow of every gambler's night. He felt the silence of blind chance absorbing all the players, who spoke only when they had to, since the only important voice here was the voice they were all straining to catch. Luck was in this room, wearing a mask of white. Everybody's luck and nobody's luck.

There were two twenty-one tables in the pale blue room but only one woman banker, whom Joe had immediately spotted. "Not bad," he said as they crossed the floor to where a blonde in a dark green evening dress was stand-ing at a table of sitting men—a Chinese, two Filipinos, a lank American lieu-tenant. From a distance the players seemed to be worshipers of the woman, but their respectfully lowered faces were bowed only in worship of the cards she was dealing them. Joe and Blacky waited for the hand to be played through.

"Hello," Joe said to her finally. "I'm Major Fenton. You know my friend Cap-tain Hurley?"

"No, I have not that honor," the woman answered in a low voice almost free of accent. "The blue chips, they are five hundred pesos, Major. The yellows, one hundred pesos. The reds, twenty pesos."

"Not tonight, not any night. I just wanted to meet you. How about a drink when you're free? A little vodka?" Joe inquired with a bold appraising smile, as if he might be induced to put in a bid for her.

"Your friend," she said, "he has the better manners, Major." She looked at Joe with eyes that were a paler blue than the pale blue walls, her long narrow face calm and composed. She was pretty, and maybe once she'd even been beautiful. Her golden hair, brushed away from her forehead, was still beautiful. But the years had thinned her cheeks and her neck. The pitiless white light showed the softest of traceries about her eyes. She might have been thirty-two or thirty-three, and she was getting a little tired. Only a pretty woman now, but in this gambler's room where she was a professional she still carried her long graceful body like a trump card.

The lank lieutenant at the table grunted. "I'm in favor of more action and less talk, Helen."

The woman's eyes had wavered at Joe's staring smile. The notion hit Blacky that she was no longer the dealer at her table. The dealer was Joe.

Why should he care about that Russky dame? Blacky asked himself in the next few days. She was no better than the next, maybe even worse. The main thing was to keep Joe away from Hanoco, and if Helen could do that, swell, Blacky thought. "Looka, bird dog," Joe had said to him. "This is what we do. You'll have Pedro phone Helen and you'll go to lunch with 'em." And they'd lunched together, a merry trio, laughing over their cocktails, and Blacky had quivered at the unmistakable sensation of knowing that the blonde Russky with the pale eyes liked him, but afterward, like any obedient bird dog called to heel, he'd reported to Joe. "One more lunch," Joe had instructed him, "and you'll unload Pedro and phone her on your own."

Wednesday morning he phoned Helen from the office, Joe grinning at him. He made a date for Friday, Helen's free day, to go swimming at the old Wack Wack Golf Club, now the Gregory Terrace, managed by the Air Force for officers. When he hung up, a clown's false smile was painted on his lips, for he badly wanted to forget her friendly voice.

"Now we're set!" Joe was saying. "I'll give Janet a call later. You'll like her, buddy. That kid's a regular passionflower. Feed her whisky and she won't care who it is."

The office filled with his laugh, the latrine laughter some men throw at all women. "What's a shack job between buddies?" that laugh was saying. Like Janet, for instance. Like Serafina, for instance. Like Helen, for instance. "Salvador Dimang's got a bungalow out of the city where we can take 'em, Blacky. After all, she might yell some at first, you never can tell, since she expects you to be her date. That gives me an idea. I'll give her a lil present. I can wangle a ring out of Salvador. He's feeling generous, what with Johnny Yen Lee almost ready to squeeze the Chinks for us. What's a jewelry fence for anyway? Right,

Blacky? Nothing like jewelry for women. A lil present'll make Helen forget the switcheroo."

His words came to Blacky, very faint and distant, like some voice cutting in on the telephone wire that had connected him with Helen. A faint and distant voice, but babbling on now, garrulous with a drunken and obscene triumph, as if gloating over every last detail of all the details: bird dog and bungalow, a wangled ring, the switcheroo....

Blacky was sick of the switcheroo, sick of Joe, and sick of himself.

CHAPTER THIRTEEN

There was a meeting at Johnny Yen Lee's that afternoon but Blacky said he was too tired to go.

Tired wasn't the word, Blacky thought as the nausea seeped into his throat. Tired? That wasn't the word by a long shot. It wasn't that he gave a damn about Johnny Yen Lee, either. It was the thought of being an eyewitness twice in one day to Joe the Lawyer's favorite little game of cross and double cross that was too much.

Cross and double cross, with somebody always nailed nice and tight. This afternoon, the Chinaman's turn was coming up. Joe would put on his act, telling how the Chinese pom-pom houses had to pay more protection money just because they were Chinese, and Salvador Dimang, with a tear in his dark brown crocodile eyes, would mumble about a bad condition, as Tommy Cruz, the perfect yes man, echoed the Filipino phoney. Any other day Blacky would have tailed along, but not today, for on Friday it would be the turn of Helen and Janet.

He left the office and rode down in the elevator. He sighed as he walked out on the Escolta. Messenger boys idled along. Slow-moving Chinese brokers, Europeans with brief cases under their arms, and uniformed Americans crowded the sidewalks, with only the Americans in the tropical worsteds pacing briskly. The tropical worsteds were only a few days or a few weeks out of America, flown in from San Francisco, the go-getter pace of the American cities still humping their muscles and bones. It was easy not to think on the Escolta, the sidewalks so crowded, the gutter a honking procession of wheels. Businessmen in jeeps, officials in limousines, and now and then a bank truck with half a dozen armed guards staring about them with the blank metal faces of men trusted with the big money.

On Quiapo Plaza, the old women were selling lighted candles outside the church doors. Jitney busses unloaded passengers; the *calesas* waited for fares. He turned swiftly, hurrying toward the *calesas*, as if he would leave his thoughts behind him on the plaza. But there was no abandoning what was invisible. Fear sat down at his side as he climbed into a *calesa* with two great red wheels and a gay striped awning. "Santa Mesa Heights—María Clara Street," he said to the driver. The fear next to him grinned like a death's head, but whether in approval or disapproval there was no telling.

God, Blacky thought as the red wheels circled under him and a hot little breeze fanned his hotter face. God, what's the matter with me? he wondered. A goddamn Russky tramp and a goddamn ring and I give myself the shakes. Hell of a lot of difference who goes to bed with her. Giving myself the shakes for no reason at all.

But there was a reason even though the man in the captain's uniform struggled not to face it. There were several reasons, and they were all the same reason: You don't sell out anybody who trusts you. Not even a tarnished blonde house gambler. Not even a crooked stockade sergeant by the name of Murdock.

At the corner of María Clara Street he stopped the driver, paid his fare, and walked dizzily down the sidewalk. Kids tossed a ball in the gutter, and a brown fat woman, the street's unofficial eye, sat at her post in the second-story window of a house painted buff.

Blacky unlocked the door of his own house, and hesitantly, like a stranger, stepped into the *sala*.

"*Hola!*" Lucy cried, running swiftly to him. She was wearing a gaudy dress, a butterfly yellow in color, her nimble feet in red straw slippers.

He felt her arms embrace him, peering down at her black head snuggled against his chest. Then she was lifting her smiling face, her lips eager for his kiss like an affectionate child's. Something tore inside of him. Groping for Lucy's mouth, kissing her, he thought of Helen.... Helen, who might yell a little at the switcheroo, so you took her out to an out-of-the-way bungalow and wangled her with a wangled ring. God Almighty, maybe Lucy'd yell a little too, and so what if she did if Joe wanted her, what if she did, what if she did, what was a shack job between buddies?

Sick with self-loathing, Blacky released himself from Lucy's arms. The red-tiled *sala* was unreal in his sight, not half so true as the Friday bungalow he'd never seen.

"Bill," he heard Lucy saying.

Bill, Blacky thought. Even here on María Clara Street there was no escaping Joe. He was the Lawyer's stooge and his name was Bill, his name was Captain William Hurley. Blacky MacIntyre wasn't his name anymore, and if he had the guts he'd admit it. "Lucy," he said wearily, "I'm beat. Where's your mother?"

"She go *mercado*, Bill."

"Don't call me Bill!" he yelled. "I hate that goddamn name!"

"I will not call Bill," Lucy promised him instantly. She stared at him, but she wasn't astonished. Nothing any man could do would ever astonish her again. Certainly not this big *americano*. When she had first met him he was a GI, and now he was a captain with two beautiful silver bars. And he had many pesos, this captain of hers, silver pesos and gold pesos, pesos for this beautiful house and for Stateside whisky. Where did the money come from? Lucy didn't know and didn't care. Nothing any man could do would ever astonish the little pom-pom girl with the scarred face.

"Lucy, don't mind me," he muttered.

"Drink?" She smiled tenderly.

"Why not?"

"Be with you in a jiffy," she said in her GI slang, and went into the kitchen.

Blacky sighed. Only now he noticed something new in the *sala* since his last visit. Dangling at the end of the long electric wire was a Chinese lantern decorated with a fire-snorting dragon. Ah, the house beautiful, Blacky thought with a moody bitterness. He fingered the native red cloth draped over the couch he was sitting on. Yeah, the house beautiful, he brooded, and the life beautiful. He'd never had it so good, wasn't that the truth? So why break his head over a Russky tramp? So he was a bird dog, a stooge, and so what? It was a helluva lot better than rotting in a stockade, a helluva lot safer than armed robbery. Here he was sitting pretty with Lucy in a cozy little house on María Clara. So why beef?

She fetched two rye hookers. "Here's how," she toasted.

He drank silently. She was silent, too. He reflected that Lucy was one girl who never asked questions. God, he was lucky to have her. And silently Blacky drank to his luck. The rye slid down his throat and he had a whisky impulse to confide in her, to speak out his heart. He decided just as swiftly not to. You couldn't trust a woman who had been a tramp.

"Know why I didn't want you to call me Bill?" he said at last.

She shrugged, her black eyes on his face.

"Bill's a bastid."

"No," she demurred.

"Yes, I am, baby. I don't kid myself. That's the only thing I can be proud of." He wondered why this should be considered such a hell of a big virtue, anyway. "That's why I didn't want you to call me Bill. But hell, you've got to call me Bill. It's my name."

Lucy laughed. Then she concentrated on her drink until three quarters of it was gone.

He watched her curiously. "Lucy, do you hit the bottle when I'm not around?"

"Yes," she admitted.

"Lucy," he lectured her without any conviction, "you want to stay away from the booze. You hit the booze by yourself and you'll turn into an alcoholic."

"Into big drinker, no?"

"Yeah."

"We have booze," she stated. "Why not drink booze?" She propounded the question seriously.

He felt a quick pity for this little stray. Nineteen years only and already an old-timer with the beginnings of a big thirst. "Yeah, why not?" he said, and patted her scarred cheek. Ripped by Jap bayonet or pom-pom alley knife—he didn't know or care much. "We have the booze, Stateside booze, so why not drink it?" he said with a sigh, as if replying to a question bigger than the one she had asked. "Here we are today! Where the hell'll we be tomorrow?" He kissed her tiny brown ear, his pity widening into love. For in this city there was no other woman, no man, no child who gave a damn about him; another passing shadow in suntans. He drained his glass to the last drop, setting the empty glass down on the floor. Hastily Lucy finished her own drink, getting rid of her own glass, too, as Blacky reached for her.

She snuggled closer to him and he held her head between his hands, kissing her on the lips. Her hands pressed against his back as if they'd never again come loose. Her hands on his back were like two brown leaves stained into a sidewalk after a rain. He kissed her eyes and cheeks, and when her black eyes brimmed, he curled one arm under her legs, lifting the clinging girl in the yellow dress and walking into the bedroom.

Lucy smiled at him as she waited for him under the tarpaulin stretched above the bed under the corrugated iron ceiling. But the rains were scant in the city now, for it was the dry season; a dry time, too, in the hearts of men exhausted by war. And the only rain was the soft patter of Lucy's hands in his hair as he lay down next to her. He stroked her smooth round shoulders and they whispered a little. They kissed a long kiss, the two of them flowing together like two drops of rain, becoming one drop of rain, and for a second he felt himself high above her, on some high place above the tarpaulin, higher even than Quiapo Church, aware of her brownness on the white sheet, the brownness of the earth.

In the twilight they walked together down María Clara, the sky copper between the roofs. In the soft copper glow, a barefooted kid chased a dog along the sidewalk. Men returned from work, their eyes slanting to the *americano* with the Filipino girl. On the corner a big black car raced by and the Filipinos inside stared at the *americano* with the Filipino girl, and because they were in a car, one of them permitted himself a sneer.

"You know them?" Blacky asked Lucy.

"They are drugstore guerrillas," she laughed.

"Come again?"

"Drugstore guerrillas. Their claim is they hide from the Japs. They hide their car from Japs. They dig hole for their car."

It'd rust," he observed. "The hell with them."

"In spades!" she added.

He laughed. "You know enough English to get by in the States, Lucy."

Her eyes were on his face. "*Hang gnang* Pier Seven!" She clutched anxiously at his arm. "You go States, Bill?"

"No! What gave you that idea?"

"You go home, Bill, yes!"

"I'm not going home, Lucy."

"No?" she said wistfully. "No?"

They were on broad Calle España now, and the copper sky had darkened enough to show the first starry crack. Under that sky, two open trucks packed with peasants roared northward; a boy in a huge straw hat yelled and brandished a placard at the American captain. "*Mabuhay Democrata Allianze!*"

"What'd that lil Red say to me?" Blacky asked.

"The *taos*." She shrugged.

"*Taos*? That's the peasants."

"The peasants," she assented. "They bring food for the strike men."

"I know. What'd that lil bastid say?"

"Say long live Democracy Alliance. *Mabuhay* mean 'long live' in American."

He was far from the Port Area, but for an instant Blacky could almost see three ships in the darkening sky—the Reuben Jones, the Marine Runner, and the Southern Cross.

"You go *hang gnang* Pier Seven and I say *mabuhay* to you," she promised him in a mournful voice.

He started. "I'm staying right here in Manila—honest, baby!" But as the words moved from his tongue, he felt the fear that had plucked at his heart on Quiapo Plaza like some finger on a string.

CHAPTER FOURTEEN

On Friday, they picked up Janet first. Calling hello to Blacky, who was at the wheel of the jeep, Janet climbed into the rear, ignoring Joe's helping hand. She dropped her overnight bag with its swimsuit and towel at her feet.

"No kiss?" Joe said to her.

She looked at him and smilingly he looked at her. "How've you been, honey?" Joe asked her.

"I should be angry with you," Janet whispered. The sun had burned her skin a deep bronze, but now her skin paled a shade, her dark brown eyes too intense, her lips stiffening at the edges. "A week and I don't hear from you!" she accused him.

"Pentagon's been phoning me every day," Joe explained, reaching for her.

She pushed him away. "Pentagon? Is that her name this time?"

Blacky shifted into second. He had made up his mind to soldier through this date. No thinking, no grief, no nothing.

The dust waved thick and yellow from under the jeep's wheels. They were moving fast on Quezon Boulevard. Blacky gazed through the windshield at a pedestrian skiping out of the way, while holding a handkerchief across his nose. The hell with you, Blacky thought, but he wasn't angry. He was calm. Too calm, maybe.

After they picked up Helen, Blacky headed the jeep north toward the Gregory Terrace Club.

"They have the best swimming pool in town!" Janet bubbled. She no longer remembered her grievances. She was holding Joe's hand between her own, happy as any woman with her lover, the sun shining bright like some private golden door opening endlessly before them.

Blacky glanced sideways at Helen, next to him, in a white cotton dress whose red buttons matched the red on her wide smiling lips, her blonde hair brushed away from her forehead. Her perfume was in his nostrils, a lilac perfume. She was a lilac blonde....

"Can you swim, Bill?" Helen asked.

"Sure," he replied curtly.

"Swims like a fish and drinks like a fish!" Joe cracked Blacky across the shoulders. "Helen, how long've you been at the Chateau?"

"A long time."

"I never before met a woman who ran a gambling game," Janet said. "It must be exciting."

"It is my profession," Helen said with dignity.

Blacky was silent, his foot steady on the gas pedal, his eyes focusing on the dusty pavement under the cloudless sky. Out on Pasig Boulevard, the houses began to scatter. A church loomed up and he stared at the Negro troops billeted in the church courtyard; two or three soldiers were talking with a Filipino laundress, her basket at her feet. He looked at bamboos and rice paddies and persistently intoned to himself, The hell with it. The hell with Helen and Janet, the hell with everybody. They sped by a mansion on a hill hedged in by blood-red *guamela* flowers, and Blacky turned the jeep into a driveway that seemed as if it had been lifted out of a Stateside automobile advertisement. There was a chain across the driveway, but when Joe showed his membership card to the MP on guard, the chain was lifted and they curved between closely cropped lawns to the Gregory Terrace parking field.

The terrace fronted on an undulating golf course dotted with playing foursomes; a course unbelievably green, greener even than the lawns. In the distance, the hills were smooth and rolling as if they too were landscaped.

"Beautiful!" Helen said, breathing deeply and staring at the hills. "I cannot believe it is Manila."

"It's the U.S.A.," Joe corrected her. "Reminds me of the golf club I belonged to back in the States."

Blacky's eyes darted to the other man's face, and Joe, noticing Blacky's look, smiled faintly and said, "When we get home, Bill, we'll play sometime."

"Let's swim," Blacky grunted.

"We'll have to separate now, girls," Joe said. "The bathing's mixed but not the undressing. Meet you at the pool."

In the officer's locker house they unbuttoned their uniforms. "You lose rank here damn fast," Joe commented loudly as he hung up his major's shirt, smiling at the officers about him changing into swim trunks or else dressing and combing their wet hair.

A sunburned officer in blue and green trunks laughed. Blacky shuddered.

They walked out of the locker. Outside, the green vista again unrolled before them.

"Blacky," Joe said as they went up a path toward the pool. "Wait!" He put his hand on Blacky's arm and nodded at a bamboo table and chairs under a huge umbrella, bright as a circus. "Let's rest our dogs a minute." When they sat down in the shade, Joe said, "Why you acting so queer?"

"Queer?"

"Don't kid me. You falling for her?"

"Who, that Russky?"

"She's not half bad."

"She's O.K., but I've seen better."

"Blacky, who the hell you kidding? I can tell what you're thinking before you think it. All the way out here you've been wearing that poker face of yours, only it can't fool me. Blacky, I don't want any more hard feelings over dames between us. I haven't forgotten about Serafina. No dame's worth any hard feelings."

"There's no hard feelings."

"Don't forget you were the one got me going on Helen. It wasn't like that Serafina dame."

"Yeah, I was the one."

"No hard feelings, you sure?"

"No hard feelings."

"I'm glad to hear that. What's a shack job between buddies, anyway?"

The bungalow of Salvador Dimang was small and filled with furniture that was too large, so that the *sala* seemed a jumble of chairs and tables. Joe, walking unsteadily over to the tray of whisky and soda bottles, was thinking that a few more shots would put him on the floor. No more drinking, he decided, setting his empty glass down and pivoting around. Seated on the couch, Blacky was frowning into his glass, as Helen, her face flushed, argued drunkenly with him, and not only with him, but with the invisible crowd that lives in every whisky bottle. Near them in a red leather chair Janet was curled. Seeing Joe turning from the table bar, she waved gaily, as if just meeting him. "Yoo-hoo, sweetie! Yoo-hoo, sweetie!" She had spilled her last drink on her dress. "Yoo-hoo, sweetie!"

"Yoo-hoo," Joe said mechanically, like a wound-up doll, his eyes on Helen, as if he were alone with her in this bungalow of Dimang's. Under the white linen of her red-buttoned dress was the slender body he remembered from the Gregory Terrace swimming pool, the finely shaped woman's body kicking up the green water, kicking up the blood in his veins....

After his private talk with Blacky, they had met Helen and Janet at the pool. Both girls had worn beach robes, their bare legs glistening in the bright sun, Janet's legs dark and bronzed like her face, Helen's white as milk. His heart had rocked at that milkiness; he hadn't had a wisecrack in him. The water in the pool had shone like an immense green stone, set between the manicured lawns and shaded by the manicured trees, and there were three times as many officers as women, and when Helen dropped her robe to the ground, the stag eyes were all on her, a tall blonde in a country where blondes were few. A blonde in a jet-black swimsuit, her hair golden, tiny golden hairs glinting on her milky arms. She might have been a statue imported from the States, except that when she moved, the curves of her hips and breasts in that jet-black suit had suddenly changed her into everybody's pinup girl. They had swum in the green pool and sunned themselves and afterward had cocktails on the terrace, watching the golfers. The stars had come out suddenly as the tropical night slid an immense wall, black as Helen's jet-black suit, out of the mountain distance. All that long day and night, Joe had been the life of the party, with Blacky silent, and yet anyone could see whom she preferred. It had only made the White Russian blonde more desirable to Joe.

And now in Dimang's bungalow she still wanted Blacky and Blacky wanted her, and Janet wanted Joe, and it was time for the switcheroo. The old switcheroo. Joe walked straight toward Helen. Smiling, he took her hand as Blacky frowned at the wall and Janet yelled behind him, "You wolf, you!" But he ignored Janet, saying to Helen, "I want to show you some books, honey. Some books in your language." But as he put into spoken words this little detail planned with all the other details, it struck him as plain downright stupid. Stupid or clever, depending upon whether the excuse would serve to get her into the bedroom. "Some Russian books," he continued.

Helen smiled with a drunk's wariness. Perhaps she was recalling all his compliments to her that day. "Bill, Janet," she invited them. "You come, yes?"

"They can't even read English!" Joe laughed and tugged gently at her hand in his own. "It'll only be a minute, Helen."

"Bring 'em out here, you wolf!" Janet called. She started to rise from her chair, but shouting insults was so much easier that she surrendered to her own whisky heaviness.

"How could I be a wolf with you around?" Joe retorted, and tugged gently again at Helen's prisoned hand. "A minute's all I'm asking you."

She arose reluctantly, teetering a little, and glanced at Blacky. He was drinking.

"You be good!" Janet yelled.

"We'll all be good," Joe promised, releasing Helen's hand. She was moving, he thought, and that was enough. Get them moving.

And it was as if the momentum he had given her was now carrying her with him down the *sala*, into a corridor, to a half-opened door. He shoved the door open, standing back politely to let her enter first. Then he stepped inside himself, closing the door behind him.

Like the *sala*, the bedroom was overcrowded with furniture, a huge dresser too close to the wide double bed, the floor lamp casting a soft yellow glow on polished mahogany. "The books?" she asked, searching about her.

"There are no books," Joe admitted, with a wide grin.

She laughed. "Janet is right. You are wolf, Major."

Joe unbuttoned his shirt pocket and held out the ring he'd been hoarding all that day. The lamplight shone on its single blue stone. In the blueness, white lines, white as the stars in the bedroom windows, crisscrossed. It was a star-sapphire ring. "To go with your eyes," he said.

Helen's pale blue eyes were amused and contemptuous both. She was drunk, but drunk or sober, this situation was as familiar to her as her own body. "The books in my language—" she said with a smiling contempt.

"The language every woman knows," Joe declared blandly. "That you know. Why kid me, Helen?"

Without a word she turned toward the door. He grabbed her around the waist.

"Let me go!" she said.

He shook his grinning head and silently, still grinning, offered the star sapphire.

"No, Major!"

"They're having fun out there. We'll have fun here, Helen. Bill's wanted Janet a long time."

"Liar!"

"I'll prove it! Bill!" he shouted. "Bill, you having fun out there?"

There was silence. Joe's face flushed. "Blacky, you having fun?"

From the *sala* Blacky's voice came low and weak. "Yeah."

"Who you believe now?" Joe taunted the blonde. "He's been after Janet a long time. Not many good-looking American girls in Manila. You're ten times better-looking, but every man to his taste, says I."

"I wish to go."

"There's no rush," he said, holding her tightly with one arm. "You're perfect, like this!" He held up the blue stone.

"I wish to go!" She had spoken quietly but her eyes had flashed toward the door.

"I wouldn't yell if I were you," he warned her flatly. "I wouldn't yell. Remember when I asked you how long you'd been at the Chateau? I should've asked you how long you'd been in Manila. Maybe you were here when the Japs were here. In fact, you were here, Helen. I've checked on you. You sang at the Nippon Café, Helen. Don't be a fool. Take that ring! Take that ring! The Nippon Café!"

She stood there, but it seemed as if she had crumpled. He picked up her limp hand and slid the ring onto her finger. "Cheer up," he said. "I'm not so bad. Trouble with you, you gave yourself some ideas on the boy friend out there. He's doing O.K. with Janet. He's another lowdown two-timer just like me. Like you, like all of us." He embraced her tightly. "I'm loaded, baby. Loaded. More rings where that's from." He held her with one arm and began to fumble with the red buttons of her white dress. "You're a sweet-looking dish for my money," he said.

From outside the closed door, Janet's voice lifted foolishly. "They're fooling around too long with those damn books, Bill. I'm going to see."

There was a silence and then Janet's drunken voice screeched. "Bill, leggo of me. Leggo of me! You're not going to stop me! Bill—"

CHAPTER FIFTEEN

Down on the water front there was still no peace.

MP submachine guns protected the cargo piled on the piers. The picket lines circled endlessly, while at Malacanan Palace anxious officials hurried between the carved lions guarding the palace doors. In the fine shining briefcases carried by the bureaucrats, there wasn't one workable plan for settling the strike. Yet the hope persisted that the strike soon would be over.

Meanwhile, the ACA, the American Commercial Agency, announced it was accepting bids from responsible persons and companies on the thousand tons of sugar. The strike couldn't last forever; one of these days the sugar would be moving out of the holds of the Reuben Jones, the Marine Runner, and the Southern Cross.

And what was to stop the Investment Company from submitting a bid? Theidea of a *legitimate bid* had stunned Joe when it first entered that devious consciousness. Then a thoughtful grin had twisted his lips as he sat in his quiet office, with Blacky daydreaming at the other desk. Here he'd been reading a thousand newspaper stories about war surplus being sold to the highest bidders, but they hadn't registered. It was his own heister's psychology, Joe realized, that had put the blinders on him.

Every man to his own trade. A pickpocket doesn't open up a retail store, and Joe the Lawyer had never conceived of himself as any Honest Joe. But one thing was sure. He wasn't the man to stay locked up in any box - except the cashbox that passed for his heart.

"Instead of wasting time sitting on our butts," he said exuberantly to Blacky, "what in hell's stopping us from walking over to the ACA offices and digging up a lil information?"

"Information about what?"

"About sugar! About who's a responsible party! About bidding on that damn sugar! Wouldn't it be a laugh if that was to be the blue-sky deal - a legitimate bid?"

"A bunch of civilians looking us over!" Blacky protested. "No good."

"Nothing's any good to you but one thing, huh, Blacky?" The blue sharp eyes shone with a secret glee at a joke he was keeping to himself - at least for the present.

Yesterday, Manuel Pangamban had told him about the house on María Clara Street. It was another detail to be filed away. To be used only, Joe decided, when he could throw that house a mile a minute like a baseball right between Blacky's big brown eyes.

"I'll go to the ACA myself," Joe said. "After all, it's an awful hot day, Blacky, and you don't like the heat." And he smiled like the most considerate of buddies.

Joe walked down the Escolta to the Hamilton Building, where the ACA had its offices, and rode up to the fourth floor in the elevator. Twenty or thirty men, Chinese, Filipinos, Americans, British, milled around a harassed receptionist in the ACA waiting room. Joe stood to one side as if he had a leisurely extra hour to everybody else's frantic minute.

Beyond the waiting room were the doors of the ACA officials - and the doors of bulging depots. On this fourth floor the cargo ships in the harbor - including the Reuben Jones, the Marine Runner, and the Southern Cross - were securely anchored. Joe breathed deeply, wondering if he'd been chasing the blue-sky deal backside forward. He glanced at the crowd besieging the receptionist; some were ingratiating, others demanding, several smiling because they believed in the smile as a business tactic.

"I have appointyment with Mist' Lane," declared a Chinaman in a blue suit.

"I have the promise of Mr. Racker!" cried another voice.

"Yesterday Mr. Lane said to me-"

"Please, sir. I was here before you."

They were well dressed and looked well heeled, but just the same they were small fry. The big fry didn't have to beg favors from any fifty-peso-a-week receptionist.

Joe had seen enough of them. He walked briskly toward the corridor leading to the inner offices. The receptionist shrilled after him, but without turning around he replied, "Army orders!" and vanished down the corridor.

He used that mouth-rolling phrase on several secretaries. "Army orders. Yes, Army orders!" Finally he was conducted to an office where an ACA official in suntans sat behind a Stateside desk smoking a Stateside cigar.

"Mr. Flack?" Joe smiled and tossed in a salute for good measure.

The official's cigar tilted as he nodded his head. His sandy hair was smooth as glass and he had round unwinking owl eyes.

Joe seated himself. "Mr. Flack, I know how busy you are, so I won't waste your time. I have some friends, Filipino businessmen, who'd like to know the procedure for submitting bids on the ACA sugar out in the harbor."

"I thought you were here representing the Army, Major." Mr. Flack spoke quietly, without surprise, as if he were used to people who invented excuses to break in on him. "My secretary stated you were here on Army orders, Major."

"Not this time, Mr. Flack. I-"

"Major, my clerk, Mr. Alexander, can give you all the information you want."

"In the Army you don't see a corporal when you can see the colonel. Since I am here, Mr. Flack, I'd appreciate your advice. A second of your time-"

"Well, sir?" Mr. Flack said coldly, picking up some papers on his desk.

"If you're too busy, couldn't we meet somewhere when you're free? Have dinner, perhaps."

"Major," the ACA man said in that quiet, unsurprised voice, "any responsible person or company can bid on our sugar stock without the necessity of footing any bill for entertainment."

Joe ignored the thrust. "What do you mean by responsible?"

"A responsible person in our definition is any individual or company who is prepared to get the sugar to the public without delay, Major. You and your friends may be aware there's a flourishing black market here in Manila. Good morning, Major. If you are still interested, see my clerk, Mr. Alexander."

Doing honest business was a headache, Joe thought in the corridor. Maybe he ought to toss in the sponge. And have Blacky give him the horse laugh?

Mr. Alexander was a lank individual with tufts of blondish hair shooting from an almost completely bald head. He was busy reading when Joe stepped into his office.

"Mr. Alexander?"

No reply.

"Mr. Alexander."

The clerk raised his face, staring at his visitor. Suddenly he smiled and apologetically lifted up his reading matter. It was a comic book. "This is one of the fantastic ones," he explained, his fifty-year-old eyes twinkling like a boy's.

"That so?" Joe stared at the clerk. "Mr. Flack said I should see you. I'm Major Fenton."

"Sit down, Major."

"Thanks."

"So you want to get in on the surplus, Major?" The clerk smiled.

"You don't waste any time getting to the point here, do you? I'm not interested personally. But I have friends who'd appreciate some information. They'd like to bid on some of that ACA sugar." He stopped abruptly, for the clerk had begun to chuckle. "What's so funny?" Joe asked, irritated.

Laughing, the clerk stroked his baldish head with a loving hand.

"What's so damn funny?"

"Everybody in town's going money-mad. That sugar, now. One thousand tons of sugar! And we have two million cases of surplus field rations we're accepting bids on. And a lot of hospital and related equipment that ought to go for three or four million pesos. Why, Major, we estimate that in a period of about six weeks we'll have got rid of thirty-four millions' worth of surplus. Money-mad!"

Joe was too astonished to speak. The clerk was now thumbing through the pages of his comic book. "Manila's more fantastic than this book. That's my honest opinion, Major. That's what I say to everybody who comes in here. Manila's more fantastic-"

"I guess so, I suppose so," Joe said, recovering his composure. "What I'd like to know is how my friends go about proving they're responsible so they can bid on some of that sugar."

"Fantastic, fantastic," the clerk murmured, as if to himself.

"Mr. Alexander!"

"You know what I do in my spare time, Major?"

"I give up. What do you do?"

"I walk around town taking notes."

"Notes?"

"About the holes cut in the barbed wire around the depots where the buy and sell's been busy. And I like to clip the newspapers for graft stories. Grafttown on the Pasig - that's what they ought to call Manila, Major. Here's a clipping that's one of my favorites." He opened a drawer and displayed a newspaper clipping. "It's from the Philippines Echo, by the columnist Alfonso Baybay. Read it, Major."

Joe read:

Do you want to buy Army and Navy surplus? Perhaps you're a buy and sell man hungry for an easy peso? Perhaps you're just an honest businessman? Well, you can't bid on the ACA's Gargantuan lots unless you were born with a triple-plated gold spoon in your mouth. But, dear reader, you can bid on ACA's uncatalogued war surplus. In an uncatalogued lot there can be anything from K-ration soup to K-ration nuts and bolts. Textiles from Batangas, airplane motors, staff cars, and four or five K-ration can openers. But there's a catch, dear Mr. Easy Peso. Eight or nine people are getting all the uncatalogued stuff because they know Mr. Arranger. And who is Mr. Arranger? Ah, dear Mr. Easy Peso, if I only knew that, I would stop writing my column.

Joe tossed the clipping to the clerk. It fluttered and settled slowly like a miniature kite. "You civilians!" he exclaimed, as if he were Regular Army. He rose. "Waste a man's time-"

"I wouldn't say that, Major. It's an experience being in Manila these days. I collect clippings like that. Sort of a hobby with me, Major. You have to admit the Baybay one's a beaut. Fantastic! But there'll be a day of reckoning. Even now Fate's walking around with his little cane, and if you have an ear for that kind of thing, you can hear its tap-tap-tap."

Joe wondered if Alexander was a genuine goofball or a religious crank; or maybe he was just snowing him. "You've been reading too damn many comics," he said, and left the clerk's office.

"They gave me the brush-off," he reported ruefully to Blacky when he returned to his own office. "The small fry haven't a Chinaman's chance."

Blacky smiled. "That's good news, Joe."

"What's good news about it? Aw, the hell with you, too!" He picked up one of the morning newspapers. All Blacky wanted to do was coast along, Joe thought. Coast along and sneak off to María Clara Street. With the town full of women, only Blacky would shack up with a pom-pom girl from the Five Sisters.

And suddenly he was no longer concentrating on Blacky. He was asking himself why Alexander had shown him that particular clipping. What was the catch, or was there no catch? Joe reached for the phone and called Phil Ide at Bilibid. He explained what he wanted to know and a half hour later Phil rang him back. The Echo didn't have a good reputation, Phil said. There were two or three lawsuits pending in the courts against its editor and publisher. Joe thanked him and considered a new possibility. Maybe that Alexander wasn't a goofball. Maybe he was just a grafter like everybody else, collecting from the suckers he relayed on to Alfonso Baybay. Still, if Baybay knew Mr. Arranger's name, that was worth money to anybody.

Joe drove over to the Echo offices; he invited the columnist to have a beer with him downstairs. And sure enough, Alfonso Baybay hinted finally that as a favor he could identify Mr. Arranger. Baybay smiled. He was a suave Filipino with a coffee-colored face and his smile was very white and toothy as he declared that such a favor was not without value. Two thousand pesos, in fact. Over a second beer Joe bargained him down to fifteen hundred spot cash.

"How is our friend Alexander?" Joe asked casually.

But Baybay only smiled and said, "I do not know such a man. Alexander?"

Joe let it go at that; he was positive Alexander would be seeing a little of the color of his fifteen hundred pesos. The phony with his comic books and tap-tap-tap of Fate!

Joe grinned as he sped off in his jeep. So he didn't have a monopoly on fraud and misrepresentation. Besides, he had no right to beef. This Baybay tip had come just when he needed a shot in the arm. The water-front heisting was ruined, and with the replacement depots emptying, the pom-pom racket was fading faster than a bleached blonde. He needed some kind of new deal, even if it had to be a deal on the level. That was the laugh of the year, but when you looked into it a little deeper, Joe considered, crooked deals or square deals weren't too damn different. There was always some guy collecting a little graft, always some guy with the in. Every damn deal depended on the in. On who you knew. On the Arranger.

"Thomas Bead, that's his name, and it cost me fifteen hundred pesos," Joe said to Pedro Dimang that evening. "The gimmick's how it's going to do us some good. With Baybay giving Mr. Arranger all that free publicity, he's going to be careful. I can't just drive over to his house. Manila's not that wide open. So this is what I thought, Pedro. You're a well-known businessman. Maybe one of your friends is a friend of this Bead."

"I am member of Philippine Chamber of Commerce," Pedro Dimang said slowly.

"That's the bet, Pedro!"

It was two days before Pedro Dimang found the mutual friend they wanted, another two days before an appointment was made for Pedro Dimang and Joe to call at Mr. Arranger's home. The address was on a quiet street between Dewey Boulevard and Taft, a square mansion behind a stone wall tipped with pieces of jagged glass that glinted like bayonets in the sun. A servant led the two visitors up a flight of wide stairs into a *sala* with windows on a garden. The servant left them and Joe studied the frescoed ceiling. It was another garden of pink and blue and rose, with lush pink Venuses reclining on dark blue capes. "This is what I call living in style," Joe said to Pedro Dimang.

"He is big shot," Pedro Dimang said nervously.

"The smell of our money's as good as anybody's."

Mr. Arranger, or Thomas Bead, was a tall Englishman in gray slacks and a white polo shirt and he came soundlessly into the *sala*; he was wearing white-laced sneakers. He shook hands with the Filipino lumberman and the American major, asking what kind of drink they wanted. The servant fixed two rye highballs for the visitors, a Scotch for his master. Bead smiled when the servant glided from the room. "Yes, gentlemen," he said, his eyes two small faded dots flanking a long nose, his mouth a tight pale line over a knobby chin.

The damn limey, Joe thought, looked like a barkeep. Yet the guy lived in a great big house out in the Pasay.

After five or six minutes of generalities, they started to talk business. "I cannot help you directly with the uncatalogued war surplus," the Arranger said. "My services are limited to introducing you to a very influential person who can be of assistance." And when questioned by Joe, he declared that his services, limited as they were, were worth ten thousand pesos.

"That's money," Joe said, "even in Manila."

"You might be throwing it away, Major."

"What do you mean by that?"

"I cannot guarantee any results. My services are purely introductory."

"I see. All you are is the arranger for the arranger."

The Englishman smiled. "You Americans have a colorful way of expressing your thoughts."

"Who is this big wheel?" Joe asked.

"Roberto Fernández."

Joe shrugged - he didn't know the name - but Pedro Dimang exclaimed, "Roberto Fernández! The adviser of Manuel de Léon?"

Bead nodded.

"Manuel de Léon!" Joe said, impressed. He'd seen the name of the Secretary of Finance almost daily in the newspapers. But ten thousand pesos to say hello to Léon's adviser was kind of steep, Joe reflected bitterly. The limey was giving them the old Chinese squeeze. "I don't like to operate on speculation, Mr. Bead."

"Who does?" The Englishman smiled agreeably.

"You're a friend of Fernández. Why don't you come in with us as a partner? Ten per cent to you on every peso we make through Fernández." And as he spoke he was thinking wryly of how he'd put over Operation Pom-Pom. That, too, was a deal where the little guys paid off the big guys.

"I would not describe that as a partnership, Major."

"What would you describe as a partnership?"

"Twenty-five per cent," the Arranger suggested.

Joe glanced at Pedro Dimang, who nodded at him. "We're partners, Mr. Bead," Joe said. "As of now."

But the new partnership was exclusive of the figure of ten thousand, at which the Arranger had appraised his services. "I cannot take any risks," the Englishman explained coolly. "I am certain everything will be satisfactory, but a slight risk remains."

"What's that?" Joe frowned.

"Fernández is an important personage, and he prefers dealing with important people who could be of possible assistance to him."

"Pedro," Joe smiled, "how important are you? Own any banks?" They laughed and Joe continued, "I have connections with officers whose names I cannot mention, but they go right up to the top echelons."

"Perhaps to a colonel or a general?"

"Right up to the top brass."

"It would be advisable to impress Fernández with that fact." The little eyes twinkled.

Joe thought that the limey didn't really believe him. But since they were or would be partners, Bead was in there pitching on his side.

An appointment was made with Roberto Fernández for eleven o'clock the next morning at his Malacanan Palace offices.

They drove to Malacanan Palace in Bead's black limousine, sitting together in the rear seat and separated from the chauffeur by a glass panel. From inside a fifteen-thousand-peso limousine, the familiar city presented another face to Joe. The *calesa* horses, kicking up dust, were the same. The dust, the pedestrians, a newspaper boy shouting the headlines on a corner, all were the same. A street sideshow with a Filipino dressed like a cowboy, a black Stetson on his head and whirling a lariat, behind him four girls swinging their hips in a come-on for the GREAT ORIENTAL SHOW; all the gaudy signs, LIGHT BRINGERS RESTAURANT, PURE FILIPINO CAPITAL, DR. RAJAH WONDER OF WONDERS, THE SNAKE AND THE GIRL - all these were the same, but now he saw the city in a golden light, as if the familiar sun had changed into an immense golden peso whose splendor touched every single person and thing on the crowded streets, as if the blue-sky deal were finally as close as Mr. Arranger, sitting next to him in the black limousine. It was all the right connections, Joe told himself solemnly as if reciting a prayer to the bells tolling on Quiapo Plaza.

Dust whirled in front of the San Miguel Brewery next to Malacanan Palace, dust stirred by the feet of thousands of peasants marching through the Malacanan iron gates, between rows of Filipino soldiers who in that thick distorting dust seemed like brown-faced dolls.

Fine dust filtered down on the gleaming hood of the black limousine. The chauffeur's hand stayed on his horn until a Filipino sergeant pushed through the peasant ranks. Bead rolled down his window. "We have an appointment with the Honorable Roberto Fernández."

The Filipino sergeant shouted at the peasants, who slowly spilled over on the lawns to open a way.

Joe stared at the massed brown faces, and above the faces, the placards dancing crazily from brown fists. "Treating all those Reds with a silk glove," he complained.

"Yes, too much silk glove," Pedro Dimang agreed.

But the Arranger said nothing, as if he were already closeted with Roberto Fernández.

The adviser to the Secretary of Finance was a tall, thin mestizo who wore his white tropical suit like a coat of mail, his skin brown like that of his Filipino ancestors, his nose hooked and aquiline like those of his Spanish ancestors. "Is it not a scandal!" he declared after the introductions. "Every week they come from their rice paddies."

"They ought to stay in their wallows," Joe stated.

Fernández nodded at the American major. "Yes, yes, Major." He waved at the high-backed chairs in his book-lined office. "My friends, please be seated."

As he spoke, the muscled step-and-lift of thousands of feet sounded through the shuttered windows like a distant thunder from the palace courtyard.

"Señor Fernández," the Arranger began in a low voice, "these are good friends of mine. Pedro Dimang is a lumberman, a prominent member of the Philippine Chamber of Commerce. Major Fenton is a friend of very important officers."

"Officers of the highest rank, Señor Fernández. I'm only a major," Joe added with a deprecating smile, "and a major is expendable, Señor Fernández. These officers, although I cannot mention their names, are prepared to be of service to any friends of mine."

"Yes, yes," Roberto Fernández said, and he waved a slim brown hand at the shuttered windows. "There is chaos, gentlemen. I am happy to meet you and I am sorry I must be so brief. I have a conference I must attend. We hope to settle the water-front situation. Yes, yes. Mr. Bead has discussed the matter that is of interest to you. I believe it can be adjusted satisfactorily." And rising from his chair, he escorted them to the door. "Today is Tuesday. I will have a decision next Tuesday on the matter that concerns you. Yes, yes. I will expect you here Tuesday at eleven, and I believe...."

The rest of his words were lost, for from the palace courtyard thousands of voices lifted in a shattering "*Mabuhay!*"

But whomever the peasants were wishing long life, the four men in the book-lined office knew it was not them.

"Chaos," Roberto Fernández said gloomily as he shook hands with his callers. "Chaos. A normal business life is impossible today."

Joe thought of the fifty tons of sugar he had lost because of the water-front strike. He wondered if something else would turn up to queer the uncatalogued war surplus deal.

CHAPTER SIXTEEN

Joe was unable to sleep that night. How could they clinch that deal for sure?

"This is what we've got to do," he said to Blacky the next morning before they went downstairs in the elevator for breakfast in the Cosmos dining room. "We promote ourselves, Blacky. We become a lieutenant colonel and a major." The words raced off his tongue, and he laughed out loud with sheer excitement. "It's a natural! It'll prove better than anything who's got the connections with the big brass. It hit me last night, Blacky, just as I was about to cork off. Here's how we do it. We throw a big party at the Chateau to celebrate, and we ask Fernández and the limey. Let them see for themselves how much the big brass love us." Joe chortled with glee. "Blacky, that's all that counts in this life. Who you know or who they think you know. Ten to one we'll be bidding on the uncatalogued stuff next Tuesday. We'll have the party Friday night."

"You're crazy, Joe. You're going to push your luck so far you'll push us both to hell and gone. Promotion parties at the Chateau," Blacky gasped, "where everybody can see us! Out in the open for the whole damn town to see! Why don't you stick your picture in all the goddamn papers? Lieutenant Colonel! Major!"

This was where he'd come in once before, Joe remembered - Tommy Cruz's house and Blacky screaming at the officers' uniforms. That boy had to be beaten into line. He'd always be a GI deep down, shacking up on the q.t. with a GI girl in that house on María Clara Street.

"Cool off, Blacky," Joe advised him softly. "We'll think it over some more. But what's there to think over? We've got the limey with us to the tune of a twenty-five-per-cent cut-in and we've got to clinch it with Roberto Fernández. You got any better ideas?" And he walked to the dark-faced, glowering man and patted Blacky's shoulder with the friendliest of hands.

There was a knife in that hand, but only Joe could see it. Or see the target at which the knife was going to be thrown - the house on María Clara Street.

Later in the morning, he sat with Manuel Pangamban in a wineshop and explained that it wouldn't look right for a major to shack up with a GI girl. The Filipino listened attentively. He was as slender as a girl himself, and he was wearing the colors of a girl, his polo shirt lavender, his slacks a grass green. No, it wouldn't look right. The future Lieutenant Colonel smiled and said he didn't want the Major to know about Manuel, so maybe it would be best if he followed Manuel out to María Clara Street in his own jeep. *Sí*, Manuel agreed. The future Lieutenant Colonel was pleased, declaring that he had big plans, and Manuel Pangamban was a part of them.

Towards twilight, the two jeeps rolled north, Manuel Pangamban in the lead,

Joe trailing him. The sun glittered from the store windows, gleamed pinkly from the small sea-shell windowpanes of the flats above the stores. On the sidewalks brown-faced girls and brown-faced men strolled together with only occasional groups of American soldiers to be seen.

The tropical city belonged to the brown people again, as María Clara had always belonged to them, even with a million GI's roistering downtown. Manuel Pangamban parked four or five houses above the house of Captain Hurley. He climbed out of his jeep, walked under the white stars salting the sky between the rooftops over to the second jeep. Manuel pointed out the house of the Captain.

Joe waited until Manuel was gone before he hurried to the door.

He heard a woman's footsteps and then a light voice questioned him in Tagalog. Monkey talk, he thought. "I want to see Bill," he replied.

"Bill?" the woman questioned from behind the door.

"Bill Hurley. I'm a friend of Bill Hurley."

The door opened and Joe stepped inside the red-tiled *sala*, to smile the friendliest of smiles at Blacky, towering above a tiny brown girl. It was just as he had expected. For how could it be otherwise, when Joe the brain was doing the figuring? Where else would Blacky slip off to - to forget about the rank he hated - but to his little GI sweetheart.

Joe slowly closed the door. "Why don't you introduce me," he said, nodding at the girl. As if he needed any introductions.

GI was written all over her, a Filipino girl with a stick of a body and a face that had seen better days, a whitish scar disfiguring one brown cheek. She was wearing a red and green dress bought in some cheap bazaar, a twenty-peso string of false pearls around her neck. A hundred-per-cent Filipino girl, Joe appraised her. "Why don't you introduce me?"

Blacky said not a word. His lips were barely opened but it seemed somehow as if his jaws had been wrenched apart.

Joe sighed. "No introduction? Well, to tell you the truth, I'd rather talk to you alone, pal." He smiled at the girl. "Excuse us, sister," he said, and walked past the couch and a table with a vase of flowers to the open door of the bedroom. There he paused, his blond head pivoted. She hadn't moved. Their eyes met and suddenly her hands came together, but whether in terror or prayer, Joe didn't know or care much. Nor had Blacky moved. "Come on!" Joe ordered. Blacky lumbered forward and Joe winked at the girl. The light of the Chinese lantern glowed softly on her perfectly matched false pearls.

Blacky shuffled into the bedroom. Joe entered too, closing the door behind them.

Another Chinese lantern, this one green, dangled from the end of the electric wire. Joe inspected it leisurely, as if Blacky weren't in the same room with him. He inspected the dark wooden bed, the tarpaulin stretched above the bed under the corrugated iron roof, the dresser littered with perfume bottles and cheap jewelry. His blue eyes darted everywhere, like fingers of light, examining, prying, missing nothing.

"You're what I'd call a prize dumb bastid." Joe pronounced his final judgment.

"Joe," Blacky pleaded. He lifted one hand.

"Joe," the Lawyer mimicked.

"Joe, listen-"

Joe ambled over to the chair alongside the bed, sweeping the shirt and khaki socks on the seat to the floor before sitting down. "What's your story?"

"There's no story, Joe."

"Don't low-rate yourself!"

"If you'd only listen to me-"

"Listen, hell! What were you trying to get away with?"

"With nothing."

"No? Never once mentions this rat-hole. Call that nothing?"

"Joe, do I have to tell you about every girl-"

"It's not the girl, and you know it. It's the house! A lil house on the q.t." He stared at the tarpaulin over the bed. "Didn't want rain on your lil innocent back, did you?"

"Joe-"

"Here I thought we were buddies."

"We are!"

"Are what?" Joe sneered and then deliberately spat on the floor. "Shut up and listen to me. You got this rat hole so you'd have a place to run off to if things ever got hot."

"Joe, you've got me wrong."

"I've got you right, but there's nothing right about you. A lot of things make sense now. All that beefing and whining about pushing our luck too far."

"Sure, I worried!" Blacky shouted. "Why shouldn't I be worried? That's why I got this house. But it was to be for the two of us if things got hot."

Joe laughed at him. "Just a lil surprise?"

"I knew you'd squawk. That's why I never mentioned it, Joe. That's the truth, Joe!"

"You don't know what the truth is!" Joe retorted indignantly, as if all his life he'd walked the straight-and-narrow. "Blacky, if you think you can snow me, you better think up something else. What a buddy you turned out to be! I give you the best deal you ever had, and this is the pay-off."

"This house was for the both of us," Blacky lied stubbornly.

"Yeah?" Joe grinned. "No fooling? Why didn't you mention it at the office today when you were crying over the promotion party? Aw, shut up! I've heard enough. This house was for one guy only. Sit down and listen to me."

Blacky hulked wearily over toward the bed. He sat on its very edge, his long powerful arms dangling between his knees. His face in the lantern light seemed stripped down to the bone of his forehead and clenched jaws. His eyes were like two protruding brown balls.

Joe looked at him. The big double-crosser was done in! As he'd do them all in, Joe thought with exultation. Every last one, from Blacky right on up to that fancy character in Malacanan Palace. "Who's the flip?" he asked.

"My girl."

"No kidding! So she's your girl! Want to know something, Blacky? I knew all about that flip and you for a long time, but I just let it ride. The hell with it, I said to myself. But we can't let it ride any more, Blacky. We can't have no Five Sisters girl spilling things to Franny and Tommy Cruz."

"She never sees any of 'em, Joe."

"That's what she says to you, but you sure?"

"I'm sure."

"What a jerk! How can you be sure about any of that kind? They don't think the way we do." He gestured at the bed. "That's all they do that's the same. Blacky, we can't let it ride any more. We've got big things ahead of us. You've told her?" He grinned as if that was O.K. with him.

"I've never told her a damn thing, Joe!"

"No?"

"No!"

"You'll go down in history as the first guy who didn't spill his guts to a dame. Anyway, we can't take any more chances, Blacky. You've had your fling. You're through with her, Blacky."

"Through?" Blacky repeated dumbly.

Joe rubbed at his eyelids like a man trying to see straight. "Do I get the idea that you love her? For God's sake, Blacky, there's a hundred like her on every Rizal corner." Blacky didn't answer him.

"That flip comes with this house, and this house goes down the drain, as of now!" Joe said with no mockery in his voice.

"Joe, listen-"

"You heard me, Blacky. We can't take any more chances. Goddamn it! With a blue-sky deal about to break, he gives me romance!"

Blacky scratched at the side of his nose as if that were the only thing that interested him in the whole wide world. But his eyes had glazed, as if he had been clubbed.

Joe looked at him. The miserable louse, he thought, wondering at the pity he'd felt for a second. Blacky didn't deserve a break. Shacking up on the q.t.! It proved you couldn't trust anybody. For some reason, Joe remembered the clerk Alexander's story about the tap-tap-tap of Fate, identifying himself of a sudden with Fate walking around Manila with its little cane.

"This goofball at the ACA," he said. "I never bothered telling you about him, but he had something, all right. He said there was a big black eight ball walking around with a lil cane and the lil cane going tap-tap-tap. That's what's happened to you. Thought you were so wise, and nobody'd find out about this private lil rat hole, and all the time who was right behind you? Nobody but lil Joe. And you! You were so goddamn sure of yourself you never heard the tap-tap-tap of the big black eight ball." Joe shrugged. "Aw, we've wasted enough time. Call her in."

Blacky walked to the bedroom door mechanically.

When the girl entered the bedroom, Joe stood up and said, "You're through with him. He's not coming here any more."

She tried to go to Blacky, but Joe seized her wrist.

Her eyes rolled wildly as she stared from her captor to her lover. Blacky avoided her beseeching eyes. A spasm of grief shook her narrow shoulders and she wept.

"You better find some other guy to pay for this house, señorita," Joe said to her. "Right, Captain? Tell her that's what you want, Captain. I'm talking to you, Captain. Tell her that's what you want!"

"Yeah," Blacky sighed.

The girl covered her weeping face with her free hand. Joe released her wrist, and this hand too, like a handkerchief of flesh, fluttered to her face.

"Get out of here," Joe said to Blacky. "I want to talk to her alone."

The door opened and closed. Only now did Lucy's hands whip from her face, as if the closing door had sounded in her consciousness, sharp, menacing as the crack of a rifle. Her lips pulled wide with hatred and she cursed the blond American in Tagalog.

"Stop that!" he yelled.

Her head lowered on her neck and still she cursed him. He rushed her, slapped her across the mouth. She recoiled, feeling the bruised lips with her fingertips. "I love him, I love him," she wailed so piteously that Joe couldn't believe that only a second ago she'd been like a fierce little brown cat.

"Shut up!"

"Bill!" she screamed. "Bill!"

But no one came to the door. She clasped her hands in front of her small breasts like a child praying. Then with a last despairing appeal, she cried with all her strength, "Bill, I love you. Come, come."

Joe shouted, "She can't get it into her head she's through!"

There was silence in the *sala*. Maybe there was no one in the *sala*, after all. Nobody but Bill Hurley, the chained shadow of Joe the Lawyer, alias Major Fenton.

The girl ran toward the door. Joe grabbed her by the shoulders. She screamed incoherently. "Shut up!" he warned her, but she shook her head frantically from side to side, tearing and kicking at him.

He ripped the dress from her body. "That's for yapping, you tramp. Shut up now!" She struck out at him, so he ripped her petticoat from her.

She retreated from him in terror. He leaped after her, dragged her to the door.

The fight was out of the girl; she was weeping hysterically. Joe flung the door open to look at Blacky, seated on the couch, head slumped, the knuckles of his left hand pressed into his mouth, as if he had gagged himself with his own fist. Joe stared at him, feeling an emotion heady and sensual and overwhelming. At that second, he could have taken the girl, but instead he forced her to look at her lover. It was the cruelest humiliation of all. Then he slammed the door shut and released his hold on her wrist. "Want to yell some more?" he asked her. "Want to tell me how much you love him?"

The girl fled - from this blond tormentor, and from the American in the *sala*. She flung herself into the bed, pulling the sheet and blanket over her head like a child hiding from a nightmare. Covered by the bedding, she sobbed.

Joe returned to the *sala*. He felt then that he could buy and sell this whole goddamn Manila town with everybody in it - but everybody!

Who was in bed with him?

On some dream bed, he could see himself sleeping on his side, while on the very edge, her back turned to him, some faceless woman slept.

Blacky awoke with Lucy's name on his lips. But there was no Lucy in the rumpled bed in his room at the hotel.

Only the whisky bottle on the dresser, only the drawn Venetian blinds penciled with hot yellow lines. Only the pangs of conscience like sun rays focused through yesterday's magnifying glass into this day's whisky-soaked and dark emptiness of heart.

Wearily, Blacky lifted his hairy forearm, squinting at the wrist watch strapped around his thick wrist. It was ten-thirty-seven. Yesterday at ten-thirty-seven he hadn't sold Lucy out, but that was yesterday, and no use thinking about Lucy or the house on María Clara. It was all under the bridge, as Joe might have said himself. His buddy Joe, good old Joe, who only wanted the best for him, the very, very best. His buddy Joe, with whom he'd come up from the ranks.

"God," Blacky muttered despairingly. But what else could he have done yesterday? What else was there to do? Heel out on the promotion party? And then what? Stick a .45 into the ribs of some money guy? That took nerve, and he didn't have that kind of nerve any more. He might as well admit it, might as well admit he was too used to the soft life. If only he had the nerve to shake the dust of Manila! The water front was a snafu, but private planes were flying these days to Shanghai and Tokyo, and if he showed cash, he'd be sure to find a pilot to sneak him on. Shanghai? Tokyo? What would he do there? Play hide-and-seek with the MP's? Maybe he ought to pull out for the States, and what would he do there? Ask for his old job in the stove factory or some other goddamn factory, punch a time clock, scrounge around for a few bucks?

Blacky knew now with the terrible clarity that sometimes accompanies a hangover that there was no escape for him. For there was damn little left of the old Blacky MacIntyre and a little too damn much of Bill Hurley.

He cursed Joe. The pitiless clarity was gone as surely as the breath of his dead mother. It was all the fault of Joe, Blacky thought to himself. How could anybody stand up against Joe? Tommy Cruz couldn't, or Salvador Dimang, or Pedro Dimang, or Johnny Yen Lee or Sergeant Kroll or Sergeant Mallinson out on Cavite. Nobody could beat Joe. Not even those two hot shots Thomas Bead and Roberto Fernández. He'd wangled the limey with a partnership and he'd wangle Fernández with the big party tomorrow night. He'd make stooges out of them, too, before he got through, as surely as he'd made a stooge out of the awol who had once answered to the name of MacIntyre. A stooge-maker and a woman-stealer. He'd stolen Serafina and Helen, and now he'd taken Lucy from him. Lucy who loved him, his GI girl, his good-luck girl....

Blacky flung himself out of bed, walked to the bottle of whisky on the dresser. He drank three or four inches, and when he set the bottle down, tears dimmed his eyes. He wept for himself, for the man who had crawled so low that he was handing out private little bouquets to the rat who had taken Lucy from him. Soft-soaping Joe even when Joe wasn't around, telling himself nobody could stand up against Joe, as if he were Superman or something. Well, maybe Joe was, at that. He had everything, looks and brains and nerve, everything but a heart. A guy like that wasn't human. Blacky remembered Joe's line at Bilibid - so long ago - about his father the police officer, and he laughed weakly. A police officer for a father, O.K., but what about a mother? He had to have a mother.

Joe's only mother was a blue-sky deal, Blacky thought, and headed for the bottle. He drank again. With the bottle gripped in one hand, he flopped down on an upholstered bamboo chair. What had Joe said yesterday at Lucy's? Something about an eight ball, a jinx following him to María Clara Street every time he went there, although he'd never known it, never heard the tap-tap-tap of the jinx behind him. Jinxed, Blacky brooded. Jinxed from the minute that Joe the Lawyer had first whispered to him in the stockade at Fernando. Jinxed by the thief who not only had stolen Lucy but had cut out his guts as neatly and unsuspectingly as any pickpocket razoring open a wallet pocket in a crowded bus.

That tap-tap-tap beat on Blacky's heart now, drawing blood, for the little cane had a point sharper than any razor.

Blacky tilted the bottle, drinking with closed eyes, but there wasn't whisky enough to wash away Lucy's tears. He could still hear her calling him, still see himself squatting like a lump in the *sala*. God!

His hand trembled on the bottle and he looked back, bitten with regrets, at the awol he'd once been, living in the thieves' town within the city. He had guts then, but that was before he'd become Captain Hurley. Good old Captain-Major Hurley roughing it at the Hotel Cosmos. God, that was the answer! The man who had doublecrossed Lucy wasn't Blacky MacIntyre, but Bill Hurley.

To hell with Joe's promotion party! he thought, and drank a few more inches of whisky righteousness. He'd show that guy! He'd blow the hell out of Manila! He knew enough of the buy-and-sell racket to get into it himself! In Tokyo! Shanghai! There must be guys like Kroll and Mallinson up there, too. All he needed was a little front, a little brass. Yeah, that's what he'd do. Blacky helped himself to another swig of whisky. What about money? Some quick money? Blacky laughed. Why, it was waiting for him in Salvador Dimang's house, up on the second floor, where Salvador kept his money in that small iron safe of his. And not only money. Helen's sapphire had come out of that same safe. Money and jewelry! Enough to buy passage, not only to Shanghai, but to the moon. And he'd take Lucy with him, Blacky resolved joyously, and he treated himself to another drink.

He dressed swiftly, his mind working on the whisky-inspired plan to heist Salvador Dimang. There would be Mrs. Dimang and maybe her daughter. Salvador would be away now. Just the wife and maybe the daughter and the servants. How many of those were there? Three, four? Hell, he didn't have to worry about them. Mrs. Dimang knew him, and all he had to do was talk her into going upstairs to the study, where the safe was. He'd gag her before she knew what had happened, make her unlock the safe, and walk out of the house with the loot.

Blacky laced his fine brown leather officer's shoes, the thought needling him that his plan was wilder than a Moro running amok. He flushed as he remembered Joe's smooth plans. Joe could be reckless, but he was never wild. What was wilder than making Mrs. Dimang open the safe? She knew him, and after he'd blown out with the loot, he'd have Dimang and Joe after him. No, first he had to have his passage on some plane lined up. And someplace to hide in until it was time to blow. But suppose Salvador Dimang and Joe would be keeping an eye on the airfields? God, if they ever got him, it would be the Sergeant Murdock treatment for him.

It was much easier tilting the bottle of whisky.

CHAPTER SEVENTEEN

"If any of my guests get here before ten, Santos, give them what they want. Drink anything."

"Yes, sir, Major Fenton. Or do I say Colonel Fenton?"

"I'm a major until the party, Santos. In fact, we won't wear our new insignia until tomorrow."

"Yes, sir, Major Fenton. Permit me to show you the arrangement, Major Fenton."

Blacky snapped to attention and saluted the Major, but Joe was already following the headwaiter, Santos, into the soft pinkness of the Chateau *sala* where tablecloths bloomed like immense roses and the faces, eating and drinking, wavered like so many pink blobs. Blacky leered drunkenly. He had already put away close to half a quart of whisky, bonded whisky. For this was the night of the big promotion party and he deserved nothing but the best.

Slowly he tagged after Joe and Santos, weaving an unsteady line down the *sala*. He grimaced at a burst of laughter from some table. He passed by the dance floor. Pink-faced dancers swayed and glided to music soft as the lighting, pink music in a pink world where nothing mattered any more.

It was a discovery that Blacky had made in the Hotel Cosmos as he transferred the bonded whisky from the bottle to his eternally parched throat. Nothing mattered. His trouble was that he had been going along as if things mattered, telling himself that Lucy meant something to him and was the big fact in his life. But suppose a man no longer went according to the facts - the big facts or the little facts? Suppose a man said to hell with the facts and just enjoyed the view?

It was an eye-opening discovery.

You just enjoyed the view.

Like the view here at the Chateau - of all kinds of guys spending all kinds of money on all kinds of dames.

Grinning to himself, Blacky reached Joe. The headwaiter had vanished. Maybe he'd dropped through a hole in the floor, Blacky speculated as he examined the view in this corner of the Chateau.

Four or five tables had been set end to end to form one banquet board. Vases of flowers sprouted out of the pink cloth, with pinkly gleaming silverware and pinkly tinted glassware for twenty or thirty people.

"Blacky," Joe said, as if the teetering Captain had been at his elbow all the time, "this is going to be a party!"

"Where's Santos?"

"I sent him off to dig up a mike."

"A mike?"

"I'm going to make a lil speech. You too. Have you forgotten?"

"I'm just gonna enjoy the view."

"What view?"

"What speech?"

"You're drunk."

"Why the hell not? What's the difference?"

Joe scowled, but Blacky only laughed. Joe waved a pink hand behind him at the crowded tables. "There's a lot of brass here tonight. That's why the mike. I want 'em to hear my lil speech. That'll get them up here to shake hands and congratulate us. Roberto Fernández'll see 'em. Blacky, you listening to me?"

"You're a smart bastid, Joe," Blacky conceded. Drunk or not, he had to admit Joe was smart.

"We'll have Roberto Fernández thinking we're pals with every damn officer in Manila. So try and sober up."

Santos joined them. A microphone would be available, the headwaiter promised. Blacky listened for a few seconds and then he started to count the chairs at the banquet table. At eighteen, he lost interest. The hell with it, he decided groggily. It was going to be a party, with Roberto Fernández and the limey Thomas Bead in the number one slot. Although Phil Ide and even Sarge Kroll hadn't been forgotten, Blacky remembered. And there'd be Pedro Dimang and Cousin Salvador, and Tommy Cruz and Manuel Pangamban, and if anybody had any hard feelings against Joe, what with Joe giving them all a demonstration of how the little old switcheroo worked, champagne ought to fix that. It was going to be a party and a half with Johnny Yen Lee and the Chinese pompom houses footing the champagne bill, but why should Johnny complain, when what he didn't know would never bother him, and besides, he'd been invited too. "I'm drunk," Blacky announced for no reason at all. And once more he noticed that the headwaiter was gone. "The bastid's got a reg'lar disappearing act," Blacky marveled.

"We've got more than an hour to kill. I said ten, but it'll be nearer eleven before we begin."

"That so?" said Blacky.

"Let's go upstairs and say hello to Helen. She drank herself unconscious the other night. Why she has to drink like that I don't know."

They walked out of the *sala*. Their pink faces changed into yellow faces on the stairs, and up in the gambling establishment into their own true faces, or what passed for their true faces. The blond, handsome, open face of the Major might have been clipped out of some magazine - the advertisement face of a man who would never, never cheat a widow or rob an orphan. And the dark Captain's face with the troubled forehead under the thinning black hair? It was the face of a loser surely, although you couldn't know what had been lost. A bank roll, probably, in this room where the roulette wheels hummed and the dice rattled and the cards whispered false promises. Some kind of a bank roll, anyway. Maybe even the single finely printed note of a man's pride and dignity.

"I paid for that dress," Joe remarked as they walked to Helen's table. "Three-fifty, and I mean dollars, not pesos."

"She looks swell," Blacky answered him.

"Why she has to drink like that I don't know."

"She looks swell. What more you want?"

Helen was wearing a white evening gown. Deft and quick, she dealt her cards to the players at her table, a Spaniard, two Americans in tropical tuxedoes, and a Philippine Army captain, the sapphire on her left hand flashing innumerable white stars as casually and simply as a child tossing off soap bubbles. And like soap bubbles they vanished in the air.

"Good evening, gentlemen," she said to Major Fenton and Captain Hurley, her voice cool.

As if she'd learned long ago that nothing mattered much, Blacky thought bitterly.

She had never reproached him, never asked any questions after the party at Salvador Dimang's bungalow. All the reproaches had been in his own mind.

Joe smiled at her. "The party won't get started for another hour. Try to come early, Helen, will you?"

"Yes," she promised him.

"Why don't we play?" Joe pounded Blacky's shoulder. "Damn it, our no-gambling rule's off. Off this night, anyway! How much're those chips, Helen?"

"The blue chips, five hundred pesos. The yellows, one hundred pesos. The reds, twenty pesos."

Joe grinned. Taking out his wallet, he counted out two thousand pesos.

"I forgot mine!" Blacky exclaimed, searching through all his pockets with a drunkard's thick-ended fingers.

One of the Americans in the tropical tuxedoes laughed. "Maybe you're lucky you did."

"Here," Joe offered. "I'll loan you two thousand. One of us is bound to win."

"You think so?" the American in the tropical tuxedo said.

"Any change is the time for luck!" Joe said.

A minute later, Blacky was looking down at the chips purchased by two thousand easy pesos. A blue five hundred, ten yellow one hundreds, twenty-five red twenties. Helen dealt the first round of cards. Blacky lifted the corner of his hole card - a seven of diamonds. All about him they were betting. Next to him the Philippine Army man placed three red chips down on his hole card while Joe bet a solitary yellow chip. Blacky picked up his blue chip and dropped it down on the hidden seven of diamonds.

"We might as well earn the expenses of our party!" Joe laughed.

The dealer in the white evening dress, like some clockwork device produced in the same factory where the cards were made, dealt the first round of open cards. A nine for the Philippine Army man, a jack to the Spaniard, an eight and a three to the two American civilians, a queen to Joe, and a seven of clubs to the top money bettor.

Seven and seven, Blacky added. He had a total of fourteen points against a possible perfect score of twenty-one. He glanced up into Helen's face. Her pale blue eyes met his own, enigmatic and expressionless as the eyes of the queen she had dealt to the man who had tricked her into being his mistress. Yet the vein in Blacky's dark tanned forehead swelled, and he concentrated, suddenly, on the seven of clubs as the old guilt pierced through the wall of whisky guarding his heart. The old guilt, the old shame. And what about his early-evening discovery that nothing mattered? So he had sat like a dummy in the *sala* of Dimang's bungalow, and in the *sala* of the house on María Clara Street, a whole vast city between the two houses that were somehow one house, for the guilt was one guilt, the shame one shame, the judgment one judgment - a nightmare judgment screaming at him out of a little brown face scarred on one cheek, and if the face altered now to a milky face with blue eyes, the judgment never changed.

The players had already made their second bets. "Captain," the dealer inquired, "you wish to bet?"

"He's dreaming," Joe remarked slyly.

But Blacky only heard Helen's low and professional voice, hearing through it Lucy's last despairing cry, "Bill, I love you. Come, come." But how in God's name could he have gone to her when he really wasn't Blacky? When he was Bill, Captain Bill Hurley, put together like any other gadget, a gadget in suntans, made for any woman's room and any bartender's bar. Blacky's brain ached and he wanted a drink badly, but there was no whisky in this room of the blue walls. So he again added up his back-to-back sevens to arrive at the same fourteen points, betting five of his yellow chips.

Five hundred pesos bet by the Captain!

The dealer was ready now to deal the second round of open cards. The Philippine Army man asked for one card. She dealt it, a king. The Philippine Army man sighed, showing his hole card, a six. With his six and nine and ten-point king, he had a total of twenty-five points. Helen raked in his chips and turned to the next player and the next. When Blacky's turn came, he lifted one finger and she dealt him a six of spades. He had a score of twenty, and she could beat him only by drawing twenty or twenty-one herself. "Enough," Blacky said. She took care of all the players, then revealed her hole card. A king - ten points. She dealt herself a nine and stopped with a score of nineteen.

Her nineteen points topped them all except Blacky's twenty. She paid him two blue chips - a thousand pesos.

"You're hitting the house!" Joe congratulated him. "That's because you'll be a major tonight."

"I think I will ask to be major," the Philippine Army captain joked.

Again the hole cards slid across the table in blind gift to each of six players. For Blacky, a queen in the hole, or ten points, but he wouldn't have played differently if he'd drawn a three. He bet two blue chips, waited for his first open card, a four, and bet ten yellow chips, one thousand pesos on his fourteen points, and asked for a second card. He drew a six. He had twenty points again. The big twenty, the lucky twenty. This round, Helen's hole card was a ten. She studied the cards of the six men betting against the house, her eyes resting longest on Blacky's four and six. She couldn't win, Blacky thought; she couldn't win and he'd already lost.... She dealt herself an eight, stopping play with eighteen points for herself. Again Blacky had won. There were two other winners, the Spaniard and one of the tuxedo Americans, but nobody glanced at them. All their eyes were on Blacky. He won the third hand, lost the fourth, won the fifth, the sixth, and the seventh hands. "Man, you're hitting!" Joe cried. The blond face was triumphant, as if he were the big winner himself. Blacky was no longer figuring out the money value of his colored chips. Blues and yellows and reds, he bet them in stacks as if this were some make-believe child's game where there would really be no winners and no losers. And he won again unaware of the players from all the games in the room lining up at Helen's table, astonished and envious and whispering:

"Ever see anything like it?"

"*Dios!*"

"He will buy the Chateau this night."

"Who is he?"

"Captain Rabbit Foot," an American officer wisecracked.

And on the twelfth or thirteenth play, a bald Spaniard with a waxed mustache pushed through the crowd, apologetically tapping the elbow of the lucky man. "Captain Hurley. Captain Hurley, this game, it is finish for this night. I apologize, Captain Hurley, for the inconvenience, but it is necessary."

"Necessary for who?" Joe demanded, while Blacky smiled dreamily. Blacky felt as if he were on some high serene wave, riding its crest under some white and flaring sky, the same electric color as the lighting in this room, a private sky, a special heaven built for one.

How many times had he dreamed the sweet GI dream of breaking the latrine crap game?

"He's got a right to keep on playing!" Joe insisted passionately, but the Spaniard only shrugged and nodded at Helen. She walked around the table to the winner's pile of chips. The crowd opened before her, then pressed in tight, pushing her against Blacky. He hadn't been so close to her since the date at the Gregory Terrace Club. Her hip touched his own. Staring down at her fingers separating his blue chips from his reds and yellows, Blacky wondered dizzily who was the winner and who the loser.

She announced the sum to the Spaniard. He pulled a big black wallet from his jacket pocket and matched the chips with pesos. "Sixteen thousand, eight hundred and forty pesos," the Spaniard said. "Sixteen thousand!" the crowd echoed, seizing on the number and repeating it like a prayer.

The crowd watched the Captain and the Major walk away from the table, and still they whispered, "Sixteen thousand pesos!"

In the corridor outside the gambling room, Joe said excitedly, "We've started on a winning streak, Blacky! I don't believe in signs and all that craperoo, but goddamn it, it never rains but it pours. Ten to one, a hundred to one, we'll be bidding on the uncatalogued stuff!"

Blacky muttered to himself.

"Once we get an in, we'll be bidding on everything! Sugar! Hospital equipment! Everything!"

"Let's get a drink," Blacky said wearily.

Joe stared at him. "You'd think you'd lost your shirt."

"One thing I haven't lost is my thirst," Blacky confessed with a sigh.

They went downstairs and Blacky paused at the bar.

"We can get what we want at our party," Joe said.

"This is quicker. A bottle whisky, bonded rye. And two glasses," he said to the bartender. He poured the whisky like water, lifting his glass in toast. "To the very best."

When they entered the *sala*, Blacky felt as if he were diving into the pink light, submerged in another world where whisky was the passport and where a man could just enjoy the view, for nothing mattered, after all.

Half of their guests had already arrived, a pink-faced crowd, champagne glasses in their hands. Blacky waved at Lieutenant Phil Ide with Kao and a fat major whom he'd never seen. Kao's naked shoulders shone sleek and pink, always pink, forever pink. Blacky smiled at Kao and he smiled at Tommy Cruz and Hanoco and he laughed when he saw his old girl friend Serafina with Sergeant Kroll, all their pink faces bubbling before him as if foaming out of some bottomless champagne glass. The headwaiter, Santos, was bowing and pointing out the seats of honor in the center of the banquet table. "Bring me a bottle of whisky," Blacky ordered. "Bonded whisky, Santos."

Phil Ide was hurrying over with the fat major. "Congratulations, Major Hurley!" the fat major said out of his pink fat face, while Johnny Yen Lee murmured, "Hap-pee, I am ve' hap-pee," out of his pink wizened face. Just one happy party or was the word slap-happy? Blacky wondered as he shook hands with Tommy Cruz and joked with Sergeant Kroll, the empty chairs at the banquet table somehow no longer empty. Roberto Fernández and Thomas Bead arrived late, but Blacky didn't give a damn, for he was pretty busy with the bonded rye whisky, feeling warm and chipper, so when Helen joined the party, sitting next to Joe, he blew her a kiss and considered propositioning Joe with the old switcheroo in reverse. He could buy her a dress, too, with his sixteen thousand pesos.

Now the champagne was flowing faster, the women giggling and the first fist fight settled, and Joe was standing up and saying, "Let's get the ceremony over and then we'll eat." Blacky grinned at the mike that was suddenly there, and Joe said, "Ladies and gentlemen, there'll be no speeches after - all the speeches'll take place now. Ladies and gentlemen, it's a treat to be with you t'night. We Americans and we Filipinos've gone through plenty together. The war! But America's going home now and things're going to be good for the Philippines from now on."

Blacky swallowed another long bonded drink and thought gleefully that Joe was drunk himself. Joe the Lawyer was drunk and making a silly speech like all that silly stuff in the papers he was always reading. "We won't forget the Philippines," Joe was saying earnestly. "We American officers won't ever forget the Philippines! I see many officers here t'night at all these tables and I know they agree with me when I say we won't forget the Philippines after all we've gone through. Well, this speech isn't going to be long, like I promised. Captain Hurley and me don't deserve being promoted, but I guess it's all the story of the lil woman who was married more than once, so every time she got married again, she said she didn't deserve it." And in the laughter, he turned toward Blacky. "I want you all to say hello and good luck to Captain Bill Hurley, now Major Bill Hurley!" Blacky laughed because Phil Ide and his guest the fat major had gotten to their feet for some damn reason, clapping their hands for some other damn reason, which made the officers at all the other tables imitate them, so it was the damnedest thing Blacky had ever seen. "Get up!" Joe cursed at him. Smiling, Blacky obeyed, reeling and staring fascinatedly at all those applauding hands. They were like the wings of fluttering pink birds.

Phil Ide and the fat major tumbled out of their chairs, hurrying to congratulate the newly promoted officers. From all over the Chateau, officers joined the procession. "Congratulations, congratulations!" they cried, shaking hands with the new Major and the new Lieutenant Colonel. "Have a drink," the new Major said impartially to captains and colonels, and a lone brigadier general. "Have a drink, have a drink," and he laughed a highpitched idiot's laugh, but everybody was feeling so good by now and the lights were so deceptively soft and muted that the officers waiting to shake his hand simply thought the new Major was feeling good, a little too good, maybe. "Have a drink!" Blacky laughed. "Faces all pink! Is your face pink?" Blacky inquired, and broke into a paroxysm of helpless mirth that he cured only with his own prescription - a hooker of whisky. "Is your face pink? Have a drink!"

CHAPTER EIGHTEEN

Toward two in the morning, the party was still going strong, and none of the survivors shooting down its champagne rapids noticed the many who were missing. Roberto Fernández had long ago excused himself, whispering to the new Lieutenant Colonel that he was positive, yes, positive, very positive, that their friendship was just beginning, and Thomas Bead had cozily shaken hands with the new Lieutenant Colonel as if to say, "Roberto Fernández means every word of it!" And when old Johnny Yen Lee had gone nobody knew or cared, or Sergeant Kroll and Serafina, or Lieutenant Ide and Kao, or Pedro Dimang, who belonged to the Chamber of Commerce and was a respectable family man, or half a dozen others. And if the party had shifted from the Chateau to the bungalow of Salvador Dimang out in the Pasay, nobody especially remembered the two limousines speeding across the deserted city under the white stars, the black expanse of Manila Bay like some empty land whose only habitations were marked by the lights of the ships at anchor.

"Some of us can go in Salvador's car," the new Lieutenant Colonel had said. "But I'm not driving my jeep. You can't drive either, Tommy. Don't want no accidents. Got too damn much to do!" So Salvador's chauffeur had helped his master and his master's mistress into their limousine, and sweated getting the new Major inside, while the new Lieutenant Colonel and Helen, Tommy Cruz and Hanoco had piled into the hired limousine provided by the obliging Santos. They all could have gone together in Salvador Dimang's huge limousine, but the new Lieutenant Colonel, noisily and happily drunk, hadn't thought of that detail. And so they had all marched into Salvador Dimang's bungalow as if it were a room adjoining the pink *sala* of the Chateau, Tommy Cruz giggling as he held Hanoco's arm, Salvador Dimang hugging his mistress, Espanita, Joe practically carrying Helen who had been unable to take the fresh air, and only Blacky without a woman. Not that Blacky was aware of his stag status. He was nine tenths out, and it required the muscles of both chauffeurs to assist the big heavy man into Salvador's *sala* and settle him in a chair. There, his head lolling, Blacky mumbled to himself.

Joe lifted Helen's legs onto the couch where he had lowered her. "This is a party," he said grinning at the survivors, while the chauffeurs carried in a case of champagne and a basket of whisky bottles.

"Too much," Salvador Dimang groaned, sitting down on the second couch in the crowded *sala*. Espanita tiptoed behind him and blew in his ear. Salvador Dimang jumped. Espanita laughed wildly, swaying, a black-haired mestiza in a black evening dress. Her giddy champagne laughter was contagious. Salvador Dimang started to smile, Joe laughed so hard he had to wipe his eyes, Tommy Cruz roared, holding his sides. But Hanoco only smiled, her slanted eyes crinkling at the corners.

Joe glanced at her as if to say, "Don't you think it's funny?" Then his eyes lingered. Her curved body was enveloped in a filmy pink gown almost the same shade as the lighting at the Chateau, her full smooth arms and neck the palest of ivory. Joe felt his heart grind to a stop in his chest. He forced himself to look elsewhere. At Helen, lying on the couch like a broken doll in white. At Blacky, who was still mumbling but now with a whisky glass in one fist for a confidante. At the row of whisky bottles and champagne bottles the chauffeurs turned bartenders had already stacked up on a table against the wall.

Better leave Hanoco alone, Joe warned himself. No dame's worth it, but what a dish! Why was she so beautiful? he asked himself, and drunkenly answered himself: Because her hair's so black, because her skin's so white, because she's Hanoco. But leave her alone. She's not worth having Tommy Cruz go wild, not with Roberto Fernández in the bag.

His face flushed and he shouted for no reason at all at the two Filipino bartenders, "That's enough, that's enough!" and crossed the floor to Salvador Dimang. "The radio, Salvador. Les have a lil music."

The long, lean pom-pom man stirred himself. He arose from the second couch, a yellow fluffy one unlike the severe dark green couch where Helen was sleeping, and walked over to a glistening cabinet. He opened its doors, turned on the current, and fiddled with the dials until dance music from somewhere in the big wide world, maybe Manila, maybe Tokyo, maybe Sydney, maybe even San Francisco, wove a blue rhythm across the room where the mumbler mumbled into his glass and the blonde imitated a sleeping beauty, where a Japanese girl sat with a faint smile on her lips....

Joe didn't dare gaze too long at that smile, for it was curved as Hanoco was curved. He was glad when Espanita glided over to him, a champagne glass in her hand.

"For me, baby?" he asked her.

"For you, the Colonel," she purred as Salvador, sighing, returned to the fluffy couch and Tommy Cruz remarked to nobody, "Too much party."

Joe took the glass and drank. Espanita moved closer, as if to dance with him. He studied her through spectacles made of the clearest champagne. Her eyes were black, her hair was black, but he seemed to see another black-eyed and black-haired woman. Hanoco, sitting next to a Tommy Cruz, so damn drunk that a few more drinks would put him under the table. A few more drinks....

"You are very handsome this night, Colonel," Espanita said boldly, as if there were no Salvador in the room.

Joe smilingly wondered if Salvador had given her the green light. Why not? Salvador had seen Roberto Fernández and Thomas Bead, and what was another mestiza compared to a big money deal? "And you are beautiful," he murmured.

She shook her head, the diamonds in her ears glittering. "We dance, no?"

"I promised Hanoco the first dance," he said. The lie flowed off his lips so smoothly that he couldn't believe it hadn't been planned long ago, in the *sala* of Tommy Cruz, that first night in Manila out of the womanless stockade.

Smiling, he gave Espanita the champagne glass, and walking over to Hanoco, he asked her to dance. She stood up and he took her hand in his own, sliding his arm about her shoulders, the radio trumpet sounding now as if it had blown from inside his brain, the beat on the radio drum his drumming heart. He squeezed her hand gently, smiled down at the small porcelain features, his eyes spinning down to the curve of soft breasts flowering out of the pink filmy gown, plunging down, down, down....

They fox-trotted round and round in the narrow space in the middle of the *sala*. Round and round, his head whirling as if on some carousel - the two brown-faced bartenders busy, Salvador Dimang smoking a cigar, Espanita whispering in his ear, Helen a recumbent statue on the couch, Blacky in an everlasting mumbling dialogue with his glass, and Tommy Cruz peering into the tobacco smoke with an entranced and childish pleasure. By God, Joe thought giddily, I can work it.

His hand on Hanoco's bare shoulder lowered to the small of her back and he imagined that hand dropping to her waist, her hips. I can work it, he thought wildly. Wasn't this the lucky bungalow where he'd worked it with Helen? Wasn't this his big night? Roberto Fernández, Hanoco....

"You're a beautiful woman, Hanoco," he whispered.

"Than' you," she said softly.

Her voice tinkled in his ears, strange and foreign, although she spoke fairly good English.

"Tommy Cruz is a lucky man. What I've always said." And his hand on the small of her back lightened its pressure for a second to press down more firmly than ever, bringing a pinkish tint to her round cheeks. "Tommy and me talked about you," he continued recklessly. "Long ago when I'd never seen you, even. You were sleeping upstairs, we were drinking downstairs." His jaws clenched at the memory, the old-new temptation. Tommy had been a dead duck that night, but he hadn't chanced tiptoeing upstairs into her bedroom, and wouldn't chance it tonight, couldn't chance it, because this was the one night in a thousand when he'd promoted himself to a colonelcy and promoted that Malacanan con man Roberto Fernández. The hell with Hanoco, he thought, furious with her and himself.

The music stopped and he sullenly thanked Hanoco for the dance. She returned to her chair next to Tommy Cruz. Joe snapped his fingers and one of the bartenders fetched him a glass of champagne on a tray. Espanita asked him if he'd dance with her next while Salvador Dimang nodded ingratiatingly. He could sleep with Espanita, Joe guessed, and Salvador would stand bowing like a pimp in the door. For Salvador smelled blue-sky deals on the horizon and the pom-pom man and jewelry fence was strictly a money player. As was Tommy

Cruz, Joe reminded himself. Instantly his heavy mood was gone. God Almighty, there was always a way to work everything. Everything! Everything!

"You dance with me, Colonel?" Espanita repeated, and very delicately she undulated one bare shoulder.

"Colonel!" Joe laughed, and with both hands he snatched at something in space before him - an imaginary microphone. He held the make-believe mike close to his lips. "Ladies and gentlemen, ladies and gentlemen-" But this wasn't his audience at the Chateau. The newly promoted Major Hurley was dozing; the blonde in white slept, Tommy Cruz grinned at the smoke, and there were only Salvador Dimang and Espanita and Hanoco to pay any real attention.

"Ladies and gentlemen, big things're cooking, big things, and I'm not going to forget my first and best friends, and by that I mean Salvador Dimang and Tommy Cruz. Champagne!" he shouted to the bartenders, his eyes shifting to Hanoco. How black her hair was! Tommy'd be easy, a few more drinks would take care of Tommy, and Blacky and Helen didn't count, but he'd have to get rid of Salvador and that tramp Espanita.

Joe walked a little unsteadily over to the dark green couch where Helen slept, sitting down faster than he intended to, surprising himself. He rested his hand on Helen's silken ankle. "I don't forget my best friends, not me," he declared. He studied the glass of champagne in his hand. "This stuff can be tricky, too! Champagne - a champagne party!" He laughed. "What a party, and it's only a beginning!" he bragged. "I'll make out, I'll make out! I'll make out when Superman goes on relief."

Espanita sipped from her glass, her black eyes above the rim shining, moist.

Bedroom eyes, Joe thought. But the bedroom eyes were on the wrong damn girl. "I'll make out, I'll make out," he intoned, "for what's Manila, what's any city?"

"What was your business life in America before the war?" Salvador asked him solemnly, as if they were both respectable businessmen.

"I had a rough deal home," the new Lieutenant Colonel said pensively, like any successful man looking backward at his beginnings. "Remember the depression in the thirties, Salvador? Did you have one in Manila?"

"Yes, yes. We have very bad time."

"It was hell for me. I got out of high school and went to New York. Champagne!" Joe marveled. "Here we're drinking champagne, can wash our feet in champagne."

"New York!" Espanita was sighing. "I hope to see New York someday, the Fifth Avenue, the Broadway."

"They'll give you the keys to the city." Joe lifted his hand from Helen's ankle and glanced quickly from Hanoco's silken ankles to Tommy's loose dangling drunkard's fingers. "Give Tommy Cruz a drink of champagne!"

"No, he have too much!" Hanoco protested.

"This is a celebration, Hanoco!" Joe gestured at the bartenders. One of them stepped forward and Tommy Cruz blearily accepted the drink.

"Champagne!" Joe cried triumphantly. "I wasn't even drinking beer in New York. Lived in a furnished room with my brother. He didn't have a job. I got a job in a store, I worked with a pick and shovel."

"You, the Colonel!" Espanita cried, astonished.

"Me, the goddamn Colonel! I didn't have a peso to my name, worked in a steel mill in Pennsylvania. A strike there, like the water-front strike here. Reds! It was rough. My brother was no good," he rambled on. "Got into trouble, goddamn big brother!" His past wavered before him for a second, and he glimpsed the lonely kid he had been in the city of a hundred bread lines where he had learned that a big brother could be no brother at all. And then, unsubstantial as any champagne bubble, the past was gone. He summed it all up: "You have to look out for yourself!"

The life and times of Joe Trent, who joined the Navy and fought as a guerrilla in the Luzon mountains north of Manila and went awol, and whatever he did, was always true to one principle: You have to look out for yourself. It was the story Blacky had always been curious about, but now Blacky was sleeping.

The bartenders refilled the new Lieutenant Colonel's glass and Espanita's glass, but Salvador Dimang and Hanoco said no. As for Tommy Cruz, he could no longer hold a glass in his hand. "Salvador, you've stuck with me and I'll stick with you!" the new Lieutenant Colonel said. "I'm not going back to the States, not me. Manila's for me. I'll go into business right here in Manila. The hell with being a Colonel! I'll be plain Mr. Fenton, one of these days." Oh, it was a dilly of an idea, Joe thought, overjoyed. Mr. John R. Fenton, with an office in the Rutledge Building! The best deal of all! He'd become a lousy civilian and forget about the damn MP's. He'd do business with Roberto Fernández and buy a swell house like the limey out in the Pasay. "Salvador!" he cried, as one idea lit up another like two attached firecrackers. "You come see me in my office tomorrow. See me at nine o'clock."

"Nine o'clock!" Salvador exclaimed. "I will be asleep at nine."

"No, you won't! You sleep now. Gwan home and sleep."

"We go," Hanoco murmured.

"No," Joe said to her. "Have to talk to Tommy. Tommy, you hear me? Tommy, I want to talk to you."

"Yes, yes," Tommy Cruz muttered.

"*Adios*," Salvador said. "Nine o'clock?"

Joe stood up, reeling, but he steadied himself to shake hands with Salvador and kiss Espanita good night. "Take Helen home," he suggested, and watched the two bartenders carry Helen out into the limousine, and he kissed Espanita again as he walked outside with her, and when he returned to the *sala* he smiled at Hanoco, telling himself there was always a way and you never could go wrong planning one detail at a time. For he was rid of Helen and Salvador and that tramp Espanita, and Tommy Cruz was as dead a duck as Blacky, and there was only one bartender left, the last detail to be taken care of. Joe focused blearily on the brown face and he said, "Get us some food. There's stuff in the kitchen." He walked over to Hanoco to say in a low voice, "Hanoco, did you know Helen used to sing at the Nippon Café?" A low voice, a blackmailer's voice. "Maybe you too," he insinuated. "And Tommy."

"No!"

"Tommy Cruz isn't his name, but what do I care, Hanoco? When a man's my friend, like Tommy, I protect him. You know Phil Ide? I had Phil Ide give me all the stuff they had on Tommy at Bilibid, all the stuff how he collaborated with the Japs." And he smiled to see her hands rigid in her lap, thinking that for all he knew, there was a dossier on Tommy Cruz at Bilibid. "Hanoco, come with me. I don't want the servant hearing us." He waited for her to rise before hurrying out of the *sala* into the corridor, and he could have laughed out loud, it was so easy, so damn easy. And when he closed the bedroom door he smiled at her with wide lips. There she was in a bedroom with him, a champagne bedroom with a champagne woman. He leaned against the door to steady himself.

"Tommy's my friend," he whispered confidentially. "My good friend, Hanoco. But what about me? Going outa my way and getting those papers on Tommy, how he was a collaborator, a spy for the Japanese. Hanoco, what about me, what about me? I ought to have a lil love too, Hanoco, what d'you say?"

She stared at him, she said nothing. In the still face the slanted eyes were frightened and too large.

"The papers on Tommy, the papers on Tommy, Hanoco. He oughta be arrested, thrown into the stockade. I'm a lieutenant colonel in the American Army, and by rights I oughta turn him in. He's an enemy, Hanoco, and that's what I oughta do, but it's for you I'm letting him alone. So how about a lil appreciation, Hanoco? It's a big party and he'll never know, he doesn't have to know."

The too large eyes suddenly filled with tears.

"What're you crying for?" he rasped. "Nothing to cry about. I'm not turning him in. That's what I oughta do, but I'm giving him a break if you give me a break. Take off your dress, Hanoco." And he waited for her to step out of her pink dress, for the champagne dream to become real. "Take everything off!" he said, but she didn't move. She stood there in silence, the tears overflowing now, trickling down her round cheeks.

"Stop that crying!" he said, rushing at her and grabbing her with both arms. He felt her breasts, her smooth bare shoulders. She didn't resist him, but still she wept. He kissed her lips and cheeks and tasted the saltiness of her tears, spitting the saltiness out.

But he couldn't spit out the fear. Sharp as salt, it stung his consciousness. Sharp, stinging, sobering. He knew he could have her and she wouldn't resist; she'd cry but she wouldn't resist. For she believed his story about Tommy Cruz.

She wouldn't resist but she'd tell Tommy. Maybe she wouldn't tell, but he'd never be sure. She might tell him, and if Tommy went nuts everything would be monked up, and what in hell for, a bawling dame. "Stop that crying, you tramp! Let's get the hell out of here! Shut up, will you? Nothing's happened to you, Hanoco! Goddamn cherry blossom."

And Hanoco trembled, Hanoco gasped as if only now realizing she wouldn't have to stretch out on the bed for this man. With a trembling hand she wiped her eyes.

"That's better. Hanoco, I was drunk. Don't say nothing to Tommy. I was drunk. Let's forget it. O.K., Hanoco?"

CHAPTER NINETEEN

In the living room of their suite at the Hotel Cosmos, Joe and Blacky confronted each other with the red-rimmed sunken eyes of men who should have been asleep. His T shirt stuck to his shoulders with sweat, Joe sat at the table, a fist in each cheek, leaning heavily on his bare elbows. Blacky, too sodden to strip out of his shirt, sprawled on the couch.

"I'll go over it again," Joe said with utter exhaustion, his voice sounding hollow, as voices do in the last hours of the night, when all the world sleeps. Sleep is a law, and the wakeful become the lawbreakers.

"I've got a feeling," that hollow voice was saying. "If we're going to do something it has to be right away or not at all."

Blacky pulled himself up from the couch and stumbled to the table. Avoiding Joe's eyes, he opened the humidor and fumbled for an Alhambra cigar. But even when he had lit the cigar, inhaling deeply, the rich smoke in his throat and lungs didn't soothe him. Nothing but sleep would have helped him. Blacky blinked at the floor lamp, casting a lonely yellow light against the heavy darkness. Out there in the night was the party at the Chateau, and the party's extension at Salvador Dimang's. Out there in the night were the pink faces, the drunken faces. Then why did he feel that some huge mocking face was pressed against the drawn Venetian blinds?

Whose face?

"Depends on what Hanoco does," Joe was saying. "Let's suppose she yacks to Tommy Cruz how I tried to make her, how I said he was a Jap collaborator. O.K., I could say I was drunk and didn't know what I was doing. I could bring him in on the uncatalogued surplus deal. That'd square things."

Blacky listened to him. Square things, Blacky thought. That was Joe the Lawyer for you. Everything could be squared.

"But we can't be sure. Those two Japs are so full of cheap romance, we can't be sure. Then what?"

"Then nothing!" Blacky said in a choking voice. "You cut him in on the uncatalogued stuff and it'll be all right with Tommy."

"We can't be sure, Blacky. How the hell can you figure how those Orientals think?"

"Tommy's not spilling on us that we're awols."

"I don't think so either. He's got something on us and we've got something on him. But suppose Hanoco knows we're awols?"

"He wouldn't tell her."

"How do you know when they're full of this romance?"

"You got something on her, Joe," Blacky argued. "Chances are she was a collaborator."

"I've let things slide," Joe was saying as if to himself. "Let things slide. Maybe it was a good thing I made a pass at Hanoco tonight."

"A good thing!" Blacky cried, astonished.

"Maybe the best thing would be to get rid of both those Japs."

Again Blacky knew what a man looked like with murder in his heart.

He wanted to protest, but in this living, waking nightmare his lips were closed by the insane beating of his own heart.

"Manuel Pangamban," he heard Joe saying from some faraway place that at the same time was this familiar room at the Cosmos. "Manuel's been my man since I let him in on the sugar deal and left Tommy out. That deal was messed up, but I could let Manuel in on the uncatalogued. Play off one against the other! Manuel will get rid of those Japs for us."

And Blacky knew that Manuel would. Across the bony chest, under the pastel shirts, the tattooed words "My Destiny Is to Be Thief" still accurately described Manuel's activities. Murder was simply another theft.

The sweat oozed on Blacky's dark haggard face. All the night's whisky gurgled in one nauseous bubble in his throat, but his brain was singularly clear and sober as he stared at the other thief, Joe. A thief who had tried to steal Hanoco as he had stolen Helen. A thief who stole for the pleasure of stealing, picking at the triangles of sex, picking at men's minds. A thief to whom everything was a deal. Kroll's gasoline and Mallinson's lumber and Murdock's life. A sugar ship, a depot of uncatalogued war surplus, and a little house on María Clara Street. "You don't have to kill Tommy Cruz and Hanoco," Blacky said slowly, out of his new sobriety. "You only want to kill 'em to give yourself a kick."

"I must've been out of my head waking you up."

"You low-down thief!"

"You stupid bastid! We can't take chances with Tommy Cruz any more."

Blacky looked with a fascinated horror at Joe's handsome face. It was calm. It was calm now because Tommy Cruz and Hanoco had been whittled down from a living man and a living woman to a detail.

"All I want from you is a loan of some of that money you won tonight."

"What?" Blacky gasped.

"What the hell do you think, what? For Manuel Pangamban! Promising him a slice of the uncatalogued war stuff's fine, but there's no money in that so far."

Blacky said, "You go to hell, Joe."

"Don't be dumb. I'm kind of flat with the party and all. Hell, Blacky, don't be a dumb jerk. All I want's a loan."

"You're dealing me!" Blacky shouted wildly. "You're not gonna deal me!"

"Are you nuts? Who loaned you two thousand so you could win-"

"You're not gonna steal my money!"

Joe pulled a handkerchief from his pants pocket. He wiped the sweat from his cheeks and brow. He rolled the handkerchief into a ball and wiped his damp eyelids. Then he said, "You're talking like a goofball, pal. All Tommy Cruz has to do to wreck us is phone Bilibid. Who knows when he'll get it into his head? We can't wait any more, Blacky. All I'm asking you's a loan of ten thousand. A lil money'll clinch it with Manuel, and it has to be done right away. And I mean right away, Blacky. Blacky, we've been in this together a long time and you tell me when I've been wrong."

"Not my money!" Blacky said sullenly.

Joe looked at him. "O.K.," he said. "The hell with you. I'm hitting the sack." Blacky watched the door of the living room close as Joe walked out. That goddamn thief, he thought. Stealing, stealing, always stealing, but not my money.

For all he had left in the world that he could call his own were the sixteen thousand pesos.

Blacky dragged himself into his own room. He lit the lamp on the little table alongside his bed and had started to unbutton his shirt when all his weariness seemed to whirl at and about him like a lasso, pulling him down to the bed. One weary hand groped for the lamp. He put it out and the night galloped across his consciousness like the hoofs of a horse. Hoofs wrapped in black felt, silent and silencing....

He opened his eyes on light. He stared unbelievingly at the single eye of a .45, an eye of steel but no harder than the two blue eyes of the man in pajamas who had switched the lamp on. Tall as a dream, huge as a nightmare, Joe stood there with a gun in one fist and a smile on his face. "Blacky," Joe said softly, "I've always been the brain in our lil team, right, Blacky? So when I say I want a loan, I mean it."

The sleep burned out of Blacky's body; he stared with hatred at the smiling lips. "So now you need a gun," he cried snatching wildly at the little table lamp. The wire flew out of the socket, pulling the electric light into an equally electric darkness. "S'my money."

"I'm only borrowing it, you crazy goofhead! Where the hell's that lamp?"

Blacky peered at a moonlit shape. "Get outa here, you bastid! I want to sleep!"

"Where's that damn light?"

Blacky leaped out of bed. He ran at the shape, pushing hard. The shape thudded heavily against the dark wall.

The cocked .45 went off more by accident than by design. A roar filled Blacky's ears and something huge and molten hit him in the shoulder, something that seemed to cut his legs in half. He crashed to the floor, to rise an instant later, charging at the shape.

There was another blast from the .45 but this deliberate shot was a miss. Then Blacky was kicking at the shape, kicking, kicking, kicking at the helpless twisting thing on the floor that was like a snake whose sting was gone.

Joe had dropped the .45 when Blacky's first heavy boot had caught him in the crotch. Groveling now on the floor, tortured by pain and fear, he was begging Blacky to stop, but no word registered. For Blacky was no longer a think-ing man. In this moonlit room, his left shoulder throbbing, the bullet turned into flame in his flesh, he was both the hunted and the hunter. He kicked madly at the palely glimmering head until the body no longer twitched. Then, panting, his left arm hanging loosely as if almost severed from his left shoul-der, he searched for the .45. It glinted darkly near the wall. Blacky snatched it up and holding it by the barrel, pounded at the head in a fury.

At last a voice at the door of the suite's living room stopped him.

A voice? Whose voice?

Blacky shuddered. For the voice he heard was the voice of the mocking Fate that all night long had been peeking through the drawn Venetian blinds at the new Lieutenant Colonel and the new Major.

"Major, Major!" the voice was calling; calling the old Major and not the new one, calling Major Fenton, who would never hear another voice again.

The manager! Blacky thought. The shot had been heard. He staggered out of his bedroom into the living room, to the door of the voice. "Just celebratin'," he called hoarsely. "Gun went off by accident. No trouble."

"Captain Hurley?"

"This is Hurley. It's all right. It's all right...."

"Captain Hurley, I must–"

"Good night! We'll pay all the damages, good night, good night!"

And he leaned against the door, panting and breathless, waiting for the man-ager to go away. But why should the manager believe him? Why should any-body believe him when Joe was in there dead? And then - a miracle! - he lis-tened to the manager's footsteps retreat down the corridor.

The sweat was thick on Blacky's face. He brushed the sleeve of his right arm across his eyes, glanced stupidly at the .45 gripped in his fist. The butt was smeared with an indescribable mixture of blood and flesh like some madman's glue. Blacky stared at that butt, he stared at his bloodied right hand. He ran to the bathroom, placed the .45 on the side of the sink, switched on the light. He turned on both faucets in the sink, catching a glimpse of some ghostly face in the mirror, numbly recognizing that face as his own. It was his own face as that horrid red hand was his own. He plunged his hand under the faucet and gasped at the water tinting pink, like the lights at the Chateau.

His left arm and left hand were useless. With his right hand he managed to spread a towel on the tiled floor. He stamped his left foot down on one edge to hold it firm. Then, kneeling, he wiped his right hand clean, palm first, then the back, like a man cleaning a paintbrush.

When he straightened, he peered sideways at his left shoulder, his mouth twisted like that of an injured child. Only then did he realize that the strange red patch on his shirt was made of his own blood.

Shaking his head, he walked from the bathroom to the living-room table; he yanked open a drawer. Inside was a sign that he took out by its little golden cord. A "Do Not Disturb" sign, supplied by the hotel management. He had some vague notion about slipping it on the knob of the door outside, but when he reached the door, he knew that plan was no good. The manager didn't really believe him, the manager was only playing a trick. Blacky hung the sign on the inside doorknob. It swung like a slow pendulum for a few seconds and then stopped.

The last clock in the world had run down for Joe the Lawyer. The last clock, the last promotion, the last deal.

Leaving only a wounded killer. The bullet in his shoulder, lodged in bone, didn't feel like a fixed thing. It moved incessantly, like a needle made of fire, stitching fire through his shoulder and left arm. He examined the red patch. Was it getting larger? Maybe a little larger. He guessed that no artery or big vein had been hit.

What am I going to do? he thought frantically. I need a doctor. God, God, I need help, I can't stay here. Lucy! Yeah, Lucy. She'll help me, the only one. Yeah, yeah! I have to go quick or they'll get me. God, they'll get me. The manager.... had he really gone away?

His head was ringing with the manager's voice. His head was a clamor of many voices, but he couldn't really hear any of them, for the loudest voice of all was the voice of the dead man.

I warned him, the killer thought piteously.

Warned him about what?

With a bullet in his shoulder and a second bullet of fear whistling through his consciousness, Blacky wasn't so sure what all the warnings had been about.

Not that it made too much difference. All the warnings were well under the famous bridge.

Now only a few things remained. The sixteen thousand pesos. The bloodied towel and .45 in the bathroom. The dead man. Himself.

And the strangest of these was himself. For he wasn't Major Bill Hurley or Captain Bill Hurley or even Blacky MacIntyre any more. With fantastic suddenness he'd been changed into a fugitive wanted for murder.

He lurched into the bathroom. He seized a fresh towel, and with his right hand sheathed he picked up the .45.

He put the towel and the gun on the floor and awkwardly, clumsily rubbed some of the blood from the butt. He'd need a gun.

And then he remembered his own .45 in the dresser of his room.

God, I'm going nuts, cleaning this damn gun. I'm going nuts.

CHAPTER TWENTY

Descending the narrow iron stairs of the fire escape, he lifted his good right hand before him as if he expected to meet one of the new and impersonal enemies that had sprouted out of nowhere when he had pounded Joe's face into a pulp. Stuck inside his belt was his own .45. He was wearing a raincoat to conceal both the weapon and his bloody shoulder; in the raincoat's right-hand pocket he carried the jeep keys. He had taken nothing else from the suite.

When he reached the street level, he leaned exhausted against the rear wall of the hotel. Before him in the Cosmos parking lot, jeeps and cars stood in black rows, ghostly without their riders, under the fading stars.

He looked about him fearfully, dashed over to Joe's jeep.

He felt better when he was on Avenida Rizal, with the Hotel Cosmos and the suite behind him. He had written the end of the brassy saga of the Lieutenant Colonel and the Major; written it with Joe's lifeblood, in weird splotched and streaked hieroglyphics that yet very simply spelled out murder. Yet, he felt better for a little while, his foot on the gas pedal giving him speed, the night air fanning the sweat from his face and giving him an illusion of new-found strength. The jeep's yellow headlights seemed to be leading him north to the house on María Clara Street. He felt as if he were hurrying down a tunnel of yellow light magically dug through the black and ominous city where everybody pretended to be asleep. Pretended only, for somebody must have seen him on the fire escape, somebody must have seen him fumbling with the jeep lock, somebody was watching him now, peering at him from a shuttered window, hidden inside a dark doorway.

Quit your whining, he lashed at himself. Think better! O.K., Lucy. Lucy, she'll get me a doctor, a Filipino doctor. Trust some damn Filipino doctor? That bullet has to come out. Lucy! Yeah, Lucy might be able to do it, Lucy and her mother. O.K., I get the bullet out....

And because he was thinking of the bullet, Blacky felt the pain swell in his left shoulder. He could almost see the pain swelling up like a sponge sucking in water. Blacky gritted his jaws. He'd soldier this trip through, he vowed, as if this lonely ride through the empty and deserted city were no different from his long-ago voyage across the Pacific. This, too, was another convoy through a blacked-out world, but this time he traveled alone.

Blacky parked the jeep on María Clara Street in front of the house he had thought he would never see again. And like a wounded beast running for its den, his left arm hanging slack and useless, he walked heavily to the door. He knocked, waited. He knocked again and felt as if he were standing in some bloody dark cave where no one could ever hear him. Unless it was Joe, and Joe was far away in the Hotel Cosmos. He knocked again, his heart fluttering in panic at footsteps sounding inside. A woman's voice called and he cried out, "Lucy, Lucy! It's me, Blacky - Bill!" he corrected himself frantically. "Bill!"

The door was flung open and he stared at the girl he had never expected to see again, the Chinese lantern hanging behind her in the *sala*, the lantern glowing like a star in his eyes, the star of his only home since the day he had left his mother in Beaver Dam. Outlined in light, a brown-faced girl in a green robe stood impaled in light. Then she threw herself at him, tears of joy in her eyes. He had turned his left shoulder and arm away from her, so she pressed herself tightly against his right side. She buried her face in the sleeve of his raincoat, her arms about his neck. Blacky grimaced at the stabbing in his shoulder. He kissed the top of her head. For one second of renewal, this girl he had abandoned was as close to him as his own beating heart.

Then he said, "Let's go in, Lucy." As she shut the door he said, "I'm in trouble, Lucy."

"Trouble." She looked at him, her eyes widening. "You are sick, no?"

"Bring me some whisky, Lucy."

She ran from the *sala* to the kitchen. In the kitchen doorway, Lucy's mother stood watching them. Blacky nodded at the old woman, and then slowly dragged himself to the couch. He sat down. He was sweating inside his raincoat, but dreaded pulling it off his left arm.

Lucy was coming toward him with a glass and a bottle of whisky.

"Pour me a drink," he said.

The bottle tilted. She handed him the drink and he swallowed it quickly.

"Bill," she said anxiously. "Your face-"

He looked at Lucy, at her mother still standing in the kitchen doorway, two tiny women in robes over their nightgowns, their feet in straw slippers. The old woman's face was a web of wrinkles, the girl's face smooth and soft even with the scar on her cheek. How was he to tell them? he wondered dumbly.

He blurted, "Get some scissors and cut me out of my clothes, Lucy."

"Scissors?"

"I've got a bullet in my shoulder."

"Bill," she keened. "Bill!"

"It's not so bad. I can't go to the Army hospital, understand? You gotta understand that! I can't go to the Army hospital!"

Their eyes met and he knew she understood him at last, finally. For why else would he be coming back to her after he'd gone away without a word? Why else would he be coming back to María Clara Street with the long black night slowly graying in the windows?

"I'll make it up to you, Lucy," he muttered, lowering his eyes in shame.

Her mouth quivered but she said nothing. She hurried to her mother. She spoke in Tagalog. The old woman listened patiently. She had lost her oldest son in the war, seen another son die of tuberculosis, seen her daughter become a pom-pom girl. Death and suffering - she had known these two terrible twins of war like her own children. So she listened patiently to her daughter and murmured only one word. "Yes," she said, and it was as if she were saying yes to all tragedy on this earth.

It was the old woman who helped Blacky out of his raincoat and then cut off the bloodstained shirt and T shirt underneath. It was the old woman who sharply scolded Lucy when the girl wept at the sight of the bullet-torn shoulder.

"Lucy, gimme that whisky!" Blacky said. "The bottle, not the damn glass, Lucy." He swallowed a long drink. "Lucy, you tell your mother to try and get that bullet out."

"No, no, no!" she cried in horror. "Bill, I bring doctor."

"I can't have any doctor, Lucy! Understand? Tell your mother to try and get that bullet out. Boil some water, boil some knives."

Lucy covered her wet eyes with her hands. Blacky helped himself to another drink. Through a haze of whisky and pain, he peered at her. "You tell your mother what I said. Lucy, for God's sake, you gotta help me, baby!"

He drank again as Lucy translated what he wanted. The whisky flooded through him warmly, but no whisky could match the fire in his shoulder.

"She says she cannot do!" Lucy cried at him.

"She can't say that!" he pleaded, tears in his own eyes. "I'm in trouble, Lucy, big trouble. You've got to help me, baby! For God's sake!" He sobbed helplessly while his brain careened madly down a score of dead-end alleys. The bullet was first, he thought. First, first! But he had so much more to do! God Almighty! He couldn't stay in this house. It wasn't safe. Joe knew about this house. He had to find a room, a safe hideaway, and everything tonight!

"No, Bill," Lucy murmured sadly. "We are not the doctor."

"Lucy, remember the Major? The American who came to this house coupla days ago?"

"Yes," she answered bitterly.

"I'm in trouble with him. Big trouble."

"He shot the bullet in your shoulder?"

"Yes," he whispered. "Yes. Lucy, I-"

But she had already guessed what he was about to confess. "*Dios mío!*" she cried.

"I had to," he said hoarsely. "But I can't go to the Army medics. I've got to hide, Lucy. I've got sixteen thousand pesos, Lucy! It's for you and me, but you gotta help me!"

The girl kissed his sweaty brow and whirled on her mother fiercely. Speaking in Tagalog, she seemed to be scratching and tearing at the impassive old woman, who finally shrugged assent.

"She will help you," Lucy said to Blacky.

He celebrated with another drink. The whisky was seeping into his nerves, blurring the faces of his unknown enemies, the MP faces, the Bilibid faces, all the faces of the law. He tilted the bottle again and smiled at Lucy, for he was

Blacky MacIntyre after all, sitting with his girl in his own house, a bottle of whisky in his fist.

In this house on María Clara Street, he was nobody else but poor old Blacky, who'd had a little tough luck but nothing that money couldn't straighten out.

And miraculously there was a clean white sheet that somebody had spread on the red-tiled floor, and Lucy was explaining that he was to lie down. Flat on his back he stared up at the yellow bottom of the Chinese lantern and wished suddenly he'd gone to an Army hospital. He wished a hundred things, wished he'd never met Joe - or killed Joe. "Lucy," he called. "The money's in my pants pocket. Take it - in case somethin' goes wrong."

Lucy dropped to her knees. She pressed her face against his huge hairy chest. "Take it, Lucy!" he said. And when she had done so, he said, "Gimme the whisky."

The old woman removed the paper Chinese lantern. The naked light of the hanging bulb blared down into Blacky's eyes. He saw dancing green discs, and the shadowy shape of the old woman fetching boiling water and sterilized knives. He felt the hot water scalding his skin as she washed the wound. He winced at the pain, and waited for pain that would make this pain nothing.

He felt the knife in his shoulder. His agonized eyelids seemed to tear open, to see the overhead bulb, blazing and immense and yellow, the yellow sun of his pain. Again the blade probed and he seemed to see without seeing the faces of the two women above him, but who held the knife and who wept there was no telling, for they were one brown, wavering and disappearing face. The knife moved again and Blacky moaned like a hurt child. He forced himself to concentrate on the bulb as if it alone held the secret he must know in order to endure the knife. And again the knife sliced through the bloody shoulder flesh. Blacky's heels drummed against the red-tile floor under the white sheet, like drumsticks in the hands of a mad drummer.

Then there was no knife. No knife at all. Lucy, weeping, wiped his sweaty face. She flung herself beside him, kissed his face and eyes. She was talking to him, but he heard no voice, heard sound faster than light. And it was a long time before the sound slowed. "Bill, Bill," she was saying. Bill - it was the word for all her love and pity.

He was too weak to answer. His shoulder was throbbing as if something alive had been grafted onto it by the sterilized knife, something fierce and cancerous, devouring his shoulder, gnawing, biting. "The bullet?" He gasped the question.

Lucy jumped to her feet. From the cabinet in the kitchen she took out the last bottle of whisky. She opened it and brought it to him.

"The bullet's still there," he said. "Oh, my God!"

She held the bottle to his lips like a mother with milk. He gulped down a long drink. Second by second, the teeth of pain rended at his flesh, cancerous teeth multiplying to feed on all his body. "The bullet's still there," he moaned.

Lucy wept to see him. She seized the bottle, and weeping she drank. Standing above them, the old Filipino woman looked down at her daughter and the American who had deserted her to return this night. The mother's eyes brimmed with pity; the special pity the old have for the young.

Suddenly, as if the bullet that remained in his shoulder had described a new trajectory to crash into the last sane center of his mind, Blacky screamed.

"You bastid!" he raved. "Yah, who killed you, Joe? Not me, Joe. Honest to God, not me. Tommy Cruz! Murdock, Sarge Murdock! Joe, he killed you, Joe! Honest! The money's at Dimang's and we can get it if you lemme show you how. Sixteen thousand, a blue-sky deal, all the money you want. Remember the iron safe on the second floor at Dimang's? Thas where the money is, all you want, Joe. All I want's my share, Joe. What's fair's fair. *Hang gnang* Pier Seven. See all those lights, Joe? Joe, Murdock's coming, Joe!" Blacky howled in deadly fear and never felt Lucy's hands trying to soothe him. "Murdock! Carryin' his goddamn head. They put him on a slab, Joe, but the bastid's not dead. That what you think, Joe, I know better. Murdock, you bastid! Who's afraid of you and your goddamn head? Hell with you, Sarge, and the whole goddamn stockade. You're all a pack of bastids...."

As the light of morning whitened the windows of the *sala*, the old woman and her daughter spoke earnestly together for long minutes. Lucy sobbed, Lucy protested, but her mother insisted patiently, "We must go, my child."

"And leave him here like a dog?"

"We will telephone a doctor. We must go, my child. We cannot help him. He has killed an American and the MP's will come and we will be arrested. We must go, my child."

The old woman packed what she could into two bamboo bags. Like wartime refugees fleeing a burning town, they walked out of the house as the first rays of the morning sun set the corrugated iron roofs on fire.

The jeep Blacky had parked outside was gone, driven off by some sharp-eyed passer-by who had noticed that the wheel chain was unlocked; a lucky passer-by who would sell the jeep in the buy and sell.

At the corner Lucy paused to look for the last time at the house on María Clara Street. She whimpered, turned as if to go to the lover she was now deserting. But the old woman seized her by the wrist. "No, my child," the old woman said, and she whispered a proverb of the people: "There is an hour to march like a lion and there is an hour to flee like a dog."

Another month had come and gone before Blacky MacIntyre was discharged from the Army hospital and removed to a cell in Bilibid. They hadn't asked him a single question as yet, but Blacky had a hunch that would be taken care of in the morning.

So he might just as well enjoy the view, Blacky told himself.

There wasn't much to see, though, in Cell Number 9. A cot with mosquito netting. A single chair. A floor of brown wooden planks. Nor was there much to see outside the single barred window. The corner of some building in Bilibid compound. And dust.

The next morning he was escorted from his cell into an L-shaped building, into a small office. A plump captain with sympathetic gray eyes and a tight mouth that contradicted the eyes smiled at the prisoner in the faded suntans while a Filipino male clerk sat ready at a typewriter.

"I'm Captain Haggstrom," he said pleasantly from behind a flat desk on which his papers and documents were arranged neatly. "How's your shoulder, MacIntyre?"

"All right."

"All right, *sir.*"

"All right, sir," Blacky corrected himself.

"MacIntyre, we've treated you right, haven't we?" the Captain inquired, as if he personally had bandaged the prisoner's shoulder.

"Yes, sir."

"Nobody's bothered you. You deserved to be left alone," the Captain added sardonically but with an undercurrent of admiration. "I've got to hand it to you, MacIntyre. You and your buddy pulled off the best job of impersonation since Dr. Jekyll and Mr. Hyde. Stand up, MacIntyre, will you?"

Blacky got to his feet and Captain Haggstrom stared at him. The Captain nodded at his Filipino typist. "It wasn't as if they were average size like most GI's. Sixfooters, both of them. And yet *nobody* saw them. You can sit down now, Major Hurley."

"Yes, sir." Blacky obeyed. In the hospital, as he had lain recuperating, he had often wondered how and when they would start asking what they had to ask. Well, the day had come, as the day always came, and he'd drawn this joker. A fat slob with a mean woman's mouth, Blacky had sized him up. Not that it made much difference. "May I ask you a question, sir?"

"Yes, you may, Major Hurley."

"All those papers on your desk-"

"They're all on you," Captain Haggstrom assured him grimly. "We know all about you, more than you know yourself, Major Hurley."

"I was only a major for one night, sir," Blacky said.

"Don't be so damned wise, MacIntyre."

"Yes, sir."

"The Provost Marshal demanded a complete investigation, and he got it." Captain Haggstrom studied his papers with satisfaction.

"I killed Joe in self-defense," Blacky volunteered.

"We'll get to that in due course," the Captain said.

"Isn't that what you want to know?"

"Sir!" the Captain reminded him.

"Isn't that all you want to know, sir?" It seemed to Blacky that he had been

waiting a long, long time for somebody to ask him about Joe. And now when
he offered the information they didn't want it. Due course! Blacky thought. If
that wasn't the Army!

"You are not to question me as to what I want to know. Understand that,
MacIntyre?"

"Yes, sir."

"We know all about *that* night." Captain Haggstrom considered the prisoner for a few seconds. "Since you've brought it up, do you want to elaborate on
what took place that night?"

"When I killed him it was too late," Blacky began, and heard what he was
saying reduced to a staccato series of clicking noises on the typewriter.

"Too late! What do you mean by too late?"

"He'd about finished me."

"That bullet didn't finish you."

"I don't mean the bullet. He'd killed me anyway."

Captain Haggstrom stared at the prisoner, and then he laughed. "You're not
getting yourself into the psycho ward that easy."

Blacky knew then it was no use trying to explain what he had learned in the
hospital: that a corpse can sometimes commit murder. He had been Joe's stooge
a little too long. A stooge, a shadow, a muscle twitching when the brain commanded. The brain was dead now. Joe the Lawyer was dead. But the jinx was-
n't dead.

"I'm not trying to get into psycho, sir," Blacky said, and he wondered vaguely if he wasn't good psycho material after all.

Captain Haggstrom had turned toward his typist. "Did you put down what
he said about his being killed without a bullet?"

"Yes, sir, Captain Haggstrom."

"X it out, please. X it all out!"

"Yes, sir."

"MacIntyre," the Captain said, frowning. His voice wasn't angry but it was
no longer friendly or humorous. It was the voice of authority and it reminded
Blacky of all the voices he had hated: stockade guards and MP's and ninety-day
wonders. "I think we've been too easygoing with you or you wouldn't be
inventing nonsense like you tried to. You take my word we know all about you
and Joe Trent. We've got a list of names a yard long of the people you went
around with, all your pom-pom and buy-and-sell friends. If you want a break
from us, I don't want any more nonsense about your being killed or any psycho stuff like that. Understand, MacIntyre?"

"Yes, sir."

"Let's start from where we found you and we'll go backward from there." He
picked up a sheet and read. "You were found by Dr. Espinosa at Twenty-three
María Clara Street with a bullet in your left shoulder. Is that correct?"

"Yes, sir," Blacky replied.

"Twenty-three María Clara Street was your hideaway?"

The typewriter was clicking steadily now.

"Sort of, sir."

"What do you mean, sort of?"

"Well, it didn't turn out to be much of a hideaway, sir."

"I see. You drove to Twenty-three María Clara Street after you killed Joe Trent. You went there to get the bullet out of your shoulder. Dr. Espinosa reports there were all the signs of amateur surgery. Is that correct?"

"Yes, sir."

"Two Filipino women lived at Twenty-three María Clara Street. Who were they? What were their names?"

Blacky looked steadily, in silence, at Captain Haggstrom. The round face reminded him now of the face of a card, flat and unreal. They were all card faces, Haggstrom's face, Joe's face, all the faces living and dead, whirling through his mind now like cards shuffled by a lightning hand: Tommy Cruz and Helen, Sergeant Murdock and Sergeant Kroll, Manuel Pangamban and Roberto Fernández, and there was only one face with any reality for him in this quiet room where the round face was called Haggstrom and the Filipino face was nameless.

Only the face of Lucy had any truth for him, given depth by the blood still pumping out of his heart. A small brown face, the cheek scarred, the face of all the lost hopes and lost dreams fading so fast in his brain. If he had believed in prayer he might have prayed to her, the one human being who had loved him.

The Captain repeated his last question. "What were their names?"

Blacky was silent. He was thinking of Lucy. All he could do for her now was to keep still. To give her the secret of her name that Captain Haggstrom wanted so much. In this moment of giving he felt that he'd become Blacky MacIntyre again. For the last time on earth.

THE END

www.ingramcontent.com/pod-product-compliance
Lightning Source LLC
Chambersburg PA
CBHW070432170726
48291CB00002B/469